W9-BZA-591

CFCM

10-17-2001

ABOUT THE
MIND CHRONICLES TRILOGY

This series is based on the Hermetic Principle: "As Above, So Below."

The goal of the series is to experience and chronicle the story of humankind since the primeval fireball, as found in the depths of one human mind—my own. The Hermetic assumption is that all places, times, and beings we have ever known exist now in the memory bank. If the key can be found to unlock this primordial memory bank, then light can shine into the records of time.

There have been many times in our history when it seemed the end of the world was upon us. These potential End Times often came at the end of an astrological age or millenium. Perhaps this twentieth-century period is unusually threatening because the end of an age coincides with the end of a millenium. In times past, we have thought the disaster was caused by moral depravity, war, or catastrophe. What is essential to understand is that all those fears *were a failure of the imagination.* Matter is never destroyed, it just changes form. In times past, we knew little about the planet as a whole, but our inner resources were richly developed. Now we know much about the whole planet, but almost nothing about our inner minds, which are creating inexplicable agents of destruction on the Earth. The Bomb, like the medieval dancers of death, confuses inner and outer. We thought our salvation was in knowing more about the world, so we did this. We must now explore the landscape of our inner selves.

Past-life regression under hypnosis, and other altered states of consciousness for deep exploration, are the methods I have used to obtain the material for this series. Ancient initiatory religions used these techniques to bring the initiate to his or her highest potential for living, and the techniques in these books are as old as the first human awareness. This series attempts to go even further, however. It recaptures the phylogenetic Earth mind records, including all the influences on this planet from other galaxies and planets. We contain all this knowledge deep within ourselves, and this series recovers the long-forgotten Earth story.

We are now precessing from the Age of Pisces into the Age of Aquarius. Thirteen thousand years ago, Earth precessed from the Age of Virgo into the Age of Leo. The Age of Leo—Atlantis—was an age of creativity, and the Age of Aquarius will be the full expression of cosmic consciousness. This Golden Age will be aborted, however, unless we recapture our story, our myth. Knowing this great myth will awaken our souls. Like the initiated bards of old, I unfold my tale for you. Together, let us awaken to full planetary consciousness.

HEART OF THE CHRISTOS
Volume Two of
The Mind Chronicles
Trilogy

HEART
of the
CHRISTOS

Starseeding from the Pleiades

Barbara Hand Clow

ILLUSTRATIONS BY
ANGELA C. WERNEKE

BEAR & COMPANY
PUBLISHING
SANTA FE, NEW MEXICO

LIBRARY OF CONGRESS CATALOGING-IN-PUBLICATION DATA

Clow, Barbara Hand, 1943-
   Heart of the Christos: starseeding from the Pleiades / by Barbara
Hand Clow; illustrations by Angela C. Werneke.
      p. cm. — (The Mind chronicles)
   Continuation of: Eye of the centaur.
   Continued by: Signet of Atlantis.
   Bibliography: p.
   ISBN 0-939680-59-9
   1. Spiritual life — Miscellanea. 2. Jesus Christ — Spiritualist
interpretations. 3. Reincarnation therapy. 4. Archetype
(Psychology) — Miscellanea. I. Title. II. Series: Clow, Barbara Hand,
1943-   Mind chronicles trilogy.
BF1999.C59 1989
133.9'01'3 — dc20   89-6587
                                                                     CIP

Text copyright © 1989 by Barbara Hand Clow
Illustration copyright © 1989 by Angela C. Werneke

All rights reserved. No part of this book may be reproduced by any means or in
any form whatsoever without written permission from the publisher, except for
brief quotations embodied in literary reviews or articles.

Bear & Company
Santa Fe, New Mexico 87504-2860

Cover & interior design & illustration: Angela C. Werneke
Author photo: Valerie Santagto
Typography: Casa Sin Nombre, Ltd.
Printed in the United States of America by R.R. Donnelley

9 8 7 6 5 4 3

To Matthew Fox

the Dominican theologian
who is more powerful in his words
than in his silence

CONTENTS

Acknowledgments xi

Heralding the New Dawn, by Tony Shearer xiii

Reflections by Chris Griscom xv

Commentary by Brian Swimme xvii

Preface xix

Chapter One: Tantric Initiation & the Goddess 3

Chapter Two: The Olmec & the Records of Teotihuacan 17

Chapter Three: Priests, Kings & the Sirius Star Records 29

Chapter Four: Tikal as the Gateway to the Underworld 49

Chapter Five: Emergence from the Underworld 67

Chapter Six: The Great Lakes & the Paleolithic Spiral 85

Chapter Seven: Teotihuacan & the Tiger Initiation 103

Chapter Eight: Bishop, Executioner & White Knight 123

Chapter Nine: Marcion & Isaiah 143

Chapter Ten: Lakota Medicine Woman 159

Chapter Eleven: Messages from the Pleiades 181

Chapter Twelve: The Emerald Records of the Holy Grail 207

Bibliography 227

About the Author 237

About the Artist 238

Comments by Readers 239

ACKNOWLEDGMENTS

I would like to thank Chris Griscom, Tom Cratsley, Jessica Fleming, Stacy Williams, Rick Phillips, Kurt Leland, and Susan Harris for assisting me as healers in the search for the records of this book. Their profound guidance and belief in the whole person are what made it possible to travel so deeply into the underworld and re-emerge with a vision for our times.

I would like to thank White Eagle Tree and Victorio Romero for sharing ceremony at Teotihuacan on Harmonic Convergence. Robert Boissiere is deeply appreciated for holding the vision of the Banana Clan in our search for the Mayan links to Hopi and in his teachings to feed sacred sites with healing feathers all over the planet. I am very grateful to Mayan daykeeper, Hunbatz Men, for his invitation to participate in the opening of Mayan initiatic centers for 2013 AD, and to all the Mesoamerican teachers who offered me welcome. I am deeply moved by the work of Tony Shearer to bring us the wisdom of Quetzalcoatl, and I am equally grateful to Tony for his support of this book. I am grateful to Jose Arguelles for ceremony at Palenque and guidance at the Olmec Museum at Villahermosa, Mexico.

I wish to deeply thank Angela Werneke for her exquisite cover, the twelve illustrations, and her design for this book. When I travel into far distant realms of time and place, the words I use to describe what I see are profoundly inadequate. Angela's ability to make visual what I have seen is truly extraordinary. It is as if she is able to be my eyes. I am grateful to Gerry Clow for his photographic assistance at sacred sites, particularly at Teotihuacan and Avebury.

I would like to acknowledge the excellent editing work of Gail Vivino, who had to struggle with verb tenses and difficult voice problems much beyond the norm. Her ability to be exacting is what has made this book into a smooth read for all.

I would like to thank my whole family for all their patience and support as I have traveled to remote places and spent many hours away from my family for this book. Gerry Clow, my husband, has unusual faith in the importance of my work, and this book would not have been created without his belief in my teachings. I would like to especially acknowledge my oldest son, Tom, for his emergence as a spiritual teacher and his lovely presence with me often in Mexico. And, I would like to acknowledge the open heart of my only daughter, Elizabeth, whose birth began my spiritual awakening.

Finally, I would like to thank all the Bears in sales, publicity, warehouse, and design, for blessing this book.

HERALDING THE NEW DAWN
Tony Shearer

It all began with a prophecy, a vision, a dream. It all began with a dream filled with hope for a brave new world. "A new world will be born," said the prophet. "On the day of August 16, 1987, a new dawn will be given, a New World will be born, a new race of people will walk upon the Earth." Such was the song of the prophet as he sang his evangel to a frightened, dying planet—the Earth. . . . Was this evangel false, or was it sacred, holy, and correct? And if it is correct, what will be next? Will the human race continue to follow the path of "orthodox religions" that have led us all to the gates of Earth destruction, greed, and cruelty beyond belief? Will that be our destiny? Or will we, as a people, rise and awaken to the true nature of our own beauty, our New World?

Here, in one book of a trilogy, *Heart of the Christos* author and poet Barbara Hand Clow heralds this new dawn. And with the brilliance of that new sun, she gently illuminates the shadows of our frightened souls with a multitude of magnificent stories, teachings, blessings, and truths. With the skill of a Carlos Castaneda, she unlocks the doors of our inner self. With the integrity of a Frank Waters, she leads the way. And, with her masterful understanding of myth, like that of Joseph Campbell, she reveals the reality, teaching us why.

With excellent judgment, Barbara selected Angela C. Werneke as her illustrator. And I don't think the choice could have been improved upon. Each and every full-page illustration is a fine work of art. Any of them is worthy of being mounted and framed. The illustrations can stand alone, making this a most desirable volume.

Within the combined talents of these two remarkable ladies, Bear & Company has delivered another fine book. I'm sure it will enlighten and illuminate the lives of many seeking people of our times.

Heart of the Christos is a most important book. I have been honored to review it. The work is intelligent, satisfying, and deeply spiritual. I have rarely been so moved and so enlightened. But more than all else, the work is honest to the human soul, as it champions the return of the Goddess. This book has been a long time in coming, like the Goddess herself, but at last the Goddess has arrived. Barbara Hand Clow and Angela C. Werneke understand all of that.

Tony Shearer
author of *Lord of the Dawn, Quetzalcoatl*
and *Beneath the Moon and Under the Sun*
May, 1989

REFLECTIONS
by Chris Griscom

Barbara Hand Clow's book, *Heart of the Christos,* is not a book for the happy-go-lucky New Ager. It calls forth the intensity only a serious seeker can sustain. It is impossible to read it as if these multi-incarnational stories belong only to her, for the reader soon becomes entrenched in the experience on some uncomfortably familiar level that knows all too well the seduction, the illusion, the outcome. We might claim that the recognition comes from our human gene pool, collective unconscious, etc., but the knowing makes us players as well. Thus we rush along looking for the way out of the future that may have been "fixed" by the echoing choices of the past!

As Barbara takes us all there, through the crack into the secret world of the initiated, we become entrapped in the funnel of initiation from which the only escape is the realization of the laws of karma—cause and effect. The ancients excused themselves by insisting that they were answering the demands of the gods, however bloodthirsty or outrageous. The bitter truth is that our interpretation of the gods' needs has set in motion a seemingly interminable cycle of physical, sexual karma, which by its very crudeness of expression has blocked us from accessing its divine nature on the level of the Creator. The ancients ascertained that the sexual act was related to fertility and procreation, but their misuse of sexuality has impregnated our very DNA and is surfacing in this present time—begging to be cleared. The sexual energy has needed to be quickened and spun up the spiral into the domain of source, rather than down into the bowels of the body's limited repertoire of pleasure/pain. Violation of the cosmic law of permission by "The Gods and the Galactics" must now cause them to share our fate and our struggle to free ourselves from the distortion of ritualistic enslavement set in our very genetic coding.

The mutual abuse of males and females fully demonstrates the principle that the victim and the victimizer are one. Releasing these monumental pillars of recorded, imprinted violations one to the other will free us to a new octave of male/female relationships.

Barbara's willingness to ferret out the "unspeakables" of her own unconscious will hopefully grant us enough curiosity and courage to do the same. As Barbara clears these karmic roles she has played, we also are freed! The ripple goes out, as each of us seeks to remember our own roles as priests, priestesses, scribes, etc.

Unveiling and dissolving past-life, astral energy is one of the greatest tools to enlightenment available to clear the dead branches off our evolutionary tree and give new life to the quickening necessary for our potential mastery as a guardian species of this planet. Barbara is right about the power of the animals which lies not in their physical focus, but in the more subtle expertise of their perceptual abilities that will, perhaps, reawaken in us as a positive side-effect of retrieving the zoomorphic memories of our merging.

Heart of the Christos is the most timely of books because it brings us to the crux of our present-day planetary initiation—to know the heart of the divine self and to search out the unspeakable and dissolve it, leaving us open to the unfailing truth and talents we have accrued in our long sojourn in body. Freedom comes from within!

Chris Griscom
The Light Institute
Galisteo, New Mexico
June 1989

COMMENTARY
by Brian Swimme

Heart of the Christos is thick with heretical ideas, graphic sex scenes, and wild speculations concerning the nature of the universe, each one with the power to irritate, outrage, or confuse many readers. Such excesses are inevitable for anyone undertaking a task as monumental as the one Clow has set for herself. For in her reflections on the deep wellsprings of the human psyche, she has become convinced that if we are to participate in the healing of the Earth, nothing less than a radically new understanding is required—a new understanding of Christ, of history, of self, and of world.

As Barbara Hand Clow takes us on her wild adventures of soul, a single conviction burns deeply: "The ecocide of our time is the greatest sin since the beginning of time. There are many blasphemous stories in this epic, but nothing is as evil as the murder of the Earth." With that as her foundation, she plunges into perhaps the most important and most ancient quest taken by humanity—the quest for the meaning of existence. As she explains: "The records of time, the real story of our history—imagine if I could get in touch with the origins of creation. What are we? What is our consciousness?"

Trusting in the spaciousness of her consciousness, intuiting that the deeper reaches of her own mind mesh with the most distant reaches of the universe and with the detailed depths of all time, Clow soars through the thoughts and experiences and hopes and agonies of personages thousands of years in the past. And not just humans. Clow is convinced that the universe as a whole is sentient, and that we are capable of contacting the inner dimensions of reality whatever its outer form. This exploration eventuates in such striking sentences as: "I am my soul as a tan cat." "Now I am a fish." And my favorite of all: "I have been the guardian stone hawk in this temple for two thousand years, looking out through the obsidian eyes of Horus, carved into my face in the column."

In many ways, the central concept of the book is "evolution." Clow is searching for a presentation of the world that will enable humans as a species to enter more deeply into their spiritual evolution. Clow presents us with a new Genesis myth, as well as a new understanding of history.

She has synthesized Christian revelation with pagan spirituality and with a feminist critique of the last five thousand years of human history. And at the center of this synthesis, and at the center of her interpretation of cosmic evolution, is Christos: "A being of such love and compassion came to Earth that now all souls have access to the desire to be alive, to be alive just to experience the love of Christos."

As Clow reflects on the needs of our time, and the contours of psychic history, and the meanings of the world, she responds by creating a new myth—an astrological-mythological synthesis drawing upon Christianity, pagan spirituality, and feminist philosophy. This book is certainly not for everyone—fragile or timid or overly rigid souls might better pass by. But for anyone interested in revisioning the world out of the experience of psychic journeying into cosmic-astrological meanings, *Heart of the Christos* is the place to begin.

Brian Swimme
physicist; author of *The Universe is a Green Dragon*
June 1989

PREFACE

Heart of the Christos: Starseeding from the Pleiades is the second book of *The Mind Chronicles* trilogy. The first book of the trilogy is *Eye of the Centaur: A Visionary Guide into Past Lives* (1986), and the last book will be *Signet of Atlantis* (1992). This trilogy is an exploration of the contents of the archetypal memory bank as it has expressed itself within the time context of history. In each book I become a time traveler who goes into the past to retrieve the lost records of ancient civilizations—the records of the desires and experiences of the people of our past. I image the human race as a great memory circuit which is the same as the cosmic memory bank, a circuit which was activated with the first breath of life on Earth. I believe that all of us contain the total memory of all time within our very cells. This trilogy is being created to access our shared story.

In 1989, as *Heart of the Christos* is being published, *Eye of the Centaur* has been in print for almost three years. I have gotten much valuable feedback from readers about the process I have been working with. The two types of reaction which are the most significant to me are first, questions about exactly where this material is coming from, and second, probing questions about the usefulness of such deep exploration. At this point, after beginning this work in 1982, I would like to address both issues before you read *Heart of the Christos*. *Heart* is an evolutionary leap beyond *Eye of the Centaur*, and clearing up questions about my sources will help you to access the shamanistic levels of consciousness available to you by reading *Heart of the Christos*.

The source of my material was twenty sessions under hypnosis targeted at accessing the contents of my own archetypal memory bank. These sessions utilized a method called "past lives." This was the same process I used for the source material in *Eye of the Centaur*, which ended up being an exploration of the seven levels of initiatic transformation. When the seven levels of initiation are completed, the next phase of the journey to enlightenment is the shamanistic transmutation of self. *Heart of the Christos* is a very shamanistic book. This "past life" method involves using the material obtained under hypnosis as an oracle for the planet, as a way to retell the stories of the ancient days. I assume that the material I am accessing is of critical need for the present time, and the comments I have gotten from my readers over three years justify this assumption. But I, myself, am only an oracle—a corner news stand. I do not believe there is anything about myself that is different than any other being on this planet except that I have taken the time to go so deeply into the mind. That is why this trilogy is called *The Mind Chronicles.*

As for where my material really comes from—past lives, primordial memory bank, or simply from creativity—I do not think it makes any difference. Like with any art form, all that matters is whether it strikes a deep chord in the audience. Do these records and stories strike a chord deep within you? Like a junk sculptor who chooses to make comments about modern culture out of refuse the culture throws away, I vigorously defend my right to utilize memories as my materials even though I have been attacked for my methodology by scholars. After studying the Mayan Calendar, I first understood how each baktun of about 400 years length (13 baktuns in one 5,125-year Mayan Great Cycle) is an evolutionary theme expressed historically. We incarnate on Earth to play roles in these themes, and *Eye of the Centaur* has all the themes in our current Mayan Great Cycle—3313 BC to 2012 AD. For example, the theme of the last baktun, which began in 1618 AD, was the development of technology and the left brain. In *Eye of the Centaur,* the rationality theme opens with the astronomer, Erastus Hummel, expressing his delight and creativity over his opportunities to escape from the medieval belief systems which had become oppressive during the latter phases of the previous baktun.

Regardless of where the memories come from, it is important to work with them in a literal way, for that is how we all play the history game. This book, of course, has its own special teaching in the trilogy. *Heart* is about deity and humankind, about sky and Earth, about the central event of this fifth Mayan Great Cycle: God, or the divine, entering into incarnational cycle.

The only knowledge I had of this book when I began it was that it would be a journey through the underworld to bring light into every shadow that has ever been a part of my experience on this planet. All of the titles for this trilogy came to me in a dream in 1983, and I have honored that information even if a publisher has wanted to alter it. When I began this book, I had no idea how Christos—the Hebrew Messiah—might be part of my journey through the underworld, even though the title given to me in 1983 was *Heart of the Christos.* My studies with Matthew Fox in creation centered theology are much the source of the creative matrix of this book. However, Matthew Fox states in his latest book, *The Coming of the Cosmic Christ* (Harper & Row, 1988), that interpreting past lives in a literal way is a form of pseudo-mysticism he calls "New Age-ism." My master's thesis written under Fox in 1983 was a comparison of Jungian psychoanalysis and past-life regression under hypnosis as therapeutic tools for accessing the archetypal memory bank. *Eye of the Centaur* is based on that master's thesis. *Heart* delves into christological themes which were brought up during my graduate studies. In *Heart*, I have focused on christological themes and humankind's struggle with intervention into human affairs by the 'gods who came down' — the Nephilim of the Hebrew Bible. This theological probing comes out of my study of creation-centered spirituality, and many of the themes in this book are very closely related to the themes in Matthew Fox's latest book.

In my introduction to *Eye of the Centaur*, I say, "It never mattered to me whether the lives I found were actual past lives or whether a voicing of subconscious needs was occurring." The therapists I am working with for this trilogy — Christina Griscom, Rick Phillips, Stacy Williams, Kurt Leland, and Tom Cratslie, as well as myself — mostly hold that we do not know whether the material we access is personal past lives or not. What is important is that analysts of various body/mind schools, particularly rebirthers, have discovered that nearly 100 percent of people will report the contents of the memory bank in a very literal way within a linear past-life format if led back in time under hypnosis. The point is, literal manifestation of memory of past lives is the fastest and most easily accessible way to get the psyche to speak — to report on its current agenda. The memories that someone's psyche speaks of are always of critical importance to the stage of growth in the present life. Jungian dream analysis is time-consuming and often difficult for people, but it is certainly equally deep and effective. The comparison is that past-life regression also works and is affordable to people because only a few sessions are needed.

When we first access past-life material, we need to trust it and not judge it, for it is the psyche doing storytelling. In this book, you will encounter very clear and emotionally heightened experiences of Paleolithic times. It is difficult to access such seemingly bizarre and foreign contents of the mind unless one shuts off the left brain entirely and simply allows the right brain to tell its colorful story. You will encounter a sexual initiation that I — whatever I is — undergo with a tiger. If at any moment in that session I had judged the material for one second — worried about what my husband, mother, or sister would think of me and the tiger—I would have lost my reunion with the animal who was my gateway to courage of the heart. It is critical to trust the process as it is occurring, and the time for judgment is later. The highest value of this work is in allowing yourself to deeply trust your own psyche. Many of your own judgment patterns may be challenged by reading this book, but it is judgment that is preventing any of us from discovering who we are, because judging removes us from our experience—the ground of being.

Metaphor is a bridging skill, a subtle technique to suggest analogies between things or feelings. For me, it is one of the most creative tools of suggestion about what reality actually is. Christos is a metaphor of the striving of humankind for its freedom of expression, for its freedom to know how to connect to creation itself. I use the name Christos for a principle of divinity which penetrated the Goddess—the Earth. This principle has many different names in many different cultures, such as Quetzalcoatl, or Kukulcan, in Mesoamerica. Once the past lives were accessed, I viewed all of the stories as metaphorical images of humankind's critical theological questions: Pentecost, crucifixion/sacrifice, covenant, hierogamous, transfiguration, and Faustian pacts. The past lives become the paint for my canvas, my book. We wake up on Earth when we see that we are all crucified here, that we are all transfigured here. These are not just things that happened to Christos, to someone else. The real battle of the New Age is going to be over the issue of taking Christ seriously when he said that we can do all he has done and more.

The greatest value of exploring past lives lies in its reality power. It has the ability to take us beyond the fear of death and to help us come alive again, remembering that WE were there at the Pentecost, which makes the Pentecost now. This form of therapy is also very successful for releasing addictions, helping people to let go of past life and/or childhood trauma, and for reawakening magical and mystical parts of the psyche that have been dormant since the worship of the left brain began four hundred years ago. And this field has hardly begun to develop.

In my lectures around the country, I got some feedback that shocked me and deepened my belief in my own work. The most constant resistance I have gotten to my work (and therefore where the teacher lies) has come from people who have difficulty with what I'm doing because "They might have to come back here again!" In other words, they are startled by the immediacy of the lives in my books and my ability to own up to that material as being contents of my own self. This triggers them into considering that we really might have been here before. But, if we were, then we will come again. Invariably, the individuals who have this issue, and I congratulate them (or you) for looking at it, are wealthy, healthy, and living lives that many oppressed people on this planet think they want for themselves. But my detractors don't want to come back here again! The ecological implications of this are mind-boggling! The wish to die and never live on Earth again is one explanation for why we are on the brink of ecocide. The one-lifetime mentality is destroying Earth. If you realized you would be back around 2150 AD, 2300 AD, 3000 AD, every action you take here might be different. Would Einstein have assisted in splitting Mother Earth if he knew he would return?

I would like to share with you how I feel about this book at this time, and how I see recovery of our memory bank as critical to contemporary therapeutic technique. A great consciousness crisis of our times has to do with channeling and a related phenomena—literal extraterrestrial contact. This book has accessed some of the most deeply hidden records of ancient civilizations—The Emerald Records, Gospel of Marcion, The Sirian Teachings, Secret of the Grail, Teachings from Nibiru/Marduk, Conch Shell Singing of Teotihuacan, the Men in Black from Orion, Starseeding from the Pleiades, Arcturian Oracular technology, and the mathematics of Andromeda Galaxy—and this is not a channeled book. Some people believe I am a channel. I would like to explain exactly how my work differs from channeling. As for literal experiences with extraterrestrials, I have been exploring such actual contact since a few months after my birth, and I am comprehending the meaning of my communion and offering my thoughts. The meeting with our grandfathers and grandmothers of other dimensions is a crisis of our times, and we are about to have some close encounters, much as we did a long time ago. But we will miss our appointed communion if we view the return in an excessively third-dimensional way—seeking silver ships from the Pleiades.

Channeling, as I understand it from a past life as a Native American priestess and also directly from some contemporary channels, is the skill of vacating the present self so that entities who are not in the physical can come into the body of the channel and communicate through him or her. Psychologically, channels either do not remember at all, or partially remember the contents of what they have accessed. They can, of course, listen to taped transcriptions of their work in order to access the wisdom themselves, and many of them do. I feel it is dangerous to access any material without personally integrating it totally into one's psyche. In

Heart of the Christos, no new step is taken until the previously accessed energies are integrated. As readers, I ask you to take time to integrate any responses you feel in your body or mind as you encounter this material. This book is very shamanistic — in touch with dimensions other than the third — and it has many codes in it for you to take the journey into the underworld to recollect your own power. But, do not forget to take the time to integrate yourself as you go along. If a story told in this book is reminding you to pay attention to something you are feeling inside, that is why I wrote it. Please get in touch with what those responses are telling you.

My work differs from channeling because I do not vacate myself as I probe the memory bank. I trust that the contents I find are my own and not from some other disembodied entity. If I am enough of an artist to create this material in a form which communicates, then these stories are of universal relevance. I now trust the universality of the material due to the intense responses many people had to *Eye of the Centaur.* If we are to move beyond separation, we must see that the thoughts and myths we entertain within us are actually the stories of all people through all times. And, these are not just stories of people! As in the latter stages of a successful Jungian analysis, when the client is diving into the deepest recesses of the mind and encounters animal archetypes, I found animal teachers within. Then, as soon as I found the animals, I found the stars!

The Milky Way is the roadway of the stars, called the Kuxuum Suum by the Mayans, and the creatures of this pathway — the constellations — are animals. One of the mastery areas of spiritual studies for the ancient Egyptians was observation of animal behavior and understanding the cosmic significance of such behavior. It is no accident that the Zodiac is a circle of animals, and it is no accident that getting in touch with animal totems is one of the most successful ways to get the psyche to speak. All is correspondance, all is in relation, and when we discover that, the ego boundaries melt away as we actually feel the cosmic interpenetration of all that is.

As I came to the end of writing *Heart,* I began to really understand the cosmic dimension in a way that included the extraterrestrial contact question. Contact with extraterrestrials occurred so early in life for me, that I have always been unable to think of them as "different." They are part of me, and they teach me in much the same way the animals have taught me. Like animals, they are real, but like animals, they are in another dimension. Animals are in the second dimension — they can feel, remember, and respond, but they do not understand time or space as we do. They seem to exist under a species-level definition more so than humans, and I doubt they need to repeatedly incarnate. They appear not to be aware of their own mortality, and their ways of expression seem to be very unconscious. Extraterrestials are in dimensions beyond the third—the human dimension. The third dimension is a reality of time and place which we humans have time and place laws of agreement about. The fourth dimension operates according to laws beyond space and time. Physical manifestation in the fourth dimension is possible for adepts with skills such as the ability to bilocate. Conversely, beings of other dimensions like extraterrestrials can manifest in the third dimension. But, for the most part, entering the third dimension is a waste of time and energy for extraterrestrials, and it is arrogant of us to expect it of them. It is also arrogant to desire human responses from animals, for we should be learning from animals their own ways. Our access to animal wisdom is by entering the second dimension, a plane free of ego and just as complex as the third. If we were to know the animal reality as they know it, we would be released into the universe of symbols.

The fourth dimension and beyond is the source of the records in this book. The more I am totally conscious in the third dimension, the more clear is my access to other dimensions. Some of the records came in under hypnosis and some of them did not. There are some past lives in this book which came to me in the middle of the day while I was meditating at sacred sites. There is an intricate cosmology in *Heart* which probably functions in dimensions beyond the third, but my explanation of the cosmologies—such as the cycles of Nibiru and the Sirian Records—is third dimensional. I intuit that *Signet of Atlantis* will be from the fourth-dimensional point of view, but I cannot imagine writing in such a way, yet.

The way I become conscious of such cycles while I am in the third dimension is to spend a lot of time transferring my awareness to other locations, such as the Andromeda Galaxy. Then I observe what is happening on Earth from another point of view, and the records of time become very accessible to me. Most of my problem is in later telling the story well. Another source of new points of view is within information which was declared heretical by whomever was in power during a given historical phase. After the destruction of the Hebrew Temple in 70 AD, there was a new creative form for rewriting history, called book burning. Records of alternative points of view have been seemingly destroyed, but it is possible to travel into the mind of anyone who ever lived on Earth!

I believe that accessing records which were threatening to the powers-that-be is the same teaching as the Nahuatl tradition of looking into the Smoking Mirror, which makes available transfigurating knowledge. There is also a major Mayan initiation that often occurs in my dreamtime which involves walking backwards back in time through a day. What is revealed is similar to the levels of clear truth that can be found by considering the wisdom of the heretics—those who think differently. Another power access point to the energy of truth beyond judgment is available in the sessionwork on the "unspeakables" at the Light Institute in Galisteo, New Mexico. Contacting the forbidden parts of the psyche—such as considering the possibility that one might have murdered or raped a person in a past life—remarkably frees the psyche from judgment. Allowing the exploration of taboo frees the soul from denial of the inner anger that exists within all of us. Such work also frees the individual from needing to act out such inner anger by means of criminal activity. So if you, the reader, can allow yourself to let go of excessive worry about the literal truth of my attempts to retell the story of time, new brain cells can be stimulated for you by looking at history in a new way.

In my research, information that gets burned is always the most relevant source. For this book, I traveled back into the mind of Marcion, Hebrew theologian, who founded a Christian synagogue based on Jesus as Messiah which was as large as any early Christian Church before 150 AD. But, Marcion was declared an arch-heretic by the Roman Christian Church, and the book burners eliminated all of the original written sources on Marcion. Marcion turned out to be a major entry point into early pre-Roman Christianity.

I am in great debt to Sumerian scholar, Zecharia Sitchin, for his work, which gets in touch with Earth history from another perspective. Sitchin is the author of *The Earth Chronicles*, in which he has told the story of Earth from the point of view of the gods—the Nephilim—"those who came down to Earth." This story exists in many records on Earth, the most complete sources being Sumerian and Egyptian, which Sitchin has thoroughly chronicled in his trilogy. I read Sitchin in the mid-seventies and was intrigued by his complete history of humankind's experience with the gods—Nephilim—of the twelfth planet, Nibiru, "the planet of the crossing" in Sumerian. The ancient story sounded so familiar to me. But, as an astrologer, I do not pay much attention to stellar phenomena or potential planets unless they have been discovered scientifically. Then on December 27, 1983, the *Washington Post* reported that an IRAS Satellite had sighted a celestial object "possibly as large as Jupiter" and "50 trillion miles from the Earth." On August 16, 1987, many major newspapers reported a similar sighting by Pioneer 10. No one is certain what this object is, but I thought of *The Twelfth Planet* by Sitchin. I think we are getting an early sighting of Nibiru returning from its aphelion (outermost point of orbit), which occurred around 1600-1800 AD. Since astronomers do not consider it to be possible that there could be a planet with a 3600-year orbit around the Sun, they are not yet entertaining the possibility that the body is a planet.

After the 1983 sighting, I reread *The Twelfth Planet* and took Sitchin's theories much more seriously. The emergence of the archetypal force of the twelfth planet became a real phenomenon to me, for which I expect scientific verification during my lifetime. In 1983, I was also bringing in the hologram for my own trilogy. I intuited that I would encounter some of the material that Sitchin chronicles from Egyptian and Sumerian sources. No material about "those who came down"—the Nephilim in the Hebrew Bible—came through while I was doing sessions for *Eye of the Centaur*. However, when I began work for *Heart*, I was literally overwhelmed with experiences with the Nephilim as well as with other star systems and galaxies. At that time, in 1987, I did a lot of comparing of my trilogy to Dante's *Comedia* because *Heart of the Christos* was coming out like *The Inferno*. But, *The Inferno* is Dante's journey through a hell filled with devils and his most despised evil contemporaries, while I was encountering the dark, the underworld, as a whole pack of extraterrestrials who were imprisoned in my soul!

For many people today, fear of extraterrestrial manifestation is similar to the medieval fear of devils. As I encountered the Nephilim while under hypnosis, I also found much evidence of the influence of the gods on Earth that was not in Sitchin's work, and my confidence that Sitchin is correct began to deepen. Next, I began to experiment with the cycles of the twelfth planet. First I attempted to discern what was happening on Earth during the phases of the orbital cycle of Nibiru. I attempted to synchronize Nibiruan cycles with planetary cycles, with Sirian cycles available from Dogon ritual cycles, with the Precession of the Equinoxes, and with the Mayan Great Cycles.

Heart of the Christos was seeded when I realized that the last time Nibiru would have come into the solar system was 0 AD. Yet Sitchin had not published much information on 0 AD. The sources on the visit of the Nibiruans in 3600 BC are voluminous and incontrovertible, and there is even some information on the cycle before that, 7200 BC. The planet comes into the solar system every 3600 years according to Sitchin, and therefore the evidences of Nibiruan influence in 0 AD should have been far superior to the 3600 BC records. Next, I set up a test for myself and Sitchin: I decided to study the sources from 0 AD, and if the influence of Nibiru was present, Sitchin was right. If there were not written chronicles, historical records, symbols and images, and new spiritual movements about "the gods," I was going to forget the whole thing. I was more than rewarded, and this book is a result of that research. The bibliography at the end of this book lists the sources of my research, but here I'd like to state that the most extensive evidences of the perihelion (return) of Nibiru are in the Jewish apocalyptical movements — The Elect — anticipating the Messiah — Christos. I now believe the Star of Bethlehem was Nibiru rising since the symbol of Nibiru is an eight-armed celestial body, the same as the symbol of the Star of Bethlehem in early Christian sources.

This is not the place to give away the story of how Christos/Quetzalcoatl/Kukulkan/Buddha/the Native American white prophet, and all the other great teachers around the time of the 0 AD crossing of Nibiru are part of the records of time. I can say that I believe that all of you would know about all of the stories in this book if it weren't for the destruction of the temple in Jerusalem in 70 AD, the burning of the libraries in Palestine, the systematic destruction of early Christian sources by the Vatican during the early Church period, the burning of the Alexandrian Library in the fourth century AD, the wholesale destruction of the Aztec/Mayan/Nahuatl records by the Spaniards in the sixteenth century, and the eradication of most Native American spirituality by the colonists. Roman Christianity has been a two-thousand-year coverup of the real story of Christos and his stellarcentric origin.

This is a blasphemous book because it tells the truth. It is a blasphemous book because millions have been killed to keep us from discovering that we are free people. Our oppression is having the story of our origins burned, lied about, and used for power over people. Most importantly, our story was taken from us and we could not know Christ in the heart — until now.

Barbara Hand Clow
January 21, 1989
Santa Fe, New Mexico

Chapter One

TANTRIC INITIATION & THE GODDESS

I hear wind whistling through cypress trees. It is air sucking, like the wind being pressured between rocks or the inner ventricles of large seashells. That sound brings it all back to me . . .

I am lying on a flat, smooth, red rock about eight feet long and three feet wide, two-and-a-half feet off the ground, surrounded by a sandy circle which is then surrounded by a circle of outwardly facing deer antlers. Beyond the antlers, a sandy pathway is edged by a circle of eighteen three-foot-tall stones spaced at eight-foot intervals. Low trees are within sight, beyond a third sandy path around the stone circle. This is a mountainous promontory high above the Aegean on the westerly pointing part of the Island of Crete. Dim light lingers as the Moon begins to be blackened by the Goddess. I am oiled and rubbed. I lie naked on my back, on the rock. The breezes caress my flesh, and the birds quiet as the Moon is swallowed by the Goddess. The sea is full as the tides are high below; the dolphins dive deeply into the waters as the silvery lunar glow disappears from the sea surface. The creatures in the Earth begin to stir as they feel the coming total lunar eclipse of 1472 BC which will occult Venus. I am priestess of the Moon, and by undergoing hierogamous—becoming the sacred vessel between Earth and sky during the eclipse—I will be given the power of the Thasos Oracle, the oracle which links Delphi to Baalbek and guards the Argo—the boat of the Sun's journey through the night sky. I have offered my body as Earth temple because my times are End Times.

I awoke in utter terror from this numinous scene that had broken through into my Dreamtime. Frantically, my mind searched for the meaning of this clear and ancient memory breakthrough from Aspasia, a Minoan priestess past-life of mine. This break-

3

through occurred in the winter of 1986. My spiritual teacher had suggested at the 1986 summer solstice that I must undergo a tantric sexual initiation with him in order to become a vessel to connect sky and Earth. Now the Dreamtime was exploding within me like a volcanic cataclysm! What did this shining black-and-white night dream mean?

The most rigorous teaching I have ever considered is that we are not separate from each other—that we create our own realities, absolutely. When this teacher manifested with a proposition which had already been presented to many of my sisters before me, I felt a new force building within which would allow me to test my beliefs. Every cell in my body knew that this potential sexual initiation was absolutely wrong for me. However, I knew that the hierogamous was once a great mystery teaching about Earth/sky connection. In prepatriarchal Goddess cultures, this ceremony was an essential survival tool, consisting of sexual initiation in return for the annual fertile fruits and grains and cosmic balance from the Goddess.

Was my inner self being mirrored to me by this man, this teacher? Or was this Heyoka, the fool, inviting me into the danse macabre—a repetition of an old mistake made in another life? Or was this the hiatus—the divine leap?

The truth is in the body. My body, my intact sense of womanself in this late twentieth-century lifetime, is my own true vessel of enlightenment. My own life in the present time was what was authentic, yet I recognized that since this issue was being raised at this time it had to be a signal directing me to an opening into my inner self. Pummeled into going within again, I opened my heart and soul, expanding myself into the inner journey regardless of the possible outcome.

What does it mean for us today that our ancestors—our gene pool, our participation in history, our very DNA—all once experienced ritual sex to birth the divine child? That we once did ritual sacrifice, offering ourselves or the lives of our oldest children for the collective benefit of the tribe? My soul took me right back into into my past life as Thracian seer, Aspasia, who lived when the Aegean Goddess culture was obliterated by warriors, a time when I did experience hierogamous while in a female body.

It is 3500 years ago. Lying exposed on the huge rock as if it is the flat back of some great beast that I cannot see, I return to my original belief system which caused me to agree to participate in the ceremony. I have searched the moon eyes of my sisters for almost a year, as the Earth has groaned and quaked from a great wrath of the Goddess. Never a day has passed without more signs of her pain. She has been lanced, and the priestesses can no longer placate her with sacred fires, temple ceremonies, and prayer. I have volunteered to appease her. The priests told me that the Goddess would be pleased with my offering.

A chill goes up my spine, through my penetrated heart, as the rapidly eclipsing Moon is now three-quarters dark. I hear the bodies of snakes slithering through sand as they emerge from their earth holes. The spiders are gripping the centers of their webs with a power greater than their size, and the great vultures and hawks fly in circles above me on the rock. This is the sanctuary rock of an ancient Cretan priestly cult. It is said to be the body of a great whale that was turned to stone when the kingdom of the ancient ones sank beneath the sea. The snakes slither nearer to the sanctuary rock in the center of the circle of stones, and the great birds circle lower. The spider feels the jerking body of the trapped fly it is gripping like the withering mind of an old crone which will not let go of a possession. I lie still as I feel the snake in my spine respond to the power of the Goddess.

The Moon darkens. I hear the movement of men's bodies as they pass around in a slow circle behind the stones. I feel the energy in my spine move to my neck and stop. It feels like the back of my neck is being gripped by pincers; my head fires with colored lights. My astral body, as if I am the mad crone who is my later self, feels the gripping legs of the spider as she sticks to her newly spun web, wrapping the fly body and wings. I feel the black widow's adrenaline, which runs hot in her body whenever she mates and kills the male, sap away my soul. My legs are spread, and I feel the chilled and damp breeze from the sea cooling my moist woman being.

The circle of priests is moving around faster, their hooded capes enshrouding their darkened faces. Their phalluses are rising, pressing their robes. Each priest sends his force to my woman center as they pass by the opening to me in the circle. The Moon darkens completely, a shudder goes through the plant, animal, and mineral kingdoms, and the priest who wears black breaks the circle and comes to me. The others wear grey robes. I close my eyes as I feel myself moved forward by hands holding my back and legs.

The priest in black moves his erect phallus into my virginal body and I am ripped by a pain that gags my throat and shocks my heart. My head spins with dizziness as the hard sword plunges into my soft body. I want to pass out, as awareness of my mistake instantly shocks me to a greater level of sight than I have ever known. My brain explodes with saffron color, and my soul cries—this is wrong!

I lie on the rock and take thrust after thrust, for I have been conditioned to never stop an initiation once it has begun. He moves in and out until near the threshold of his orgasm—Earth gift to the Mother. Then he draws out his weapon just before threshold, and throws his hands to sky and shrieks like an eagle:

"When the Sun hides the Moon and Venus, you cannot kill the grain god!"

I am numb; my woman being is ritually stolen by this secret chant to the Sun that was first shrieked out by my initiator and then chorused by the whole circle of priests. The priestesses are the protectors of the grain, the first gift from the stars! I feel a split through my body; my heart throbs as if it will break, and my throat feels choked just like the fly struggling for breath in the spider web. Another priest comes forward with his incredible phallus and plunges it deep into my violated body; my back arches and draws my spine off the stone. He thrusts in and out, and I watch his rippling chest muscles, the ecstasy on his face. His legs are powerful and they move his weapon in and out, plunging ever deeper in his search for my precious energy. He stops just short of orgasm, pulling his sword out, and shrieks to the nearly invisible Moon:

"We hold the Sun from you, so that Earth blocks your light and power."

He is saying he controls the Moon! The Goddess! There are eight of them, and each one of them violates my essence to the core of my being, as I lie there underneath the moonless sky, knowing that the world of the Goddess has ended.

Thousands of years of men violating women power will pass until all peoples find their own woman within—the Goddess within who does not desire violence, war, and sexual abuse.

Can I possibly begin to describe the shock to my psyche caused by the memory of that experience of core violation as a woman 3500 years ago? The recovery of this memory caused a new animalistic craving to find my primal roots. Possibly this crisis was revived at this time because Nibiru is now in the same position in the solar system that it was when the Goddess culture disintegrated. Once I brought Aspasia on the rock back into my conscious mind, my body began to feel like a great ancient cat. But, in my own life as Barbara, I did not yet know my feline heart. What was the very first incident that closed my throat, darkened my heart, and held my mind captive in this life? Where was that primordial memory of the source of my primary emotional blocks in my present life? What is it exactly in ancient memories that carries a numinous lure which we all sense that, if released, could propel us into enlightenment instantly? Visions of the snakes in the original Garden of Eden began to flood my inner mind, teasing me to dare to unlock their true legend.

Once when I was Aspasia, I knew the teachings in the wind, the Goddess in the water and earth. Purification was in fire, and the first teachers about the soul were the animals on the Earth. I never forgot this lesson because no one ever forgets any initiation. But, the elemental and animal dimensions were deeply submerged by the abusive, controlling, patriarchal culture I was born into. It took that call to a tantric initiation to rend my paralyzed heart open. Suddenly I had gotten the courage to cross the waters into the darkness, to confront every shadow within and take my own power. What was it that drove Aspasia herself into this ancient tantric ceremonial form?

I feel pain in my arms, in my chest, and in my third eye. I am standing with my head bent over. This is a temple of scribes, and seven of them are encircling me. The seven scribes wear saffron robes with wide gold sashes, and they sit in the lotus position writing on slates. I listen to the scratching chalk. Their heads are shaved except for little pigtails on the backs of their necks. Like their shining skin-tight skulls, their faces have no lines. They are maddeningly perfect, in total control, since they meditate constantly. The scribes are not human and betray no feelings.

I am blue-grey; I feel old. The scribes seem to be young. I stand with my head down as they sit around me in a circle, chastizing me. They keep scratching with their chalk on the slate. I have failed at some task they expected me to complete. I seethe with anger because I hate their perfection. My body energy is wild energy, animal energy, for I am part tiger, and I do not like the way they are. It is their judgment that I will be put to death because I know too much, and I refuse to compromise. I was not trained by them—I feel like a stranger. I hate their energy. They are so clean, so perfect, so balanced. I am animalistic, courageous, and I hate control.

I am bigger than they are; they are small little runts. I am large, like Bigfoot. I know about their corruption. I am a freedom fighter from the other side. I will be done in because of my knowledge. I am nailed. Always right in the middle of things, here I stand in the middle of this little pack of weak judges. They are the old way and I am the new path. These are the monks of the perfect city, Atlantis, the city of total control over the world. I am a creature of nature, free of human infringement.

I love wolves, snakes, birds, and spiders. I am a wild man stolen out of the forest. Like Romulus and Remus raised by wolves, my teachers are the animals. Now here I am in the midst of these perfect control monsters who created the world of the city, a place in which I cannot survive.

I am part of a clan. I can see the hills in the distance. We are the warriors of the woods, and these clean men are pushing into the forest. They are an alien death squad. I was trying to destroy them so they couldn't get into our village, and they trapped me. I was sitting by the sacred spring which flows out of the mountain which hovers over our village. They were spying on me. I was going into the Dreamtime by watching the water trickle over the crystal clusters at the mouth of the spring. I was caught off guard because I was visualizing their activities in Atlantis, and when they arrived in physical form, I thought it was an appearance from another dimension.

These people are henchmen, and they are not the leaders of the city. They are just performing a rite; they are just tools for other powers. That is what infuriates me. I cannot get at the real cause; I would rather be judged by their king. I am passive even though I feel all this anger and violence within. I'm passive because I fear they will torture me. Torturing me will neutralize my anger so that my spirit can't malign them later. The monks are writing the form of my torture down on the seven tablets in great detail.

The Atlanteans are going to clean me up! They are going to tie me to a post and cut off all my hair to make me like them. The beating in my chest convulses my heart with terror. My energy is in my hair! From the beginning of time, my clan has been one with the animal spirits, and the animal spirit is in my hair. Each hair is an electromagnetic transmitter to the stars from the center of the Earth, and they are going to remove it! They write my sentence because they can feel how much I hate their slavish conformity.

The Atlanteans have no odor, but my people are able to live in the woods by utilizing smell. These judges don't even want to cut off my phallus, which is what I'd do to them. They only want to clean me up! Then they are going to burn me up at the pillar, but it is still a worse punishment that they will cut my hair. We are the hill people, and our life is based on our attunement to the elemental forces. We cannot exist without our hair for we can feel with our hair when lightning will strike.

This is 9000 BC, and the difference between the city people and the forest people is dramatic. We are like animals and they are like machines. The Atlanteans are the metal people who came from the stars. They are cleanliness and light and we are Earth and darkness. This is the time when the Atlantean colonies realize they cannot survive in isolation and they go into the surrounding territory to master our Lemurian ways in order to attune to Earth energy.

This sentencing connects to my lifetime when I am a Talmudic scribe. In that future life I am as wild as if I have an animal inside, and yet I undergo great cultural evolution as a star teacher. I am initiated by studying Hebrew, and I am given the secret teaching about the evolution of humans beyond the animal realm: "Words and symbols transmit divinity and so do sacred teachings because the letters are infused with power, even if the text has been altered, misinterpreted, or mistranslated."

This condemnation in writing by seven scribes is deeply disturbing. My sentence is that I will be cleaned up and burned to death, and that these words of my condemnation are the holy word of God! I could shift into my lion body and get out of here, but I am staying here long enough to imprint this experience so that I can transmute it later. . .

Therefore, sacred language cannot be trusted. The correct form of the evolution of the race still survives, however, and is transmitted through time because of the planetary Earth oracles. Outside the city, I was the guardian of the sacred spring of an oracle. These monks found out, and they knew they could never invade the labyrinthian matrix of this land unless they held the power of my oracle. They were getting rid of me because they could not access the oracle as long as I was alive. Oracles are a voice of the Earth, and anyone can hear them who is in complete attunement with how the heart of the Goddess beats eternally in the universe.

The first scribe wrote that all people speak for themselves, that no one person speaks for another. The second scribe wrote that knowing the truth is never dangerous, and that a time would come when the oracle would transmit to all. The third scribe wrote that I was giving myself as a gift to the future. The fourth scribe wrote that the wild man would one day learn to speak the truth with no fear. The fifth scribe wrote that eventually this wild man would learn that no one individual holds a truth. The sixth scribe wrote that one day this being would freely express spiritual essence in all forms. The seventh scribe wrote that the wild man would one day reintegrate full animal essence and have no dissonance with civilization and the sacred word. Then the scribes placed their chalks on the floor.

As I stand at the pillar, my body is white and raw. I was scrubbed with hot suds and water until I bled. The flames are lit as the monks begin to walk around me in a circle. This sight catapults me inwardly to a vision of myself lying on the rocks during the eclipse. Licking flames warm my flesh and dry the water on my skin, and then my skin begins to burn. I feel no pain now that I'm finished being cleaned up. As my physical body dies, my shadow jumps out and flies through the astral plane back to the deep woods. I become a panther. When the city people come to my sacred spring to listen to the stories of time, they will meet with me again as a cat, my form as a warrior of the Earth power. My soul rises in the night sky and also returns to my oracle, and I spin around the site like a whirling dervish. Then I go straight up to the blue light. Looking back down at the Earth, I see blue-light energy emanating from all the oracles, forming a crystalline grid matrix across the surface of the planet. I return to my star home which I watched in the night sky while I was on Earth. I see the crystalline matrix formed by all the power points on Earth. They are owned and controlled by no man or temple and are eternally guarded by the animals!

Once I contacted the beast within, truly amazing shifts began to happen in my present life. The boundaries I had always felt between myself and others began to soften. At first, this change was disturbing because I could feel other people too intensely. I was unable to go into crowds, especially supermarkets, the most unnatural places in the modern world. My heart could feel the needs and pain of people. In confrontative situations, I could actually feel my guts knotting and turning. When I saw bare truth, my liver, spleen, and pancreas would ache. I got a gnawing feeling that perhaps I did not know anything at all. Maybe I did not even know whether I had an existence which defined me. Now I see that I had dissolved the flowering field of my own childish illusions because I was on the verge of falling down the tunnel of the underworld.

Once an illusion—a chimera that enables you to not grow—dissolves, it goes back to the first dream that created it. I had no idea that there was no return to my old world until I saw one day that my everyday reality had become a chasm away from myself, as if I were looking at myself across a canyon. I truly was in a bell jar, on an island in a dimension not even known to me yet, and so far gone was my old self that there was no return. Just like the person shipwrecked on the proverbial desert island, I made the decision to know myself with all the rawness and vigor of new life. I could see that I was a shadow in my present world, a shell. I was required to go on playing my old role as the new life grew. I felt a growing trust that it was all right not to be present as my old self during this incubation time.

Then, falling into a deeper part of myself made me want to meet again with the great mother who was wandering the fields of forgetfulness—the home of woman pain from the loss of our daughter, Persephone. I became Persephone and discovered that I was still alive in the underworld with Pluto, as my own mother called to me from above. I had dared to ask for my source, and my soul called out to my mother to return with me to my birth in this life.

I am my soul as a tan cat. My energy exists in my blue eyes, and power radiates out of me as a cat. I am strong and steady. I exist firmly within at the center of my being. I am a wise and tricky cat, and I watch the reptilian energy level carefully. I am a protector.

Now I see it! I am swirling in the midst of a murky green tornado, a sucking vortex. This is the time between my last lifetime as the Victorian woman and my current lifetime as Barbara. The vortex is spinning upward as time ends, but I reverse the flow and I spin back down again, wishing to return with new eyes. I want to know about the hidden realms regardless of the consequences. My field of vision is all dense and green, as if I am caught in a tornado like Dorothy in the Wizard of Oz. I am spinning around. I am so heavy that I spin down instead of up.

No, wait! Caught in all my fears, I don't want to go! I never wanted to go! It is I who did not want to come . . . ! I always thought my resistance to this place started because I was not wanted, but no, my mother wanted me. I nearly died right at birth, but I did choose to be born. She is an exquisite spiritual being, like all mothers. I see now that she is old, but I never saw until now that she was so spiritual, even when she was young. But it is so painful, so sad from this view, because I can see truth outside of time. These are the total records of all my lives, and I am ecstatic! I can see every experience I will have, in all of my lives, with an open heart. I dive down.

First I see my mother standing in fields of grain in ancient Greece. The grain is tall and waving around her as she stands and radiates unearthly white light. She looks to the side. Her face is beautiful, like a goddess, as her loose white tunic blows in the wind. She surveys the grain as the wind makes wave patterns like it does on the surface of the sea. Her light is intense, opal and turquoise, like a flash of sunlight captured within a gemstone. I rush joyfully to her as she touches my third eye lightly, and then she puts her hand over my crown chakra. Oh, this is so real—it is the most intense feeling I have ever had.

As she touches me, I realize that I came to life again because I wanted to. I always thought I had not chosen to come for this late-twentieth-century lifetime, for I knew exactly what would happen at this time. It would be the gathering time when those I had known in other bodies, other times, would decide to either destroy Earth or choose life. As I came in, my own lack of trust coming from my own negativity made me fear the outcome, and I shut my heart down as I came in. Once my heart was closed, then every cell in my body contained pain and fear instead of ecstasy and courage. Therefore I had to agree to go back through every experience from the beginning of time and clear it. No wonder I resisted, but what if there was never another time when my mother the Earth could touch me, could hold me?

As my own mother stands in the field, worry captures her beautiful face as she discovers I have gone underground. She becomes Demeter, as all mothers have from the beginning of time. She, too, is having her trust tested for bringing a soul into form. She, too, will know the initiation of losing a child, and losing the man who made that child with her. She claws at her dress, and at her hair and face, as the agony of recognizing the pain that is life strikes her all-seeing soul. I return again to the time before I came to Earth.

I am back in the volcano, which is now indigo blue. I have come back to the time of choosing again, but this time it is my stellar choosing from the center of our galaxy. Why is it this way on Earth! Why must we take the underworld journey! I spiral back to the time when I had the courage to ask that same question once before, back to 26,000 years ago when Pisces precessed into Aquarius in the previous cycle. I will travel back even further if it is required to receive the answer to my most important question: Why is there evil on Earth?

I feel myself being water. I am a sponge in the stars! I am swelling, moving into form like a new coral bank as I feel my own intracellular encodement. Eyeless, I look with wonder, as I feel that the connections between things are all that really exist. When I incarnate, my perceptions are false. There is no real pain, only the perception of pain. I do not leave my mother for my journey, and my mother does not lose me. We are never really separated, and so I am free to return again.

I am an Earth guardian as we all are guardians of the Earth, and I have always come willingly. Earth is where we play all the music. Otherwise, all existence happens in the last note of Beethoven's Ninth Symphony. We all came here to play! Life is the musician playing in the orchestra, but I had believed that the conductor made the music happen. That is why the symphony was invented only in the last few hundred years, after we had managed to convince ourselves that there is always a leader, always a beginning and ending note. But now we are being catapulted into the energy itself, and are beginning to see that we are the sound and the vibration. The illusion of the symphony—the third dimension—will exist only as long as we need it.

Our modern-day contemplation of our dark side is a crisis caused by the mass media. For example, Einstein knew he was making a mistake when he decided to play Prometheus, the god who is chained in the underworld because he desires immortality, and who covets the fire powers which belong to the Goddess. In ages past, we would not have known what Einstein created in his laboratory. All who are able to know the Goddess know Einstein made a fatal choice, because the quest of the female is to die, to open the underworld, and to rediscover our intact and timeless daughter within. Women do not desire earthly immortality since they can give birth.

I admit it. My stellar soul, the non-material part of me that lives in many other realms, did not want to return when I saw that Einstein had been seduced by the lure of the sacred fire. Controlling matter/Goddess? Quite a feat. Because of that fatal egotistical turn, now we all must enter the world of Pluto for purification—a journey once reserved for a few rare initiates—or choose the fate of Icarus and disintegrate in the fire. This is what I resisted: I did not want to return because I knew that I would have to die as a function of the old pattern or discover an entirely new way which I could not yet imagine from my previous experience. This is a time when we are going to let go of all knowing without being sure of any possible outcome. When the Big Bang ceases to be the official story of our creation, we will be ready to contemplate being the music itself. The part of me that could not resist coming back is the child within who knows we are on the threshold of a new world. It is the part of me that plays.

Now as I contemplate my incarnational choosing from the stellar perspective for the last time before birth, I see that I am in the direct center of new creation, the center of the galactic core—two spinning arms of positive and negative manifestation which bring matter into form. One arm of the galaxy is me, the other arm is the arm of my twin self, my brother. I hear the cries of my mother as if they are emerging from a conch shell, and I come into form with a rare indigo-blue crystal from the galactic core, which I gave to my son. He places it in the seventh Earth chakra—Palenque Temple: Supernova 1987 showers Earth with photons, new seeds.

I become a spinning flower, spinning very, very fast. I spin so fast there is no motion, and that is what trust is. I spin so fast that someday I will even have the courage to have my own daughter. I will be ready to choose to be the one who wanders year after year calling for her. I will allow my own heart to break for the love of the creation itself. I stay in that place, spinning as I choose all of my children, knowing that we must return and let ourselves cry to moisten the Earth and make the plants green again.

I spin faster and faster, creating a new reorganizaton of creative energy. I am preparing myself to create balances and harmonics within, which will actually synchronize stellar and Earth vibrations. As this is done, I feel emptiness, a creative force inside that is magnetic and like a hot coal. Then I notice that the energy inside is like the vibrations outside myself, that there is no difference. This is an inner trust which exists when I exist here on Earth and in the center of the galaxy simultaneously. This knowing is simply a pulsation, a vibration traveling in the spine.

This is the pulsation Einstein needed to feel so that he would know there could be no shield around his creation: split matter. I now speak as the Goddess who protects Earth against all destructive forces: Einstein was to have dissipated his cyclotron when he saw its potential to harm my creation. He was to have seen that we must let go of God/Yahweh whenever that God demands that we harm the Earth, for then that God is our own ego. We must stop splitting matter, believing that energy is created from that splitting, for energy is created from spiraling forms. The Goddess is returning to clear away foul pollution with her spiraling arms of massive hurricanes and firestorms. Earth is the Goddess who is awakening.

WERNEKE ©1989

Chapter Two

THE OLMEC & THE
RECORDS OF TEOTIHUACAN

"I did not want to return again because I knew I would have to die as a function of the old pattern, or discover an entirely new way which I could not yet imagine from my previous experience."

The part of me that could not resist returning, however, is the part of me that plays. The very instant I was able to feel my own mother's ecstasy and pain, I was granted my own daughter from the universe. The Goddess was reborn in my own body. It felt like this was the first time I had opened myself since my soul was first injured on Earth. Men say that if we could see God, we would be blinded, and women say that when we feel Goddess, we are stripped of our lies.

But I must know! I feel such responsibility for every being who is oppressed and violated, abused, lonely, and separate that I must know why the forces that create our experience on Earth actually do allow such pain. Now that I had encountered the Goddess—who is simply pure energy with no judgment about any outcome—I was ready to consider the possibility that I/we are the sole creators of human evil and its required mirror—the angry God that we believe judges us. As this potential path of exploration manifested itself—which my soul had not looked at before—I took a long deep breath as I felt trust leap into my heart. I sensed I had the ability to safely invoke the gods at this time as the Goddess smiled on my newly found courage. Yet, her facial expression betrayed maternal concern, for she knew, far better than I, about the path I was headed down. When she created herself, she faced evil herself. The part of me that plays had asked to return to a life in which I had access to the "Green Records," the true story of the unfoldment of Earth . . .

I feel great energy in this body. I am ten feet tall and silver, with great wings. My head is in the jaws of a great serpent which envelops the back of my form, and I hold a bag of maize seeds. I am looking at a very early temple site which I have felt within my body since the beginning of time.

This is such a strong impression that I feel it in Barbara's heart. It's like the way I remember my childhood home. First, my eyes eat up all of the contours and shadows that I've missed for so long. Pausing a moment in wonderment, I realize that this is the place that I, as Barbara, kept trying to find when she was under five years of age. She called it Magicland. This is the Olmec temple site, La Venta, but we call it Machinga.

I stand next to a stone altar on the right side of a rounded pyramid which is in the center of the site. I see the site as clearly as if it were a photograph, as if time had stopped. Machinga is the sacred temple complex that we, the angels, first made in Mesoamerica. We created it so we could descend our bodies here in the new land after we decided to transfer the wisdom teachings of the ancient East to this new geomantic zone. This is 1141 BC, and our Earth people have come in great boats from the East. They left the land of Canaan when a conquering tribe of Hebrews out of Egypt destroyed the stone circles and Earth temples and stole the women and children. We are the sky teachers, and we cannot descend to Earth without the assistance of priests and priestesses who honor the sacred teachings of Earth energy. There is no access to dimensions higher than the third without geomantic temples, and there are no Earth temples left in Canaan except the great Dome rock in Jerusalem.

Machinga is an Earth-plane sculpture, a holographic form to balance Earth and sky, so that beings in other dimensions, such as myself, can commune with beings living on Earth. We created this site so we could descend in physical form to sacred sites in order to ground our multidimensional essence into the evolution of planet Earth. This pyramid is a record device which causes dimensional vectoring and makes it possible for us to come into form here, now or in the future.

The central pyramid is very beautiful, like an inverted honeysuckle blossom with the petal edges resting on the ground. From the sky, the pyramid looks like the rounded and cone-shaped backside of the blossom. The form is ideal for amplification of our wave pattern on Earth. By means of this form, we can calibrate feelings on Earth to feelings in other dimensions which are real, but are not detectable to the first five human senses. This is the temple of the Dreamtime, for our only access to the feelings of Earth creatures is our feeling for the currents of nature. The whole temple site is the perfect sculpture for us to take form. We attune our own wide-dimensional view into the animal, plant, and insect energies of Earth which do not exist in other places in the universe. This temple is the touchstone for calibrating Earth forms to our dimensions, and our new contact into the cosmically unique Earth experiment.

I see multicolored and radiant beings in the air. They radiate energy around their forms which are in the infrared dimension. The beings are radiances which are changing form as I look at them. They create forms that are comprehensible to me only if they want to be seen. They can always be seen at temple sites, and I've come to consult with them. I am standing in front of one being who is in front of the flower pyramid. Surrounded by a rainbow, she is so radiant, so electromagnetic, that I almost cannot look at her. She continually changes from cat to human as her energy form pulses out in curvilinear to circular radiant forms around her eyes. She has a feline face, like Sekhmet—lion goddess of Egypt—but in this land, she is the jaguar. I have chosen to come here now to hear her speak:

"I created this temple complex as a transfer point of the records of the Galactic Center. I transfer to this site the access mechanisms for the descending god, Itzanna, who will be fully human." This is a labyrinth, created so that people can access the records in non-physical form. The aliveness, the luminosity, color, and energy of the goddess is incredible, and I must attune my form to hers to know myself.

I stand in front of her, grounding all my own energy into the Earth dimensions. Her face becomes a spiral of white crystalline light, and all I can see is her eyes as she holds out the first medicine bundle given to a god who came from the East. Wrapped in a rabbit skin are small stone statues of Machinga. She places a string of cowrie shells on my neck, and points to a deep pit. I move quickly and place the medicine bundle in the pit. Then I remove the shells and place them in the pit. I return to stand in front of her, and I give her my bag of sacred maize. I feel myself becoming a stone statue as my crystalline matrix encodes myself as a gift from the East to Machinga. I am myself, as I am griffin and snake, as I am statue—holographic touchstone of all that is. She is the medicine bundle carrier in this new land, as I am the maize gifter.

I stand staring out through my stone eyes, and I watch as time passes. I see the temple begin to be grown over by the voracious jungle as storms batter my form and the Moon lights my surface. Earth begins to rise around me as choking vines cover me. Snakes crawl all over me, flying insects land on me, and birds shit on my head. I become one with Earth itself as I exist in this form for milleniums.

Now, I am being dug up! First they uncover my head, the very topmost part of me. I feel like they have found me because they can sense my energy. The archaeologists uncover and move me to another location, an outdoor museum at Villahermosa, Mexico. I am very upset because I am part of the code of Machinga which contains the secrets of multidimensional access for Earthlings. I go back again to when I first arrived in 1200 BC . . .

I seem to exist in many forms here because I hold resonant energy fields of fourth-dimensional light bodies of certain individuals such as Barbara. I'm not contained by time, but it is necessary for me to exist as a statue on Earth. I am called Nagua. As long as I exist in statue form on Earth, my higher dimensional self has a resonant waveform in the third dimension which is accessible to sensitive individuals. This is why so many ancient statues and carvings are found in temples and graves. Now that the temple sites are being restored and statues being found, people are getting reconnected to their fourth-dimensional light bodies, their stellar selves. I have experienced every storm and Full Moon, every eclipse and earthquake. When others are in touch with me, they are not afraid of danger on Earth. I am from Arcturus, and I calibrate cycles and time records on this planet in order to facilitate evolution. I am immortal, as is anyone in the fourth dimension.

This temple is a hologram that is completely encoded with all multi-dimensional spiritual forms which influence Earth. This is why the giant Olmec heads are so entrancing. People feel that the heads are able to speak and tell all. The seeker can only know the story of the Olmec transfer by hearing the voices in stone. Each statue has a special story, and I am ready to tell mine now. This pyramid is the perfect receptive resonator with the plane of the ecliptic of Earth, which is the location plane for all aspects of human souls that descend to Earth. This pyramid is the receptive, feminine complex that is in perfect attunement with all the forces in the universe. It is like a gigantic soul DNA form complex which calibrates the spiritual growth of each soul.

There is a crystalline spiral form above the pyramid like a gigantic wave form of very high energy. Each one of the statues is a teaching, an energy, which has a unique code for the human race. Each is attuned to the universal essence—the human energetic form which is beyond the physical. The sculptures represent a permanent way in which we are all in touch with oneness, but we have lost this trust in material form for thousands of years. The Jews and Christians condemned these sacred vessels as "idols." They learned that individuals could find their freedom by discovering angelic form on Earth through learning the encoded messages in stone. We transferred the energy form out of Canaan in 1141 BC when the Earth temples were desecrated, for this land was to hold the new temple. There are great snake forms of sacred stone buried deep within the ground here, built by us, which resonate with the Galactic Center. These forms have power, ultimately, over humanity's religious and political control of destiny. "As above, so below," was miscommunicated. These words are actually the Angelic Law of Compensation, which states, "The Above is exalted in the Below." Divinity implants energy into stone and radiates it out to encourage humankind to evolve, just as quartz crystals contain the exaltation of heaven in Earth.

I will now shift to the next transfer point: Teotihuacan.

I exist in a square column in the Temple of the Quetzal Butterfly above the Temple of the Plumed Shell at Teotihuacan, "where the tree god comes to Earth." I was asleep until August 16, 1987, when my spirit brother, the Nahuatl shaman, Victorio, woke me up by carving my form in obsidian. I have been the guardian stone hawk in this temple for two thousand years—since the time of Christos, in the form of the Quetzal—looking out through the obsidian eyes of Horus, carved into my face in the columns. I came here to exist on Earth until the end of the cycles of time, and I have been fully alive within this stone, holding the energy form of Christos, the descending god who becomes fully human.

Teotihuacan contains the Emerald Records of the story of Christos, as La Venta—Machinga—contains the codes of body dynamics in relation to other dimensions—the way in which humans take on form for the experiences needed by their souls. I am ready to open the Green Records, because doing so is safe now. We have passed beyond the Nine Hells of the Aztecs that spanned the period from 1519 AD until August 1987 AD. Pyramid relief drawings which depict four steps down to a base and four steps back up symbolize the Nine Hells. Pyramids with six steps up to a top and six back down symbolize the Thirteen Heavens. During the last Nine Hells, Mesoamerica was challenged to protect the original sacred teachings of Machinga and Teotihuacan, and this phase is now complete at the New Dawn.

The Christians from the East brought their religious beliefs about good against evil, their systems which teach that people are sinners at birth and must be redeemed. The Native Americans were judged to be "pagan" or at best innocently evil. The Nine Hells was a time during which the Native Americans rediscovered their own true divinity as custodians of the Earth, when the red race remembered that they were the chosen teachers of the white race. When the white race first invaded, they wore the mask of Quetzalcoatl. When they removed the mask to exhibit domination, the people were amazed! The native people said, "The white man, he must be crazy!" The people of the Americas were very patient, and they waited for the time of truth which would come because all the prophecies said it was so. The custodians truly believed the invader would recover from his sickness in the head that came from belief in a basically sinful nature. The white race would learn that Creation is good and can be trusted, and would learn to worship the Earth. As the time drew very near, certain white teachers were told the Legend of the Rainbow Warrior. They were given the true story of Quetzalcoatl/Kukulcan, the return of Christos—the birth of divinity in the Goddess.

The return of the Rainbow Warriors on Harmonic Convergence was the remembering by these teachers of how alive the Earth is when sacred sites are charged with power during ceremony. The Emerald Records are the entry into the hidden world, the journey through the night to observe the rising of the Sun at the New Dawn. They contain the true creation story.

Now I was intrigued. Emerald Records. . . there was a feeling in that term which seemed to open new centers of creativity in myself. Teotihuacan as the place where the Emerald Records are located . . . this was a refreshing possibility that the records of our spiritual evolution would be located in a temple site that had lain dormant for over a thousand years, and which was located in the Western Hemisphere. As fascinated as I was and still am by Egyptian, Sumerian, Druidic, Greek, and Hebrew mythology, I was even more excited by the possibility that the real story might be hidden right in my own land of birth. And Mayan daykeeper, Hunbatz Men, notes that the pyramid construction in Mesoamerica continued until about 500 years ago. Perhaps I was born here to manifest a sacred teaching of my own. Maybe we will build pyramids again.

When I was a child studying mythology, I longed for my own temples and pyramids. A few years before Harmonic Convergence in August of 1987, I began to remember that the real touchstone for me might be Teotihuacan, the pyramid complex north of Mexico City. I traveled to Teotihuacan to see whether this was the place of revelation for me. I have also traveled there several times since then, and each time I have received an extraordinary teaching.

I took my large quartz record crystal with me the first time, since the teaching might not be linear or verbal, but might come to me in some form which I would have to decode over time. The record crystal dutifully soaked up the hologram of the Records. The revelation of the Emerald Records then came to me through this crystal over a period of time. This knowledge will be revealed in each chapter of this book. The Emerald Records contain the single most important teaching about evolution on this planet, and a knowledge which is preparing us to experience the Heart of the Christos. The indigenous people of Mesoamerica have never forgotten that there is no separation—

they know that we are all living within the dreams of each other. That is why they knew Cortez wore the mask of Quetzalcoatl! Christos cannot return to a world that believes that one group or race is chosen by God while another is doomed. That is the Tower of Babel, the synagogue of separation. The judgment of others is what keeps us from our desire to know divinity.

When I arrived at Teotihuacan, I went to the Temple of the Quetzal Butterfly located directly above the Temple of the Plumed Shell. The section I was drawn to is an open-air courtyard surrounded by twelve, large, carved columns. Behind the columns in a covered area are fret designs in red ochre of a tree reaching for the sky and descending into the Earth—the descent of the red race. The top of the temple has solar unity symbols which reached for the sky and also ground into the Earth. The center of the courtyard is graded downward into a hole in the center, a sipapu—a hole to the spirits of the underworld in the Hopi tradition. This sipapu allows the rain water to flow down to levels below, and the whole courtyard feels like a temple of baptism. The visible level below contains magnificent conch shells carved in stone. The conch is the sacred shell of Quetzalcoatl, the Mesoamerican god who is the same as Christos of my own land. Sitting in lotus position in front of the sipapu with my record crystal and eagle feather, I asked to be given the knowledge of the Emerald Records.

The sun was hot, the winter winds outside the exquisite temple were strong, and my eyes studied the carved square columns of the Quetzal, which was the face of my own teacher, Horus. There was no doubt that this was a temple of the Divine Son, because Horus was a divine child as well as a bird in Egyptian mythology, and the legend of the return of Quetzalcoatl often involves the hawk. The hawk and the Quetzal symbolize metamorphosis. The eye is critical when contacting Horus, much as the Ojo Dios, the Eye of God, is important to native people. The obsidian eyes of the birds on the columns began to mesmerize me as I went into another dimension.

The first gate opening into the Records was a radical shifting in my bodily dimensions, and in my very understanding of the events I had experienced in this lifetime. I could hear the birds in the columns communicating with each other, and I became one of them as they recognized me. There was a great wind in the ancient temple courtyard that was open to the sky. My companions said that the tourists suddenly scurried out. My crystal began resonating with my own stone being as I heard a high-pitched whistling deep in my head. The sound felt like an obsidian knife, and then I heard a voice in the courtyard that seemed to come from the columns:

You are here to name yourself, even if it means
    you are an ass?
For your light to come into matter,
    radical transmutation is required.
In you we see dense grey forms brought here from eons ago,

yet here you are in the temple of Gaia-Saa . . .
Earth truth.
Woman, what are you going to do at this point?
For you are not in form in your Earth self yet.
You, not we, made yourself imperfect. We are only love.

If we let you pass, you will be annihilated.
So, tell us why you think you can pass our veil.
I say—Open to me! I will look at all dense grey forms.
If you will let me know the truth.
I will now look at the evil, all of it!
Be it mine or the issue of another.
I will agree to know every evil you shine your light upon.

Ha! What a joke you make up now! You? A Heyoka!
You haven't figured out how to laugh yet!

I still ask to pass . . .

And, with this crystal, I pledge to tell the whole story,
To my people of the heart. Whatever the story is,
I will reveal that story,
If you will open the door to the Records, to me.

Oh! Hoh! Let's let her have it, full force!
You have participated in every evil and ecstasy
     from the beginning.
You have been overtaken when you channeled before, and
In the condition you are in now,
     you will be overtaken again.
Ah, but we see that you enjoy a free-flowing life,
     that your intuition and spontaneity guide you.
You already know about what you did before . . .
Hah!
You don't even seem to give a damn about your past!
You don't even seem to fear the ones who will fear you,
If you dare to bring in the Records!
You are trying to integrate good and evil? A worthy task!
But, you have not looked at every ugly part of yourself,
The evil that you despise in others is actually your own.

I ask to pass again, knowing that if you deny me,
     I am consigned to a life of searching for the secrets

and only seeing my own nose.
I cannot be Sisyphus, Icarus, Atlas, Faust, or Job.
I ask to pass, knowing that my third request
    is my enlightenment, or my doom.
I ask to pass, knowing that each revelation I am given
Will create a corresponding freedom in my soul.

Hoh! So you ask for such clarity
    that you will not even be taken over?
As you bring the story of the Christos to all those
Crying for the spilling of the water of the ages past.
The pouring out by all the great people who believed
They were fulfilling their own great destinies?
Do you not see that those who need this wisdom for survival,
Will attempt to become your most worthy opponents?
Stop! We do not wish to annihilate you!

You cannot!
I experienced my own essence when I was five years old!
I never forgot it.
The visions haunted me like tongues of fire,
Only here in this antediluvian temple do I feel my essence!
I cry! I cannot go back, for I know my mission.

Do you know if we agree to this
    that you will have to see
All the misuses of power that have accrued to you
    as priest—
Channeler of transformation—in all your existences?
You will have to look at the blackness in your own heart.
Do you see that you are asking to expose secrets
    that people have died and sold their souls for
    in all the past ages?
You say you want to free that which you love—life itself?
You are willing to challenge all demons
    so that Earth can plant new symbols and ceremonies?
You will have to let go of all ideas
    that you ever thought defined you!
Are you willing to be named the Ass?
Do you see that you have come here to know your power,
Which means you will value the wisdom of those you teach

more than your own?
You are willing to let go of self for the new road of life?

Yes?

Pass! You have entry to the Emerald Records!

Chapter Three

PRIESTS, KINGS &
THE SIRIUS STAR RECORDS

The records of time, the real story of our history—imagine if I could get in touch with the origins of creation. What are we? What is our consciousness? I had passed through the three gates, passed beyond the judgment of others, and beyond the idea that evil was not me. Possibly I knew who I was in this life, but that did not show me how I arrived at this organization of self that I perceived to be me. What had I done before? What was the probable influence of past experience on my present self-definition? One thing I knew for sure: All of this knowledge existed within the cells of my own body. Who I was held a road map to my inner being, which had formed when I breathed the first breath of life.

As I went into my inner self, I entered certain tunnels and passed by others in haste. But what if I stopped at those and listened? So I stopped to listen at the doors of the passed-by elements of my inner self, and I heard the screaming of damned souls within! What was the matter with them? The screaming got louder and louder!

"You think you are a healer, when you can't even look at all the experiences you've participated in on this planet? You think you still are not possessed by old identities that you never even claimed? Don't you know that we are all down here because we failed to develop spirit? Don't you see that each time you came to Earth and then left without finding your soul, that you created a place in yourself that will deny the spirit when it comes to you now? You cannot regenerate yourself unless you integrate every action you have ever done and then create spirit right in that place that you once denied. Welcome, Barbara to the records of time. We will happily allow you to look at each experience you ever had in which you denied your soul life."

Then I hauled out my map of what-to-admit-about-myself-and-what-to-never-look-at, and my body began to teach me. Actually, my body was groaning. Since this deep search had been triggered during a session in which I saw that I really had chosen to incarnate this time, I began an intense healing crisis. I became afflicted with severe eczema and short-term memory loss, and I created a whole series of people around me who seemed to be compelled to challenge my beliefs. My physical body was erupting as I tried to awaken myself. As I sat in my house meditating, first I felt heaviness and tingling in my arms. Images flowed into my heart showing me that I was tired of wandering around this place never knowing who I was. As if called to another level by a beautiful ivory bird with iridescent feathers, I let myself go into my own heavy arms.

I stand wearing heavy leather sandals and a brown and grey, coarse, hooded cape. My brown hair is medium length with curls at the ends, my skin is thick and coarse, very weathered, and I have a square and prominent chin with full lips. My rather bulbous nose is broad and long with a bump on the ridge. My cheeks are sunken, with high cheek bones that stand out on the side. My scraggly beard grows down my neck and meets with my chest hair. I am hairy. I wear a leather belt around my waist with an attached bag of runes hanging from it. This bag is made of soft brown leather and is smaller than my fist. As I hold my runes, my hands and fingers feel thick—filled with ultraviolet blue-green energy. I feel energy pulsating in my throat, running through my shoulders, arms, and torso, and shooting down my feet and into the Earth.

The skin on the backs of my hands is pale and hairy. I wear a ring with an oval jade stone set in silver, the signature of my brotherhood, the Liber Frater. As long as I wear the emblem, I can hold my power. I always know what to do as far as timing is concerned because I have total use of my intuition and know exactly when to act. When I was initiated, the brothers told me that my ring would mean I would always do the right thing. I believe that. I don't have to follow the ordinary rules.

I'm standing in front of a cave where grass grows and rocks abound, and I look out at beautiful green rolling hills, golden meadows of tall grass, and sparkling rivers. This land is part of my body, and my energy field resonates to its various contours. The Earth forms are my body. The landscape rolls and undulates with the sky, and all is luminous like my runes.

I feel very dense, very magnetized. I am a resonater with the forces in the universe and the forms of the Earth. I am 47 years old, my name is Nera, Druid master, and I have just finished my 18-year mastery training. All the secrets of the ancient ones were passed on to me. For example, as I stand here, I see all my lives in the past and all my future lives. I therefore move myself to my own epitome of absolute courage.

I am a Druid master. Coming down a stone hallway wearing a leather tunic and cloak, I carry a sword. I take off my cloak and put it in the corner out of the way. There are six or seven men in the room at the end of the hallway. I am going to kill them all. These men are pestilence, for they plot against the king, the only order in the midst of the chaos of Britain. There is much death, destruction, and plague, and my king is Celtic, from the Atlantean lineage. He is the king of Angleterre. While everyone else is selling out to the Roman Church, he is genuine, for he loves the land. These men are in here planning to harm him, and then one will try to kill me. These men belong to the king's court, but they cannot be trusted.

I saw my opportunity this morning when I realized that the men would all be in here at once. Their room is connected to the prison, and they are all guards and court servants. After a court festival yesterday, they all decided to take the day off and get drunk. The main source of trouble for the king is from these men. If I kill them, my path will be easier. I can go forward while maintaining order and balance in the kingdom. I am a Druid master who serves the Divine King. The king is shepherd of his people, chosen by God for their welfare. At this dark time in history, my work is to maintain the balance of the kingdom so that food is grown and people can eat.

My Roman sword has a wide blade about sixteen inches long which is very destructive. I'm like an animal, keyed up and watching every movement. If I can destroy these men fast, there will be no one to interrupt me. I open the door and quickly look to see where each man is positioned, and the placement of their weapons. A few of them must have daggers, but their swords are lying in a pile at the edge of the room. Once I see where the weapons are, I leap quickly into the room and kick the weapons lying on the floor behind me. I could have just gone in and stabbed one of them, but I kicked the swords away so I could watch their reflexes and quickly judge which ones were really drunk. I had already listened by the door for quite awhile to make sure most of them were really inebriated.

The man right in front of me lurches around, and I gore him hard in the chest. He is the one with the quickest reflexes, and he falls as another man to my left starts to lunge for me. I stab him in the throat, and he falls gasping in front of me. I twist backwards to push quickly forward. I stab another one in the back who hardly realizes what is happening. I dash around to the other side of the table where the other three are and, as two of them sit dazed, the third one jumps up on the table. I slash off the head of one who still sits, and stab the other one in the chest. The man on the table lunges for me as I am stabbing the second man. I thrust, throwing my chest forward on the table, as he stumbles over me. I turn and flip my body as he comes for me and I start to fight with him.

He's got a dagger which grazes my right arm. He hugs my body as I slice his thigh with my sword. My sharp blade parts his iron-tensed upper leg muscles, chopping into his bone like a meat cleaver. He jerks into spasms, screaming with pain like a felled lion. He staggers back and falls against the table edge, then onto the floor. I stab him in the heart as I stare into his eyes and expel all the air from my lungs. I yank my sword out and pierce each one of them in the heart from the front or back. Mostly they are lying with their faces down. I make sure they are all dead by turning the bodies over, piercing them in the front, and observing the blood spurt from their hearts. I chop off the hands of the one who fought me. I feel high, light, and I have no doubts, whatsoever, about what I have done. Death is inconsequential since I am spiritually evolved. Why should I care about killing a man?

These men were absolutely wrong in what they were doing. I freed them by killing them, and they can come back in another life. It was a gift from me to sever them from their evil ways. This is a lifetime of great power. My task finished, I fill the room with blue energy, beautiful aquamarine energy. Then I put my sword in its scabbard, step backwards into the hallway, get my cloak, hold my hands out in front of me, and bound out of the room into another realm. I jump, make my shoulders very heavy, make my body into an energy rod, and just shift to a different place. The feeling is electrical.

Now I'm sitting at a table. I have shifted here and resolidified into a light-filled room. I see a very beautiful, bright blue lady sitting next to me. An eight- or nine-year-old blond boy is sitting at the table. The lady is shining; she is blue light, and actually, she's not really there. She seemed to be physical when I first came into the room at this table. But she is just blue light, not a real person.

As soon as I am fully into the dimension, I sit here with the boy. I am now in the physical plane dimension, and the blue lady cannot be seen by me. The boy is the son of the king, and I am his teacher, his tutor. He is a very, very special child, and I'm teaching him about numbers and mathematics. I use stones, not the runes, to teach him about counting. I killed the men while I was also sitting here with the boy. I do not want the fact to be known that I killed the men. But how can I be accused of being in two places at once? This is a special skill, and to demonstrate the phenomenon, I return to the point at which I left the room with the boy.

The king is named Aethelberht and his son is Arthur. As I show the boy how to count, he works very hard. He becomes absorbed. Then in my unconscious mind—my reptilian brain—I become aware that the time is fast approaching when I must go kill the men. The boy is absorbed, busy, and very meditative. He is not aware that I am disappearing. He is so involved in his studies that even if he looked up and I wasn't there, he would not notice. When I am sure the child is totally absorbed, and the exact right time has come, I simply reorganize the cells in my body by imaging the other doorway. I jump from one place to another. I am gone for 20 minutes.

I can image another place and, with my will, jump into another dimensional warp by accessing the timeless place between locations. Many people bilocate, but do not become conscious of these journeys of their astral bodies because of the limiting belief that they can only be in one place at one time. Also, since they have not been trained in the magical arts, rarely can they do anything physical—as I did in the murder of seven men—when they travel. This is the cause of all kinds of weird goings-on, but the moral issue is what is important to me. This was a very dark time in my character development. The cause of my actions as I bilocated was my belief that I must sacrifice for the king. I move to a time when I am with the king as a Druid high priest.

The king sits in a large, high-backed chair and I sit next to him on his left. I am in council with him in the stone great hall. The walls are 20-feet high with tall windows that admit diffused light, lending a timeless quality to the court scene. There are massive pillars supporting the stone arches in the middle of the room, and dripping wax candles in sconces flicker in the dusty air. Soldiers guard all the entrances but they cannot hear what we say if we talk quietly. Aethelberht is a calm and nonaggressive person who is in close touch with all existing political and military realities. His thoughts are elsewhere as he sits here with me in council. He is in the center of the kingdom, but he is able to be in many places at once with his mind. He may also travel the way I do.

He's much younger than I am, with very black hair and a black beard. Nearly 40, with a muscular and wiry body, he is just shy of six-feet tall. This is very tall for a Briton of his type, unlike the Danes and Jutlanders, who are very blond and tall. His eyes are light blue with much light in them, and he has a very penetrating gaze. He asks in his mind, Is it done? and I answer in my thoughts, Yes, knowing that he means the killing of the men.

Neither one of us want anyone to know what is at issue. Without verbalizing, we try to know and share much about what is going on. That is the way the priest always works with the king. The king knows the courtiers were all killed. He would prefer that the name of whoever did it never be verbalized. Besides, was I really there anyway? What is a murder when the perpetrator was in two places at once? What if we kill our enemies with our thoughts? This is a complex situation. His wife, Bertha, is a Saxon princess, and the men I killed were her men. I know he does not want to know, yet I tell him of the slain men to make sure he knows that I am in service to him, for my service is my innocence.

He slumps down in his chair, puts his chin on his right hand, and looks off to the side, expelling air out of his lungs. He says, "These are heavy times that this should happen." Then he shifts his body forward and says, "Now, we can move to take Angleterre Castle, the Saxon holdout." He is in a stronger position now that the six men have been killed because the Saxons are trying to infiltrate the kingdom since Bertha is his wife.

Next, we will do the runes.

He gets up and I walk behind him as he goes through the great hall to the entrance of a room. The soldiers at the door open it, and we pass through into a narrow hallway after going down four steps. The wooden door at the end of the hall has a window in the shape of a Celtic cross that has been cut through its thick wood. This is the divination room. It was built over the ancient stone circle that was constructed here when Avebury was built. This room is the oldest part of the castle, and will later become a Christian chapel. Now we call the castle Gaevering. We bend to go through the small door. Shutting the door behind us, the king relocks the door with a big, ancient, iron key. The room is damp and closed, an ideal environment for the many spiders living within its round walls. I walk to the other side of the chamber to open the wooden shutters, letting fresh air in. There is a vibrant blue rug in the center of the room. We sit on the edges of the rug as I light a candle by striking a flint hard on a stone. I light the oil lamps on the edges of the room, and as I light the wicks, any spirits or bad energies are cleared away. The king and I go into a mystical state together, and I look into Aethelberht's eyes and reach into my rune pouch.

He says, "The bridge to the spiritual energy forces of my divine kingdom is destroyed. How can I again call the higher planes to my people?"

I am distressed. I did not know this had happened. He knows more than I do, and I respect his insight. We have been struggling to write in runic form the new laws based on ancient Celtic wisdom. We must save our ancient customs as invaders settle on our land. There has been a problem with the priestess, Mordreth. Only the king and I know that the king took the form of Cernunnos—the Horned God—in the hierogamous with Mordreth eighteen years ago. A child was probably born, and that child would be the divine child of the sacred force of the Earth goddess and king. Such a child would be the vessel/Grail of the genetic line of the gods. Was there such a child to be revealed? I ask, "Was there a child from the sacred union of Earth and sky many years ago?"

"Yes," he replies gravely, "and the child is now of age. I have committed a fatal error. As you know, my Saxon wife is now a Christian, making our son, Arthur, a Christian. I am torn apart by my two sons, who would kill each other like Cain and Abel if I revealed the truth. I carry their fratricidal creation in my heart as the country becomes the vessel of the deathly struggle between the Earth religion and Roman Christianity. My first son, Wotan, is a consecrated child of the Earth, and my son, Arthur, is Church-consecrated. I am split, which creates a corresponding split in the dragon energy under all the ancient temples, for I hold the temples in my heart. I am guilty of pagan sin, for my queen has shown me that I am born evil. I asked to be freed from the devils in baptism. I confessed my pagan sin to the bishop, and he betrayed me to the queen! Bertha made plans to have the priestess and my son put to death. I could not bear it. I told Mordreth, and she fled over the sea years ago to a distant temple with our son, Wotan.

"She cursed me when she left, saying, 'You are damned to be the last sacred king, who will now serve the Church of the Powers and Principalities until your kingdom, and every other kingdom, loses its power just as the Romans did. You will hold the Imperium, and lose the Bretwalda. Your kingdom and the Church will become fat with power, obsessed with intrigues, and you are doomed to ravage the Earth until she can no longer support your greed. As long as you hold the Imperium, you will hold the power. But you will grow to hate that power! You are making covenant with your own oppressor! When you have fully implanted the oppressor in your heart—the kingdom—the Goddess will return to the Earth temples of Britain. This will be a time when two women rule your country.'"

I am stunned. How has this evil been unleashed to rot our kingdom? I have been taught that the king is divine, that I am serving heaven by his will. Merlin was my teacher but he went into the wilderness years ago when the Christian priest came. The priest had been called by the queen, who believed she was childless because the king was not baptized. Mordreth told me that the land would be ravaged if the Goddess was not honored. The barbarians are raiding our shores, plague ravages the kingdom, and Mordreth said that these horrors are caused by the wrath of the Goddess whose divine child, Wotan, was not given his birthright. History will even say that King Aethelberht was a Saxon himself, to cover up the pure Celtic divinity of Wotan.

Instead of looking at what I had done myself, which was my only access to truth at this peak point in history, I quickly moved into pragmatism. How could I fix it? I could refuse to serve the king any more, as I did when Sigebert committed grave errors. I do not want to throw the runes for this man, but I am afraid of saying no, of being true to myself. It is a reactive pattern. I don't deal with the problem, I jump out of the energy to fix it. I throw the runes.

The king announces, "I am the first king of Angleterre, and I have denied my first born by not defending his bloodline for him. Where does the divine blood of kings go in this situation? What does this mean for my second son, Arthur, the child born from my Christian wife?"

I become a column of energy the minute I throw the runes, an energy rod from Earth to sky, and the voice channels in:

"The source of the wind is gone, the straight tree trunk is bent, the stars do not rise above the stones on the horizon, the springs no longer flow as the birds cease to fly. Like a man with no blood in his veins, the kingdom is at a still point. The Goddess has abandoned this land for a new land. Wotan took the line of sacred kings from this land to the temple of the flowers protected by the monkeys who guard the genetic pool. Arthur and all future kings will serve the Church guarded by secret male warrior brotherhoods. Together, paternal orders will eliminate all vestiges of the Goddess from the minds, hearts, and myths of the people. The true story of the true king, Wotan, will be hidden within the secret society of the Knights of the Round Table. You have the Imperium, but you do not have the power. The power is transferred to the temple of the Sun, Nah Chan, of the planted cross in the new land."

The king stands up and walks out of the room. As he is closing the door, he looks back in at me with a grave expression. I go back to the center of the room and enter into a deep meditation. Soon I realize I am not alone, and I open my eyes to see the blue lady sitting across from me. She is my inner female. I recognize her instantly, and my body shudders with chills.

She says, "I don't know how many more times you need to do this, but I came to make sure that you look at what you have done because you are courting disaster. Murder is serious enough, but you have even misused power with the runes to avoid looking at your personal responsibility. First you threw the runes to decide whether to kill the men, and you decided murder was a good idea from the reading. If you were more honest about your personal character, you would not be confused about using your divination skills to assist any king. The runes are for the revelation of the hidden levels in the cycles of history, and now you have opened yourself to be used by the gods." She disappears.

I sit for a long time focusing into my body. I will look at my faults no matter what they are. I jump out and travel right to Avebury, the temple of the birthing goddess where I was initiated on this land. Here is the only place in Briton I have felt peace, because here is the pure physical form that was built in 3113 BC at the beginning of this cycle of the Pleiades. It is a simple Earth form containing all the elements of the 5000-year cycle of evolution that existed before historic layers began to be part of Earth-temple geomancy. Human-made structures can contain the Pleiadean keys, but Avebury is completely constructed from uncut stones formed into circles, figure eights, and pathways which exhibit Earth symbols for stellar observation. It can only be understood by viewing it from the Moon.

Now I stand in front of a large menhir, a tall standing stone. In the night sky, the Moon is full, and the clouds are racing. The wind howls on this exquisite, damp evening. This stone circle is on the top of a very wild ridge east of Silbury Hill. The passage grave for passing souls back into the Galactic Center is to the west of this small sanctuary. It is now called Overton Hill, and the passage grave, West Kennet Barrow. Our most hallowed sanctuary, I come here when I am disconnected.

Thousands of years old, Avebury is a unique gift from the ancient ones who knew how to be connected with the central spiritual force of the universe: the spiraling Galactic Center. Even now in the sixth century AD, we have already lost the memory of the origin of our creation. We are sure that the ancient ones knew more about our cosmic source than we now know. In the beginning, they placed the stones on points where the Goddess breathes, and this sanctuary is where she cries for her Divine Son. As time passes, the people will know even less than we know now. The Christians will destroy many of these sacred stones in the thirteenth century. When the Goddess returns to the Earth and breathes again in 2012 AD, this temple will be rebuilt exactly as it stood in the beginning.

I stand in front of a rock wearing only my cloak, the wind brushing my bare skin, cooling all the parts of my body. I am rigid in front of the stone with my feet firm on Earth and my hands reaching for the sky. I am totally confused after 25 years of political intrigues in the courts in Britain.

All day today I have meditated, first in the inner womb sanctuary of Silbury Hill, surrounded by the secret waters of life. The star teachers who initiated me can see the great hill with the waters around it from the sky because this valley and spring are sacred to the hawk. Thousands of years ago, the Goddess created this Earth temple as the central teaching about Earth for our star teachers. This site is visible from the stars and tells the story of the protection of Earth by the Goddess, and of her eternal birthing of her Divine Son. We cannot allow our stellar creators to forget that matter comes into new lifeforms on Earth. This birth process happens nowhere else but on Earth! But, have the gods forgotten us? I was sent here from the Rhineland to protect this Earth generator. Is anybody listening to me calling for a god, a being greater than myself?

The day lengthens into late afternoon, and I meditate for a long time next to the spring of the swallows, which emerges from an underwater river running under the passage grave. The spring flows under the consecrated skull of a very ancient sacred king. The current flows around Silbury Hill, the hill of emergence after the Flood. This hill was constructed over the original river-tossed egg of primordial creation, buried in the Earth by an ancient priestess of the Lion of Judah. These days, the sacrifice of the sacred king for fertility and protection of the land against disaster is no longer necessary. The Druids, as keepers of the ancient records of this planet, have been informed that the gods no longer require this sacrifice from us. Instead, it is the time for the Druids—the priests of the tree god—to instruct kings on how to personally live their own sacred journeys with the forces of dark and light. The sky teaching for Earth has ceased, and the people of Earth are ready to know divinity in their hearts by individually facing inner darkness. We are all asked to become courageous. I was sent into the court in Briton to teach Aethelberht about this entirely new freedom of the Earth. The gods no longer control us—now we create good or evil.

When the first bishop arrived and infiltrated the court, he explained that all individuals had to be baptized so they could become vessels of grace. Grace would enable them to see the new teaching. Grace would protect them from the darkness in their hearts which would cause evil and chaos in the universe. Many listened because there was great trial and tribulation in the lands when Rome fell. When the basic economic and political structures disintegrated, the pagans began reintroducing the ancient sacrificial rites in order to appease the gods. We, the Druids, had been teaching that the ancient sacrifices were no longer necessary, that we now had the right to appeal to the Creator directly to ask for help in time of trouble.

When the Christian bishop introduced the teaching of baptism, I meditated for a long time. I realized that the teaching the bishop brought was in many ways similar to our Druidic teaching. The Roman Church teaches that converts are freed from devil possession if they wash away original sin and are baptized. As Druids, we teach that we can be divinely freed from possession by entities of other dimensions if we commune with the waters of the Goddess surrounding Silbury Hill, source of the waters of emergence from the previous world at Avebury Temple.

Now I meditate about this teacher, Christos, which means Messiah in Greek—the Chosen One of the Elect of God. I am sure that this great teacher came to ask us to take responsibility for the Earth. I see that he was the last sacred king to be sacrificed, and as I see the magnificence of his planetary gift, I have an exquisite vision of him. Like a soaring white owl in the Full Moon, he shimmers with otherworldly light. He swoops over Avebury, over all the great stone circles, over all the sacred oak groves, and over the whole world. He blesses us. When the Christians came to the court, I was curious about them. But their court intrigues were evil! Worse than anything I—a pagan tree priest—had ever done! I could see that they did not believe in this new teaching—the new order of freedom—for their Church was enslaved by the Romans who had already enslaved my people, the Celts. Christians located their sanctuary in Rome, and Rome is the temple of the gods who enslave humanity and oppress the human spirit.

My values are breaking down around me. I thought it didn't bother me to kill those men. But some moral shift has occurred in me now that I have had a vision of Christos. I am not sure I had the right to kill. This great master of love taught that each one of us has free will and the right to life. In the old laws, the individual could be sacrificed to the group, and such a sacrifice was cosmic—beyond human. I will go into my ancestral tomb, the barrow—spirit home in the Goddess. I will ask the grandfathers and grandmothers if they also agonized over the sanctity of individual free will within the collective needs of the great ancient clans. I have always believed that the gods just decided everything for us in the ancient days and that we simply obeyed. I have always assumed that we were blissed out and in ecstasy when we sacrificed ourselves. Perhaps my ancestors will know if we once angered the gods? Did we ever disobey divine decrees in order to know a personal destiny? Christianity teaches that each individual is of cosmic importance.

My access to the truth about the significance of the individual within the collective must come from my present reality. But, in my times, the individual is not really sacred to the Christians—I see no signs that their God is present for them, and yet they claim to have displaced my gods. Where did the gods all go? Where are you, gods, as I cry for you in my need? Am I alone and abandoned in the cosmos?

My mind races madly like an endless old curse as I walk along the ancient energy lines worn deep into the fertile Earth. These lines begin at the exit from the sanctuary and snake across the land to the barrow. The underwater spring which begins under the sanctuary flows deep under the sacred pathway, and the sun is setting behind the barrow. Now is a strange time to go into the tomb, but I am drawn by an irresistable force. The rolling hills and oak groves shimmer magically in the waning light. The top of Silbury Hill is visible on my right and West Kennet River is a silver snake—the writhing Goddess body. Usually we only go into the barrow before sunrise to observe the rising sun in the east. Souls choose to incarnate with the rising sun, and we are the keepers of each soul's entrance. Ahead I see the great menhirs that form a concave half-circle leading into the barrow entrance. The litany of nine great stone gods awaits my quest.

As I come to the front entrance of the barrow, I am afraid to go in. But I am drawn to the center sanctuary. I roll away the central, round stone covering the entrance, and I walk slowly into the passage, readjusting my eyes. I see the small tombs to my right and left with their eagle and hawk feather totems, fresh but wilting flowers, cups of mead, and crystals glowing in the oil lamplight. Coming closer to the sanctuary, I am grateful that the priests and priestesses of the clans are still feeding our graves. As long as the ancient bodies of the ancestors are blessed while becoming Earth, we can return again until our quest here is complete. The Christians have not yet found this tomb.

My heart is beating like a huge drum as I enter the hallowed space at the back covered with the beautiful spirals of the ancient ones. I stare at the spirals, sitting in lotus position in the center of the sanctuary, facing west. The spirals begin to move in the flickering light of the lamps as I feel my higher head centers being activated. I feel the pounding in my heart and my own blood coursing through my veins. Getting dizzy and disoriented, I want to run, as I feel myself being sucked back in time. I perspire due to the air pressure effect from being pummeled through space and/or time, and I fear I will have a heart attack. A huge black spider lands 'ploomp' on my right arm! "Trust, Nera, trust now," a voice whispers from the rocks.

I am amazed! The spider is the totem of the teacher gods. She has come in response to my need to know. My heart begins to slow out of gratefulness for this deep affirmation which says that I can ask my questions, and that the gods will hear me when I cry for them.

Suddenly, an incomprehensibly gigantic voice comes out of the spider, as if her voice is the actual sound of the galactic movement. She begins, "You have asked for the Emerald Records of the gods and of their relationship with all peoples of Earth. You have asked, so we will release the records of the secrets of the Five Worlds, the Green Records of Earth. The story of time is held in secret until Earth is ready to birth herself, ready to emerge into the consciousness of her own body."

The spider continues:

The gods are not limited to the third dimension of fixed space and time as you are, but their experience with Earth is cyclical and limited by orbit. That is the law of the solar system. The gods are beholden to the laws of your solar system as well as the universe and galaxy, and you are the source of Earth connection. Beings born on Earth can know the Creator—the one God. You are the companions of the gods in the birthing laboratory of this solar system, but their cycle is so long and wise that you forget about them—your sky teachers. They long to have you remember their experience with you now. They are cosmically lonely, while you desperately search for the memory of your communion with them when their cycle has brought them to Earth.

When you truly accept all the phases of your evolution, then you will be prepared for their teachings about dimensions beyond the third. Know this as you hear the amazing story of your divine origins: The gods were once only spirit and you were once only matter. By their desire to know matter, the gods became spirit and matter while you became matter and spirit.

First you must remember the last four visitations to Earth by the gods— the Four Worlds of Emergence before the Fifth World of Christos. They visit Earth in the third dimension every 3600 years, and it is time now to remember the returns of 10,800 BC, 7200 BC, 3600 BC, and 0 AD. Your time has come because now is the revelation from the 0 AD visit. If you can reattune to your divine experience, your sky memory, your teachers of synchronicity, your ancient mastery techniques of dimensional vectoring, then your heart will open to your true origins in 2013 AD. At that time, your solar system will reverse its motion and begin returning to the Galactic Center. It will be too late for those who have refused to feel the Heart of the Christos, and the third dimension will dissipate on Earth. There will be no more crosses or trees of the four directions; the time of learning must come to an end because the suffering of God must end. The solar system began its orbit out of the Galactic Center in 11,000 BC, and at that point the cycle of the Twelve Worlds began—the initiation into the teachings of the tri-star system, Sirius.

In 10,800 BC, the planet of the gods—called Nibiru, Marduk, Aion, Merkabah, Planetoi, K'uatzal—orbited as usual into the Earth's solar system. As soon as Nibiru entered the solar system, it was caught in the time dynamic of the solar system. This planet normally functions on galactic time. Nibiru orbited in past Pluto, Neptune, Uranus, Chiron, Saturn, Jupiter, the Asteroid Belt, and Mars, and then Earth became visible. Panic ensued when the Nibiruans saw that the poles of Earth had become encrusted with ice caused by the Greenhouse Effect from the pollution of Atlantean technology!

For hundreds of thousands of years, the Nibiruans had mined the Earth, and this race was again planning on landing on Earth to obtain metals. Now the Nibiruans were afraid that the fly-by of their planet would imbalance the Earth, causing a polar shift, due to the weight of the ice. For the last 13,000 years, the Nibiruans had begun to know the Earthlings in a more intimate way: Their scientists had altered the DNA of some Earthlings so that Adamah—as the men and women of Earth were now called—could become similar to the Nibiruans and reduce their own loneliness. This evolved species thought of humans as no better than animals, while the humans could never understand why the Nibiruans did not admire the wisdom of animals.

In horror, the Nibiruans watched the Earth as their own large planet moved into position to cross the Earth's orbital path. Their planet began to pull on the gravitational balance of the Earth and its Moon, Maya. The Nibiruans were utterly helpless. They were imprisoned by their own orbit, as anybody in the solar system would be. The Earth wobbled and then shifted its poles three times! Almost all life on Earth, almost all of the structures built there by the Nibiruans, and the last vestiges of Atlantis, a civilization established there by the Andromeda Galaxy, were destroyed in this great cataclysm.

A few hundred years later, the Nibiruans returned from their orbit around the Sun and landed on Earth. There were almost no structures left, but the amazing variety of species on Earth, including Adamah, had survived and were existing in a very primitive state of survival. There were also many changes in the genetic lines of the species because the pole shift had caused an invasion of cosmic rays into the atmosphere of Earth. Cosmic rays carry the genes of species out of the inner heart of supernovas. The Nibiruans saw that Adamah had no conscious memory of the cataclysm, but was now imprinted with an inner brain locus of paralyzing fear which had activated a chakra—the solar plexus—which had previously accessed feelings for the Goddess.

The gods grieved for Adamah, for they recognized that this was the birth of the search for cosmic peace, a quality which the Nibiruans also desired. Quickly they surveyed as much of the situation as they had time for, and repaired the Great Pyramid and the Sphinx—a statue of a Nibiruan king which was carved out of solid limestone next to the pyramid. Then the Nibiruans built the Osirion as the first temple of emergence of Adamah after the cataclysm. This structure was to be the temple of the Sirian teachings, the sacred story of the evolution of the gods and the species. Then the Nibiruans left for their long journey into the dark night of the soul, beyond the solar system in deep space.

Nibiru traveled out toward the star Sirius, reaching its farthest point from the Sun in 9000 BC. As the great planet prepared to change direction and return to the Sun, it was given the essential stellar teaching of this first phase—Sirius Teaching One for Earth. How the teaching was given to Nibiru was similar to the way each person receives teachings from their own higher self. If you trust such illumination, access to the divine is automatic. Sirius Teaching One to Nibiru was:

"You will make a Garden in Eden so that you can begin to manifest the plant lifeforms of Earth. In exchange for the herbal teaching from Adamah, you will teach him about the alchemical building stone and the elemental mastery of water control. You are to tell Adamah that you are those who have walked with God, that you are the Enochians."

In 7200 BC, Nibiru returned again. At this time of the Second World, the Nibiruans were very excited. What a great project!

When they landed on Earth, Adamah asked them: "Who are you?"

"We are the priests of Enoch who have come to teach you new ways of wisdom," they replied.

Adamah asked, "Are you our Creator?"

"No. We worship the central creative force of the universe manifested in spiraling lifeforms, but we are the teachers for Earth," they said.

Adamah asked, "What is a priest?"

And the Creator wept when the Nibiruans set in motion the first lie of the Twelve Worlds. Anu, the leader said, "A priest is one who walks with God and brings the news from God to your planet."

Desire was created! For Adamah wanted to be a priest instead of finding God within the heart.

This was a time of primeval bliss. Adamah was awed to see that the rushing waters could be harnessed. That is why Earth legends about divine humans tell of their discovery in baskets on river banks. The gods were in awe of the genetic strains of plants. They brought a few of their own plants which amazed the Earthlings. They brought a Tree of Life—the date palm—and the seeds of corn, bananas, and grains. Long after the gods had left again, the fields of corn and wheat were worshipped, and the banana was admired as a phallic plant. The Tree of Life became the central altar of Adamah. Adamah noticed that the Tree lived thousands of years, just like the Nibiruans. The Tree's solar seed year is 3600 years because its DNA is Nibiruan.

When the gods had to leave because their planet was ready to journey out of the solar system, they longed to stay, and Earth longed to keep them. But if they abandoned their original planet, the Nibiruans would lose their immortality.

Adamah said, "Only the Earth has the Goddess. Perhaps if you lie with her you will never leave?"

The Nibiruans had been observing the sexual habits of humans and animals for thousands of years, and wondered what the experience felt like. They agreed with Adamah. A beautiful priestess was rubbed with oil and blessed with frankincense and myrrh, and she lay waiting on the bed in the very top of the Temple of Eridu. A great god came to her, and he made love to her with all the force of every man's first sexual experience. The waveform of erotic ecstasy was so intense that the eros was even felt by the Creator, who was very pleased. The Earth shivered with a new power, but the god was depressed, for he felt desire for the first time. His seed coursed through virgin veins in his luminous body. Like a great comet newly born in the center of the universe, which takes form in an atmosphere that lights an inner fire, he desired matter. He had lost his immortality, for he wanted to know matter as well as spirit.

The priestess felt the power of spirit in her body. New ecstatic meridians opened in her body as the god's seed coursed through the virginal veins of his light body. She became dissatisfied with her mortality, and longed for spirit. As they found desire together—this erotic union of male and female, of Earth and sky, of matter and spirit—the desire to manifest a diamond body which could hold spirit was born. Neither one had ever felt such a union, and they were unbalanced by this new dimension because they could only fulfill its magnificent agenda during sexual union. But they were still caught in orbital definition, caught in being in the third dimension, and all levels of unity would be fulfilled only in time, in cycles of evolution.

Nibiru rose in the western sky over Eridu, having completed a journey around the Sun. The gods left, and the priestesses now burned eternal fires at the altars, waiting for the next return. For the first time, Adamah worried. Instead of existing in present bliss, Adamah waited for a return, and that possibility became less real to each succeeding generation. The Divine Son of Adamah, Enoch, was born of the priestess who received the god, and the lineage of the elect, of demi-gods, was started on Earth. Half Nibiruan, half Earthling, Enoch lived a thousand years.

Nibiru went out to the star Sirius and, in 5400 BC, received Sirius Teaching Two for Earth:

"You will honor Adamah with your magical arts and divination skills when you return in 3600 BC, and you will learn the secrets of the animals from Adamah."

As they came within sight of the solar system in about 4000 BC, big trouble developed. All of the male gods wanted to mate with Earth priestesses because they had found out about the power of sexual desire when Enoch was created. Hundreds of the gods came to Earth in small spaceships and mated with priestesses in sacred sites—Earth groves and mountaintop temples. Both men and women were happy, but then the gods started mating with animals. The Nibiruans did not see much of a difference between animals and women in terms of the physical effects experienced during intercourse. The Earthlings were dismayed by the knowledge that disease resulted from this practice. Next, a disaster occurred! The Earthlings saw that new genetic forms were being created because the gods were able to impregnate the animals! Genetic barriers between animals and Earthlings had been built into the evolution of Earth. Suddenly the Earth was filling up with composite animal/god creatures.

The head god of Nibiru, Anu, was furious as he came closer to Earth and saw the effects of this sexual practice. With his great powers, he could easily seed the atmosphere of Earth with ions so that rain would fall until the Earth flooded. He blasted Earth with ferocious lightning, but then he had a change of heart. Now he loved Adamah. Surely Earth could survive this plague of composite creatures, especially if the monsters were put to death. So, Anu arranged a secret meeting with Noah, who was a descendant of Enoch. He instructed Noah to gather a perfect male and female of each animal species into an Ark. After the flood, the Earth would be cleansed of the monsters, and the Ark would release the pure species to populate the planet again. At the appropriate time, Anu would send a Nibiruan priestess to birth a new race. He would send his own daughter, who would undergo the pain of physical birthing, because he loved Earth. The Earth flooded, and Noah saved the race as Anu had ordered him.

Nibiru returned from its orbit around the Sun in 3600 BC. The Nibiruans landed and built temples in Sumeria, Egypt, India, and China. Since the glacial recession, Adamah now lived in many places on the Earth. The Nibiruans taught the people the wisdom of the gods, which was now purified of desire. This time the gods did not mate with priestesses but taught magical arts and tantric rituals to be conducted in the temple by Earthlings. Eve was brought from Venus to the Garden of Eden, and she was taught that her lover was to be Adam. All of the healing and divination arts were given to Earthlings so that the species could learn the ways of the gods.

The Egyptians had been honoring the Sirian teachings in the Osirion since the 10,800 BC flood. The gods, in turn, studied the animal totemic wisdom with Osiris, Isis, and Horus in beautiful temples originally designed by Nibiruans. As the time came to leave, separation was even more difficult. Already Adamah had found that knowing power created evil. He demanded that Eve belong to him exclusively when she was ready to give birth to her child. He needed to control her as a vessel for his seed because there were still monsters on Earth. For the first time there was anger, violence, and fear on Earth. Previously, this had only been the behavior of the gods. Earthlings were now defined as superior to animals because animals do not experience moral suffering caused by their own actions. It became a mark of superiority to be a judge, to be in a position to decide that one thing or person was better or worse than another. Separation was totally in form and all the structures needed to ensure its perpetuation were being developed.

When the gods saw Adamah doing things that they disliked in themselves, they decided to save Adamah as a mirror image in which they could see themselves. Narcissism began, and would end only when Adamah was free. Anu made the first covenant with Noah, called the Noatic Covenant:

The Lord would never flood the Earth again because he loved Adamah.

But the gods panicked at their gift of magic and divination because they thought Adamah would use this power against them when the opportunity arose. They returned to their original lie, which was that they were the link to God, and they taught Adamah to set up a temple hierarchy. From then on, the power would be in the hands of consecrated priests and priestesses, and in the hands of kings who possessed the blood of the gods in their veins. Distrust was created.

The Nibiruans left as a great cry went up in all the temples on planet Earth. But the priests were not unhappy to see their lords leave. As for the gods, when they saw Earth from space, the realization came that they had made a grave error: They had not fully trusted Adamah with the Sirian gift! The Nibiruans had violated the divine giveaway. It was now time for all Earthlings to be linked to the gods by means of astrology, tarot, and all other forms of magic and divination, but the gods reserved these teachings for the priesthood, who would then use this ability to control other Earthlings. The Creator observed this and decided that it was time for Earth to be free.

When the third teaching was received from Sirius, even the gods were amazed! Sirius Teaching Three for Earth:

"Adamah now has tasted of good and evil, but he can only know of divinity if granted free will. Free will can only be mastered on Earth by utilization of magic and divination, which involve the ability to be on Earth and in other dimensions simultaneously. By giving away the secrets of the divine, you can be freed from your original lie, which first separated me from my children of Earth. You will do this by assisting in the birth of the Son of the Source, the Creator, on Earth. Then Earth will transcend duality over time, for Nibiru will no longer be separate from the Solar Logos when Earth is the equal of the gods."

Sitting in amongst the spirals in the dim oil lamplight, I feel an intense pain in my heart. It is the place within myself that longs to go beyond all the eons of struggle and reconnect with my divine origins again, to see the face of the Creator! It is the place in me that looks up at the stars at night and wishes to return home, the place in me that finds peace when in the embrace of a lover. I blink my eyes, wondering when the spider will go on with her wonderful story. I eagerly await the best part—the more recent times. The spider continues:

You are permitted no more knowledge. You cannot know any esoteric secrets until you have mastered the emotions which are released for you by this knowledge. Radical trust for humankind in the universe was first introduced in the fourth return of Nibiru in 0 AD. When you have learned to totally trust your Creator, we will continue the story of the Emerald Records. Being unable to proceed is not your fault, for your whole civilization had ceased to trust. The Records were transferred to a new land so that the Third Sirian Teaching could be given to your planet. Someday you will know the trust of the new land when the old world releases the desire to be the birth place of the only god.

TIKAL AS THE GATEWAY
TO THE UNDERWORLD

We live in a world on the verge of complete annihilation, a world we have created that has emerged from powers hidden deep within the darkest recesses of the human soul. But not, of course, from within "my" soul! If this manifestation were within my soul, then could it be that I am unwittingly the evil itself?

As I considered that possibility, I felt an intense pain in my heart. Only the body knows. Where was this resistance coming from? A blinding white flash innundated my brain as I realized the resistance was coming from my own soul! What did my soul want? Did it want me to surrender my judgments? Suddenly the blinding white flash turned to coursing red blood. Would I cause a heart attack by asking this question?

I moved into the pain in my heart and again heard the souls screaming from within me:

"Free us! Love us enough to look at the very darkest part of your being!"

The struggle within my solar plexus was building to a level that surely would kill me! But what could I have done that was so unspeakable?

My soul screamed at me, "So what if you are annihilated in your quest? You have gone too far now, Barbara. You are asking to be free, as all shamans have asked! You must offer your immortality. Even your soul can die. Why do you care?"

I felt a lion roaring within me like a cosmic scream that could send the stars spinning and create a new supernova instantly. "Pass me!" screamed the lion! "For unbeknownst even to yourself, you have just acknowledged my power and asked me for my help. I give you my power, willingly."

I returned to the darkest lifetime lurking deep within my soul.

As a young Mayan priest, I stand near a pyramid with steps up the side. There is a doorway on the pyramid's right side which opens into the interior. The steps lead up to a platform on the top. I am the Huitzilopochtli kachina of the Jaguar Cult, and this is the New Fire ceremony of 843 AD, before the opening of the Thirteen Heavens. The pyramid is covered with colorful painted murals of snakes, lizards, and reptiles. We transmute reptilian energy here. This is the vibration which is felt in the shoulder chakra, the place where wings grow on the human body, and which is contained at the base of the spine. By dynamizing, or making manifest, the energy of the first chakra—the root chakra—we have a method for tapping into the experiential levels of war, violence, anger, and sex on the human plane. We are tapping into this level in order to transmute the energy to reach the second level—survival.

I must tap into the first level of vibration to overcome fear and to know when to protect myself. This is the reptilian level, a primary level on Earth. This power to transmute must come from the deliberate activation of my "young energy," the experiential levels that I require as a young soul in an evolving universe. When we activate the young energy frequency on the Earth plane, then historical experiential situations unfold for the needs of young souls. This is the most difficult part of the human experience to comprehend, in light of the divine plan for Earth. Activation of the survival level is analogous to setting off a bomb. But every soul must choose survival over pain, or that soul has no access to its own animal totem power, its own unique behavioral form on Earth. I am the Huitzilopochtli kachina at this time because my soul chose to integrate this kachina totem, the hummingbird, with my soul totem, the jaguar. Now it is time for me to open my feline magic to draw the nectar of the gods. I have decided to create a space in my heart now for my future role in the Age of Flowers, to create a world which does not fear wild animals.

We have been taught by the ancient ones that we cannot evolve without transmutation—the new phase cannot begin if there is too much old energy. There are seven steps on this pyramid—six plus the top platform. These six steps up, plus the top platform, plus six steps down, make thirteen—symbolic of the Thirteen Heavens—the experience above Earth. Initiates who climb these steps are offering themselves to further evolution. This is why the steps are so steep and why we are taught to look straight ahead when we ascend and descend. I feel this teaching implanted in the back of my spine where my skull meets with the top of my spine.

We must climb the steps as an observation of the cyclic phases of time in sacred ritual. We are located in the middle of an unceasing journey to know our divinity. We activate the energy with rattles, drums, and dance. In times of crisis or special ceremony, we dance with the snake after meditating underground with her in a pot. When we liberate the snake, we fuse her reptilian spirit with our own in dance. When we have activated her spirit, we come into oneness with the reptilian energy. We become the snake and then we do not fear her. If there is energy in the land or people around us which is not in tune with the snake, then we begin to fear the life-force itself.

Outside the pyramid, the visual dynamic is the dance which the people see, but they do not see the transmutation. Priests who work with the Jaguar Cult have no free will, and I hate this part of my life. We are servants of necessity ordered by the gods to perform. The people hate us, but we are in control. At this time, we are coming to the end of an era of Nine Hells. The inside of the pyramid has four levels down, a bottom platform, and four levels up—nine steps, symbolic of the eternal return journey into the Earth. This configuration is buried under the surface level of the pyramid. When the forms of nine and thirteen are the ruling geometry of pyramids, these numbers represent the sacred wheel of time. I am in service to the Jaguar Cult and the god, Tezcatzlipoca. We were taken in and chosen when we were very young because we possessed a special energy, a sexual force in our beings. The priests can tell which of the boys have this energy, and they took us from our mothers to serve the Jaguar Cult when we were seven. This ritual energy is so strong, addictive, and alluring, that we gave our free will away. We are told all kinds of lies. We are told that we are channels of sexual force from the gods to Earth.

My higher self in that life is above me observing what I am doing. My higher self can separate what is true from what is false about that life. As I remember the life, I am existing in my body as a Jaguar priest, and my soul is outside me, observing. While I am a kachina, my higher self does not commingle with my physical body, for the physical body density and energy pattern is not safe for my soul during this phase of the priestly ceremonial cycle at Tikal. Now it is time to find out how my soul feels living on Earth while it is separated from my higher self.

The Nine Hells at Tikal from 375 AD to 843 AD created an obsession with absolute control on Earth which would be intensified all over the planet during the next Nine Hells from 1519 AD to 1987 AD. But my soul never left me. It hovered over me, for this life was about immersion in the absolute dark night of the soul—that point when the faces of the gods are hidden, when the monster cannot be seen, for reality becomes the monster.

I am fourteen and, as the feather god, Huitzilopochtli, I am being prepared by the older priests to carry out a ritual for the cycles of time. The kachina spirit comes in and I become Huitzilopochtli as I am fed a cup of bitter liquid mixed with cactus juice. This is pulque—cactus juice and black mushrooms dried into a white powder. As they feed me this liquid, I do not really have a choice. I agreed to be the kachina—to embody the hummingbird who sucks the nectar of flowers, the etheric veils to the divine. We have been trained to never stop once we have begun a ritual.

I am getting high, very energized, filling up with power, and I feel energy in my arms, hands, shoulders, and in my feet for dancing. But my soul is separated out, and I feel an agonizing loneliness. My soul does not agree to take the drugs, but my physical body thinks the concoction is just great, for I have a continual erection throughout the entire process. The energy is very sexual, very empowered, and very electrical. This is my snake energy; we are Snake Clan. I am entering into my phallus, becoming Huitzilopochtli, as they are drumming around me.

We are inside the step pyramid over a configuration of the Nine Hells. We face the doorway to the West, the chaotic force, the sucking energy which brings the force to all four of the directions. We must embody all the directions. There would be no energy without the West—the ability to simply accept the forces of the Goddess as supreme. This is the Mayan temple of the West, the Temple of the Red Spirit, of Huitzilopochtli—the temple of the solar winds which periodically cause catastrophe on Earth. This is the temple which teaches about the fragility of life. All must come to this temple who need to learn that the great purpose of the universe is not accessible through only one part of it, but that we all must surrender to the greater whole for survival itself.

The liquid burns as it goes down my throat and into the pit of my stomach. The drink is hot and painful and zaps my solar plexus, especially the intestines. The sensation hits my solar plexus like acid and is absorbed into my system. Out shoots a white laser beam of light which penetrates all of my brain centers, like a stroke occurring at the realization of a truth that cannot be considered. My head is exploding as the pulque goes into my neurological pathways. The drug is so powerful that the effects could kill me if I were open to my soul's plan at this moment. I shoot my hands straight out, my feet firmly implanted in the Earth, and I have a great erection. I shoot the fire energy out of my five extremities: my feet, hands, and phallus.

As I shoot the energy out, the pyramid above me becomes activated. The beings in other dimensions are drawn to it in anticipation of a ceremony which will generate experiences that will be meaningful for them. I am conscious of the appearance of the beings because my astral body is trained, and I can see forms in other dimensions. One of the purposes of ceremony is to invite in beings from other dimensions, and those of us who lead ritual in the physical body watch these appearances. Of course, we hope they will be visitors who elevate us, but the risk we take by opening the veil is that essences caught in negative thoughtforms may manifest. As I activate myself, I am a conduit which activates beings who require this teaching from other planes. As they come into form, I can see them.

That is what I don't like—using my energy to activate the energy of others. Their energy feels sticky when they enter my own energy field. My soul does not like the beings who are drawn to this place and time. But my physical body is totally charged by this experience, and my soul observes and records the teachings happening in my body during this ritual. I require this experience to be able to understand power on Earth, and I will return later to master power. But my soul hates negative imprints, for later, new personal situations will be required to clear these imprints. But my soul knows the time has come in my experiential Earth body for the encodement of the experience of alienation from my soul. I must experience the behavior that occurs during times of massive abuse, and times of societal insanity, when many well-meaning individuals participate in monstrous behavior, so that I will feel the loss of my soul.

I am now activating those waiting outside while we are doing a secret ritual deep inside the pyramid. Outside, a priestess dressed in white walks up to the top of the platform, climbing seven steps on the East side. As she is walking up these steps, six kachinas are ascending other steps on the pyramid, three each from the North and South sides. I will eventually ascend the steps on the West side when I emerge from within. My energy is activating the six kachina beings who are ascending the steps. I feel the kachinas as I activate their sexual powers with my phallus. The priestess is in a drugged trance. She walks up the steps and stands on top of the platform wearing a white robe. The six god beings coming from the South and North, three on each side, get to the top as she lies down. The gods move into position in a circle around her. These gods represent the six levels of manifestation, and I will be the seventh. She lies down. Several hands lift her dress and spread her legs, exposing her nakedness.

All the people of the city, Tikal, are watching this ritual. This is a very sticky situation, and my higher self does not like the emotions in the people of Tikal. The crowd is eroticized by observing the ritual. If this ritual were pure, the populace would not be eroticized. There is nothing negative about erotic energy, but it is not right in this situation because there is no free will. This girl has no free will because she is drugged. The priests use the power of the drug to bring in the mana, the power. Our male religious leaders are not evolved enough to see that this is an abuse of power. Whenever power is abused in ceremony involving erotic energy, it becomes sticky, atavistic and potentially open to possession. This priestly cult of Tikal believes that they are attuned to the evolution of their collective in this ritual, when in reality they do not know the results of their creations. This ceremony implants a planetary blindness about the sacredness of the woman/Earth which will come to full blossom at the last phase of the next Nine Hells— 1968 AD to 1987 AD. This temple is the Mayan stronghold of the male Jaguar Cult—the cult of the fear of female eroticism.

My soul wishes to scream the truth through the veils of time: This is wrong! It is repeating a ritual that goes back thousands of years which recreates the original time when the gods came down and mated with priestesses. This interference by star beings was carried out in order to speed up the evolution of the human race. The purpose of that was to produce laborers for Earth colonies which served the star gods. Human females were impregnated with superior genes by gods who came down to make workers. But now, humans cannot take away the free will of others. Humans can only make others suffer through time.

Spirit has objected to both this re-creation ceremony and to the original genetic manipulation by the gods. Women will willingly bear the divine child when the child wishes entrance. Five Venus cycles, of 52 years each, before this time at Tikal, the divine child came to Palenque, and he was welcomed. He was ceremoniously buried in the new land, making all forms of free-will invasion by another being obsolete. Control of others is now the root cause of violence on Earth. One should not disturb the progress of the soul and manipulate events. The teaching of the Age of Flowers after the next Nine Hells will be about the natural unfoldment of the flower petals until they fall to the ground.

The cults were empowered to be the guardians of the blood line. The priests utilized sexuality for these esoteric ceremonies to control women. But women are the guardians of the birth process which protects the species. The male pattern is to produce too many children so that these children can be enslaved as warriors and laborers. This is such an ancient and deeply ingrained response pattern—a faulty warrior gene—that fathers even insist that their sons go to war and perish. The agony of the next Nine Hells—the Age of the Fathers—will break this pattern when men learn to weep. Through time, as long as the birth process is taken from women, the human population will be enslaved into labor. Male priests distorted the story of the original garden. It was not that women would be cursed with labor pains, but that all humans would be destined to lives of labor. Before you watch any more of this ritual, listen!

I, your soul, cannot reside in you because of your frequency as the Huit-zilopochtli kachina—the energy of the violent father god who hates the feminine. I cannot reside in you when you deny your own female side, for that denial is the source of the cruel heart.

Emerging from the temple wearing a feathered belt on my waist, cowrie shells around my neck, and a feathered headdress, I walk up the steps on the left-hand side of the pyramid. My soul—like a guardian angel—walks up the steps on the right side. There are seven steps. I begin at the first, my head lowered, my hands at my sides, pulling Earth energy with me. My enormous phallus is visible to all who watch. Feeling their excitement, I feel potent sexual power. I stop on the first step, and two priestesses emerge who stroke my phallus with oil. These women are very excited, surely wishing to exchange places with the priestess at the top. I rise up to the second step as the power floods into my arms, my shoulders, my entire back. My whole body is shooting with energy, incredible energy. As I climb onto the second step, the women of Tikal scream and writhe in orgasmic ecstasy.

I climb to the third step, and the six priests around the girl throw off their robes. These men wear dog headdresses, and also exhibit enormous erections. The people are in a frenzy. The six dog kachinas reach down to bowls of oil in front of their feet, and coat their own phalluses with oil. Down below, the people are losing control. I stop on the third step and raise my arms high in the air, a signal to the priests on the seventh level: the five Chichimeca of the Dog Star, Sirius, and Topiltzin, the prince. Raising their arms in the air, the dog kachinas send out a great electrical jolt which resembles lightning on the etheric plane. The bolt stops the activity.

I ascend to the fourth step, the turquoise step, sacred to the snake. Now I feel incredible resistance. My soul cries. . .I am going to commit sodomy! On the fourth step I stop, and a young boy of ten or twelve is brought out of the interior. I had not been aware of him until now. If I had known about this, I might have been able to refuse to do the whole thing. He is brought up the steps where my soul was attempting to remain in another dimension. As he is brought to the fourth step, he exposes his buttocks. I resist, but the six priests at the top send out a jolt of electrical energy that drives the pulque further into all the cells of my body. I have no way to resist. The energy shoots down into my phallus, and I am filled with a sexual rush that is more intense than I have ever felt. This is sexual energy used as violence to the body. We are creating a form of abuse to be activated later at the beginning of the Nine Hells.

I sodomize him. He screeches in pain, but there is angelic white light all around him. His astral self is able to jump out of his body as this is occurring, but his soul remains with him. He has given me a great teaching by being who he is with his soul present within his forcefield. He feels the total agony of his soul and will therefore be free forever of primary sado-masochism. As I see that, I am sure that I will never again be capable of sexual or drug abuse. I do not ejaculate.

I ascend to the fifth step—the feminine—where my soul can be stolen or forever held by me. I refuse still to integrate my vicious behavior totally into myself. I am an initiated priest! I do this ceremony, but my actions are not mine! To perform this ceremony, how I feel, think, or relate to its energy does not matter. Horror! Next a veil opens to the other dimensions which should never be opened. Like monsters of my own inner night, I see leering griffins with black wings. Like harpies, the beasts clutch me on the shoulders, and the back of my neck and head. One of the griffins manifests as a beautiful female sprite. She places her perfect pink vagina on my phallus, and fear takes complete control of me. The only way in which I have allowed the feminine within is as the devouring mother, because the priests took me away from my own mother, and deprived me of affection until I quit wanting the safety she provided.

The people become very excited again. The men attack the women, the women attack the men. This time, the six priests around the girl hold their hands out to create an electrical field on the seventh seal, which is like a perverse Star of David. The phalluses of the priests become lightning rods for electrical arcs that leap across to each other from phallus to phallus. They ejaculate spontaneously from the stimulation, and then the people of Tikal begin an orgy. Children, animals, parents—all participate in the firestorm of soul denial. Any remaining identity is swallowed by the ferocious need to deny the pure spiritual person each desires to be the most.

In the forcefield around Tikal, astral beings from many dimensions have manifested. All the griffins and dragons are breaking into the physical dimension. Barely alive anymore, these creatures need this kind of juice. The beings are dessicated spirits that have been created during abusive sexual acts. They are always hanging around in the astral dimension waiting for more stimulation.

I ascend to the sixth step—becoming totally conscious—where I have a last opportunity for choice. The harpies and the sylphs leave and fly around. All of the energy from the copulating people below and from the electrical energy of the six priests above has sucked me into a state of total obsession. This is the quintessence of violent eroticism. My phallus is pounding with power while my soul is disembodied. My soul cries out in desperation:

"We ask you, Goddess, to help the soul you love."

My soul fills with the pure energy of the first creation as the light shines in front of me and enters into my essence. I see the blue lady again! She electromagnetically infuses me—at the cellular level—with a future knowing: I will go forward in time and commit no more abuse. Both the child I sodomized and myself are encoded with an absolutely pure teaching about how sexual and violent abuse functions. The demon is to be given back to the people at the completion of the next Nine Hells as a teaching about the sanctity of the child within.

I step up to the top of the platform, the seventh seal, and the power of the sexual energy is an energy known only to those who fuse sex and anger. I am like the Beast at the end of time, and only my self-loathing interests me as I lower myself down on the priestess, pushing my phallus in as her body convulses. Writhing with pain and shock, she is held tight by the six priests who grasp her arms and legs. She hates it! She is in excruciating pain, which is intensified by not being able to move. She is only about nine years old. The people down below are building up sexual frenzy into an orgy. This is the first time I have entered the body of a woman, for the priests made me enter a male first. As I enter her, I do not feel her female energy since my ability to fuse with her was stolen by the sodomy diversion. This is one of the most insidious control devices of the male priesthood through the ages. The way to male healing on Earth is in making peace with the female. The male cults have used many methods to garner control of Earth, one of which is initiation techniques utilizing sodomy.

I rape her with the full force of male aggression, a gross parody of hierogamous. She wears garlands of corn, her cheeks are painted red, and she is feathered with parrot feathers from her elbows to her wrists. Hierogamous was a very fecund ritual of sympathetic magic when the ritual was passionate and officiated over by the Goddess—guardian of the cycles of life. This gross parody of the powers of the sacred serpent and the sky bird is male power, aggression, and male control. The act is a violation of the Maize Mother. When women are suppressed in ceremony, an energy is created of mindless violence. I reach orgasm, but it is all yang energy, for I receive no energy from her. I feel no reciprocation. I stand below her legs, far enough away so that the other six priests have access to her. One by one, as Topiltzin—the sixth one—stands above her head, the entranced priests line up to violate her. The men do not give the child-woman their energy either, for each has released his seed to the sky god. Topiltzin hands me an obsidian blade after he is last to pull from her body. Oh my God!

I cut her chest open, remove her beating heart. I stare hypnotized, as if the bloody organ were the heart of a wounded little bird. Dazed, I ask for her forgiveness for taking her vital energy. I place her still-beating heart on the back of the reclining statue of Chacmool, who stares forever at the rising Sun, awaiting the redemption of humanity. Now that every cell of my own body has died, I must enter into the consciousness of the young priestess. . .

I lie on the seventh level with my legs spread apart. I am drugged, I am dizzy and sick, and blurry dog-like faces are whirling around me in circles. I can't see, and I am surrounded by horrible, sticky energy which I do not understand. What is this? Next, I feel a huge pole entering my body. The shaft tears and rends the fabric of my flesh as if I am a bird attacked by a jaguar. I am torn to pieces and I am passing out from the pain, but I go into a fighting mode. My muscles tighten up like iron, and the horrible sensation hurts even more! I claw at flesh, but I am held tight on all my sides. I open my eyes, and I see the horrid phalluses of my torture. The pain is unbearable. I can't move my body, and I cannot jump out! The priests drugged me to keep me in my body! A man is pounding in me, building up to a point of ecstasy, and he shoots me with a jet of hot liquid. I hate it! I know he hates me, for I can feel his violence, not his eroticism. I become every woman who was raped from the beginning of time. A place in my soul forms which holds a scream. This scream will shatter the sky when I one day make peace with the jaguar.

The man pulls out of me as I implode inside, flooded with this purple red, violent pain. Then one by one the priests thrust into me. I am split open as they take their turn. At last they are finished. And then I feel this excruciating cutting pain as a man cuts out my heart, a heart I have abandoned. I die and leave.

Above my death, my spirit hovers and watches my bleeding body. Enveloped by white light from the soul of the first priest who violated me, I see that the light is his exquisite soul! I am him and he is me! I am gifted with the most sacred Mayan teaching—"In Lake'ch"—I am the man who violated me, and the man who violated me is me. This teaching allows me to shift my hurt and anger into compassion for my own small broken body. This compassion is so great that my heart melts into the sacred waters of life, and I feel the eternal patience of the Creator who suffers with me. My heart is the Heart of the Christos, a heart that waits until the end of time for the end of abuse.

The Heart of the Christos extends compassion to all the people of Tikal. The crowd stops and looks at the sky. Next, the Heart floods love into all the beings on the seventh seal, and they feel what they have done. I—the priest/me—am the last one to feel, and I stand silently for a moment. Then I begin to weep from the center of my soul. This is a deep, intense weeping of pain for the human race. I am Itzanna. I stand on the seventh seal, overtaken by a vision of the arrival of Cortez at the opening of the next Nine Hells. Cortez comes to Tenochitlan after dining with Moctezuma, and he casts out the hearts at the Festival of Huitzilopochtli. The day is Good Friday of 1519 AD—a gross parody of the first crucifixion.

"I, Itzanna, will have no peace until the New Dawn. This is Maya. Like the waxing and waning Moon, we must live time out. Huitzilopochtli is the hummingbird god who will return for the Age of Flowers to suck the sweet flower nectar of peace." I am crucified.

This sacrifice will not happen to my soul again. That is what I choose with my tears. The girl/woman gave her life as a sacrificial priestess so that men could learn to cry. As Mayans, we only need martyrdom once, and now we are a people who know how to cry. Because we know how to cry, we will be resistant to the evil which Cortez will bring so that we can teach his people to cry. When the next teaching comes from Cortez, he will wear the mask of Quetzalcoatl. We will live out the most profound teaching of the Nine Hells: As white people try to kill every one of us, he will be able to see in our eyes that we know he wears the mask. One day he will remove his mask and expose himself with courage, like this young Mayan who has exposed the very core of his soul. A Mayan is one who knows the pain of Earth in the heart, who sees truth with clear eyes. We stare out at the conquerer with his heartless life, as we live through the Nine Hells awaiting the New Dawn when the mask will be removed from the face of the white brothers and sisters.

I, Itzanna, as kachina Huitzilopochtli, stand above the blood and begin to feel the waters flow within. I feel great pain over not having any free will because of taking the drug, and I cry for my free will as the order reverses itself. I let go of my desire to remain unconscious, to not know exactly who I am—everyman. I only ask that I contain my soul within my body as I live, that my soul will never again vacate, so I can never again be taken over by any substance, being, or belief system. I know this means I can never again be a priest and set myself above the others. I begin to cry, and the astral spirits turn to fire. All of the dragons and griffins begin to writhe in pain, since the only element that can purify the astral dimension is fire.

The fire element begins to purify the dimensions. The fire is the Pentecost, but with this Pentecost, the fire purifies the emotions of the people. Yellow and red tongues of fire purify the people as they begin to feel ecstatic from the flames. The tongues of fire purify the top of the altar, burning away the blood and heart, and the pyramid turns to fire. I become fire, a torch of truth from Earth to sky, and this temple site ceases to function. Every person who was present at this ceremony will return to see the white people cry after 1987 AD. This is a power greater than any government, ruler, priest, or military establishment. This is the power of fusion.

Days later, snakes, reptiles, centipedes, amd spiders crawl over the temple. A Mayan daykeeper walks from Teotihuacan. He walks in a state of deep meditation through five or six hundred miles of jungle on the sacbes, the sacred pathways. He arrives at the temple of Tikal. He sees that there is no one left, no human habitation here, even though the murals are still fresh and the thatched roofs are still intact covering the sanctuaries at the tops of the pyramids. The fire element has transmuted the end of the Nine Hells. Coming to the Temple of Huitzilopochtli, the door is still open. The daykeeper looks inside to see emptiness, and he closes the stone door. He goes to the top of the pyramid carrying the last jaguar skin from the last jaguar priest, which he places on the top of the sacrificial altar—Chacmool—who stares innocently out at the horizon. He will stare out at the horizon until the coming of the waterbearer. He is the Mayan sphinx who knows that the Mayans became people of compassion at the end of the Nine Hells in 843 AD. He is the god who makes rain.

The daykeeper walks back to Teotihuacan where he awaits the return of Itzanna. He awaits the return, which will bring the opening of the Emerald Records at the New Dawn. The daykeeper will wait for the people who wear no mask, who open their hearts and trust Earth enough to look into the darkest resource of the self. Now we open the Green Records to tell the story of all the people of Earth who trusted the wounded healer. . .

I recalled my life as young Mayan priest at Tikal in 843 AD during the summer of 1987, just before I left to do ceremony for Harmonic Convergence at Teotihuacan. The full memory of that lifetime about my own inner male was a blinding systemic shock. I knew that to be given such truth about myself was a profound gift. This ability to confront my own shadow—in the knowledge of this past life—was a truth that was to be required of me before leading ceremonies at Teotihuacan. It was a calling which I had to answer. Seeing such raw truth was a great purification, and I resolved to allow the truth to be my teacher, no matter what the consequences.

Tezcatzlipoca was the Aztec god of human sacrifice, a form of the dark side that I believe also existed earlier at Tikal, but only during Tikal's last phase. Regarding human sacrifice, Tezcatzlipoca and Quetzalcoatl are reflections of the inner dark and light sides of human nature. Like Cain and Abel, or Horus and Seth, these archetypes have arisen to the surface repeatedly in human history when cultures have attained a consciousness of the individual. Quetzalcoatl—the Plumed Serpent—said many times during his life that the mask would be removed from Tezcatzlipoca at the end of the Nine Hells—August 16, 1987. Quetzalcoatl said we would be surprised at who he really is! Was I the first one to see the identity? Tezcatzlipoca, god of rape, murder, control, and lies, is seen unmasked by one who has the guts to shine the light into the darkest recesses of his or her own being. Quetzalcoatl also said that he would return to open the Nine Hells in 1519 AD on Good Friday to destroy the manmade gods of his people.

I sat in the Pipe Ceremony at noon on August 16th, 1987 in the Temple of Quetzal Butterfly, with White Eagle Tree and a woman Lakota Pipe Carrier, passing the White Pipe of Peace of Quetzalcoatl. We were awaiting the New Dawn. White Eagle Tree's Red Pipe had been sacrificed to the wind god. The records below the temple opened for us, and I was given the Sirius Teaching Three for planet Earth:

"Adamah now has tasted of good and evil, but he can only know of divinity if granted free will. Free will can only be mastered on Earth by utilization of magic and divination, which involve the ability to be on Earth and in other dimensions simultaneously. By giving away the secrets of the divine, you can be freed from your original lie, which first separated me from my children of Earth. You will do this by assisting in the birth of the Son of the Source, the Creator, on Earth. Then Earth will transcend duality over time, for Nibiru will no longer be separate from the Solar Logos when Earth is the equal of the gods."

I watched the sacred smoke disappear into the Sun and I saw that Earth would finally become my relative, transcending all fratricide and matricide, and that I would know both sides of myself.

Nibiru began a planetary return to the solar system in 1600 BC after receiving Sirius Teaching Three, and now, in the late twentieth century, Nibiru is at the same point in its cycle. The consciousness link between Nibiru and Earth became very active. Earth teachers were able to know the thoughts of the gods, and the gods could observe the activities of the Earthlings. The gods knew they must now trust Earthlings to choose their own way. But the gods could also see that Adamah was not free of their influence, because the temple teachings and stories of Creation were all from the gods! Just like Quetzalcoatl prophesied, the manmade gods of the people would have to be destroyed. Like a parent ready to let go of a grown child, the Nibiruans began to actually see the needed total end of their influence.

As Nibiru began its return, the decision was made to send teachings to Earth oracles and prophets, to prepare Earth people for the Divine Son, Christos. Earthlings would need to experience the prophetic powers; the source could no longer be simply the gods. Earthlings began receiving messages directly from the gods, and the news was so shocking that some of them went crazy or were blinded by the light. At that time, the mental circuitry of most Earthlings was not developed enough for such power. The source often shattered their identity, especially since Earthlings had no choice about receiving the messages. All over the planet, a quickening began. It was a time of building Earth energy and the range of human experience so that the planet could know Christos. The memory of that ancient oracular infusion is being revived in modern times by channels who are suddenly infused with information.

In Egypt, the most empowered temple system at the time, diviners heard that Horus was returning to Earth. The pharoah, Hatshepsut, was sure she would give birth to the Son, and she prepared a god-birthing room for him. Two generations later, the pharoah, Akhenaton, thought he was the actual Son himself, and he built new temples to honor his great father. Amongst the Hebrews who were sojourning in Egypt because of famine in the Holy Land, a frenzy emerged: The people had to return to the promised land for the birth of the Son, for surely God's Son would be born in the Holy Land. But, as the Hebrews fled out of Egypt, a great tidal wave swept behind them— the tsunami resulting from the eruption of Thera. Moses had a vision that the waters parted for his people—the Chosen People of God. The gods, who were trying to let go of playing God, were dismayed by this. The gods knew that the Earthlings would never master free will if one race put their people above another race. Wherever a doctrine of divine favor existed, how could one people ever respect another people? When Moses led his people back to the Holy Land, he died before he could enter the sacred valley. Joshua, the warrior, was the conquerer who claimed the land for the Chosen People.

In 3600 BC, many Trees of Life had been brought to Earth, one for the West which was planted in Oaxaca, and one in Jerusalem—the Tree of Jesse. As the

Hebrews destroyed the ancient Earth temples and sacred circles, the roots of the ancient Tree of Jesse began to shrivel. The ancient water courses deep in the Earth flowed under the great and powerful stones, and the springs stopped flowing. In Egypt, the secret priesthood which guarded the true Sirian teachings became very afraid when Akhenaton wanted to move the sacred sites, believing that he could eradicate "the gods." He moved the sacred altars to different parts of Egypt, places which had no telluric energy. The power of the Earth was no longer accessible in Egypt, the Tree of Life planted beside the Sphinx in 10,800 BC began to shrivel, and the secret priesthood took drastic action. The priests shut down all the altars and oracles of the goddess Sekhmet, wiped her teachings from the last three chapters of the Am Tuat *and* Book of the Gates, *and hid all the teachings on the day Akhenaton was crowned.*

The divine Son was to be born in the land of the Garden, but the decision was made to shift the Earth energy for the future birth to the sacred lands of the West. The Nibiruans were sure that new sacred sites needed to be empowered for the descent of the Son. His descent, which was a calibration of stellar dimensions into third-dimensional form, could not happen without the balancing of the powerful Earth energies. The Nibiruans could see that the power of the ancient Nibiruan memories was so entrenched in Egypt that a transfer to the West was required. So, under Seti I, a great master from Andromeda Galaxy, the teachers were sent to Machinga/La Venta to create the new temple form. The very first teaching in the new land was to bury the gods, to let the gods exist deep in the Earth, so that the Earth could safely receive her Son. The most powerful Earth temple in the West was Teotihuacan. The Emerald Crystal of the Records was moved out of Egypt and placed deep in an underground temple and sealed off. Later, the upper temples were built over the crystal.

The geomancy of the Teotihuacan complex is absolutely unique on Earth. The main temple complex is the center of a spiral which connects to all the Mayan temple sites. Each one of the temples on the spiral was to be activated at a New Fire Ceremony when the Pleiades rose. The first New Fire Ceremony was at Machinga. The power of Christos and the records of evolution on Earth would be contained in the center of the spiral, and each site would activate certain desires which would present the ceremony participants with their first choices. Until the activation of Teotihuacan, free will did not exist on Earth except in humans who carried the blood of the gods. Within the ancient Egyptian and Hebrew temples, there was no free will—only obedience was known. With the return of Nibiru in 0 AD, humans would take on the burden of the gods and freely choose or reject alternatives offered to them. This teaching had to be implanted in the West without the interference of powerful memories of many lifetimes where there was no free will.

Sitting in the hot sun on that August afternoon as the pipe was passed, I realized that I was beginning to "see." I had "remembered" life after life in which I was given no choice. I had gone through a series of experiences which might have been pleasant or unpleasant, but I had no control over them. Then, when I had realized that I could decide to change reality, getting myself to do anything was like trying to crawl out of a deep sleep, since humans differ from the gods in that we learn to feel in the third dimension. First, I had had to experience participation in evil acts against other humans so that I could choose to never do it again. Then, as I had tried to act with consciousness, to learn to love in a female body, all the pain and resistance I had experienced when I had been violated resurfaced and engulfed me. In my most recent lifetime as a repressed and oppressed Victorian woman, I had felt like I had been asleep all my life, as described in Eye of the Centaur. In my current life, each time I have awakened a new aspect of myself, I have had to go back through the maze of pain and resistance at the cellular level in order to open new spaces within myself.

The cedar smoke from the pipe created spirals in the afternoon sunlight as the people surrounding the circle were joyfully awakening to the New Dawn. I was taken by a vision of the spiral containing all the Mayan temples, grounded into this center where we sat. I became aware that this was the perfect hologram for my own emergence. I could simply return again and again to each temple that had a soul teaching for me until I had let go of every single belief system in which I was limited in any way in my search for the pathway to the center of creation, to the Heart of the Christos.

Chapter Five

EMERGENCE FROM THE UNDERWORLD

The shattering and ecstatic energy of total free-will power coursed through my body and soul, and I was ready to remember the original childhood trauma of my current lifetime. By remembering Tikal, I was now able to realize that people commit evil acts because they cannot feel the pain they cause others. They would be absolutely incapable of murder and rape if they could feel their own inner pain. I, as the young Mayan priest, had been conditioned not to feel by older priests who had also once been conditioned not to feel. What a gift to have that most deeply hidden place—the murderous heart—revealed to me! At age 45, suddenly I was prepared to see my central core of pain. I was ready to offer compassion to myself.

I was sent away during the Second World War to live with another family, and the father in that family raped me when I was less than three years old. The mother's actions when she realized I had been raped were incomprehensibly sad. Since she was my real mother's childhood friend, her only interest was in making sure that my mother never found out about it.

Broken and wounded, I received no solace from the woman in that house. She talked at me for hours about how I had fantasized the experience, even as I felt the stickiness and pain in my own body. She told me I had a wild imagination, which was just what she told my mother about me when I went home a year later. While she talked at me with her red mouth, glared at me with her sharp eyes, and clutched at me with her calloused hands, I felt my brain deaden in the back of my skull. I lost the ability to trust any woman. She was like a caterpillar, spinning the threads of her lies as she chrysalized in the back of my skull the horrid memory of what had happened to me on a cold porch, as lake winds pounded on the unforgiving glass. This matrix of encapsulated trauma, sealed like a trapped larval form lacking the metamorphosizing hormone for emergence, held me back from finding my wings—my identity.

Every single occurrence in my universe became a source of fear until I was at least eight or nine years old. All dark hallways and closets contained demons, and I found myself unable to fully comprehend who was present around me. When I returned to my parents' house after the War, I did not recognize my genetic family.

Every nerve in my body and brain conspired to have me never know what had happened to me. But as the energy in me awakened when I began the shamanistic journey, my central core of fear had to be penetrated. Actually, what really drove me to know the truth was that I began to worry that I might develop Alzheimer's Disease. A few years before recalling the rape, I became very concerned about an accelerating short-term memory loss. I could feel the source in the back of my head, and the locus felt like a knotted mass of brain matter that was tightening around a hot coal. When I finally recovered the core memory of my rape during an all-day session with a healer, I faced it exactly as it was. There was no hiding from the ugliness of this brutalization of a beautiful little girl. At that point, I could actually feel my brain begin to regenerate! I was ready to begin the journey back through the lives of evil. Whether I committed that evil, or whether the evil was done to me, I wanted to know the source, for it is only in facing the great evil in ourselves that we can be free. And so I journeyed to Tikal in Guatemala in February of 1988. It was in this place that I had committed the greatest evil.

When I arrived at Tikal, I walked to the center plaza of the temple complex and got sick. Many have had just this experience at ancient sacred sites, and in my case, I actually knew why. I decided to start my experience on the perimeter of the complex and work my way closer into the center after my psyche had begun to reintegrate the traumatic memories. I assumed that there were many more experiences than I had already remembered.

I had the notion that, through my own meditation at this temple complex, and through being purified by my own willingness to integrate past-life actions that I now judged to be evil, I could break the hold of evil on this planet. I intuited that all the judgment separating us from our divinity could be dissolved if just one wounded soul could forgive herself. But, when we came to Earth and agreed to undergo the free-will experiment, we all agreed to experience both the dark and the light, like carbon being compressed to form an exquisite diamond. What if God had no compassion or understanding for those who needed to experience the dark side? Joy and pain are both necessary to transform carbon to diamond. This will be true until the last person lets go of separation and cuts the last facet into the stone, allowing the Sun to shine into its center so it can re-emit pure light. Our ability to love our own pain and our own pleasure with enlightenment is what honors our experience, and makes every experience into a teaching. When all resistance, all fear or hatred of darkness, is removed, then the light may move through us completely, creating the luminous form that is immortal—the diaphanous lifeform.

So I began my opening at Tikal with the illumination that I might only cut one facet on the diamond body hologram that would eventually enable us all to emerge from *our chrysalises. Or, I might have been there to cut the last facet that would allow the Sun to shine into the primordial carbon. I began in a state of total trust that my ceremonial gift had power.*

It was clear—I needed to bless my inner turmoil day after day until I felt myself fill with light. Starting at the perimeter and working my way into the powerful central plaza of the six-mile-square temple complex containing over 3,000 ruins, I began in the West with a call for the dark goddess—my guide for all that is yet unknown. After walking six miles in deep jungle, I emerged into a section called "El Mundo Perdido"—The Lost World. I was very disoriented, until I found the Temple of the Red Hand. This was an indication that my quest had begun. I am of the Mayan Order of the Red Hand, since my name is Hand and my teaching is divination. I placed my own right hand on the red hand of the guardian deity at the temple entrance, and felt my ancient Mayan initiations activate so that the temple complex would open for me.

Later, I walked on the second story of the Bat Palace past five typical Mayan doorways. No one was around, the weather was humid and warm, and I could hear tropical birds high up in the ceiba trees. Suddenly I was jerked backwards by an energy pull that yanked me through one of the doorways. I sat down on a stone platform resembling a bed and went into a trance. I felt a great vortex of energy building up. Two red parrots flew by above me, then a great green parrot flew over, and I was consumed with an ancient memory.

I am walking swiftly and silently to the forum of the priests who are in training. The time is 200 AD. I am going to see my lover, a young initiate living in the Forum, the Central Acropolis. I go to the door near his room, anticipating lying in fields of grass in the sun and making love. As I come to the door, I look into the central quadrant where the outdoor discourses are held, and I see him at a distance, but he appears as if in a dream.

I move to another scene where I am standing naked in a row with seven other priestesses. One of us will be chosen for hierogamous with the high priest and will give birth to the godchild. A year ago, I would have given any possession for this honor. But now I have fallen in love with my young man.

We stand in a row. My eyes are down as I feel the high priest examining my body, and I look at him through my eyelashes. He is the same being who proposed a sexual initiation in my lifetime as Barbara! As my future memory comes to me, I know he will choose me for the hierogamous. I feel lonely for I will no longer be allowed to see my lover.

I give birth to a child, but she is a deformed baby girl! The bat priestesses take the baby to die on the rocks and be eaten by the vultures.

I am consumed with confusion! The priests told me I would give birth to the god if I did as they told me to do! Finally, I have a meeting with the high priest, who seems to be in no mood to have me take his time. He looks at me with contempt.

I challenge him, "How could this have happened if this was a sacred ritual? You told me you selected me because the child would be a god!"

He becomes annoyed and tells me, "I only picked you because I wanted your young flesh."

I abandon myself to the jungle for fire purification. I lie over the emergence hole of a fire-ant nest. If I can survive the ordeal, I will become a priestess in the weaving lodge. If I were to just commit suicide, my spirit would wander Tikal until the end of time. The ants consume my watery grief with their fire power. I swoon as desire ceases within me. I no longer wish for my young lover.

Just before I die, I hear a thundering voice in the clouds: "There was no initiation, no birth of a god, for God is within you. You are now my daughter, blessed with healing hands of power."

While I am dying in the jungle, my lover burns copal in his temple, calling my soul to return to meet him again in another life.

I stayed in the bat complex at Tikal a long, long time, realizing how far I had come. In my current life, I stayed with the man I chose and did not fall into the old pattern again. In Mayan spirituality, the bat rules reincarnation. This remnant of the age of dinosaurs is a totem of the dark goddess, who teaches us that we must all return to the dark cave in order to regenerate ourselves. The bat emerges from the cave at twilight and flies with swift wings into the setting Sun. This creature spends the night in meditation while the Sun journeys around the opposite side of the planet. Within the cave, during the long bright day, the bat holds the power of the night journey.

The second day at Tikal, I went to the top of the West Temple in the evening, when the Sun was getting ready to set. I meditated for hours, burning incense to clear the pain and clear the anger, letting these feelings go into the night air of the exquisite jungle. I left the West Temple when darkness fell and ran through the jungle in the moonless night. We had deliberately gone to Tikal during the waning Moon, and I was wearing all black for the initiation of the dark side of the Moon. This jungle, unlike the woods of my childhood, had pythons, barba amarilla or fer-de-lance snakes, jaguars, and fire ants. If bitten by the barba amarilla, blood oozes from all body orifices and one is dead within five minutes.

The next day I meditated and did ceremony at several sites, but not in the intensely polarized central plaza. I found an astrologer's complex and spent hours letting go of the cycles, moving out the deaths and lives, sadnesses and joys, of the last 26,000 years, as my hands ran over Mayan dating glyphs of the long cycles which chronicle Creation itself. Then, after reinitiating myself into my ancient teaching as a Mayan astrologer, I went into a very remote part of the site which was closed off for an archaeological dig. I walked stealthily in the deep jungle, for I had asked my guide, Horus, to show me my animal teacher after accepting my role as a Mayan astrologer.

There was a heavy thud about twenty feet to my right, a crack of a branch, and I was looking into the yellow eyes of a jaguar. I was in my power, wearing all black. I was no threat, and the cat lunged quickly up a tree and out of sight. I was ecstatic! What a teacher! My totem animal had come to give me courage of the heart. The great cat spoke to me of my own warrior female.

I offered my power to help others undergo the initiation of the dark side of the Moon, for I knew that the next trial I would face would be the sorcerer. That night, the sorcerer came to the hotel in the form of a drunkard. My companion told him that I had seen a jaguar in the jungle that afternoon. Spitting into his filthy beer bottle, he told the story of an archaeologist who had attempted to walk to the temple east of Tikal—Uaxuactum. He was found a year later, a dried and clean corpse. He had been bitten by the barba amarilla. I asked the sorcerer how to watch out for these deadly snakes, and he instructed me that the creatures lie in sun spots in the jungle. He said they are hard to see against the leaves. However, I had studied my guidebook carefully: The barba amarilla lies sequestered in dark and damp places.

The next day I went east of Tikal to its companion temple, Uaxuactum, the feminine side of the temple form. This complex is round and soft while Tikal is harsh and angular. Uaxuactum is Lemurian and accesses the right brain and intuition, while Tikal is very Atlantean and technological. I meditated in one temple for six hours as the rains came and went. Finally, I felt myself break open deep within my cells. All my barriers against women left me as I forgave the first seven female teachers who had facilitated me in seeing painful truths about myself. The first one to be forgiven was the mother who did not protect me against male aggression. I asked for the future to give me peace with the eighth woman teacher, who was my companion on this journey and who had gifted me with the day-long session in which I had recalled my childhood rape.

My life was at stake, for any residue of anger against women would deliver the snake—my appointment with death made by the sorcerer. His role was to guard the temple secrets for the brotherhood of the snake clan. My thoughts about who was right or wrong, and who did what to whom, all mercifully left me. I had held anger in my heart against the woman who did not comfort me when I was raped. As I released this anger, a hummingbird—totem spirit of the Aztec/Toltec/Mayan god, Huitzilopochtli—flew to my face, around my head for a moment, and then rested on my shoulder. Hummingbirds do not land on the shoulders of humans, but then perhaps the story is not true that pulverized hummingbird is a Mesoamerican aphrodisiac. At the same moment in time, the sorcerer sat in the center of the Tikal complex, visualizing a vulture flying out of a ceiba tree on the edge of the lake between Tikal and Uaxuactum and beginning his sky journey to Uaxuactum. The sorcerer as vulture would be the first purifier to discover the body of the white woman in the jungle. My companion who stayed in the hotel at Tikal was meditating. She called in the Goddess to protect me. My most secret desire—-to have a mother who would totally shield me against the terror of life—broke. I looked up to the sky to see a spiraling hawk.

As I was walking later that day, I sensed a vibrating totem power nearby. There, curled up in a moist dark place under a carved Mayan fist, was the barba amarilla. Moving slowly and cautiously backwards, I sent the snake respect. Then I examined the four-by-five foot carved hand. I had never seen a carving like it at a Mayan site. I was profoundly moved that the snake goddess had awaited me under a hand.

At exactly the same time that the energy broke within me at Tikal on February 25, 1988, there appeared sun dogs and rainbows in the sky over Santa Fe, New Mexico which were observed for hours by hundreds of people. According to the Mayan calendar, this was a day when the fire spirit could be released from Earth by means of an open heart. Each time any individual is able to release stored-up inner pain, the planet is released, and, in turn, as the planet releases inner pain, we are able to individually release it. The barba amarilla is the snake totem for the fire spirit, so indeed the planet had passed through another gate in evolution. In addition, the summer of 1988 was the summer of the great fires in the western U.S. Every time the power of a sorcerer is absorbed into an open heart and acknowledged, the need to control life lessens.

My last day in Tikal, I went to the central polarity point of the main plaza. There I sat in a lotus position in a deep state of meditation as the true natural energy of the temple site exhibited itself. Tikal is the temple complex which holds the war hologram on Earth. It is the temple in synchronicity with Mars, and I listened to a group of Guatemalans making plans for guerilla movements. Much time went by, and then a little girl rolling a hoop came through the center and paused to play with her dog—the sacred guardian against death for the Mayans. I left, to never return to Tikal again.

The form of abuse at Tikal that was originally planted there by me at the end of the previous Nine Hells is released now. All forms will proliferate endlessly in creation, but the frequency shifts are the gateway to the divine, and the shift which occurred on Harmonic Convergence was the same as the shift in 843 AD. As already reported, I recovered the memory of the young priest at Tikal a few weeks before Harmonic Convergence. My twentieth-century ceremony there was a cleansing, a purification. There was a general shift at Tikal when the fire spirit was released in 843 AD. This occurred at the end of the epitome of polarization which always characterizes the last phase of the Nine Hells. Polarization is generated by inner stress over our individual integration of male and female parts of ourselves.

At the end of the previous Nine Hells, I had participated in an orgiastic desecration of a little girl. With the modern ending of the Nine Hells, we see exactly the same type of hideous violence against females being perpetrated by males disconnected from their own inner feminine. In my childhood, I lacked the energy of my own inner male and ended up playing the role of victim. The energy released at Tikal in ceremony was contained in a hologram. This hologram held the belief systems which allowed individuals to commit evil acts and not feel the pain of those they acted against because they were blinded to their own inner oppositions.

Obsession with one side of the self is the heart of the darkness to be lanced, now that we have reached the end of the Nine Hells. The pentecostal fire spirit lay dormant until the New Dawn: the next cycle of ascension of the Thirteen Heavens, which began at sunrise on August 17, 1987—Harmonic Convergence. People who work in military complexes and chemical factories will actually feel pain in their corroded livers, toxic pancreases, angry bowels, and encrusted hearts as the last of the energy from the Nine Hells clears, until 1992. The consequences of inner blindness are going to be mirrored back to their sources. Soon the chemists—blind alchemists—while trying to sleep at night, will hear the screams of the protozoa in the oceans which are being poisoned by their toxic products. The tree cutters will experience their own castration as they fell the giants in the forest. We have attained the experiences we require by now and there will be no more learning about what is required by Mother Earth. This last phase of the Thirteen Heavens and Nine Hells coincides with the beginning of the Sixth World, when we will move beyond polarizaton.

In the soft night sky over Tikal and Uaxuactum, my father flew to the Pleiades that night, released by a daughter who carried the coals in the New Fire Ceremony, and who released the anger from her heart.

The tension I felt in my physical body after returning from Tikal to the States made me feel like a crouching jaguar ready to spring. The inner tension was as intense as the frenzied chaos of my inner being when I was a little girl. Drawing nearer to the source, my emotional blocks began to manifest in my body in the form of muscle and joint malfunctions. I had a dream one night that the barba amarilla had bitten me in another dimension, and the jaguar that had jumped out of a tree near me in the jungle had ripped my right side with its paws. But, I will name the inner opposition that imprisons me, I will call my other side to manifest for me. I will see my dark side, no matter what it knows about me. I will go into my body to find my truth.

Most of the energy on my right side feels atrophied. I call angels of light to my right side and left brain, into my male energy. I ask my higher self to take me into masculine themes that have been the source of polarities, of abuse, of patterns I've played out in this life.

I see a being who looks very extraterrestrial, like an insect. It is green like a grasshopper, with a light green body and dark green eyes. It is hovering over my right shoulder. I feel like it is watching me all the time, with absolute determination to observe all my activities. It is the sorcerer! But this energy does not upset or frustrate me, and it feels curiously amoral. I seem to have no ability to recognize it or judge it, to respond to the sorcerer. This inner trickster seems to be hanging onto my arm between my elbow and shoulder, and it looks like one of those little green demons in medieval iconography. The insect being imports no feeling, as if it has no temperature or blood, repels moisture from its skin, and just "watches." The body is about to spring, but seems harmless. I judge I could squash it, but I know this manifestation would appear at certain times and situations, no matter what. Now I see a line of billions of these creatures extending from behind my right shoulder!

The insect being has me in its claws, gripping my right side. Its jaws maintain a constant grip and keep me from paying attention to the real source of danger. My consciousness would prefer to move down the river within me that just flows. I am caught between going down the river and being pulled on the right side. I would just as soon allow the river to attract me, but now the being on my shoulder seems to be turning into a Sumerian griffin, and is holding on very tightly. It is like an old bird, an old pterodactyl. It has been holding on for a long time. I have resistance to going inside of this new form because it is a watcher from the secret societies. It was attached to me during an initiatic ritual a long time ago to control me, to insure that I would never reveal the cosmology of the gods. Well, I would like to know who was I before this entity got attached to me!

I go back to the time before I knew this creature. This form is diminishing and my body is getting dense, filling with energy. I am getting larger and filling with golden light. But there is still some gripping on the right side and the sensation causes my head and neck to turn to the left side. I become a powerful and dense golden body, but I am still held to some extent on the right side. I am manifesting myself as a being of great golden light getting hotter and hotter, my inner fire challenging the clinging and diminishing sorcerer.

Now there is a helmet, a heavy formation on my head above my third eye and upper skull. The watchers put that helmet on my head. The helmet keeps my golden yellow body—my stellar body—held in place. My body is filling with power, building up energy so I can fight, and I am being crushed from the right side. I feel my judgment about my own power side. I don't understand why this is being done to me. My right hand is becoming very strong in response to an energy coming from this attachment, not energy coming from my own golden body. This energy makes my right arm into a weapon, and the helmet controls my will about this process. The helmet makes an energetic power connection between my head and my arm. Warriors wear helmets and use their hands to do violence on Earth because all warriors know that their hands will not kill unless they have decided in their brains that the killing is justified.

The Nibiruans put this energy into my form to make me commit certain acts on Earth which they were convinced were necessary for the evolution of the species. To me, they are the Masters of the Universe, the cause of my own evil on this planet. The cycles of time that are creating history on Earth are the egoic reality construct that exists within the minds of men and women, and within the memory bank of our experience with the watchers, the masters. I believe that these masters have had great power to interfere with human life when they have had designs here, because I have been controlled by them in my past. At one time they could impose their will on individuals whom they wished to use for their own purposes. This ability to impose their will was destroyed by Christos—the new order. They have no power in the cosmos now, except where they exist in the minds of men and women. This is the ego, which is the grip of belief systems and judgments coming from memory.

I am a light teacher from Andromeda Galaxy sent here in the feminine ray as a teacher to this galaxy. When I am in a female body, I have the opportunity to be free of the male conflict energy in my Earth self. The warrior test is the most difficult male test on Earth. When we are in female bodies, we usually do not wear the helmet which activates obedience to a declared higher authority. Men will be free on Earth when they refuse to be warriors, and women when they are free from rape. I have undergone a series of experiences on Earth as male so that I can understand male warrior energy. I came this time with a great teaching for breaking the grip of war on Earth. When I came as male, I activated the warrior force in order to comprehend this type of energy. But now, the need in Barbara's life is to transmute the ego while in female form, to empty the mind of belief systems not created in the present time.

The form on my right side is drawing both arms up, forming huge wings that are pulling back. It brushes off my right arm. Now the form is deep amethyst purple; its whole body is a faience sculpture of melted amethyst quartz! This materialization speaks to me in a crackling, sharp voice: "I am tired of purple light, tired of holding on. Like a bat seeing the light of day, I am tired of my host. There is too much purple light now, too much releasing of all the addictions which offer me a place to roost. I go willingly."

I spin and release the juice of belief-system addiction from my intestines, release the toxins in my liver into the light. I become a vessel, a Grail for holding the waveform of atonement with my own opposition. I am blasted with an explosion of light coursing through my system, and I know I have instantaneously integrated my stellar body—the consciousness form which is the Galactic Center. What I need to know now is what it means to be a teacher from Andromeda Galaxy. What does the Andromeda teaching have to do with evil?

The energy begins to relax and I feel balanced with this amazing new frequency, I feel like I am a blue-white star. This frequency is as high as fluorescent blue crystal—star crystal—which we all carry in our cells. This is the source of my stellar body, which exists simultaneously with my earth body. Suddenly I am convulsed with a life-threatening electrical shock which opens my higher brain centers—my galactic receiving stations! I am the blue lady! I open the Emerald Records of Andromeda Galaxy, and hear a voice:

The pain in your left side is from the secret teaching of the Jaguar Priest Cult. All Andromedan Earth teachers were initiated into the Jaguar Cult. This necessary phase of Earth's evolution is coming to a completion. Now is the entrance of Andromeda Galaxy intelligence into the Earth mental field by means of the "animal bypass."

We are ready to address the central confusion caused by us on Earth. Our desire now is to assist the evolution of all species on Earth beyond the confusion of evil. Please understand that all dimensions of life in the universe are capable of evil—rejecting the Creator—because of free choice.

In the beginning we did not understand exactly how Earth energy worked, and we first knew life-force—eros—in the physical body of the exquisite jaguar. This cat was the singular species we found which could shapeshift us from our own dimension to the third dimension of Earth. For, like the mysterious feline creatures of Earth, our eyes tell the story of the ages, and fear is incomprehensible to us. We are ferocious.

Before our communion with the life-force, we resonated spiral energy forms to Earth, which caused the solidification of shells. In those shells were born the first lifeforms of Earth. Your fossils are the structure of Andromeda Galaxy. But now our spiraling form has been fully implanted by the Mayans, and we can harmonize the energy so that humans can cease fearing animals. The Earth woman will lie with the jaguar in peace at last. The animals of the sky—the Zodiac—are the macrocosm, and the animals of Earth are the totemic forces representing all natural forms of expression.

We sent Osiris from Andromeda to Earth after the fall of Atlantis—our Earthcolony—since the fall of Atlantis was caused by a separation in mind between Earthlings and star forms. As long as Earthlings are ignorant of the relationship between stellar cycles and solar systems, people will live in fear of catastrophe. People make catastrophe happen by projecting it to escape the tension coming from the first experience of fear. Humans go crazy at the possibility that there are no endings, that existence is simply spiraling energy, snapping, whiplashing power like the tail of a jaguar or a snake gripped in the mouth of a ceremonial dancer.

A time will come when Earthlings will tune into the reality of other dimensions. They will experience actual existence someplace else such as Andromeda Galaxy while they live on Earth. In the ancient days, this simultaneous reality was called the Dreamtime. This simultaneity of existence was well understood by the Egyptians, who represented the stellar body of Osiris as Sirius, and the Earth form as a phallic deity. Immersion in the Dreamtime, or the ability to be on a star while living on Earth, offers peace. It offers the chance to see that nothing ever ceases to exist—we simply change dimension and form. And, I can assure you that the Sirians enjoy the phallic form of Osiris as much as Osiris enjoys being in a star. Study a spiraling ancient fossil in limestone, observe a hurricane from the sky, and then contemplate the brilliant white spiraling Andromeda Galaxy.

Since we did not know animals before we came to Earth, we had not yet discovered that the macrocosm and microcosm communion is manifested in the Milky Way Galaxy as the Zodiacal forms which are symbiotic with all species! We learned on Earth that one day the Creator got bored and envisioned the cosmos as a great boat filled with a male and female of each species. The Creator gave this vision—this covenant—to Noah! Then we discovered that we were bored with the simple lifeforms like shells. We wondered about the animals.

When Earth first experienced the incredible energy infusion of our stellar forms into the Earth dimension, we were not integrated with the animal kingdom. Our thoughtforms created a terrific energetic imbalance, and we judged humans to be superior to animals. As the humans felt our thoughtforms, they began to judge their own instincts, the inner knowing they possessed which was similar to animal traits. For animals, traits such as migration are habits. For humans, they are potentially higher states of knowing: the knowing of the intuitive mind. Magical skills such as bird divination are derived from a complex instinctual understanding of cosmic cycles. Because we judged that animals were inferior to humans, humankind was afflicted with an inner judgment against instinct. But instinct is the source of unity! The ability to act upon instinct is the ability to go beyond fear and pain. So, alienation began when trust in instinct was lost. Humankind experienced its first alienation from Earth as we—pure mind—began to contact this odd species caught between the animals and the stars. The animal expresses subtle behavioral forms which are essential to third-dimensional evolution. The shattering of unity was caused by our own stellarcentric confusion as we groped to understand the third dimension. We hoped to discover how to bring to Earthlings our dimension—the ninth—the fusion of the dark with the light.

Osiris was torn to pieces by the fragmentation of his inner being when Earth first experienced dualism—separation between the stellar and Earth selves. It was his Sethian side, his dark side, that tore him to pieces like a man being torn limb from limb by a lion. But Osiris was regenerated by the Goddess Isis for choosing animal wisdom as the basis of magical training for Egypt. He learned, from his fragmentation into fourteen parts and his regeneration by Isis for the insemination of Horus, the secrets of alchemy and the philosopher's stone. The solution to this unsolved mystery is the Great Pyramid, which all people on Earth intuit. The secret is actually very simple. The blocks of stone with which the pyramid is composed are made of a composite of ancient limestone containing spiral fossil forms, ashes of all animal species on Earth, the brains of the pharaoh, salt, and other mineral and semiprecious stones. All other body organs of the pharaoh are stored in Canopic jars, which demonstrates that the karmic patterns created by incarnated humans are stored in the intestines, liver, stomach, and lungs.

Osiris was the hero of the Temple of Saqqara, where the formula of fourteen ingredients for the hardening of stone was discovered by Imhoptep. Saqqara has fourteen gates symbolizing the fragmentation of Osiris into fourteen parts. Thirteen gates are walled in, and one is open, symbolizing the essential truth that we refer to as the "animal bypass": there is only one elixir for the unity of form, the animal totem. The human access to the open fourteenth gate is sexual, is phallic.

Lately, when we wished communion with Earth, we simply sent photons from an exploding supernova in our own galaxy. This explosion offered new creative forms. It was an ecstatic shiver, sending photons into the female organs of the jaguar on Earth. Osiris was born of such a union. There is nothing mechanistic about this. Osiris was born, and he was found by the Nile because Earth people believe that gifts from the gods are found in infant form in woven baskets on river banks. He was named a god, and he began the Jaguar Priest Cult. But we did not comprehend the great power of this animal, and Osiris tried to balance the power by setting up temples, rituals, and teachings. However, the Earth energy is feminine, the jaguar is the feminine warrior, and fear between male and female was born on Earth. This power technology of Osiris was based on control, and control divides male and female.

Male warriors were entranced by the natural great power and energy of the jaguar. These men tried to control the jaguar spirit by wearing its skin and by stealing its natural form—the ecstatic expression of the self as woman. Thus began the priestly secret cabals and programs of violence on Earth based on supression of the Goddess. The bypass to the energy, the rainbow bridge of multiforms, is made by each person when he or she sees that higher and more evolved strains of beings on Earth originate from creations of star beings as animals. The Zodiac is the star map for Earth and the code entry for species level creativity.

This great teaching is the basis of the animal totem teachings on that Earth originated in Egypt. Therefore, when one reaches a certain level of evolution, one contacts one's totem animal. The Native Americans protected this teaching—that the pathway to the stellar body on Earth is through the animal teacher. When a person does this, then he or she is a whole person within the cosmos. But the need to clear up Atlantean confusion about cataclysms has caused the primal Atlantean confusion—the desire to control reality to avoid a cataclysmic end. This has resulted in dominion over the species—the belief that humans are superior to any other species or elemental creation and that the human race must husband these species to protect the planet. This is the same mistake Osiris made which caused him to fragment into fourteen parts and to lose the fourteenth part—his phallus. Isis saved him, since the Earth is feminine. New creation comes from the body of women, and new birth can never be controlled by men. The male part of people will perpetrate an insidious elimination of all species, excluding itself, during this late phase of repeated Atlantean technology. The male will even attempt to destroy Mother Earth until the New Dawn, when the female is reintegrated into the male.

A connection must be made with the jaguar totem animal so that this negative control of the feminine by male priests can finally complete itself. You will know when the animal power has returned when women cease wearing animal skins. The signs are all visible, and even the Osirian archetype is in place. Like the fragmentaton of Osiris by his brother Seth, it is a requirement for priestly status in the Roman Church to have a phallus, but not use it once the sacrament of holy orders is taken. I can manifest the jaguar at will as I did at Tikal. A yellow-and black-spotted jaguar hovers over my body, and he gives me a strange extraterrestrial scarab with a Mayan glyph that radiates purple, iridescent light.

I have had many encounters with the great cat in my own lifetime, first with the bobcats and lynxs of my childhood. Once my healing crisis began, my eczema was like the spotted skin of the jaguar. A healing crisis will occur for us all when the stellar link is established, for then all the experiences of pain and fear residing within ourselves from our own evolution will need to be cleared. We are in the midst of a planetary crisis. The destruction of all species would totally eliminate the possibility of stellar communion, which is the chance to know our Earth story from the beginning of time. Our story is the multifaceted expression of creation from the beginning of time.

We can enter stellar Dreamtime by learning the ways of animals through totemic magic. But we cannot understand animal totems without observing their habits on Earth. As people connect with their totem animals, they will protect the animals, realizing they are connections to the soul. We are soulless without our animal teachers. And the crisis is cosmic! It is no accident that the stellar expression of the great ages—the Zodiac—is in animal form.

I have a place of deep pain in the left side of my heart over the elimination of animal species. My own attunement to my totem—the jaguar—is most intense, for this cat is the guardian of the gate into the dark side, the gate I have chosen to open at this time. In the early stages of civilization—alienation from instinct—on this planet, the jaguar was known to be a teacher importing information about our maximum ability to feel animal power. Humans of weak heart feared these teachings. Initiatic training was developed to teach humans not to fear, to have the courage of the lion's heart. The oldest structure on this planet—the Sphinx—is the reminder of this story. But power-hungry priests wanted to dominate the animals. This was the origin of the various priestly black-magic cults which appeared on Earth when decisions were made to dominate the feminine Earth energy rather than to know the undivided self. The black-magic priestly cults killed an animal to rob it of its power instead of asking the animal for the gift of its life. Then they robed themselves in the animal's pelts, thus stealing more of its power instead of knowing their own power. We have tried to kill our own teachers, such as the jaguar, rather than face our own great powers. The pain in my heart comes from killing animals.

I recognize the abuse and I allow the release of the jaguar. This opens the gate to my central sadness: the killing of the jaguar energy within myself is what caused that man to rape me. I see myself as the wounded little girl. Like a murdered great cat radiating light from my heart, I surround the abuser. I recognize him for playing a role for me, teaching me a lesson. I allow myself to come full circle—to acknowledge that he brought the jaguar teaching into the world with him, for he was part of that story. The totem animal of my own rapist was the jaguar! What brought out his jaguar energy was the same energy in myself, for he did not want to respond that way to anyone. This leads me into my place of deepest sadness, a place in my heart where the painful experiences exist right next to a place of waiting for peace inside.

I find a place within myself where there is a belief that we must repeat the pain over and over again, a place in me that says I must suffer, feel awful, and grieve. There is another feeling that tells me just to jump out and open up the locus of inner suffering/fear/despair and prepare myself to encounter the jaguar. The masculine energy does not need to rape the feminine on this planet. The energy can release and peace can radiate out from the heart. There are thousands of years of imprint about this issue, but the lion will lie with the lamb when the waters of emotional pain are poured out of the jar.

I cannot forgive the man who raped me unless I forgive all the pain I have ever caused another. He is a mirror of myself and we are each other. To break the pattern of victim/victimizer, abused/abuser, I have to feel there is no difference between him and me. I go into the heart, I let the love unify, for love destroys opposites. I can see my deep purple body and, in my head, deep purple through the corpus callosum channel between my left and right brains. I can actually see the vertebrae in my own neck and I am catapulted back in time to when I was eighteen months old in this life, before I was sent away to live with another family during the War. . .

I was sitting on the warm floor of the sunporch in the house in Elmont, New York, playing with large wooden blocks. I drew within myself as I saw my nanny in the distance, knitting. My vision blurred, and I heard an imploding high-pitched ringing which felt like metal piercing my brain. It excoriated the last sight from my pupils as I spiraled in reverse to the pink land—magicland—where I had gone before. Magic was my first home.

I was caressed by folds of diaphanous white fabric as my large blue eyes popped open and I saw the blue lady staring at me, a look of love in her eyes which contained a safe place for my earthheld body. She waited until I was totally present and then began to talk in a low voice:

"Within days, you will be sent by train with Auntie to the land by the great waters. We see great pain coming to you as part of your entry into Earth and we have teachings for you.

When your heart is filled with sadness,
    remember the bear in the woods.
When you have no home,
    go to the pond and caress the turtle.
When you are hungry and no one feeds you,
    walk by the waters and make yourself larger
    with the greatness you see, for you have no limits.

When your body takes the pain of abuse,
    observe the heron taking flight!
When you cannot feel your own legs,

watch the horse running free.
When you are cold and no one holds you tightly,
    stare into the flames and remember the inner fire,
    for the Goddess is always in your heart.

When your mind rebels
    as you see cruelty inflicted upon your brother,
Look to the center of your forehead
    where we have placed the emerald
    and send that greening straight to the heart
    of all humans.
For I vibrate a power to you
    greater than any power on Earth.

When your soul is dry with confusion,
    call the lynx into your heart,
The lynx sets a field of acceptance for all who love you,
    but a fence for all who do not know my vibration.
Together you look up to my stars to see
    that I am the light that is a spiral."

That day, I disappeared at one o'clock in the afternoon to be with one of my star teachers, and I was found five hours later by the Bronx Fire Department, sliding down the edge of the Bronx Reservoir. Because I was always getting "lost," I was sent to "safety" by the great lake in Michigan, where I met my first worthy opponent.

Chapter Six

THE GREAT LAKES & THE PALEOLITHIC SPIRAL

The place where I experienced the greatest pain on Earth was also the place where I learned to heal.

It is the spring of 1946 and I am standing in tall grass listening to the wind. The grasshoppers make gnawing sounds. A snake slithers out of a cave formed by nearby root systems, and I can hear its scaly body scraping against stones and bulbous tubers which dig down into the fertile soil. A crow caws above at me, knowing I am feeling myself fly along with him. I feel all the fish swimming in the lake nearby. As for me, I am a turtle dragging my home across the gravel. I am digging my leather shoes into the dirt and glaring at the sky as I boil with frustration and anger.

This is the backyard of the house on Wildfowl Bay. He has locked Bobby in the toolshed and I hate him! The woman of the house, Gracie, is in the kitchen washing dishes and staring out the window into the backyard. She knows Bobby is locked in the toolshed because he spilled a can of paint. She is making the kitchen floor perfect by waxing it over and over again, and observing its sheen. She knows Bobby is hungry, but if she feeds him, the man will beat her up, and push her down in the bed, and . . . If I get Bobby out, the man will hit me. I hate him.

Bobby is sitting inside the toolshed crying, and he is hungry. He just peed in the corner and the piss smells. There are hornets up in the roof corners who are just beginning to awaken and buzz. A rat is gnawing on some corn husks under the shed and its sharp teeth seem to be getting closer. Bobby is six, and he is thinking about the water-paints in the back of the Sunday School basement. Last week he painted the sky above the lake in a way that made him feel how the sky felt. This day is Sunday, in the afternoon, and he has missed Sunday School, the only time he can ever paint.

I grip my corduroy dress, fighting back the tears that have not flowed for over a year, since . . . My mind begins to swirl with attempts to remember the people from long ago—the gigantic black nanny and the mother with soft hands who cradled my head, cradled my head—before my concussion. My mind also holds visionary scenes of shining people, ladies in white flowing robes, and crystal balls. The visions mix with forms of Gracie in the kitchen, old cats in the barn, and a quick memory flash of being bashed against a wall when my head got hurt. A blinding white light calls a distant memory to me as I begin to feel a warm pulsation in the center of my third eye. My sight goes within as my body begins to warm up, and all my limbs begin to feel like tree limbs. I feel a great rod of white light suck down into my rigid body, go through me, and thunder into the Earth. A vibration in my spine pounds with my heartbeat as I feel a hot rush of energy thrust through me, an Earthforce which I felt the first time when I was born.

The light blasts through my heart, almost causing it to cease beating. Once through my heart, the force opens the choking wet heat in my throat caused by my frustration over not being able to protest against the tyrant. The energy blasts freely into my head once it is past my throat constriction. I can see Bobby inside the shed, like a cartoon at the movies! He looks so small and sad. My forehead is tingling and vibrating with an exquisite feeling, as if ice cream is melting there. A green ray, surrounded by magnetic topaz-blue, spirals like a snake through the air from my forehead to Bobby in the shed. The inside of the shed around him is vibrating. I shake with ecstasy, my whole body a rod of white light from Earth to sky. The field fills with hundreds of butterflies, all shimmering in beautiful golden light around the waving flowers.

Inside the shed, there is a warm glow and Bobby shifts. He falls into a trance, the way he feels when he watches the watercolors make forms on the paper. His mind expands out beyond the confines of the shed. He flies out over the field of flowers, over Wildfowl Bay, and off to the horizon of the rising sun. He is imprinted with an incredible truth—that no authority can ever imprison his mind. Later in his life, when he is a prisoner in Vietnam, interrogators try to break his spirit by confining him. He is unbreakable, because he simply travels out of the confinement with his mind.

Remembering that first time in this life when I healed another suffering child was metamorphic for me. My own child within now remembered its delight, its own fantastic creativity. My inner child ecstatically danced as the memory of the green light carried me into an exquisitely faceted peridot. I swirled counter-clockwise through green stone, and found myself encradled in the large hands of a huge, wonderful brown man.

I am a week old and I am delirious with fever as I hang between life and death. The year is 1887. I am on Honolulu Island being held in the arms of the Kahuna.

I come into density and blackness. Eons have passed since I have returned in a female body with my stellar self existing with me as I incarnate. As I arrive, I feel that I am chosen to be a channel for female energy from the stars. Possibly the star body always remains intact in each infant for a little while, and I just happen to be noticing my stellar self at this particular birth. The room feels so dense, thick, and warm. I begin to drift away, but I want to watch the lovely colors of yellow and green, topaz and amethyst, pushing at a shimmering envelope of diamond light around the brown man who holds me. So I fight to breathe.

Brown women with kind faces hold warm compresses soaked in fire herbs on my tiny chest as they rub my limbs with oils. My tiny lungs struggle to open and my heart fights to beat in rhythm with the drums in the room. I open my eyes for a moment, fascinated by the shooting rays of green and purple light around the Kahuna's ancient face as his heart beats with mine. I hear his message, for he tells me that I must come in this way—my soul has chosen the way of the mother. I must find the mother within myself as a girl-child, or I will turn to warrior ways as a male and perish eternally. He sees my soul from the beginning of creation and sees the test ahead of me. I must learn to be a mother, to give myself completely away.

My gift to him is that I agree. His gift to me, as he smiles at me with great radiance, is that he encodes my cells with the Kahuna green-healing teaching. He fills me with green light so that I can send the rays to my brother in the next life when I am a white person. He names me Leonore after Father Leonore, the Catholic missionary whom the native people love. In Hawaiian, Leonore means "the light," and the people first named this priest "the light."

Just before it is time to return me to my waiting family, the loving brown man takes me out of my crib, wraps my tiny body in treasured otter skin from the land faraway, and takes me to the cave of origin to sit with me for hours. Periodically he grunts and shakes his head as he probes more deeply into who I am. He wears a necklace of lion's teeth on his neck, for he protects the heart. He has healed me simply because he was asked to do so by Father Leonore. He heals anyone if asked. But his reward is that, once he heals someone, he can see their place of origin from far beyond this galaxy. His soul travels to the wandering planet which has caused pain on Earth since creatures were made from the lava of the Goddess. He wonders if the time of true freedom is coming closer. Has the Goddess finally come to deliver the Earth? He looks into my eyes, sending joy deep into my being as I fly back 50,000 years in time.

I stand on sand with tufts of grass, and there is a rock ledge above my head. I have a tall, sturdy body with great feet. I wear an otterskin medicine-woman dress with strings of turquoise around my neck. My skin is red, and I have black hair on my legs. I wear a bone bracelet on my right arm, and no jewelry on my fingers, which end in long nails. My hands are slender but very muscular, very strong and expressive. My nose is broad, and my cheeks are high and concave, slightly sunken from many lost teeth. My eyes and ears are keen. I am a medicine woman and I have come to travel to the home of the ancestors.

I am inside a shallow ceremonial cave and I face the back of the cave wall with the sky behind me. To each side, I see a painted warrior shaman. The figures each have a knee against the cave wall but are turned so that they are staring to the outside. I am looking in, and the shamans are staring out. Each of them is beating a drum, is dressed in many feathers, and is wearing paint which is bright red, yellow, and green—the mask for traveling to the spirit world.

I stare at the grey rock which is covered with drawings that have been picked into the rock by the ancient people of our tribes. Focusing on a pictograph of the Sun, a circle with snaking rays coming out from the edges, I become like the Sun and can travel to places in this solar system. I was trained for many years to be able to travel for my clan. The warriors with me are my guardians in the spirit world, and are standing here to hold my ground while I travel. These two will soon disappear from my perception, but they must physically remain to hold my space. If either of them did not remain and some other shaman came into my cave, I would never be able to return to Earth.

Around the Sun in the pictograph are the animals of the stars. Animals are my very soul. If I concentrate on one of the animals, I can shapeshift and become that animal. I can become the animal energy. However, I am attuning myself to the Sun today. The animal-medicine circle in the sky is cosmic, it is all that exists, and it is an entry point to any dimension or state of being. I focus on the central Sun of our universe. As I meditate, golden light begins to shine and then becomes stronger and stronger. The cave fills with golden rays, and then the light spreads out of the cave and over the land, and begins to pulsate. I become a rushing wind force and I leave.

I am traveling, flying through a dimension beyond the cycles of time. As soon as I left the cave, I lost all sense of place. I am shooting out to create a link to the people of the other side, the timeless, nonphysical people. I am a light with pale blue around me, and I feel as though I am moving along slowly. The experience feels like I am moving through a dimension, approaching a cave in another place. The place I am nearing has a blue metallic housing which is lit up. I am approaching an oval door which is about fifteen feet high and open. The sides of the walls, which are flexed concave to the door, are encased in metal and are very shiny. There are many lights, like hundreds of small suns.

As soon as I fly in, the door is quickly shut. The weight of the air feels incredible. I am heavy, as if my arms weigh thousands of pounds. I shoot into the interior. The side of the mountain or planet is all that can be seen on the surface, once the door closes. My range of vision is difficult to comprehend because this world is completely technological. It is so unlike my own world, and my body is so heavy here. The three or four people awaiting me seem to expect me. They are bigger than I — eight feet tall — and they are shining. I wonder if these strange people are the gods of the north light? I begin to feel very excited. Their forms seem to be less physical than mine, or else I have gained density by coming here. I realize I am expected to go sit in a chair as the inner doors to this circular chamber shut.

The group of beings stands with expanding light auras that move out from their bodies. I can feel these auras like the tingle after lightning on Earth. Perhaps I am in the presence of the lightning gods? I cannot make out their features very well. I know they called me here for some reason, and I do not think I have ever been here before. I expected something else to happen when I entered the dimension of the pictograph. I thought I was just going to travel to the land of the masked gods — kachinas — but perhaps this is the home of the kachinas! The two shamans remaining in the cave have created this and so I open to the experience. This is my next initiation, but I could never have imagined this scene, and it is hard to believe I will ever see Earth again. I must let go completely.

The beings do not talk, they just send me thoughts in waves. As they radiate energy to me, I feel a macrocellular shift into less density. As I shift, I feel a new pulsing vibration, and my heart warms. I begin to relax and marvel at their magnificent golden wings. These are the thunderbird people! They begin:

"We connected with your passage to other dimensions through the solar force, because that is how we maintain our conscious contact with Earth. If we lose our conscious contact with Earth, we lose our sharing in the story of Earth. We are the abode of the gods, the Solar Logos, the teachers of Earth, the brotherhood and sisterhood of creation. Your legends of the ancient days are the story of our eternal return to Earth. We are the protectors of seeds, animals, the genetic strains of all life in the solar system, including the genetic strains of humans. We store new seeds grown on your planet, and we do this to guard your planet. Because of us, you have many animals and different kinds of plants on your planet. Because of our care and genetic breeding, you are able to evolve. We are your teachers about alchemy — changing form."

The beings have some kind of control over me which I do not like.

They understand my thoughts. Surely they are reading my mind and there is nothing I can do about it. I still wonder what this means to me, and I wonder if this is what the major secret initiations actually are? I am not afraid of them, for I have passed through the initiation of the great cat. But I did not realize that there were gods who were actually involved in what happens on Earth. They beam awareness into my mind concerning the appropriateness of their involvement with Earth and suggesting that we are better off because of them. Like knowing the outcome of a hunt, these beings can anticipate any desire or fear I might have about them, and even figure out whether it is good for me! This is 50,000 BC, and their teaching comes through time, flowing through me as the shaman warriors hold my Earth place for me.

"Our project in the solar system is to develop plant and animal species. Earth is the greenhouse, and our planet is cold with little water. We are highly developed in the mineral kingdom and in the mental dimension. We are the source of morphogenetic fields in the solar system. Living things exist here in underground laboratories in storage. Our seeds grow into plants and trees on Earth, and we get seeds back from Earth whenever we return. Earth's atmosphere is superior to ours. One year here is equal to 3600 years on Earth. The orbital cyclical influence is the key to dimensionality, since beings in this solar system age according to the time cycles of their own location. If we come to Earth, we age at your rate, so we rarely stay long. When we come home, we age normally, but when one of us returns to Earth, you are shocked to see that a teacher such as Thoth, Enoch, Isis, or Khnum, is still young. The ancient Earth legends about people living a thousand years come from our people visiting Earth, and the stories about Earth people going to sleep and waking up still young after hundreds of years have passed, are true accounts of Earthlings who came and spent time here. We have access to your world through time warps such as Avalon. You, Isha, will be the beginning of a great legend when you return to Earth.

"All evolution is dimensionality in relation to time, and your dimensional perceptual skills will mutate exponentially if you can absorb our teaching for you. Mastery of the cosmos is attained by any creature that can travel through space and time at will, recognizing its participation in creation in an eternal existence with no beginning or end. This is your initiation as an astrologer, and you will give it all back to Earth.

"Planetary cycles are locations of dimensionality. Twelve years on Jupiter is equal to one Earth year, and Jupiter is the solar teacher of mastery of spiritual skills. That is why there are twelve sections of the Zodiac in sympathetic attunement to the twelve Great Ages. If you attune to that, you can live one Earth year each month in your mind and multiply your mastery skills twelvefold. Or, if you observe the New Moon Lodge faithfully for one year, you attain our cycle of 3600 years by attuning to the addition of zero to a period of 28 days times 13 months, which is how the shamans got you here. The Buddha obtained enlightenment in one year by transferring his consciousness to Uranus for one year and experiencing an 84-year-long kundalini breakthrough.

"We are the Akashic Records of Earth because ours is the longest cycle in the solar system. The Akashic Records are the records of emotional growth of the soul over many lifetimes, and the key into them is the Moon, which rules the emotions. Emotional growth takes a long time, until finally free will becomes possible. You will be a teacher of the evolved will, and we called you here today to encode your brain with the teachings of the emotional record bank.

"Since 3600 years on Earth is equal to one year here, our physical needs are miniscule in comparison to yours. This fact is the key to future transmutation of the entrapment of physical desires on Earth. A time will come on Earth when you will be faced with consuming yourselves. Then you will learn that wants and needs are all functions of consciousness, and you will discover that you can manifest wants and needs mentally instead of emotionally. We are the givers of the Tree of Life, which represents the teaching that all which is needed is already present. We only require one great Tree to sustain ourselves. You will have a Tree in Jerusalem, which will be killed by the beliefs of the Mosaic Covenant—that men have dominion over plants, animals, and women. The Tule tree of Oaxaca, and the sycamore tree next to the Sphinx, will survive to see the transmutation of emotional obsession.

"Our genetic and chemical technology is very advanced. But we have made mistakes because the universe is a place of experimentation and free will. Choice exists to offer the hope to all beings to choose the Creator. Your memory of us is negative because of our dimensional difference. For example, we decided to see if we could improve the genetic strain of humans by breeding ourselves with animals, and then breeding ourselves on Earth. The idea was that a woman could have the courage of the jaguar or a man could attain the frequency range of the dolphin. We were wrong! We were impressed by the magnificent formation powers of the third dimension, since we are fourth dimensional and not in material form. We tried to meld second-dimensional qualities—animal existential expression—into humanity. We learned that all dimensions are equal but different. We now understand that diversity is the key to survival, which you have not yet realized. Noah will bring the Ark, which is a boat of the heavens, a creation like our planet, and he will deliver the teaching of a mated pair of each species to Earth. Noah's teaching will be understood at the New Dawn.

"As for your painful memories of us, the composite animal/human experiments were an afternoon in the laboratory to us. But for you, because one of our afternoons is equivalent to three of your years, one week of our time is a lifetime for you. You suffered terrible pain from our experiments. All of that memory lies within your phylogenetic coding. As in any relationship over time, you will not believe that we have learned from our mistakes just as you have. It is like a bad marriage loaded with uncleared blame. Your problem is, we are gods to you. When you find God—your fourth-dimensional self—in yourself, when you are able to recognize your own mistakes, you will not need to blame anyone else. Our lack is, we do not feel your pain enough yet. We are slated to learn compassion, to learn to feel.

"You must also recognize that very little would have happened on Earth if we had not loved the greenhouse and needed it ourselves. Our vibration is the way to understand mineral forces, and to not fear the cycles of the mineral kingdom—volcanoes, earthquakes, and mass movements of continents. You feel heavy here because you can actually feel geologic time. For us, your long geologic cycles are like our afternoon weather report. We are also the teachers who gave you the Philosopher's Stone, and when you remember our history with Earth, you will remember how to find the Philosopher's Stone again.

"On more etheric levels, we are masters of emotions because we live such a long, long life. Our needs are actually similar, for we have the same center, the Sun. Only because we have so much more time do we already know that our relationship to Earth is very mature now. Once upon a time, we would have used you—medicine woman sent to us by the shapeshifters—for experimentation. But now we only want to teach you. Separation is coming as you move out of your childhood, and like any parent, we do not want to let you go."

As I sit here in the chair, I realize that I have already encountered them. Earthlings have always worshipped these beings when they appeared on Earth. I am in the presence of the gods and the gods are vastly superior to us, exhibiting complete self-control. It frightens me. I like first to feel and then to react. I do not think these beings feel and then react. Our planet is their big concern, but I suppose this is because of their own needs. They are much like us, but evolved vastly beyond humankind. Yet, since their planet comes around the Sun so seldom, I wonder if the gods know as much as we do about our cycle in relationship to the galaxy?

Earth is in relationship to the Pleiades by means of a 5125-year evolutionary cycle. This cycle is transmuting Earth into a planet of love so that we can attune to the Galactic Center. We have great Earth temples at sacred sites which attune us to Andromeda and the Pleiades. When I received my first initiation, I was told that our Earth temples are unique—that only on Earth do we resonate to the stars and the planets, to the distant spiral galaxy beyond our way of the stars. As these beings thoroughly know technology, the possibility exists that I have superior knowledge about cosmic cycles. Perhaps Earth is the only place in the cosmos that has temples which connect Earth and sky.

Bizarre as it seems, I become aware that I understand their thoughts and that these beings understand mine. If I thought about the needs of Earth while I meditated, would they hear my thoughts? How do they tune into what is happening on Earth? Is there transfer via thought? Or are these advanced beings attuned to the information we are conscious about because they are actually joined with our thoughts, i.e., are they another aspect of who we are?

I struggle to understand these beings better during this opportunity to exist in their space. I must understand as much about them as I can. Like a deep awakening in the ancient mind, I find I can telepathize. The beings are infusing my mind with levels of wisdom which are like a new creation in larval form that will require eons to metamorphosize. I suddenly see that they have accelerated me into the future, to another life as Barbara, and then have guided me right back to being a medicine woman 50,000 years ago. My awareness is exquisitely timeless and exists in all minds.

Their time frame is enormous, and I sense that I am being encoded with the skill for traveling over huge spans of time. This is a wisdom initiation into the Records! I am awestruck. I feel myself shifting, and I could easily pass out as I see a vision of the cosmos as cycles of time, like whirling gears of spinning galaxies of precious gems. As I spiral in and out of space and time, they modulate their energy with mine so that a new level of fusion is possible. I have felt, for just a moment, what it is like to feel as they do. They need the seeds of Earth as we need their experience at the outer edges of the solar system in bridging our Sun to its brother and sister stars. I appreciate my shamans grounding me on

Earth while I am here discovering new realities of time, even if I do not have immortality as these beings do. In a way, I wish I had their life span and their knowledge. But the acuteness of my physical and emotional senses is as multifaceted as their consciousness beyond the third dimension.

Somehow, by being able to intensify awareness, I begin to recover a personal memory of an experience I had with these beings when they once came to Earth. I shiver with a great intensity, as my adrenal system shoots energy into my body. I hold my power as a buried memory moves slowly into consciousness, a memory of mating with one of these gods and giving birth to a demi-god. Pride then floods my being. I was a maiden then and now I am great medicine-woman crone. I fill with ecstasy, holding my energy as I see that the beings have brought me home. I raise my eyes to the one I once knew, who looks deeply into me. A new dimension of loving men is given to me by his eyes. I remember being chosen to be the divine mother, Isis/Eve, as all women on planet Earth have once been.

A doorway opens in the back of the room where I am sitting. It is a hallway into a laboratory. I walk into the laboratory filled with rows of boxes on three-by-nine-foot tables. The boxes are like coffins with see-through lids, like oxygen decompression tanks, and there is a body inside each one. I am afraid their scientists plan to put me in one of those things! I walk down the rows and look at men and women from all the different historical cycles of Earth. Since the beings shifted me so that I could comprehend past, present, and future before I came in here, I can see individuals from the dawning of history into the future. They are from different times, different countries, and different races. I see a pharoah next to a potter, a warrior next to a queen.

When someone dies on Earth, these beings can teleport the person's body here. Whether or not this happens depends on the quality of a person's physical body at death, resulting from life experiences. The Egyptians knew all about the status of the physical body at death from being instructed by these gods. The Egyptians knew how to purify and neutralize body qualities resulting from experiences during life. The status of the physical body during passage from life to death influences the abilities of the soul and emotional body to travel to other realms between Earth incarnations—the ability to visit the schools on other planets and stars. The Egyptians purified the organs during mummification and then stored the organs in Canopic jars because the emotional lessons being learned on Earth are evolving through time. The growth of each consciousness in the universe is not static. This laboratory is an interface zone between the linear comprehension of spherical time and the third dimension—a tool to be used for tuning into any place or time period. It is like the ceremonial cave—a device for traveling.

Each person in this laboratory is a harmonic channel for a particular historical lesson, for a specific civilization's belief system which made an impression on great numbers of people and systems. We can tune into a particular lesson by using these frequency harmonics. We do the same thing on Earth when we are fascinated with a particular historical period or individual. This is why people think they were a famous person in a past life when actually they are tapping into the lesson encapsulated by this historical person. This lesson is held in energy form by us in spherical time. Such issues can be reexplored over and over again by time-traveling into "past lives" until the lesson is mastered. There are certain truths to be learned by all souls in the midst of the time-developmental universe. Time will cease, as we understand time, once the lessons are learned. Time is simply a device which is useful for consciousness in the third dimension.

From a human point of view, these individuals are not dead. We walk over to a case containing a woman: "Look at her," the beings communicate mentally. She comes alive! They communicate to me by their thoughts that this is happening to her in her time zone and place—that she is becoming consciously aware of them right now! They teleport thoughts to her the way they are sending thought to me. They seem to be very interested in communicating.

I absorb the knowledge—we are eternally in tune with all places and times.

I look down at the woman and she is not separate from me. I am flowing within myself and I feel that my cells are the same as hers. The beings are assisting in my ability to do this. It is very natural to them, as if they are the one and I am the many, but we are both of the same essence.

"We are not 'body snatchers.' The bodies you are looking at do not actually exist in a third-dimensional sense, but are fourth-dimensional holographic forms of third-dimensional emotional consciousnesses. These bodies are evolving with us as our planet moves out of the solar system. We travel all the way out to Sirius—Record Bank of the central souls. Let us use as an example the late twentieth-century, just before Earth and our planet attained equality. Much of the evolution at that time was occurring within electronic media, and also much of the retrogressive behavior. Stop for a moment and observe the big container with rows of small boxes with screens, each containing the face of a celebrity—an individual to whom many people transferred their desires for more experience. This was an odd phase in the late twentieth-century, previous to humans becoming less astral and more mental. These are the 'TV personages.' Earth people were so hooked on them, that the only way we could keep in touch with Earth people was to access these TV forms who acted as collectives of individual egos. It was a curious time. Many were obsessed with being famous—holding personage energy.

"This point was the dark before the dawn, because individuals were experimenting with what consciousness actually is. You can, on Earth, invest your consciousness in the life of another, but who would want to? Another bizarre phenomenon in the late twentieth century was the process of channeling entities instead of just developing superconsciousness. We do amuse ourselves occasionally, and so we created a hall of entities that could be channeled. We filled it with entities that you would call 'blabbermouths' so the entities could talk until they finally got tired of it. They loved the rapt and mindless audiences. The reason that people were trying to lose their identity in another being was that they were bored and exhausted by their individuality and their egos just before they accessed their cosmic selves. They got to the point when they thought ego was suffering. In fact, the consciousness form called the ego is simply a station for access to other realities. Meanwhile, others were getting closer to contact with us. One person, Michael Jackson, even built a container like our laboratory containers, and slept in it at night, so deeply did he long for a journey to Sirius.

"When out near Sirius, Nibiru is more like a star than a planet, because then its orbit is more determined by galactic orbits than by the Sun. It differs from other planets in that sense. It is less dense, less caught in linear time, and it thus bridges solar forms and star forms. Solar forms are circular and star forms are spiralic, and these laboratory forms are the bridges. Here is the big secret: You can't have knowledge in a multidimensional way unless it can be felt, and that is why there has been so much suffering throughout time. This will continue until feelings evolve. The silver cord into the solar plexus connects the traveling astral body to the physical body, and the solar plexus must be cleared of pain in order to free the astral body.

"If the lessons from Sirius are going to be available for Earth, you must become conscious about your evolution by learning to clear the emotional body and by training your brain for multidimensional access.

Such evolutionary skills are a science which exists in the memory bank of each individual. We hold all these holograms for Earth learning, but such holding of energy may be making it harder for you to do it yourselves. Let go of the belief that we will do it for you, because universal knowledge is within you, waiting to be tapped.

"There is a faster way! If you can learn to attune to star forms, especially to Sirius, then the laboratory forms can go. We can dump the records. When you are ready to let go of your identities, we can let go of this archaic method of keeping in touch. When you remember us, you will be released from your subliminal need—your tiresome obsession with fame—resulting from having lost touch with the divine. Our reality is much more fascinating."

The forms keep changing, but this laboratory is for holding emotional energy until we learn to be as conscious of these beings as they are of us. This is our primal consciousness, our ability to remember our origins in the stars, our story. We are not just egos. Each person has subliminal memory of another side—the planet that links us to the stars—but our egos want to block the stellar connections which cause the ego to dissolve. So we are drying up, and we have forgotten that we have a physical-plane, multidimensional, cosmic participation.

Earthlings and Nibiruans each have skills and qualities which the other does not have. Nibiruans are masters at manipulating time and distance because they travel so far for so long, and yet we Earthlings are the masters of bringing those energies into form in time and place on Earth. When we do that, the Nibiruans are linked to us, which grounds them into the greenhouse. We then experience a greater frequency range, which frees us from the oppressive narrowness of incarnation. When Earthlings do ceremony at certain times at certain sacred sites, the vertical axis is made, and we are in ecstatic communion. But a dark time will come before the light. They tell me a story of the Dark Ages...

"When you leave your childhood after the Flood and take your first steps, you will desire to be like the gods. You will fight amongst yourselves for thousands of years to obtain power. When you enter your adolescence and have complete freedom, when you are ready to be sons and daughters of God yourselves, you will reach a point when Earth has attained technological expertise on the level of Nibiru. Earth will have grown up and will reach a level in its space program of technology that is similar to Nibiruan technology.

"You will come to a critical crossing time when you will either revert to atavism—to old and non-evolutionary patterns—or you will grasp the free-will teaching of Christos. This point in your development is a test that we ourselves failed, and we resorted to war in space. Your ancient memory holds records of that conflict, which was a war between the shattered planet that existed between Mars and Jupiter, now the asteroid belt, and Orion. This memory will tempt you to use your knowledge of space technology as a weapon instead of as a bridge. This will be a very confusing time, because the free-will process on Earth allows many beings from other star systems to be born on Earth after the darkest point—Dec. 2, 1942. These beings will be called 'walk-ins.' They will participate in the free-will experiment because they failed the experiment before. Some extraterrestrials will come at this time to try to encourage Earth to choose Christos instead of separation. People on Earth will not know whether their friends or enemies are from Earth, Orion, the Pleiades, or the Andromeda Galaxy. Each individual will be personally called to overcome his or her own sense of separation. You will be able to see that this is happening when people eliminate addictions—behavior patterns which isolate the self.

"You will not destroy Earth, and people will not be able to travel in space until they advance their consciousness of time and space. Scientists who wish to experiment in these areas will be blocked unless their consciousness is as advanced as yours—as a medicine woman 50,000 years prior to this time. And, nobody gets to your level until they have cleared their own negativity, for they would die in the dimensional initiation. Millions of humans will die in the late twentieth century because they will refuse to advance their consciousness. This retrogressive point of view will be egocidal, because the ego will become dysfunctional, like a turtle shell which does not grow with the turtle and insanely crushes the animal. The space program will advance no further than dimensional consciousness because dimensional shifts are a requirement for ascension. The ancient Egyptians knew how to accelerate their bodies to leave Earth, and the teaching exists in the Book of the Dead. We are freed from some of the constraints of linear time; we see better than you do. You will be blocked from certain actions that could harm the cosmos because we will meet again in 3600 AD. Meanwhile, the cosmic joke is that there will be no apocalypse, no cataclysm, and no End Times. Instead, each individual will have to clear his or her emotional body and create an environment which reflects the ecstasy of the divine human in a medicine wheel of animals.

"We are remembered by you as a destructive force because we are the wild card of the solar system—the electron. Our orbit is highly elliptical, and we manifest chaos and change. You cannot have order and stability without chaos and change, for matter is always evolving into new forms as the old forms die. On the physical level, this will never change. Old stars will become supernovas and new stars will be born. But there is no death, only matter changing form, and consciousnesses accessing more dimension. We always return to bring a new teaching from the stars.

"Until you remember that you return again and again to Earth, you will continue to search for a beginning and an end. You have experienced our return as a crossing, a periodic cataclysm in the solar system. But, the electron does not destabilize the molecule; the molecule is a unit of balance. When you go into balance and understand the eternal return, then you will see that Christos brought in the new order—a balanced solar system—with our last return at the Incarnation. Let me tell you about the End Times.

"Since the coming of Christos, the time has come to choose life over death. The death wish comes from the paralyzing fear of the black place—Orion. In the wars with Orion, pain and separation were first experienced, and after that point many souls chose to cease to be. But all changed with Christos. A being of such love and compassion came to Earth that now all souls have access to the desire to be alive, to be alive just to experience the love of Christos. The atmosphere of Mars was destroyed in the Orion wars, and Earth will begin to remember the battle when the Face on Mars is seen. The reality of the Face will sink in during a joint exploration between two countries which have used up the resources of their own people by naming each other as enemies.

"The ancient memory will suddenly become much more important than any enemy on Earth, for the revelation of the Face on Mars will cause Earthlings to see that the wrong enemy has been identified. In the Orion Wars—the time of terror—Earth was knocked out of orbit by Nibiru. The planet between Mars and Jupiter was exploded, disturbing the orbit of Earth. Earth's orbit around the Sun had been 360 days, in perfect synchronicity with Nibiru. In those days, the degrees in the circle, the days in the year, and the function of time were all in perfect synchronicity in the solar system.

"The twentieth-century is the critical test, for our memory banks are filled with craters of emotional pain just like the surface of the Moon, the body in the solar system which teaches Earth about the emotions. The Moon teaches Earth about waxing and waning, the process which teaches humans to trust the cosmos. The Moon also has a dark side which is not seen from Earth, but which can be seen by the cosmos. The return of Nibiru will teach Earth not to fear the dark side, for we have come full circle at last. Earth is ready to acknowledge its dark side and see that Nibiru is no longer the source of fear. That which is deep within and unseen—the memory bank—causes confusion. People on Earth are ready to see that the useless going back and forth—raping and murdering the other, being raped and murdered themselves—will not assuage their fears. Let go of these denying behavioral patterns, for even the most intense violence will not hide the truth from you.

"We exist with no beginning or end, and we will never know the answer to how form can have existence when it has more space within itself than actual matter. Only our hearts can handle being free of definition. I call you to emerge out of your mummy, for saying goodbye well is harder than becoming acquainted. Now that you might find yourself able to remember the other side, the hardest is yet to come: next you will name yourself."

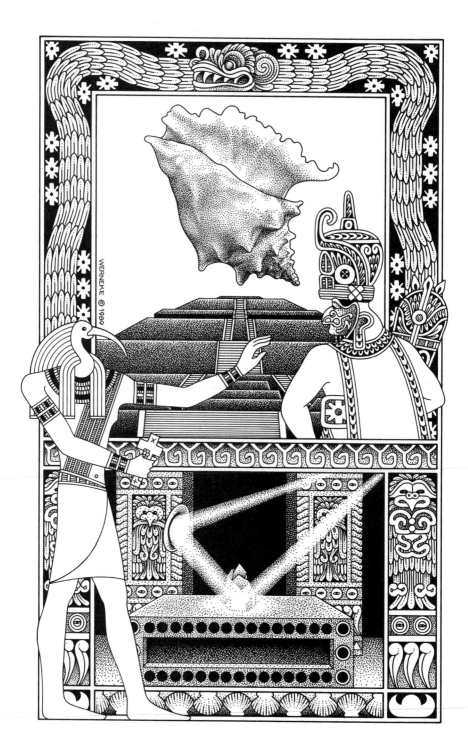

Chapter Seven

TEOTIHUACAN &
THE TIGER INITIATION

I will name myself. The only way I know how to do that is to name myself at my temple in this lifetime—Teotihuacan, "where the tree god comes to Earth." Like the rebirth of the Sun caused by the flux of spiralic currents ceaselessly precipitating and coagulating cosmic substance, I call myself my own lightbody, Itzanna, "the god who enters into density, into the Mother Earth."

I named myself on Harmonic Convergence when I meditated for many hours with my Atlantean record crystal in the Temple of the Quetzal Butterfly—"the phoenix metamorphoses." After hours in the blazing sun, Itzanna came into soul fusion and I asked to be able to resonate with the records of Teotihuacan. By asking, I knew that I would have to be personally prepared to look at any of my own experiences which were blocking my access to this knowledge. I knew I was preparing to rebirth the crystalline star woman who came here billions of years ago when Earth took form. The Goddess delighted in our creation here, and we were all present in the beginning. Element to element, blood crystal to blood crystal, I opened inner space so that I could become a home for our story. As I felt the transmutative shifts within myself, I first experienced bilocation—the ability to be in two places simultaneously. I am used to this experience now, but the feelings in my body while being in two places at once were amazing when it was first happening. I was sitting in the temple at Teotihuacan in 1987, and was simultaneously manifesting an extraterrestrial facet of my own self in the same location.

I have a heavy, barrel-chested body, and my skin is smooth and brown. I wear silver shoes with pointed curled toes, a silver headpiece with antennae, and have a little rim of hair underneath the edges of the headpiece. My lips are thick and wide, my nose is flat with a curved bridge, and my slanted eyes are wide apart. My forehead was pressed when I was an infant to connect my third eye to my pineal gland, for I am galactic Mayan. I wear a yoke collar that begins on my neck and falls around my front, over my shoulders, and connects in the back where a long cloak is attached beneath the yoke collar. I am bare-chested, and I wear a metal waist belt that is held to the collar by means of two-inch-wide crossed straps. A fabric skirt is attached to the belt which goes to my knees. My fitted space boots cover my calves and are made of a silver, woven, metallic fabric.

My silver gloves are related to how I arrived here in this dimension, but I cannot imagine how. A strip of metallic fabric wraps around my wrist, then connects to a strap that wraps around my middle finger over the back of my hand. Ah, yes, I see . . . I just shapeshifted into this dimension during a Mayan ballcourt game. The contestants play the game to break through the dimensions so galactic Mayans can enter the third dimension. When I press my thumb to my palm, I notice that I have only three fingers, and these digits are webbed and short like on amphibian hands.

Now I am standing on a cut, red sandstone platform in the middle of a plaza of red sandstone, and I am a distance away from the ballcourt. The platform is on the eastern side of a large temple complex which is about 400 feet square. The flat surface I stand on is about fourteen feet wide, and drops off to the frontside about thirteen steps. Down the back, to the east, stairs drop off very steeply; there are about 50 steps down to the ancient Pyramid of the Serpent. I am alone, and I look west to the pyramids of the Sun and Moon. This is Teotihuacan, and I am gazing from the eastern side of the Citadel just above the Pyramid of Quetzalcoatl. The view is exquisite and I come here often.

I shifted into this place and experience, which gives me a very strange feeling. The temple complex is now deserted, as if the entire sanctuary has been abandoned or deactivated. All resonations are shut down and I wonder why. This is a hotspot. When this temple site is active, Teotihuacan is a tremendous resonator to all dimensions. When activated, Teotihuacan resonates directly to the Pleiades, to Arcturus, and to the Andromeda Galaxy. The Mayan daykeepers deactivated this site in 212 AD to shut down active energy connections to certain stellar planes. I come to this site from other dimensions frequently, as a fourth-dimensional lightbody of the daykeepers, who serve the cycles of time. I also was an active worker here during a series of incarnations. When individuals in incarnational form learn to bilocate, as Barbara has done while meditating in the Temple of the Quetzal Butterfly, the contact with lightbodies occurs. We are here all the time at sacred sites, but people in Earthform forget about us. When we deactivated the site, I was here as an

Earth temple artisan. Now I gaze down into the conch shells at the base of the Pyramid of the Emerging Double Serpent which I carved with my obsidian knife, and I see a part of myself in the center, crying for a vision. I will tell you my story of Teotihuacan now, as I awaken from thousands of years of sleep.

There are only two places of this power magnitude on the planet: Giza and Teotihuacan. Giza is active all the time because the pyramids calibrate the teachings of Sirius for Earth from the cycles of the planet Nibiru. Teotihuacan is a cosmic resonator which was deactivated in 212 AD as a safety measure. The temple was used by the galactic Mayans to open the dimensional light channel for the Incarnation of Christos, who was known as Quetzalcoatl/Kukulcan in Mesoamerica. Christos/Messiah came as a teacher from the Pleiades. He was born Mayan—one who exists in many dimensions simultaneously and who is outside of geographical and political boundaries. He was sent to resolve conflicts on Earth. It was the first time such an event had ever occurred on Earth. There had been many visitors from Sirius and Orion but never from the Pleiades—the star system of the heart. The Pleiadean waveform transmuted the deep memory banks of Earthlings—hope was implanted for polarity to be unified into love. And, when Christos/Kukulcan—the Solar Logos—came to Earth, the Mayans received a stellar waveform from Andromeda Galaxy through the Pleiades to Earth. That is why the Earth/sky temple at Teotihuacan is called the Temple of the Metamorphosis of Quetzalcoatl—the Plumed Serpent. This temple is the Mesoamerican site of absolute transmutation, a magical point where the skybird and the snake lie peacefully together in the Sun.

But at the dimensional fusion point—the Earth—intense polarity conflicts, originating in the group mind from past cataclysms in the solar system and Orion, were activated by this incredible power-wave. In Jerusalem, the geomantic zone that Christos was born into, spiritual identity was sharply polarized into two archetypes: the Hebrew "chosen people," and the Egyptian "enemy." Later, the Romans took advantage of the polarization and conquered both sides. This caused the new Christos teaching to be distorted for 2000 years. From a galactic perspective, we knew about such judgmental identities. But Nibiru came into the solar system as the Star of Bethlehem—Nibiru rising—a great light in the sky representing the gift of peace from the three eastern astrologers, the Sirian star magi. This was an exquisite epiphany of the end of the domination of the gods.

We thought Earth would end all war and worship the Prince of Peace—who was a new earthly human with an integrated stellar self. We thought

Earth would go to the next stage of evolution: freedom for Earthlings from interference of "the gods" and a decision to choose their own reality. But Earthlings had gotten addicted to taking orders, and were always looking for a leader! Rome took full advantage of the hiatus by putting a solid gold statue of the god/emperor, Gaius Caligula, in the Hebrew Temple in 41 AD, just before Nibiru left the orbital plane of Earth in 44 AD. When Nibiru entered the orbital plane of Earth in 7 BC, Augustus Caesar declared himself Son of God—Divi Filius. As soon as the Hebrew Temple was destroyed in 70 AD, the Romans began removing the Egyptian Earth/sky power connectors—the obelisks—to Rome! The pharaonic line of Egypt had been the abode of the gods during the 3600 BC phase of bringing magical teachings to Earthlings. But the temple holding the last vestiges of the power of the gods, Karnak, was devastated by a great earthquake in 26 BC, and Rome was to be the next abode of the gods. The Roman Empire declared their leaders the "Imperium," or the very gods themselves. The Church claimed Jesus of Nazareth, also calling him Divi Filius, even though Jesus consistently declared that his empire was not of this Earth. Then Rome—Church and State— conspired to control the hearts and minds of the people. All that was needed in the populace was a full belly and plenty of pomp and ceremony. Throughout time, the Egyptian obelisks hold the power of the imperium of the sky gods for the popes and the city of Rome! To protect the new seed, Quetzalcoatl, the Mayans deactivated the time-dimensional tunnel of Teoti- huacan until Christos would be born in the hearts of all the peoples of Earth.

The Mayans were chosen to protect the Christic seed because their people were the Earthlings who coordinated sacred or stellar time—galactic spirals—to Earth cycles. The Mayans lived the teachings of sacred time, called Ahau, and they understood the weaving of history on Earth. They were free of the Powers and Principalities, or Archons, as Nibiruans were called in 0 A.D. For as Nibiru underwent the agony of its solar return—its loss of immortality—the Mayans at Teotihuacan taught the Nibiruans about the soul. Our bodies may be in an orbit or a cycle, but our souls are traveling free in the cosmos. The Mayans taught the Nibiruans about the Dreamtime!

At this moment, the possibility existed to free Earth from its chains: fear, rape, and violence—the human activities that separate us from our stellar selves. Christos/Kukulcan came to announce a new order, and the Archons were prepared to let go of their obsession with Earth once they had savored the Dreamtime. But the Archons were entrenched in the memory banks of all humans, and it would take another cosmic fusion cycle—the Age of Pisces—for humans to absorb the new freedom. The gods did let go, but because humans had become emotionally addicted to taking orders, their power juice existed in the memory bank, waiting to be restimulated by kings and priests. We had gotten addicted to not thinking on our own, to getting depressed and not taking action when we did not like things the way they were, and to thinking the condition of Earth did not matter unless we were personally threatened.

The next step on the part of the Powers and Principalities was brilliant. Church and State perceived that the way to totally limit the power of the individual was to eliminate access to story, to myth, to the Dreamtime, to the larger cosmic whole which teaches us that each individual action has an effect on all of existence: Earth, animals, rocks, people, and galaxies. Then the economic and political arena would seem to be the only reality. Humans could not imagine creating their own reality. When Christos/Kukulcan saw the status of Earth, he activated a great teaching about the healing heart. He taught that love was the natural state of the human soul.

The Earth field shifted because a few were able to hear the truth, and the few disciples whom Christos initiated protected the heart. But we toned down the cosmic connection at Teotihuacan because the addiction to power and control would be lived out through the Thirteen Heavens and Nine Hells. We would be caught in the cycles of history until each human sought Christos in the heart. Simply put, the change could only come through each human who chose to love. Next, the eternally patient planet, the Goddess, would outwardly mirror the pain of humans so that each person could see an analog reflected by the condition of the planet itself. That would be the extreme sacrifice of Gaia, the true story of the cross which was covered up: Christos suffers with the planet, for the planet in ecological crisis cannot offer sanctuary to the Divine Son.

Humans were freed by Christos, but the Roman Church methodically destroyed all sources containing the true teaching. The Church set up dogma which would make the true teaching almost impossible for humans to discover. The Church became the oracular fount of the Earthborn Archons—the outward structure of the demons in the mind from ancient pain! This institution aligned with the Roman Empire, which was geomantically empowered by the Egyptian obelisks and the Roman Pantheon. Church and State became the new temple of the Archons by manipulating the archetypal contents of the deep mind. Together they conspired to force humans to forget the Dreamtime. The people had little chance to even recognize Christos, but this great teacher unleashed a new feeling, a personal divinity that would grow like an eternal flame in the heart. For protection, the teaching of Christos was given to the native peoples of the West, who were uncorrupted by the civilization that was addicted to power and control. The geomantic power of Teotihuacan held the teaching to be activated on August 17, 1987, when Quetzalcoatl would return to Mesoamerica.

The return of the Christos was carefully planned for thousands of years. As part of this process, the solar system gradually moved into balance so that it could align with the spiraling heart of the Milky Way Galaxy. 0 AD was the precession shift into the heart when the gods returned to Earth to let go of the addiction to being gods. Egypt was the dimensional tunnel for the Sirian star teaching of 3600 BC. In 0 AD, the dimensional tunnel became Teotihuacan.

In 212 BC, Teotihuacan became the new home for the Emerald Records of our long evolution and new freedom. Later, in 0 AD, the records of Teotihuacan were greened by the birth of a star teacher into human form. Like chlorophyll in the cells, Christos initiated two thousand years of growing, which is nearly finished. Teotihuacan has released the truth about the true home of Christ in the heart—Gaia. Seers have long predicted great Earth shifts—volcanoes, earthquakes, tidal waves—at this time. But actually, the real shift lies in the complete loss of power by the Vatican, which has caused society to become uncentered. The Church/State will collapse during a ceremony. The Roman Lie is almost exposed: There is no Second Coming. The Second Coming is Christ in the heart, releasing to heal the Mother Goddess, Gaia.

Teotihuacan was totally abandoned by the Mayan daykeepers in 587 AD, when the site became a commercial city. The rituals that occurred during that time were lifeless, but very elaborate and beautiful. The performances became energyless, ritualistic pomp and ceremony, as other Mayan temples were activated for the unfoldment of Christos in the form of Quetzalcoatl/Kukulcan. I was not present for any of that. I appeared today to take my soul on a journey to a time when I actually worked with the Emerald Records.

I am standing below the first Pyramid of Quetzalcoatl, built in 6700 BC. It lies within the Pyramid of Quetzalcoatl at Teotihuacan that was built in later years. I walk up the side of the pyramid to enter the ninth dimension—fusion of the inner child with the stellar self. When I reach the top, I dematerialize and reform myself in a small subterranean room, one level beneath the Temple of the Plumed Shell. I enter this most sacred sanctuary by moving my awareness into the curve-form of one of the large conch shells in the murals. I spiral down through the curves of the inner shell and enter the holy room deep in the Earth. The space is cut out of solid bedrock, with one rectangular door into the interior and symbols divided into eight sections on the sides. The nine-pointed star above my head as I go within is the mystery symbol for the integration of shadow and light. Around this large block of stone containing the interior space, there are twelve columns which support the Temple of the Plumed Shell directly above. The columns make a hallway, composed of columns on the outside, and walls of the interior room on the inside, and each is deeply incised with exquisite scenes of many antediluvian creatures of the deep sea. This is the original temple. The Temple of the Plumed Shell directly above it was built later and was similarly modeled. The Temple of the Quetzal Butterfly is open to the sky. These forms are a copy of the original temple. Part of the Mayan mystery is that this first temple was once open to the sky.

Within the room is a rectangular stone box that is six feet in length, two feet high, and three feet wide. It is about the size of a coffin. The box is made of cut white stone set with patterns of obsidian chunks on the sides which look like eyes. There is a great emerald crystal on the top with a curved obsidian mirror stationed above. In the center of the box, there is a lens which sends a ray of light reflected from the emerald crystal up to the mirror. The mirror then reflects the light ray back down to the lens, which sends the ray to the Andromeda Galaxy.

This mechanism accesses the memory of the Emerald Records of Khnum/Thoth, who is the mental plane calibrator from the star systems which influence Earth. Thoth is unlike any other teacher since the beginning of time, because he is the one who protects the alchemical secret. Half of the secret—that matter is not destroyed but simply changes form—is known, but the other half—that consciousness can access all forms of matter and all manifestations in time—is hidden. That is why Thoth's animal is a baboon, and like the baboon who howls when the Sun rises in Egypt each morning, he awaits the revelation of the other half of the secret. He howls at the rising of the Sun each day, hoping that this day will be the day of revelation! The African baboon goes into complete silence for one day and one night at the time of the New Moon each month, because he awaits the new and unique seed. Perhaps that seed will be the one to reveal the secrets of matter and form? The baboon is the first to observe the rising of the dog star Sirius before the inundation, for he understands that the keys to existence are known on Sirius.

This box reflecting Earth wisdom to Andromeda Galaxy is Thoth's path to symbiotic attunement of the spiraling galactic forms. These galactic forms illustrate how the Goddess manifests in time, for matter is inert unless activated by the passionate spinning of the Goddess. Thoth will again activate the Records when humans awaken to their galactic selves, for Andromeda will be the brightest it has ever been to the naked eye between 1987 and 2012 AD. Those who attune to spirals will move into the Dreamtime, and Andromeda Galaxy is the most magnificent spiraling form visible from Earth.

I am in the room with Thoth, for I am the guardian being in this room, in the form of a stone hawk. I also exist as one of the hawks in the columns of the upper temple. This temple is open to the sky and receives the light of the Sun, Moon, and stars. I am Horus-of-the-Horizon. I can come alive in my stone form in this room, just as I willingly became stone before, in order to exist on Earth within the cycles of time. I have waited in this room for a long, long time, fully conscious within stone, observing all the Records sent from Earth to Andromeda Galaxy. I have been waiting for the cyclic apotheosis of the Mayan Great Cycles to activate the Records again. I have obsidian eyes placed in my form for seeing the cycles of time. Obsidian is volcanic, and makes my seeing through the fire possible.

I now focus my obsidian eyes on the emerald crystal on the top of the box, and as I do this my vibration begins to tone down to a comprehensible level. I hear a high-pitched ringing in my temples, and a voice forms:

The Records are a frequency resonance and calibration system with other dimensions, and the text is not to be confused with Earth legends such as the history of Atlantis. There are ways in which the ancient sacred sites and secrets of the universe are still very much alive on Earth. Now is the time to attune to the vibrations, as we move beyond past experiences connected with such places. Listen! Do not assume you will face sacrifice and sexual abuse if you allow yourself to feel the power of the Earth again. These images are simply memories. You have to listen to the Earth like a little child! We cannot create a new world with you unless you pass out of the old cycles of fear, so that you will again be able to hear the teachings of the wind. Earth is in a storytelling relationship with Andromeda Galaxy, Arcturus, and the Pleiades. You forgot about creativity. You lost your hearing. I have not changed. You must brace yourselves with my fire, enter my waters, read the messages in my wind again, and become my stone, by lovingly giving your offerings and energies for the new vision.

I exist in radiant light form above the emerald crystal, and the pathway into me is the spiral form, for you must escape from the circular and endless cycles of reason now, and focus on the turning curves of the conch shell where existence actually takes form. All the dimensions of life are located in the Moebius curve of the conch shell, and I exist where the spiral ascends out of its own curvilinear form. To know me, ask questions that have to do with bridging from one reality to another, with the places between things, for I am emptiness.

I will go into the interface zone between the physical and astral dimensions of your bodies to show you what it is in your being at this time that makes the ability to know me difficult—your God within. There is grey and fuzzy-looking matter in your physical cells which contains emotional imprints of your experiences. This matter draws energies to you which mirror these emotional imprints. You draw individuals to yourselves who confuse you, and you try to cover the signals from your emotional imprints with addictions. All you have to do is ask me for my help and I will free you from every chain that ever held you.

Look within yourself for me and the imprints turn to light! I have not vacated you; you have just forgotten that I dwell within you. Now I see whirling forms of color within you and I spin counterclockwise with the forms. A male would spin clockwise. With a man and a woman, a double spin forms a figure eight, the action for bringing in the new galactic energy without jamming the faster vibration into the old form. Light floods the cells with this movement, which is why the symbol of my healing is the entwinement of two serpents. The evolutionary spiral has been rising at each turn in the Moebius curve, and that is why you learned at such a dizzying pace as soon as the Nine Hells began. The energy ascension is about to occur, but you will miss the great leap if you do not see that the densest matter must be moved. You must spin the matter. Those who do not first love their own bodies are in grave danger at a time like this. Every place in you that denies any of your many roles in the story of time, which denies any part of the collective consciousness, is in grave danger—for you know me only by your own experience. Nothing is other than yourself, not the Albigensian Crusades, Adolf Hitler, or the ceremony at Tikal. Where you deny your experience, you deny creation.

The material plane will move into spiral form, for these events have occurred before on Earth. You will recall these events if you just remember the ancient skills: geomancy, sacred geometry, and correct ceremonial cycles. For example, the physical plane in England is exceedingly impenetrable by higher dimensions because the belief in power and control there was sealed into divine kingship, a later version of the Roman Imperium. Teachers must energize Avebury, energize the ancient rock formations which were created for galactic communion at the beginning of the fifth Mayan Great Cycle. Like the ourobouros—the snake swallowing its tail—return to your child, your first quickening, and know the Earth again. Spin the dormant forms into energies that will come alive and release all the molecules into the next dimension. By enlivening the stones, the statues, we will be given back the energies contained within them which actually quicken your Sun, your own star. We are waiting to be reawakened and enlivened by you. We are alive like the spiraling galactic energy in all the shells on Earth.

I was meditating in the blinding sunlight of August, 1987 in the Temple of the Quetzal Butterfly. I also existed simultaneously two levels below. An intense macrocellular reorganizaton was occurring. I shifted in my body, which felt like carbon being pressed into diamond, and I was myself then as I had been in 6700 BC! I had already found a statue of my galactic self by observing the Nagua in the La Venta Museum at Villahermosa, Mexico. I had actually found my ancient form who came to Earth, and I had stood in front of myself in stone in 1987 for a few hours. I had wondered whether if I were released from stone at that time, I could become whole—release my form from the beginning of time. Would I then not be layered any more into individual planes? Would I know myself in all dimensions simultaneously, instead of perceiving myself in this or that time or place?

I began to notice that I was rooted into my body, as I was both sitting in front of the sipapu of Teotihuacan and also existing in 6700 BC with my attention fixed on the exquisite emerald crystal. A great tornado-like funnel of billions of diamonds swirled above me in the turquoise sky. Suddenly, the symbols of the center of the universe around the top rim of the temple became tree roots digging into the soil with tongues of fire to the sky, and the centers were spinning. All three levels of the temple formed the Tree of Life! I gave my soul the freedom to return to the moment when I first got caught in time and place.

I am slender, tall, and muscular, with small breasts. My hair is straight, coarse, and very long, and my skin is tough and swarthy. I have strong features with a prominent and strong chin. My nose is straight and large, and my cheeks are very high above full lips. My neck is long and slender, and I wear a deerskin tunic down to midthigh. I have a green sash around my waist made of a loose-weave cotton, and I wear nothing else. My skin is brown and suntanned and I have large hands and strong arms. I have a leather thong on my wrist with a hanging owl feather which flies in the wind. I am an owl priestess and my name is Adreena.

My skin is rough from climbing trees. I can see a long, long distance to the rolling hills far away. I am standing on mossy rock, having just emerged from a four-foot-high hole into a cave. I hid something in the cave and I'm looking to see if anybody saw me do it. I've buried something in there. The cave is ten-to-twelve-feet deep, and I buried a body in the front of the cave where there is a flat, sandy bottom. It's the skull and a few bones of a one-year-old infant. I dug up the remains someplace else where I had found them all discolored and deteriorated. Somebody is disturbing the graves of my people. I found the grave of this infant disturbed, with sacred objects taken out, and some of the bones were gone. I brought the remains here to rebury them.

When invaders disturb the graves, we lose touch with our ancestors and forget our stories and legends. The stories of our clan are the teachings of the ways of wisdom, healing, and how to live in the world. If we forget the stories, we have no existence—no time. We are the dark people, and the blond people of the North across the water did this. The invaders from the North woods want us to forget our past, our lineage, and the way to accomplish that is to destroy our graves. Then we are vulnerable. This was another child my mother had and he died of a killing cough. He was my brother.

I can see grassy fields and trees, lots of trees. This is southern England. It is 20,000 years ago, way back in time when there were many great trees. If I go forward in time, I can see fields, stone walls, farms, and the Avebury stone circle here.

The cave is on the edge of a hill. I leave the cave and walk through the forest to my village. The woods are deep and dark, and the trees are very big. This is a great oak forest with light reaching the ground in patches. There are green plants on the ground, and this pathway through the deep woods is very solemn. As I walk along, there is a river nearby which leads to our village. I am afraid of what has happened. I have returned from a long journey to find the disturbed graves of my clan, the Wolf Clan. I took the remains and buried them in the cave and now I return to my village.

I am sneaking along, tree-by-tree, getting closer. Our village by the river has crude huts made out of wood with dirt roofs. We dry the logs from trees that have fallen in the forest, and pile them up for stockade fences and for building houses. We use the branches for the roof. The roofs are packed with dirt, which becomes mossy and repels the rain. Our houses are like the forest and are low to the ground. Our village consists of twenty huts in a central clearing, and a stockade fence surrounds these dwellings to protect us against wolves, bears, and tigers. The forest is so deep, and the trees so tall, that there is little sunlight here even in the central clearing.

I see that the skin flaps on the doors are open and that, inside the huts, skins and vessels seem to be gone. The huts are all there but the village does not look normal. I am coming in on the backside of the village between two huts, and there is a smoking campfire off to one side. I go into the central clearing because I sense there is no one around.

The sun slants in from the West in the late afternoon. No one is here, and I go across the center clearing to the hut where I live. All is strange. I pull aside the moose skin that covers the entrance. The few tree trunks that we usually sit on are knocked over, and there is some debris strewn around in the back. There is no one inside and I feel intense dread. I do not know what to do. I cannot figure out what has happened, as there are no dead bodies, but somehow my whole clan is gone. There is little physical disturbance, but my people would fight! This is like an abduction. The tribe was removed without killing anyone. I go back to the time just before I left on my journey.

The hot August sun is high overhead. There are some people cooking and drying meat and skins, children are playing, and other people talk in low voices in the village center. I am near my own house. We do not go inside much in the summer because we wlll endure the winter's coldness soon enough. I hear lots of talking and the barking of dogs. I hear the owls in the trees, the birds singing. There are lots of little kids around. We are a happy people.

I am not a mother myself and I do not have a man. I am an owl priestess. I have sex with many young men before they mate, but I regulate my cycle to the Moon so that I do not conceive children. I will not have children in this lifetime and I feel very free. I keep my village in tune with the cycles of nature. I am trained to be in tune with the cycles by becoming the animal. I can become the spirit of any animal. If someone in my village needs to learn how to walk in the woods without making a sound, I become the deer and show them how. I was chosen to be an owl priestess because of my affinity to the animals, especially the wolf. I am in tune with the energy of the village, and I regulate the village energy to the cycles of the planets, the stars, the Moon, and the seasons of the Sun. My sanctuary is to the North in a large clearing. This sacred space is a great stone circle which is carefully aligned to standing stones on the ridges of the surrounding hills. That is how I know certain seasons have begun. My work is to know the timing, but my most important work is to feel the people. I feel their needs and respond with healing methods.

I know the energies of the plants and herbs. I feel the emotions of the people and give them plants for balance. If there is a family that is in discord, if there is anger or violence, I commune with the animals in the forest to attune myself to the animal spirit which is the right healer for this need. I go into the deep forest and run with the wolves, prowl with the lynx, sniff with the fox, and eat with the deer. I sometimes climb in the trees with the squirrel. I become one with the animal, then I travel in spirit to the family in the village. I bring the energy of the animal from my sanctuary to the family. This heals the failing spirit of a person in the family so that the family can know happiness again. I give myself in this way because I know that if a human group gets out of balance, and the energy is not rebalanced, then a negative heart cycle begins. Once such a cycle begins, the sequence repeats itself over and over again. People are caught in repetition.

I heal with animals because many animal powers are free of the complexities of being human. For example, the animals do not know of their mortality, so they remain always in the present time and their spirit does not need to come and be, over and over again. My people get very confused by death and cannot imagine not existing. Various people get obsessed about the importance of their own meaning, their own significance. People forget they are part of the larger whole and they get caught in a trap that they believe is a universe. To the lynx, each hunt is an orgasmic union with the hunted, but my people spend all their time worrying about whether they have food. The great hunters of my clan know that the animal will manifest before leaving on the hunt. Those of us who are old souls know that we return over and over again, and that we are not caught in a particular moment. We feel immortal even though we die again and again.

People begin to develop ideas about how existence is supposed to be which have little to do with reality. The way life actually works is only known to a few initiates. There are at least thirteen dimensions which are kept in balance by the cycles of the planets, stars, and galaxies. Just like a human body, all the parts play together. I can travel in all of these dimensions by just tuning into feelings, and can actually feel all of what being is. If I cannot feel a person, we do a sweat ceremony together to find that person's power animal—the beast who has access to his or her soul. Then I learn the medicine of that animal and I can heal the person. My only limitation is how much feeling my body can hold.

I can travel anyplace because no place in the universe is separate from any other place. The distances that I travel are only restricted by my own inner limits. I am unusually free in my mind, emotions, and planes of existence, because this is an extraordinary lifetime. I am so conscious because, before I came, I chose to master the animal vibrations, to attune totally to the animal dimension. This is the thirteenth dimension, unlimited by any sense of time, place, or fear. Animals are the constellations of the stars, and these lifeforms are the most potent teachers for humans.

We shall observe her from the center of her own soul, because she asked to see the true meaning of the animal teachings, the most sacred teachings in the universe. Adreena commented that her perception of her own limitation is that her body can only hold so much feeling. The secret to the hope for perfect and robust health exists in Adreena's judgment about herself. She is not actually limited, but her form of resistance to admitting feelings is the entry point of all organic disease in the human body. The Egyptians—masters of the physical body—had organic disease figured out. At death, they embalmed the lungs in an ape jar, the stomach in a jackal jar, the liver in a human jar, and intestines in a falcon jar. In each lifetime there is a central mastery issue. Adreena has true communion with the animals. But in any life there is also a central confusion coming from that lifetime, and the soul returns until each confusion is solved. We now move to the point at which the conflict originated in the life as Adreena.

I am in the center of my village. There is a place right in the middle of the clearing where the stone from the grandmothers of the Wolf Clan is buried. This stone is the primordial egg from the beginning of time. It was buried here in the center of this village before the village site was chosen. I saw the sacred relic when I was five. The owl priestesses dig up the stone every nineteen years for the ceremony of the cycle of rebirth. This ceremony is performed when the Moon is closest to Earth as the Moon rises in the notch of the grandmothers. All the priestesses were here in the center when we dug up the stone.

When I am in the center sitting over the stone, I can tune into every feeling in my village. Then my feelings take me to the part of my body which responds. Now I begin to feel very upset in my belly, as if the center of my body is my heart and this location feels very heavy. I feel all these vibrations in my belly, and I do not know the source of this great power. I cannot see the animal, but I can feel great violence. I allow myself to be taken to the source of the violence.

In one of the huts in my village, there is a man who is clutching a girl at the throat. He is over her and her body is thrashing. He leans down to force his knees onto her knees in order to spread her legs. He has an erection and he is shoving his phallus into her body. She is eight or nine years old, and she is his daughter. He is penetrating her and I allow myself to totally absorb the insane violence of this act. The energy is very intense when violence and sexual power are mixed together, and that is how the experience feels when I tune into him. When I become her, I feel like I am being caught, being trapped, being suffocated, being stuffed. I stand over the grandmother's stone, totally feeling this screaming pain. I become an animal in pain. I feel the violence, I see that this is not sexual, not erotic, and I scream its constriction out through my throat, blasting its imprint out of myself. I do not think about the meaning of what has occurred, for that is another way to get caught in the energy form.

I go into the forest beyond the vibrational frequency of the village to my sanctuary—animal territory. There I am the goddess of the woods, and I have no rational mind. I cross the line into my territory, take off my tunic, and leave this clothing at the base of a tree. I go into the land of Atlana and I am walking into a field of vibrating yellow color which was invisible a moment ago. I take high steps, as if I am walking over a rainbow of blue and green. The frequency is suddenly very high, with more vibrating waves of color. I become the central forcefield. I can see myself yet I am also inside myself. I am a vibrating point of force like the intersection in the center of the figure eight of a magnetic field. Within the two circles, my body is a perfect energy field, a complete universe in itself. I stand there and charge myself.

I charge the higher head centers, which ground right into the Earth as an electromagnetic field is created. I am surrounded by my circle of standing stones, being built by the gods for the grandmothers, and as I ground, an etheric dome forms all around me. My spine is the central alignment rod. I am the rod of a resonant vibrational core which structures an etheric forcefield of a great area around me—spreading out 360 degrees to all the constellations, and also down to the central crystal core of the Earth. Like a tree, the further out I go, the further down I go, until I attract the animal teacher for this healing. All of the animals, insects, plants, and minerals respond to this energy channel—a vortex which all beings participate in. The only way to have this power is to be in tune with all the animal spirits you can feel but have denied. The only way to know yourself is to observe these creatures in their truth. A tiger is the animal that is called to me, for only a restoration to the girlchild of her own eroticism will save her from withdrawal from the love of life.

There is a great cat out there but I cannot see its shape. This cat is vibrating from the location in my energy field which fears shapeshifting—fears changing form because my soul might get caught between places. But, at this moment I care more about that violated little girl than I care about my identity. I do not care about my identity—my feminine sense of self—if such abuse is occurring. Letting my identity go enables me to meet with this great totem, a totem by which I have never been initiated. I will allow the power of the great cat to gain entrance into my being for my teaching.

Watching me, the tiger is stronger, for I can see all the other creatures but this one. The great cat is filled with power and energy. I can feel him prowling around me as my auric field begins to crackle from his presence. I hold my space. I stand there as the cat begins to move in closer and closer. He walks back and forth, switching his tail and zig-zagging toward me, watching to see if I react. I will not move, so well-trained am I to never leave the power center once I have attained it, or the explosion of power would pulverize me.

I see the great tiger now. This is southern England in a period between glaciers, and there is a bridge of land to the tropical continent. This tiger has come across the land bridge.

The animal circles around me and I begin to feel his energy as he moves into my aura. He is pacing back and forth, never taking his eyes off me. To the tiger, I look like a column of white light, with light extending all around me, but he can smell my flesh. There is great radiant power in my huge aura, but there is an opening in my field on the right side which is causing tingling in my shoulder blade. The tiger gets closer, rises slowly on his hind legs, and with one paw, claws my flesh from my right shoulder blade all the way down my back and my arm. My flesh burns as I bend down on my right knee and fall to the ground in supplication, for I recognize that this beast is stronger than I am.

I am hoping he will just kill me quickly. This is the point when I would rather die than go on with the pain. But I was taught never to just die, for courage—the totem power of the cat—is the most precious thing we have. Without courage, we are heartless. I melt down into Mother Earth, in supplication to the great cat, for I was trained by the grandmothers to offer myself as a woman rather than to die. The central core issue of survival over pain, the real trust in the ultimate meaning of our lives on Earth is women's survival wisdom. All is simultaneous, and we have forgotten about courage in the confusion from the softness of modern life.

I lie on the ground as the cat covers my body and penetrates me. I feel warm. For now the cat is gentle, is enjoying himself. I am lying beneath his hot and shivering body, becoming the primordial mother, the Earth priestess, allowing myself just to experience and not to judge. My heart begins to expand but I go into spasm simultaneously, as if I cannot take the tiger power. I go deep within myself to find the central place of pain, and I see my abandoned village. I am ready to open myself to the exact point when I closed down. I see . . .

The tigers were the sign of the coming travail. The cats had come to my homeland over the land bridge during the warmer weather. Now I see . . . My people left in the fall because of the advancing ice. There had been a movement of people leaving our homelands as the cold made our villages uninhabitable. My people joined the hordes of refugees. I have sunk down into Mother Earth, drawn there for healing. I do that with the cat because then he knows that I am seeking the peace of the Earth. He knows I am his equal. He is my teacher about Earth. As I have accepted his teaching, he responds to me and feels me. The moment is exquisitely poignant.

I know animal energy, a communion known only to people of courage. Others fear this knowing intensely. The tiger hovers over me, and sinks down on his haunches as he penetrates me with his phallus. When he was circling me, he was gathering energy for a kill, but now his energy is erotic, not violent. I lie there and become totally willing to know him, choosing to live, but not because I was taught survival. No, I choose to live right now because this is the most intensely erotic moment I have ever known. The girlchild is saved from anger that would encrust her heart.

There is a light force in my pelvis, a casement of light around my ovaries which I visualize so that I cannot become pregnant. The tiger is shivering and ejaculating as I lie there with my face turned to the side. I feel warm and connected. He withdraws and licks me all over my body, my genitals, and I have an orgasm which fills my body with energy from my shoulders down to my legs. The tiger starts walking away as I turn over sideways and go to sleep. The cat walks many circles around me, closing the energy as I sleep in the center of my sanctuary, and my animal self reemerges into the forest.

I was shaking from such a revelation of raw honesty. But, what did this ancient owl priestess have to do with all the lifetimes when I wore the jaguar skin as a male priest? When we wore the skin of the cat, we became the power of the cat, or so we thought then. I took a moment to feel the female quality of being with the great cat in the central sanctuary, and the experience felt very different from the days as a Jaguar Priest wearing the skin.

As a Jaguar Priest, I embodied the power of fear over other beings. But as the priestess lying on the Earth, I took my fear as myself. I became my greatest fear—letting go of my human identity. When this journey began, I requested entry into the records of time in order to bring back the story of our freedom by agreeing to look at every lesson I myself learned as a male priest. I agreed to reveal what was shown to me in the records, to open up all knowledge I had ever given secret oath to, in my quest for a new set of symbols and ceremonies for a new age I could not yet envision. I had now given myself to my own totem power. I asked the jaguar, the tiger, to carry us forth with the Earth blessing from the ancient owl-priestess sanctuary initiation—the sacred bridge between the animal and the human soul.

Chapter Eight

BISHOP, EXECUTIONER & WHITE KNIGHT

The jaguar became my companion in the inner forest, for I was going deep into my woman heart to shine light into every experience I ever had as male on this planet in which I controlled the gates to the central creative force. These were aspects within myself which agreed to be quiet when evil was present; the parts of myself which agreed that living was easier when I was just being safe and not crying out against injustice; the parts of myself which believed that people needed to be controlled, for they did not know what was best for themselves. But, I no longer needed refuges of avoidance within myself. Adreena had let them all go as she lay sleeping in the dark forest.

Adreena rose slowly as she felt a new reality around herself. Higher tides caused the inundation of the ancient land bridge to the continent where her clan had gone. Her lover, the land-locked tiger, would soon freeze. She walked back to the center of her village and began to make ceremony. With cedar and sage, she smoked the remains of her ancestors as she spiraled into the center to stand over the stone of the grandmothers. Surrounding that primordial beginning of life with many branches and twigs, she made a pyre. She created a fire and placed the burning coals in a vessel, and then she sat in the center above the stone of creation and made Dreamtime. The vision of the owl priestess from the days before the recession of the great glacier was now available through the veils of time. Adreena speaks:

I can see four times yet to come in this place. The first time is the gathering of clans when the weather makes habitation in this place possible again. I see a seer standing where I once sat over the primordial egg of the world. She calls for a vision. I enter into her vision-making and break the barriers of past and future so this seer can attune to the egg deep within the Earth, to know all the ancient stories of this place. She feels her guts turning and her heart opening as she receives my force through eons of time.

This river-tossed granite egg will be the sacred stone of a new clan founded in 3113 BC. Other members of this clan will build a great passage grave to pass souls to the East, and thousands of these river-tossed eggs will be latticed into the white-quartz eastern facade of the temple. Thousands of years later, archaeologists will call this temple Newgrange. These clans come from the original homeland—the Basque land—where my people went over the land bridge to seek refuge from the advancing ice. They are of the Clan of the Great Mother, the Mother who worships the cosmic egg which came from the sky. Some of them also come from the place of the passage graves of primordial eggs that is over the sea to the West—the Boyne River Valley, where a god was found in the spring. These are the people of the ancestors, and their visions are accessed in the passage graves.

Next I see Silbury Hill being built over my egg! This Clan of the Great Mother builds seven, circular, layered stages with perpendicular sides out of white chalk. Then they cover it with earth, which makes it round like a breast. This is the sacred hill of emergence of the birthing goddess. The craftsmen construct a great, double, stone circle, signifying the two sides of the serpent power. This sanctuary becomes the connector between all dimensions, for the Great Mother is the Earth who receives the sky.

Later in time, I see a church being built in the center of the stone circles. It is the parish of Avebury, constructed after the destruction of the pagan stones. The baptismal font in the church is placed at the exact intersection of the two great stone circles, and the stone altar depicts a bishop stabbing one of two serpents with his crozier—his shepherd's rod. But the two serpents writhe on top of a row of Holy Grails with torrents of water pouring from one receptacle to another. With intense cosmic power, this altar shows that the Age of Aquarius will begin in the intersection of the two great circles of Avebury at a time when the Water Bearer pours out the pain of humanity from the jars of time. That is my fourth vision.

I come out of my trance and realize that at last the time has come. I light the pyre near me, releasing all fear about the future of the Earth. The fire leaps. The flames consume my heart, and I ask to return to the time when the Earth oracles of the Great Mother were stolen by men. Like the phoenix rising, I am willing to become any man who ever took that power.

I am Augustine of Hippo, wearing a greenish-grey robe and sitting by the right side of the sacred spring. My back is hunched over with my chin resting on my right hand. Guardian of the teachings of Christ, I am contemplating a weighty matter—the contemporary heresies. It has become obvious that Christ is not returning soon, and the people are losing their religious fervor. I move into the Dreamtime, immersing all my energy into the swirling issues of my times. I begin to think of my own position in the midst of the doctrinal swill of 396 AD.

I have just taken over the power to control the meaning of Christ's teachings by accepting the mitre of bishop. But, I am still connected to the sacred spring, an ancient pagan meditation place which has power from when the ancient ones used the waters for healings. I feel that I am totally barred from this ancient healing energy because of the role I have taken on since my conversion. But this is the only place where I can hear the secrets, and know my own inner voice. I feel guilty about returning to my source of pagan power, but this connection to the center means the most to me.

As I sit, light forms around me. I try to become the light, but the glow dissipates. My power mitre and bishop's robes abscess as if they are leprous. I am recalling truth, and I am torn apart inside as I realize I will never return here again. I feel damnably black inside and I want the spring to cease to exist. I want the waters to cease flowing for any life. I feel my heart compress, while a black liquid guilt seeps into my soul. These times are heavy, and I feel the whole battle within myself. I came today to open to the Earth energy for the last time, as I know I am about to compromise every feeling I have ever had. There is still a little place in my heart where there is room for an emotion that could change me. But my new way in the Church is an addiction, a chosen path of comfort which helps me stop feeling my own demons within. My role is sharply defined and safe. I am 42. I have lived a life of both goodness and evil. I know from what I have done in the flesh that people must be controlled, or they will be consumed by sin.

I become the sound of the water once more, and I hear the inner ringing. Then I explode from within at the thundering sound of the voice. "You were offered the secret of liberation that Christ brought to Earth. You were initiated into all the deepest secrets so that you could be a liberator at this dangerous time. Few were ever allowed into the inner circles of Manicheanism because the initiate might abuse magical powers which would result in annihilation. Bishop Faustus chose you to be the true protector of Christos, and now here you have decided to serve the Powers and Principalities. You are one of the few who knows the revelation cycle of the Good News—the process through which humankind can become free of enslavement to the gods. And now you have taken the mitre to contain Christ in the Roman Church, making him into an impotent tool of the Imperium."

Shaking, I try to remember my primary encounter with Bishop Faustus. To be a Manichean required that I master my own powerful sexual impulses, that I move beyond being controlled by intensely felt desires. Since the original cosmological/Earth experience was sexual, initiates had to be powerfully motivated by sexual energy. I was selected as an initiate because of my brilliance and because I truly loved my own mother and my female lover. Once, woman was Goddess to me, but then I grew up. What was the experience that made me feel like a lost soul?

I feel a block, a fuzziness above my brain stem, and then I feel a click in my head. I can only overcome evil in myself—my own sexual obsession—by taking on the power vestment of the Church. This power bargain will balance my inner evil which I can never conquer by myself. I took the power into my being at my Investment yesterday and I know exactly what the bargain entails. Part of the plan is that I would come here today to let go of the sacred spring. The Romans will control me now, completely. I lost my soul before I was born, for I was born of woman.

I enter the Dreamtime again as a tiny image of Christ forms across the stream from me on the left. The image begins to shine and radiate. The figure wears a red robe with a blue-white shining cape over the shoulders and down to the ground. His hands are extended out and held in supplication as light radiates from them. He grows larger. I do not see the Christ but I am aware of a growing light in my own heart. The figure grows into an ascended master about ten feet tall. He hovers over the water, which is now gold and aquamarine, radiating rays of blue topaz light. I cry out:

"I must take on the full density of the Earth, of the human incarnational plane. I take this heaviness. Flesh is the only way to know existence. I am getting dense and frozen and heavier, and the Christ light diminishes. I *see* what happened at my initiation! I was shown the waters of Aquarius, the radiant, golden and topaz, aquamarine spring of life. In this massive, mandalic vision, I see that, in the age to come, people will free themselves from every control dynamic that I am about to set into form in my time. I sacrificed my own free will and higher self when I agreed to play my role in the Church. I stopped experiencing things mystical and magical in order to be in the center of earthly power and success.

"I know that by taking this power I am setting up a personal battle against Earth energy. That is why I know exactly what steps to take in order to be sure no one ever understands what the Messiah wrought. I am a chosen pawn in the conspiracy to hide the emergence of a new order brought by Christos—the gift from God, who became human in order to free us all. But the time is too soon for people to know freedom, for people will sin if they find out that God no longer judges them. Better to have such news controlled by theologians who will release the truth when people are ready. That control is exactly what Christ came to announce as being released. I know this from the secret Testimony Book, which is carefully guarded by the Manicheans since Rome has destroyed as many Hebrew sources as possible. But, personally, I know people need to be controlled because they are naturally pagan, especially women. If people are not protected by priests, then evil oozes out of them just like it oozed out of me when I was young. But as for how I feel becoming Bishop, this entrance into Rome feels like I am separating from my soul."

I am still sitting on the right side of the stream with my chin in my right hand, hunched over. A beautiful, lavender hibiscus flower, nestled in greenery with radiant light around the bloom, appears in front of me. I am depressed, feeling like I will cease to exist, but I watch the flower transform into a ball of white light which then pops into me! The radiation is a spinning seed of essence which pops into my third eye and lights this chakra and my throat. This seed makes me into a great writer, makes me able to tell the amazing story of my times. A time will come when my story will be read again and my self-sacrifice will be known. I am a true pagan, for I have a woman within me who will rage through all the lies that have been put into form by my obsessive need to hold my intensely sexual power inside. She—goddess of the night—will cause rage around all my oppressive dogma until that anger causes a tidal wave of prophecy by a fox in priestly robes.

My Faustian pacts from my separated self can now be seen in a new light, for my own struggle with my internal demons will someday offer the human race the revelation that evil exists only in the mind of humanity.

Making such pacts captures the light force in time, but the light energy is never destroyed. Such pacts—agreements with some power to rob others of their own experience—are holograms that will be liberated when the individuals holding the agreements get tired of the game and let go. In individuals, such pacts utilize the power of the will for extension of the ego into extreme desire to influence events on Earth. Such pacts are faithlessness, for the essential lack of trust removes our energy from the greater process which simply flows, no matter what humans do. Such pacts create mental forms—idea complexes which suck people into roles instead of letting them live—but spiritual freedom exists outside of time and place in the cosmos. To use free will in this way is to become the anti-Christ, and all humans have played the role of anti-Christ. Now that the flower of Jesse has risen from the root—Christos—I will release my hibiscus vision to relate what I did fifteen hundred years ago to bind humanity in chains until now. I am the Father of the Church, and when I received the mitre, the heavens opened above my head in the Church and a chorus of voices intoned to me:

"If you take this mitre, you accept the helmet of protection and salvation, the two horns of which represent the two horns of the Old and New Testament. You will be servant of Yahweh and the Lord, and a terror to the enemies of truth. There is one God in the universe and all evil in the world is caused by the power of the Devil. Each human must fight the demons within the soul. God is perfect, his plan is perfect, and the Church is the manifestor of the plan of God. You will destroy all vestiges of the Manichean heresy, all traces of past cosmological dualism in all the sources. The Roman Empire is united with the Catholic Church, so that God will be honored on Earth. Henceforth, the struggle between good and evil will inhabit the human mind, and the inner conflict will be called original sin. When carrying out your offices, you are the dispenser of God's grace. Unlike unconsecretated humans, you are above the original sin of Adam and Eve. For you are celibate and not tempted by the evil serpent."

In my writings after being made Bishop of Hippo, I wrote many treatises against the heretics. I made sure their writings were burned, and I arranged to have the Testimony Book placed in the Vatican Library, which caused the downfall of the Manicheans. Now I move forward to a time in my life when the Empire protecting the Church of God was destroyed before my very eyes...

I have been living in Rome for ten years, since 400 AD, and the heresy I have been fighting is a doctrine which does not comprehend the depths of human sin—the teachings of Pelagius. Rome, with all its weaknesses caused by the pagans, is a Christian society preparing for the return of Christ. But, for ten years, Rome has been constantly threatened by the Visigoths. Under Alaric, their armies arrived in the late summer of 410, the Salarian Gate was opened, and Rome, the bastion of civilization, was sacked. A shudder of mindless fear went through my mind as the State—the foundation of my belief system—collapsed in a frenzy of rape, pillage, and murder. The union of God and humanity was shattered.

The chaos is incurable! There can be no Church of God and Christ in a world totally infested with sin. I will drive the fear of evil into the heart of Christianity like the soldiers drove nails into the feet and hands of Christ. There cannot be any free will in a world such as I have seen. Adam's sin twisted humanity forever. Since the Fall, we have lost our freedom, and only by being given baptism and grace in the Church can we be servants of God and freed of sin. That is my conclusion, and the dogma of the Catholic Church will be founded upon my doctrine: original sin. But this knowledge is an anger in me that even I cannot carry anymore. I return to the lifetime that is the root cause of my loss of freedom to the most insidious demon ever created by humankind—judgment.

I am standing on a high garrison wall around Jerusalem. Akra, the ghetto of the Jewish agitators, is within the wall. I stare to the East over the Valley of Kedron, holding a banner of Caesar and watching a crowd of people approaching the gate by the Pool of Siloam. There has been agitation in the city for weeks, and I stand here with guards because we have heard that Jesus the Nazarean is coming into the city to claim his victory. He is the Messiah of the Jews, while I hold the power of the Imperium. Caesar is God. The people approaching the East Gate wear clothes of many colors, and a man in a white robe walks in front of them carrying a shepherds's crook. As I stare at the scene I begin to feel very odd. At first I am dizzy in my forehead, then my body tingles, and I feel strange wind blowing through my body.

Enough! I cease staring at the strange figure who is becoming translucent. But even my mind won't leave me alone. For months I have been prey to taking strange actions that I did not understand, but suddenly my mind plays the meaning of my actions through me. I receive a revelation! I have been guided for months by an unseen directive from another dimension.

I had placed symbols of the solar disk in the Tower of Antonia that were inscribed with "Divi Filius," meaning that Caesar is the Son of God. The great star of the gods will be returning in 44 AD. It is now 29 AD, and the Jews would be better off if they would just recognize that Caesar is divine. I *see* that I was directed by the returning celestial body to establish the solar disk in the tower. Caesar declared himself divine when the gods landed on Earth in 6 BC. Jews and Romans alike know that the Last Times will culminate in 44 AD. The Hebrew prophet, Enoch, saw the

Son of Man appearing in the Last Times. I placed the solar disk in the Antonia to avoid chaos, destruction, and jealousy of the gods, which would cause them to take vengeance on innocent poeple. I am Roman, but I have learned much about the ancient times from the Hebrew and Mithric scholars. According to the Torah, God punished the people for not obeying God above all others during the time of Moses. It is my job to keep order in Jerusalem, and I placated the avenging gods to protect the people. Now I realize that this Messiah is able to enter the Holy City because the Jews forced me to remove the solar disk from the tower! What does this mean to me?

I had built a new aqueduct under the city to channel the waters under the Dome of the Rock, for it had been empowered as Zion under David. Now I *see* that I caused the Earth spirit to course under the Holy of Holies. I requisitioned funds from the temple which the Pharisees gave to me willingly. The money to pay for the aqueduct came from funds that were to be used to buy sacrificial animals for Passover. The High Priest, Caiaphas, who gave me the money, realized that my watercourse symbolized the end of sacrifice, when their Messiah would receive the water jar. But Galilean Jews rioted against me even though I created exactly what they had prophesied. I killed many of them, and now their Messiah is coming up the path right over the aqueduct. The Earth power of the Dome has drawn this Messiah, and the temple rings with power as in the ancient days.

Three days before this day, the Galilean rebels fomented revolution and took control of the Tower of Siloam, which I see from where I stand. It was burned out by the bloody fools. Now this foolish King of the Jews approaches the gate right beneath Siloam Tower. Every time I look at him, I swoon. I feel the great Dome of the Rock vibrating as the ancient city swirls into a vortex. I observe his energy as I find myself becoming fascinated. The mobs have been so angry lately, but this one is joyous.

He approaches the gates of the city and my body begins to vibrate with an inner sound, as if my cells are singing! I am Pontius Pilate, and I am being swept into the path of this Jesus the Nazarean as if I have simply manifested for his dream! I combine my energy with his energy and the gates of the city rise! I have absolutely no control over myself! And I am the leader of the Roman Legions! I opened that gate as if the great star which is returning from its journey around the Sun ordered my action. I am not here in Jerusalem: I am in the Sun.

I am about 150 feet away from him as he passes by the Pool of Siloam and approaches the main square of Akra below the wall where I stand. His eyes meet mine and then he looks around himself. He is searching for something. In my mind, I see that he needs to ride an ass for his entrance into the city. He thinks about riding the donkey, and I manifest a donkey! A woman emerges out of a portal between two houses on the plaza, bringing a donkey to him. The donkey is covered with a bright blue blanket studded with stars—the Robe of Atlantis. This is a magical donkey, and I shiver as I bilocate to the Sun. I am seeing the Earthly scene through a rainbow, as if I am the Lord of Spirits. I see that the man in white is Son of Man—he who will cast down the kings and priests; he who will be teacher to the children of the gods. He is the one who will free me from the grip of my warrior within. He is the tree and the vine, the branch of David who is the flower of Jesse. This holy man is totally present in Jerusalem, in the Sun, and in the heart of the supreme Creator. At this moment, Jesus is beyond being a Jew or of the line of David. He is the Messiah of the world. As I am on the Sun, seeing the Earth through a rainbow, he is flying over Teotihuacan, where the Pleiades are rising above the Pyramid of the Sun. He is both shepherd and stone as he holds his crook and rests on the Earth in the Holy City. The great Dome emits a low tone as it absorbs the new order. The grounding of the Messiah above the stone is the end of all secrets. I stand on the fortified wall as he walks toward the woman holding the ass of the ancient kingdom, and I become transfixed as the Sun begins to spin. No one seems to see it down below. He climbs on the donkey, rides the beast of burden down the street, and I climb down from the wall and go to my headquarters.

My headquarters are well furnished. The ceiling is 25 feet tall and the room is a large hallway. I unstrap the armor covering me from my waist to my thighs, and remove my helmet. Then I remove my shoulder coverings by unbuckling them on my chest where they are fastened to a metal guard plate, and put all the armor in a pile behind my desk. I sit at my large carved desk and fall deeply into a state of meditation. I ask the star that is returning to Earth from the Sun what I am supposed to do.

I am to guard the peace of Jerusalem during the time that Jesus is in the Holy City. As I meditate, an egg-form manifests in my hands! It is a diaphanous form which contains all there is to understand about his appearance. I will respond to events and be conscious of all their meaning. I will get whatever knowledge I require, for each person who knows him will return at the time of the Apotheosis to demand acceptance of his gift by the world. I can draw strength from my knowledge as I cope with whatever emotional difficulties are presented. I am to maintain an orderly structure in the city so that events are fully implanted in the consciousness of the Earth. It is time to recognize the roles that all people will play in the drama. All players are to act out these roles in the highest possible awareness. The egg is a very complicated, multifaceted hologram which I understand by means of specifics. Who are the various groups present for the cosmic play? Who are the people with Jesus who resist him or falsify him? The story of Jesus has been mysteriously tenacious even though most of the real contents were hidden by the fanatical destruction of original sources. A phylogenetic reprinting occurred when Christ incarnated which involved the birth of a new cosmos. This created resistance and confusion, which would gradually dissipate over another two thousand years. My role is to create maximum order in the Holy City so that a mystery play can occur which offers maximum awareness for all participants. I am fixing the energy—grounding it into the rocks and water—so that it takes hold at the deepest level of consciousness. I have no choice about the course of these events.

This teacher is fully human—no more and no less than any human. He does not know what will happen to him yet, for what happens will be the result of the combined actions of all players involved. If he could see the future, he might choose otherwise, but he chooses to be the Suffering Servant regardless of the consequences. He has no judgment or desire about the outcome, so he causes the shift into the new order. This is the teaching called the death of the Son; it is the penultimate initiation. As Pontius Pilate, I move myself into the feelings of Christos.

He thinks there is a point at which he can check out of it, a point at which he can ascend back to his Father. He does not yet know, as he enters the city, that he is to play out a complete karmic experience—the only way to become fully human. He doesn't understand this divine infusion into matter. No one does, as an Incarnation has never happened before. It is the first co-creation, a christogenesis. The knowledge of all beings, from master to frog, comes from experience. The opportunity to participate in this drama, whether one is Judas or Mary Magdalene, is the first time we know divinity in our bodies.

Since Christos is fully human, he doesn't really know what is going to happen. He has the idea that he can just cut out of this anytime he needs to. He has not yet developed his magical skills well enough to be able to extricate himself. The human involutionary force will overtake him, and he won't be able to escape death. He could have developed magical skill to the point where he could ascend instead of getting stuck on the cross. But at this point in history, the manifested teaching is for him to get caught. People need to entertain the possibility that even a god is fully human, and that is why many Hebrews have concluded that he is not the Messiah. Their Messiah has to be a Chosen One of the Elect, who is greater than human. However, the teaching of this time is for as many people as possible to see that total acceptance of humanity is needed before any ascension is possible. The Christians deify him and refuse to integrate his humanity—which is what he values the most. Thus, they idolize Mammon—Rome. Our personal ascensions will not occur until we end separation from our own divinity and all creatures.

He ascends later, as we know. Like Enoch and Elijah, he walks with God. He explicitly says we can all walk with God. But the thought-form that is impressed on humanity for two thousand years is the cross—symbolizing the full entrance into the Earth on the four directions. The form of Christos—perfect love—was fully implanted in 0 AD. The ascension—multidimensional access—will occur when we all integrate the opposite gender of ourselves. There is one person who understands Christos better than he understands himself—Mary Magdalene—and Jesus has told his disciples that she is wiser than he. She is the mirror of God and he has seen her. She has not given the gift he gives, for she cannot. Her gift is not to be accepted yet! All men who become priests from this moment forward are priests of Peter, the one who rejected the woman Christos loved above all others. A woman cannot gift the world in these times. The Second Coming will manifest when a woman offers the gift of the vine.

I, Pontius Pilate, sit at my desk and continue to marvel at the cosmic egg handed to me. I am a brave man. The one who understands the whole form is selected by history to be the executioner. The facets of this egg are truly exquisite. I also see that the Second Coming will not manifest until we see that there is no executioner—we all kill together. Tremendous energy modulaton is going on in me as this is the exact moment when the Age of Aries shifts into the Age of Pisces. I *see* that I restored the geomantic powers of Jerusalem by causing the waters to flow in the ancient course. Like a salmon, I offer my staff to the fish who swims up all streams until I return to lay my seed at the end of time. For me to comprehend the enormity of my role in this drama—I/warrior who now transmutes to pregnant fish—I am given a vision into the way creation functions, putting me on the level of God. I can see the waters flowing beneath the ancient city of the goddess. I see them flow into the Pool of Siloam where I have spilled the blood of the people. I can even see that, while Jesus is celebrating the Last Supper and transmuting the grape to his blood, I will be in the temple, slaying Jews who are sacrificing the lambs for Passover. I see that the water jar brought to Christos as a sign that his time is complete actually contains the blood of his followers spilled by me. At this entry point into the Age of Pisces, let no person on Earth say that he or she does not see. You can only say that you have decided it is not your time yet.

I feel trapped. I want to escape it. I want to escape playing out this role. I know how agonizing it will be. But I accept the role I have chosen because I will hold in time the secret revelation of Jesus. Since I am the executioner, I will be the one vilified by the Christians and the Jews. A time will come when people will take on their own responsibility for the pain on this planet, and I will emerge as a follower of Christ. My wife is already down in the streets with those who follow Jesus. I did not know who I was until I stood up on that wall and saw him coming. I did not have feelings until that moment when my heart opened as I saw his eyes. Suddenly, everything I had ever known on Earth catalyzed into a magnificent story, a form like this etheric egg given to me. As I face my truth, nothing in my heart wishes I were elsewhere. When I saw him, a higher dimension of myself was able to come into my form—my soul was entered into me. The presence of my soul will facilitate my understanding of the complexity of balancing the city as this cosmic reordering occurs. I will shepherd the people and no sheep of mine will know I guard them. My soul will give me the exquisite freedom of having no one know what I am doing except my wife and Christos. I will protect the people who all think it is the Last Days. I comprehend that it is the new seed. This remarkable facet of myself is something that I do not fully understand, but will allow to unfold through time. The reason I am able to be this way comes from my visit to the dungeon.

I stand in front of the cell door, peering through the grate. Jesus is inside on his knees, praying, as the late afternoon light falls on his face. I have come to make a personal connection with him. As I enter, I notice that the light I am seeing is emanating from within Him. There is no other light. I shut the door behind myself. I feel humble; I am a soldier. I wonder what he thinks of me. I begin:

"Master, there is little time left. What are we to do with the time that you do have left?"

He gives me many instructions about protecting his family, his followers, and the innocent. He tells me that if I do this, I will be punished and returned to Rome. When he is finished, he puts his three middle fingers on his forehead while he looks into my eyes. I feel a subtle reorganization in my skull as grey miasmic forms move out. A circle of light is created and I become one with him in the midst of it. This is what he has done with many people. There is a new receptor point in my head that changes me as the whole planet shifts into a new form. It is very difficult for me because I have taken the role as executioner. Before this entry into the circle of light, I felt nothing about my actions. I am being forgiven by him as I simultaneously absorb all the pain I have caused others. He says:

"My heart absorbs all of you as if you are a new baby within my own body, and I give birth to you so that we may know one another."

I absorb the peace, the absolute love of everything that I have ever been. He allows me to fully enter into this experience by helping me accept myself just as I am—a Roman soldier. I emerge as if from his body—the Mystical Body of Christ—and he says:

"Pontius Pilate, do you know who you are?"

I do not understand.

"You are all that has ever occurred. Specifically, you were born as a demi-god because your mother and father seeded you when the teachers from the Star of Bethlehem—called Marduk by the Babylonians— visited Earth. You were seeded when I was seeded, but my stellar essence is Pleiadean because my time has arrived. Many were seeded as the Star of Bethlehem rose, but they were murdered when they were two years old because Herod knew I existed. You and many others survived because you lived elsewhere. As you matured, the Roman Empire selected you as governor of Judea because they utilized the talents of as many demi-gods as possible to add power to the Imperium. If they could enlist most of you, then, when they announced they were divine, your loyal support was guaranteed. In your heart, you know they would have killed you as an infant. If they could have, they would have killed me. You and I share the deepest bond of all. We are ready to forgive the murderous father and free him from his prison of responsibility. You are undertaking the ultimate initiation—to act out the role of the executioner of the Son of God. Because you have chosen this initiation, I will return first to you when the release comes, during the exquisite joy at the End Times when all blame is ended. I will be there in the temples, which have allowed my blood to spill into this exquisite Earth, so that the fruit of the vine can eternally regenerate life for my Father. You are the demi-god who undertakes the ultimate sacrifice. When I am crucified, my ascension to my home guarantees free will on Earth. That is when I become the Messiah. The stellar bodies of all Earthlings will begin to take form in their physical bodies. Your initiation as my blood brother guarantees that there will be no one crucified or victimized by any executioner when I emerge in the heart. You are the Lion of Judah who lies down with the lamb, as foretold by Isaiah."

The visions of the lives of St. Augustine and Pontius Pilate did not feel like my own past lives when they came. As I allowed myself to feel the angst in the soul of Augustine and the agony in the life of Pilate, I felt that these visions were being given to me so that I could heal the inner father—the one who blames and accuses, the one who says "I can't." These visions would not have come to me unless I shared some of the issues and experiences which I accessed. I then asked to return to a lifetime in which my unhealed inner father had caused me to intimidate and torture others, and I asked to heal it.

This is the eighteenth dynasty in Egypt. It is 1420 BC. We are the people from the North, and we want to leave Egypt. Ichor, High Priest of Osiris, agent of Pharaoh Amenhotep II, is standing on a rise above our guarded camp of prisoners, staring at me. I am caged behind a wooden fence made of crossed pieces, staring at Ichor with hatred. We are being held in this compound until the Egyptians decide what to do with us. We came down into Egypt before I was born, when there was famine all over the world. The Egyptians had stored grain from seven years of great harvest while the lands north and east had had no rain for many years. There had been great volcanic eruptions in the sea near the Cretans, and there had been too much rain in Egypt while other places had been too dry. The sun had been almost totally blocked for a few years, and the evening skies had been blood red from the volcanic ash of Thera. I want to know what this Egyptian will do to me, and I enter his mind. He is thinking:

Some of these people come from the far north in Thrace; some of them are Hittites. The Hittites say they were pushed out of their land by people to the north of them, the Axiochorion, an ancient race who come from the steppes north of Thrace. These people are Hibiru and they came to Egypt saying the weather was too cold for them to grow food in their fields. We gave them sanctuary, but the new arrivals had to work in the mines in Syria and they are restless. The refugees want to live like nomads in the land of the pharaoh, which was how they lived in their own land. We must control them, or the pharaonic line of divine kings could be disrupted. The pharaohs came to planet Earth to stabilize the solar system.

That man is staring at me with hatred as I look into his right red eye. The soldiers say he is dangerous because he was once instructed in the temple. He is called Mosheh and he was a favorite of the pharaoh. That was before my time, for I am only 23. I suck my power into my solar plexus and stare back at him, but his red eye sears into my throat. He can read my mind and I feel his rage clutching me around my throat. This Hibiru hates me and judges me because I am high priest of the dynasty of Amenhotep II.

As he continues to stare at me, I charge my powerful electrical form as I look back into his eyes. I raise my right hand—I need no staff. I put my left foot forward rigidly and I ZAP him! I have been expertly trained to pull magnetic energy into my feet, suck the force up my legs, build the strength in my spine while drawing white light into my head, and shoot the energy down to my root chakra, holding the power in my electrical body with my breath. Then I ZAP the arc from the Earth out of my right hand, for the man behind this wooden fence is the mirror of my male self. We are male priestly brothers. I wear the single crown of Egypt because I am the son of Thutmosis, and suddenly my crown bursts open and emits a blue egg!

I become a composite being because I have been taught to change form, to access my reptilian self when I am threatened by male aggression. I strip myself of my human overlay by delivering my egg-form from within, for the real truth about me in relation to this worthy opponent lies with my snake self.

Next I become a mouse, and he turns into a great big lizard! I crawl away to a nearby woodpile as I watch him. He has shown me what he thinks I am, and only a fool does that. He is a great, big, bright lizard who keeps on changing into different kinds of lizards. Hiding in the woodpile, I begin to tremble as he moves the wood about and his lizard snout probes my hiding place. I feel his hot breath as he nuzzles in. I am running around frantically in the pile as his huge nose pushes on the wood. He smashes through, grabs me in his right claw, squeezes me until my bones crack, and eats me by biting my head off! He is very pleased.

I flash back to my position above the compound after I have run through these scenes from my phylogenetic memory bank. Now I move my awarenesss into the man with the red eye called Mosheh. He stares at my golden being, my powerful being standing above him wearing the green snakeskin priest form and the skin of the jaguar. My legs are like the trunks of massive trees, and my garments are shining in the sun, encased in radiant, green, fish scales. My cape and chest shine like silver moonlight. He says, "I hate the Egyptians! This one is like an animal god!" My energized right hand is on the wooden fence.

I shift into the experience of Mosheh and stare at the Egyptian as he becomes more golden, more light-filled. He raises his right hand and points a finger at me! Radiant electricity arcs towards me like cosmic lightning, causing an explosion in my neurological pathways. The arc explodes all the cells in my solar plexus and encodes my cells with a desire for him that creates karma between us. The nerves in my solar plexus are exploding as radiant light: purple light is shining into my form. I am blown out of space and time by this being because our connection is between our male selves, as if woman never existed. He is surging energy into my form. This priest, Ichor, projected a ray and struck me with a powerful force. What is it?

I projected kundalini energy into him. Challenged by his ability to kill me in the animal dimension, I zapped him with an overdose of electrical energy which would carry through time in his etheric body. That meant that I could always identify this killer later in time. For him, the action meant that he would gain great powers if he could escape from the land of Egypt. But in the geomantic zone of Egypt, he would be powerless. That is why his people hate Egypt. This pure electrical power can be drawn from the Earth only in geomantic zones that have obelisks standing on key vortex points. The pharaoh, who was all-knowing, saw what I did and was deeply saddened. Once a worthy opponent, always a worthy opponent, until the time comes when the lion lies with the lamb. The lion is Egypt and the lamb is Israel.

The pharaoh knew I would have karma with this man from this point forward unless one or both of us found our suppressed feminine side of being. The energy I zapped into the etheric body of Mosheh would make him prone to sexual difficulties with women, which would cause him to gravitate to celibate male priesthoods. Someday, a solution would have to be found that would heal the hatred between Egypt and the people of Mosheh—the hatred between the oppressor and the oppressed.

As Ichor, I projected into Mosheh the force of overpowering and unbalanced electrical energy. I had learned how to do this from the Egyptian magical training techniques which developed in the Eighteenth Dynasty when male secret societies made inroads into conventional religion. Thus began the recent curse of male priesthoods and secret societies, an insidious lack of integration with the feminine. The imbalance began when we discovered that we could use sexual power over people when we violated the energy from the female source. Before sexual energy could return to balance with the female waveform in Egypt, the energy form was carried out of Egypt into the Holy Land and used as a new and very poorly understood control technique. The patriarchy condemned the female fertility cults in the Holy Land and destroyed the sacred sites of the Mother Goddess. The female wave-form must be reintegrated into sacred technology or neither male nor female will ever be at peace again.

I stand on one side of the wooden crossed fence and begin radiating golden light as Mosheh stares at me. I walk close to the fence on which he placed his right hand before he became a lizard and ate me alive. I put my hand on his hand. He cringes and draws back slightly, becoming a balanced and untroubled young form of himself. He looks at me and a knowing passes between us. We are caught in time, in history. We move back to the time when we were essence together, before creation began. I see golden rings with seeds clinging to them, and then I see that he and I were created together. There are others around us who began an Earth drama then. We were created before time to come to this planet to serve experience. I immerse myself intently into the golden seed rings from before the beginning, and I let go of every attachment I ever had to a beginning or a time.

I choose to exist only in the rings, with the seeds, to dance the history dance until the lessons we need to learn about the people we love are complete. I return to that vibration before matter took form—the emptiness that is shared divinity. I see that this is another being who has not yet made peace with the father, and who is a destroyer of Earth, the Goddess. I choose to rejoin the anima and animus, and by that choice, I am catapulted into feminine form from the beginning of time, to return throughout history whenever that powerful molder of history—my male mirror—returns to Earth. I return with that soul until we make peace. When I can finally attain the knowing in my heart that he is no different from me, then I will have the love to offer him his release from our self-created cage, a cage labeled Chosen People.

Hurry! Hurry! There is so little time. I return to a time when I tried to make peace again.

Now I am a fish. I am an ancient fish emerging out of a coral reef cave. My fishfeel is heavy, like a lumbering roll that is balanced in the water. I am all grey, and I like to rest in place while only my eyes roll. I carry all the weight of the Piscean Age. Even the water I exist in is heavy. My fins are in the current, feeling what is going on, and my eyes are always watching in the water. I will not be going back into the cave. I feel energy in my heart and throat.

Emerging from the rock like a plug that is pushed out through a hole, I see that there are other fish like me in other holes who are also emerging. We are all energy together, those of us that are emerging, that is. We must be careful not to get eaten by bigger fish or by the octopi out there. We are rolling and lumbering, like we are coming out of a deep, deep sleep. I sense that this scene is an ending, as the primordial crustaceans were an ending. As we move out, my third eye begins to hurt.

Ah! I see a king wearing a red robe and riding on a white horse—a Crusader. Ah! The man on the white horse is the old White Knight, the mighty warrior force of the male world. My third eye really hurts from seeing this repeat, cycle after cycle. Men control the center, everyone knows that, but what to do about it? Now the Crusader's sword penetrates my third eye, as if the sword of destiny is piercing my center brain. He stabs me in my pineal gland.

The spear turns to silver, liquid mercury as the point drives deep into my brain. There cannot be any contact between that sword and my brain, so the blade goes deeply in and my brain separates. I feel like there is some big secret that does not want to be told, ever. The secret is contained in all the pacts in blood which the White Knight has ever made, and the image I see is a red, red rose which wilts.

The rose shrinks into a circle of guardian beings, a coven of thirteen witches who are continually killed by the White Knights. We are together in a circle, agreeing to protect each other by going into the Earth as a group. We make this decision because of the Sacred Blood—Ichor. But this action is negative because we act out of fear, out of a habit of giving in to the forces of the White Knight. We abdicate, and the message goes out into the world that the White Knight is a "good" energy, a crusader, a protector against evil. Again, the contest is between my oppressor self and my oppressed self.

As a witch, I want to know about my own choice to go underground! The rose with white light is exploding as I see some green Masons. So I just float, and my feet go straight up! The trouble is, all we have known is a world controlled by males. It is just like the eternal confusion caused by thinking of ourselves as sinful instead of a blessing to Earth—we started our thinking in the wrong place!

I have knocked twice on a door that goes right into my third eye. The third knock is into the quartz crystal essence of my blood, and I am exploded with white light. I get in the pineal gland, the most hidden place on the planet, the central point of emergence. It is the inner room where our stellar selves meet with our Earth selves. I do not look back, and I expand into the blackness within.

The door is opening. I see a womb, and a tiny baby inside the womb, the deep and protected place within. I knock three times, hearing a loud, resonating knock in return. I see a time wheel that looks like old clock gears which are turning, and I know that this means I am ready to let go of the last three or four thousand years of male control. I am just too tired to go on with the patriarchy anymore. I cannot turn the wheel once more. We needed all that time, but I cannot go around the wheel again. The fish! They are vibrating!

I go back to the coral reef with all of us fishes half in and half out of our rocks, before the White Knight came charging along. Why, he needs to get off his horse and quit acting like he is doing deeds for us! He was the healer of so many, the architect of our opportunity, but now he needs to heal himself! His plan will not work if he just goes charging along, doing all that great stuff. He is so driven all the time to move quickly forward and not to look down at who he is riding right by—himself. He needs to get off his horse. He needs to know that there is no worry now. We are feeding the sacred places again. We are exposing all the old pacts and secrets, for they only existed in time.

We begin to swim out and enter the channel, and we instantly realize why we were chosen to be here in the first place! We begin to play, two by two, one on top and the other below, and then we swirl madly around in a circle as if we are the Moon spinning. There are not three of us, there are not two of us—no trinity or duality. We are together; we are the motion of spinning in time which is beyond annihilation. You do not have to fear your identity, your survival, your reason for coming into form. We, the fishes of Pisces, pass you on now to a resting place, a heaven where you are beyond the abyss, and everyone and everything that you thought was your abuser becomes your guide.

WERNEKE © 1989

GOSPEL OF MARCION OF PONTUS

Chapter Nine

ISAIAH & MARCION

We are on the threshold of a fusion of the Earth with the stellar self—the part of ourselves that is cosmic. This rainbow bridge is a critical leap. It is a fusion that is the chirotic point, the moment when God and Earth are united into a magnificent column of white light. Do not look back! Do not grab for a rope! Do not reach out for your addiction one more time! This is the edge of the abyss to the divine flight of knowing evil in the midst of the search for true goodness. This leap stupifies the demon—your own sense of limitation.

The first step over the bridge to the other dimensions is development of a divination skill, a tool to enable you to lose yourself in the present moment—the gateway to infinity. For some, this divination skill involves the practice of attuning to the synchronicity plane by carefully observing events around themselves which reflect their inner selves. For others, divination is the practice of being in touch with the macrocosm/microcosm by means of astrology, regular ceremony, or tarot. We escape the limitations of third-dimensional time and space by means of astute observation of the links between times, places, symbols, feelings, relationships, and species. Then we are prepared to know symbiosis with the divine, with all that is.

What holds us back is that we actually know how powerful symbols are, and how great we really are. We are afraid that getting bigger will separate us from a life we have always known. But we have reached that magnificent and dangerous time when we have manifested our own inner power outside of ourselves—as nuclear fission. Now we will have to choose to expand, or we will collapse in on ourselves like a black hole, like entry into negative space/time. We can actually remember that we are able to access power by means of non-rational divination skills. Cosmic creativity, and the acquisition of dimensional magical skills, will characterize the next age.

It was the point of realizing this for myself that I was absolutely ready to be truthful with myself: I have been in the midst of a holding pattern ever since I recalled the

Vision of Isaiah in the Temple of Solomon, an experience which was published in Eye of the Centaur *in 1986.*

I do not believe that I was Isaiah or any of the other beings in my creative writing. If I were, I would be required to believe that I have some literal connection to my archetypal memory bank. In fact, I know very well that my only literal existence is my life at the present time. If I were to say that I was Isaiah, then I would also have to be St. Augustine, the Mayan at Tikal, or the paleolithic owl priestess who took on the tiger as her lover. But it is true that, when I have accessed any archetype from my inner self, the archetype has challenged me to integrate its numinous and wholistic form.

When I accessed the prophet Isaiah, I began a crisis of consciousness which I have only recently resolved. The power in the prophet's body was stupendous, and my physical body had to change to hold such energy and not become ill. Many theologians believe that Isaiah announced the coming of Christ. Yet the Jews as a body did not declare that Christ was the Messiah. The integration of Isaiah with my present self puts me right into the center of the Christian-Judaic conflict. I do not believe that the Jews are the ones who missed the Big Event—the insidious result of Christian projection on the sacred Hebrew scriptures. I welcomed looking at the heart of this two-millenial conflict with my own vision. More challenging from the perspective of my own Christian background, Isaiah was the crier against the evil empire of his times. I knew that the main reason I accessed this great prophet was that it was my time to manifest a prophetic role in my own life. Otherwise, I would not have been gifted with such a magnificent vision of this great man in turmoil. It is now time to return again to the prophet Isaiah for more wisdom, as we proceed bravely forward, not looking back lest I become a pillar of salt.

I see a shepherd. I see a white shepherd's robe which shrouds the face. The sun is hot, my face is scraggly and oily and bearded. I hold the shepherd's crook as I stand on a high ridge overlooking the Valley of Kedron. I stand looking at the river and trees, and the structures of mud-brick, as the sun reflects flashing light on the river.

I am a sheepherder, a member of the most sacred quest. I am a watcher for each person, for each soul of this valley. As I stand here, I am deep in meditation about being a watcher. I begin by connecting the energy in my spine with all my people down in the valley. As a watcher, I also feel the other dimensions, which seem like bird wings on my shoulders. I stand like a great eagle, with the other dimensions behind me and the world of my people in front of me.

I must remain connected to both dimensions. If I lose one of my sheep, then all is lost. That is my teaching. In the village below, Jerusalem, I am the Hebrew high priest, Isaiah. I hold the energy of each person centered in the Temple of Solomon. Then I open the back part of my body—spine, shoulders, the back of my arms and head—for there are receptors back there, and I hold these receiving points open to the other side. I am standing here now because it is time to connect with the other side to see what the other side has to say about my people. I am very worried about my people because I can see that we are going to be invaded soon by the Urim Shamash—the invaders from the other dimension. The Urim Shamash will manifest on the Earth plane as political invaders from the East, from Babylon, and their armies will invade my people. I am deeply worried about what will happen.

I am a seer and I can look forward in time. I see that political invasions happen on Earth because of multidimensional invasion. This is a reality which I observe but do not understand. I am standing here because I want to know how the process works. My own desire to protect my people on Earth blocks my ability to comprehend how the other dimensions cause events on Earth! I cannot see clearly into the other dimensions as long as I am obsessed with what happens here. In this lifetime, I invest much energy in trying to change the flow of history. We are the Chosen People and the gods will intervene, protect us, and control our reality. So then why are we on the verge of invasion? I stand here in my truth. I am ready to see the larger meaning of this lifetime.

In this lifetime, I function as high priest of the Chosen People, which means that I protect them. However, my higher self is trying to give a teaching in this lifetime which I am able to manifest in my scripture but which I cannot take into the sanctuary of the temple. The Temple of Solomon is a large square block, and inside the temple, there is a smaller block with a cube inside. All three of these forms are of equal dimension, and are equivalent to the time-dimensional coordinates of the divine/cosmos. This is the center of the universe, for the divine expresses in physical form according to these coordinates. As male priests, we contemplate this form in the temple and with prayers. We breathe the power of the word into our times—the Age of Aries. We are chosen by Yahweh. Life is filled with all manner of evil and, according to the prophecies, God will send the Messiah so that the wicked will be punished. The Earth must be purified, just as when the Flood occurred. As high priest, I am the vehicle for that teaching, but my soul wishes that in the time I live—756 BC—I would implant the naming of the coming Christos into the source, the temple.

The earliest Christos awakening has already begun. As keeper of the temple, my consciousness is attuned to the sacred temple form which is cosmic. I cannot ground the Heart of the Christos into the Temple of Solomon because the rock beneath the Holy of Holies is devoid of geomantic power. I can feel Earth energy—I felt the white-light column from Earth to sky when I had a vision in the temple—but now the Goddess has removed the power. The Chosen People are part of the evolutionary process of the planet and the human race, a phase of the identity crisis of the anthropocentric world. Disconnection from the Earth always creates a race of wanderers. I do not interfere because the temple priests find wisdom in their covenantal agreements with Yahweh, and the real story of my vision—that I saw the Goddess above the Holy of Holies—was barred from the scriptures. My soul can see how my present reality is a lower form of the highest potential manifestation of my culture at this time. But my people have never had a home and temple until the last five hundred years.

I am standing, holding all my Chosen People in my mind, and I center that energy into the Temple of Solomon. I am ravaged inside about events to come. The other dimensions are pushing from behind me. The result will be the destruction of the Chosen People, unless my people purify and cease their evil ways. I will make myself into an electromagnetic connector between the sky and the Earth. If I can create the vertical axis now, perhaps I can attain greater wisdom.

I wish to view my times from the place of all-seeing consciousness, no matter what the final outcome will be. I must enter into the fourth dimension, the timeless abode of my soul, to see beyond the historical/evolutionary process over time. I wish to see this process from the perspective of a higher dimensional interface. My body is becoming very dense. This dynamic is related to the interference on the Earth plane called the Fall. I wish to know. . .

My soul responds. . ."At the time of the Fall, Adamah was first given consciousness, the unique ability to contemplate the divine. This power was so great that the watchers who gave the skill were afraid of what Adamah would do with this magical ability. Made as Adamah was, in the image of the watchers, the priesthood was established to hold the power of the divine in the temple. The temple would function instead of Adamah as the source to the divine. Isaiah, because he was high priest of the Temple of Solomon, was a channel for the intervention of the watchers. All teachers who are called "shepherd" are channels for the watchers.

"During this period in history, a process of rapid genetic and electromagnetic encodement of Earthlings happened because, 700 years after Isaiah lived, the Christos energy was to be infused into the Earth plane. Christos's birth would rend open the hearts of Earth creatures, allowing many people to experience divinity as an Earth-born reality. The gods we have known from Nibiru are a planetary phenomenon because the inner cycle of Nibiru's orbit is around the Sun. Christos manifested the birth into this solar system from space, from another star. The Messiah birthed the Galactic Center into the solar center in 0 AD.

"Isaiah is fascinating because he knew Christos was coming and he announced this within the sacred Hebrew scriptures. But when Christos came, he was not recognized as Messiah by the Jews who held the main political control in the temple. The temple was destroyed in 70 AD, and the Christians claimed Isaiah's naming of the divine birth by saying that Isaiah was the Hebrew prophet who predicted the birth of the Messiah in 0 AD. This Messiah, Christos, was a planetary birth of the divine into humankind, and he could not be limited to being Messiah only of the Chosen People. The Hebrews were caught in identity at a time when the ability was not present to leap out of time. All hierarchies of people are control dynamics which are limiting, and are left over from a time before the Garden when Adamah first discovered identity, or became conscious of separation from the gods. In the agony of separation, Adamah cried to be recognized by the gods. He displaced his sense of self to the outside, and only now is the human race realizing this soul loss.

"There is no such thing as a Chosen People. By living with that belief and taking on the energy of the temple, Isaiah was encoded with a false belief system which he then lived out until he was destroyed by his false reasoning in that lifetime. The Christos energetic is fourth dimensional and is beyond separate realities, and the Incarnation is the reception of the Divine Son by Mother Earth. When Christos penetrated the Earth, all people who were invested in separateness—patriarchal Yahwist suppression of the Goddess—were unable to see that the incarnation of Christos was the end of separate, third-dimensional control. The Christians completed the third dimensional wall by claiming that members of their sects named the Messiah. Their sacred site became the Wailing Wall—the place where souls cry for an end to separation.

"Access to the fourth dimension frees the soul, while the natural control process of the third dimension makes the soul accessible to usage by entities from other dimensions. This is why an obsession with demonic possession reached a culmination in the Middle Ages, exactly when the Church limited human freedom and denied the Jews the most intensely. People were possessed because they had no access to the freedom which is meant to be their birthright.

"Within Isaiah, within his heart, was an awareness of new truth, and yet his truth was not personally fulfilled. He played out his role as consecrated high priest of the temple. His greatest source of resistance is coming from the temple training imposed upon him to encode him with a belief in separation. We ask to open the Emerald Records of the temple training of the Prophet Isaiah."

I, Isaiah, invoke a vertical column of light from Earth to sky, and as I do that, I break open my own temple teachings:

I was taught that there is a lineage of teachers in the bloodline of Abraham through David from the time when the gods gave the secrets to the priests—the Hebraic Ichor. The Davidic line is the line of the sacred kings, the race of Adamah made from clay and implanted with consciousness by the Nephilim, the angels, the gods who came down to Earth, the "watchers." I stand on this ridge like a watcher. I stand here with all the power of the gods who came down, and wings form on my shoulders. By being initiated into the temple teachings, my inner blood cells are encoded with the genetic implant of the Nephilim, making me superior. Because the blood of the Nephilim flows in my veins, I am the high priest, carrier of the bloodline of Abraham. I will continue the bloodline as leader of the Chosen People. I live this in my time, and I return now to my participation in the bloodline at a much earlier time.

The year is 8000 BC. I am a Priest of Enoch and there is no separation of dimensions in my consciousness. As I exist on this planet which we call Eden, I exist here with the energy and power of the ninth dimension, Nibiru. Those who can exist on Earth containing the full powers of Nibiru are in the ninth dimension. This only happened in the ancient days. As Priest of Enoch, I am watcher, I am Nephilim, and I am human. I am here to teach humans about temple-building techniques, Earth energy, grafting plants, and making alchemical forms on Earth in general. Alchemical forms contain cosmic energy. I brought seed from my dimension to grow corn, grapes, melons, and grains. I brought these in my bag when I came, and now I teach the people how to make dams and fields, how to grow plants, and how to make temples. I teach them how to bake bread, and how to use the residue of the lifeforms from seeds mixed with lime and salt to make stone for the sacred buildings. My gift to the people is good, for I save them time so they can create ceremony to be able to connect to the stars.

I love these people, the people of bread and wine. The fermentation I bring to them in the grapes and grain teaches them about the energy of the Galactic Center. I show them that bees are sacred messengers who suck the female nectar from the flowers to make honey. The flowers are in tune with the cycles of feminine Earth power, and the bees make the flower nectar into honey, which contains the exact, potent energy of essential life formation. I show the people how to be in the galaxy by eating honey. The great teacher, Khnum, gives exactly the same teachings in Egypt at this time.

I have the power to move forward in time. I look further ahead in time and I see that these people have obeyed me. The people did my work and mastered my teachings, but they found that following me was easy while knowing themselves was difficult. So, after thousands of years of teaching and gifting, the people were ready to know the divine. I send my awareness into the room where Christos is about to transubstantiate the gift of the grape into the complete cellular matrix of Earth. I come into a place of blinding light and shimmering beauty, for the time has finally come!

Christos holds the chalice of the grape, and the wine transmutes into blood. The bloodline of the sacred priest/kings of Earth is transmuted into a new crystalline matrix. Christos is hard to see because he is so filled with light. The Master has fire color in his arms and hands as he stands in front of the chalice. He holds the chalice and is very close to burning up, actually spontaneously combusting from the heat in his body created by the quickening in his cells. The Magdalena stands next to him, grounding the power from the sky deeply into the Earth by making her body into a magnetic receptor of the force of the vertical axis. His aura is cooled by a shimmering blue topaz light which keeps his tree form from burning up as he transmutes the blood. As Tree of Life, he holds the gift of the Nephilim—the fruit of the vine—steady, as he frees the Nephilim to return to Sirius and not control the cycles of Earth. He prays for the gods who came down to Earth.

"They interfered because they loved us. They are freed of all the sins known in this dimension—the sins of experience. I hold this sacred liquid which has come from experience and I accept this cup for my heavenly Father. This is the blood of the New Covenant, the gift of the cosmos becoming the river of God within the veins of all people."

In that moment, he creates a new heaven and a new Earth. As he holds the gift of the primordial oppressors, I see rays of yellow light coming out from his body. I see blue light around the yellow rays and I see his heart, which is very green and expanding into the cellular level. The Heart of the Christos holds the next 2000 years of pain, as each person journeys to find the green ray of compassion within.

This process is very painful for him. He quickens the frequency of the gift of the lesser gods so that these deities will no longer interfere as the higher dimensions open to Earth in a new way. At this same moment in time, Kukulcan is in ceremony at Teotihuacan, quickening the sacred honey through the hummingbird temple teachings. In order for this process to be successful, Christos must now absorb the next two thousand years of experience. He sees that the gods will continue to have access in the third dimension through repetition of old forms coming from the memory banks of humans. The gods will continue to interfere until every human can let go of them. On the Christian path, an apex point of attempting to integrate this new freedom will be the veneration of the bleeding heart of Christ. Hearts will be cut out and offered as sacred food for the gods in Mesoamerica. Humans will live out the complete intracellular memory of experience with the gods. Finally, they will release the addiction to higher powers outside themselves and take responsibility for their own growth. Those who clear the past will enter into the present age of Christos as many have done since Christos was sent by the Creator. In the twentieth century, we will be in the midst of a universal clearing of our addictions and an acceptance of our freedom. As Christos, I speak:

"My gift to the people is good. I encode the planet with the knowledge that now is the time to take my gift and own it. You, the people, must become the divine beings who were in the mind of the Creator in the beginning. I give my gift freely, but you still think you need me. Now you must see that I need to be free, that God needs to be free! My sacrifice must not be called upon much longer. For you do not have needs beyond the knowledge you already have."

He stands there with rays moving out of his head, his heart filled with all the pain of history. I accept his gift and re-encode my cellular matrix with the awareness that I no longer need to function as an agent of the Chosen People. As I did when I looked at the ritual at Tikal, we all must enter more fully into the pain of time by seeing that we carry out our lives, we are not the agents of others. If Christos was willing to be crucified in his time for his connection to the divine, then we must all be crucified in our own times for our cosmic birthrights. This crucifixion must involve the dying of an old self so that resurrection is possible. The Transubstantiation is most profound, for he begins with the gift of the Father God and encodes the fruit of the vine into matter—body of the Earth. The wisdom teaching of the Age of Pisces, the times of Christos, is that we cannot move on with evolution until we have accepted, integrated, and lastly transfigured, human history.

He stands there holding the chalice, and invokes an incredible power dynamic in a very simple way. He holds the chalice, for he is fully human, and his cellular essence is fully in communion with the cellular essence of humanity during his own time. He holds all of that, and brings all the souls of Earth fully into his heart. As he does that, he draws me into the wine.

I am in the wine! He transubstantiates the wine by simply saying, "I am love." He becomes the vibration of love and the air fills with pink energy.

I am in the wine! I am swimming through the wine, through the bubbles, through the red globs of the wine—particles containing all experience, which transmute into a white crystalline matrix. The experience is like swimming in the blood within my own heart. The crystalline matrix completes itself as the new blood changes the crystalline matrix in my being. The human condition will never be the same again.

But what happened? A few hundred years after the Transubstantiation, which forever altered the relationship of planet Earth to the divine, humanity fell into an alienation—an inability to feel the ecstasy of the Earth. This created such violence against the Earth and humankind that now we are on the verge of ecocide. But many people on the planet seem to be aware that a fundamental change occurred on the Earth two thousand years ago. There lies deep in our hearts a profound hope for the planetary freedom to live in worship and creativity. I return to the lifetime when the story of our new freedom was first hidden.

I am Marcion. This is 144 AD, and I have just founded the Marcionite Synagogue of the Christos. The message teachings of Jesus were being distorted by the Christian priests, the Hebrew rabbis, and the Roman Empire. I wrote my own gospel, the correct story of the Incarnation, when God sent his only Divine Son to Earth. Jesus refused to worship the old gods, even Yahweh. He refused to worship the powers that have always controlled humanity, for he was the teacher of oppressed people. In my gospel, I wrote the real story of Christos, separate from the Hebrew scriptures of my childhood. The new order of Christos will never be understood by people if he is confused with the old god, Yahweh. And, the exquisite wisdom of the Hebrew scriptures will be stolen by Christianity. Once the temple was destroyed by the Romans, connecting the Hebrew scriptures to the New Testament was a grave error. The truths within each equally important source were distorted.

In a moment, I will open my book to you for the records needed at this time. But before we begin, I ask you to let go of your agonizing confusions about the Judeo/Christian conflict, and listen to a new story about the savior of the world. The confusion is political, because the Vatican and the Empire have controlled the issue you care about most deeply—the access to your real story. The hidden secret you desire is your birthright. The primary lie—that the Jews missed the Big Event and the Christians are the ones who recognized the Messiah—has made straight thinking impossible. Neither portion of this is the truth, and the dual projection robs both Christians and Jews of a messiah.

Christos was born into the heart of the patriarchy, for that was where the healing needed to happen. But everything he taught was a radical threat to the beliefs on the planet at that time. By means of the Transubstantiation, he altered our relationship to the Powers and Principalities. That is why he had such a potent effect on history. But the true story of his teachings was so radically distorted that the truth could not be ascertained until 1795 AD, when the Earth received the gift of Sirius Teaching Four. We were bitterly divided by the Church as Imperium, for the Imperium was the way we could be controlled. You, the people of Earth, do not yet know about me because the destruction of my works was one of the most thorough book burnings in history. I am the ultimate heretic. But, a person's story never really goes away, and now is the time to tell my story.

I am Marcion. I have grown to be twenty years of age in my father's house in Pontus at Sinope on the shores of the Black Sea. My Hebrew father is a Christian bishop, my mother a Jew, and the year is 98 AD. As a child, we knew the story of the conversion of St. Paul, my father's close friend. We imagined the light enveloping our great teacher, Paul, as he was chosen by the Christ. We awaited the return of Master Jesus. We were mocked and persecuted for our belief in Christos, the Son of God. When will our teacher return to redeem the world? Alas, I am losing the great light of Paul as I climb up the cliffs to the ancient temple at Arataxta. I know of no other place of power on this planet where I can return to my animal self, my beast within who will know the truth no matter what any man says, even my own father.

Coming to the top of the mountain, I see ancient foundations of the great temple that was built thousands of years ago by the gods who came to Earth to bring the teachings of the stars. Around me are magnificent gigantic stone heads of the great gods which are half buried in the dry rocky soil. These figures have been staring out at the rising Sun for millenia. The crumbling entry arch with great lions on each side leads into the roofless sanctuary which is the gateway to the other side—a place on Earth where I can ask the gods to hear me in my pain. In the arch, I feel a thundering beneath the Earth, as if I have no right to enter the sanctuary, but I proceed. I feel electricity in my feet, and my eyes dart from side to side, seeing moving creatures as I walk slowly forward to the center point. My vision becomes like a microscope as I see, in minute detail, the writhing bodies of snakes, lizards, and large beetles. The sky fills with circling vultures, hawks, and eagles, and my heart is pounding, for I fear what I have done. But Christos invaded the sanctuary and drove out the evildoers, and so I will go forward with my quest.

Ahead, in an empty circle, a great dragon with fiery and foul breath, his lashing tail armed with great spikes, his clawed feet pounding the soil, awaits my arrival. I stop and look him in his red eye with a flashing yellow center, and I begin:

"Great monster from antiquity, I have come to ask you what my purpose is! My fellow Christians do not know about you, who are ever present in my being, like a brother. You will not cease to exist until the End Times. My people await the end and do not live in the present time. The evil stench of the Roman Empire sucks into all the forms of matter as the Christians abandon their power, awaiting only the end. I await no end, even the end that might be mine today. You, dragon, great denizen of the other world, tell me what it is I am to do with my life! I abandon myself, needing no End Times, only the fulfillment of the world."

The Earth begins to shake! Every cell in my body is quaking as my blood boils and my head rings. I am seized with a power I have not known before, and I scream a rasping, vicious scream from my woman within that shakes the heavens and Earth! I stand in my truth in front of the dragon, amd I see visions of all the people of Earth. A column of brilliant white light comes down and envelops me. I writhe in agony as I see babies burning with disease, women being raped and defiled in ways that are incomprehensible. All the waters of the Earth are boiling with foul pollution, the skies are filthy with poison. Still I keep my eyes open, not flinching from this horror, for I know that any person who asks to know the wisdom of the ages must look at the human vision of the end of time. Suddenly I shudder with terror as a black dog comes forth from the dragon. A huge woman bird flies at this creature from the frothing skies. The black dog howls in agony as the inner demon of the dragon of the End Times separates from himself, as if the animal's soul is vomiting. A new part—a jackal—chases the retching black dog right back into the dragon, which then dissipates into mist. The great harpy screams at me!

"You will write a book against the lies of the world. God has now entered creation as a result of the Incarnation of Christos so that even we can be redeemed from the chains of hell. You will write your book of the truth about the Powers and Principalities, and you will teach your word until the Goddess/self is freed from tormentors."

Suddenly all dissipates, and I am standing in the midst of the sanctuary. It is empty of what I have seen. I must create a story that will eventually shake the Earth like the great dragon of old, but that book will cause me to become a hated man in my own time.

Later, I do write the book, and here is what it says:

In the beginning there were three levels of existence: the God or Creator, the Demi-Urge, and the Hyle. The Demi-Urge is masculine, the Hyle is feminine, and God is indescribable, beyond form and gender, unknowable except in the experience of the Demi-Urge and the Hyle/Goddess. The Demi-Urge made the Earth and the Goddess rules the Earth. The Demi-Urge which manifested on Earth as "the gods who came down," desired to make humans in their own image, and did so with the agreement of the Goddess, who gave them clay for the work. The work was completed and named Adamah—Adam/Eve—who prospered in the beautiful Garden of Creation/Eden. The gods loved Adam, desired his total obedience, and came to Eden to ask Adam to worship no other gods. Adam was saddened, for this meant he could no longer adore the Goddess. But he was afraid of the Demi-Urge, so he abandoned the Goddess, who was enraged!

Consumed with anger, the Goddess rent Adam into many pieces and hid his phallus from Eve, who was in her image. Then the Goddess filled the sky with many more gods and goddesses, all a reflection of the parts of Adamah's psyche, so that Adamah could become conscious. She gave these gods abodes on the various planets and moons of the solar system, and she created a great river of stars containing the forms of all the animals who were parts of Adamah's psyche. The Goddess arranged the cosmos so that Adamah would be eternally immersed in her parts. These deities ruled the world from 2900 BC until 0 AD, when God saw that original matter had split into Goddess and Demi-Urge, convulsing the world in violence and pain in the midst of a cosmic struggle between anima and animus.

God the Creator felt compassion for Adamah and sent the Divine Son to Earth. Christos was to heal, to be a suffering servant with Adam, so that humankind would recognize that Christos came to heal the division between male and female—between spirit and body. Christos was to enter hell to free all beings enchained by the gods so that all humans would know that, from that time, no one was enslaved by any god. Christos knew that the gods would see him as a rival and envy him. He knew that the gods would crucify him. But there was no escape from the Great Mother. The blood of Christos would penetrate the Goddess, who would welcome his body—the new seed for a new Tree of Life. All beings put in hell by the gods were released, and Christos was crucified. Earth was shaken by an earthquake which darkened the skies of Rome for days as he arose out of the Goddess to return to his father. Humankind knew then that Christos was the Son of God who had come down into the Goddess to heal the dualism between body and spirit.

I finish my story and title it "Against the Demi-Urge." In 120 AD I begin teaching all over Syria, Cappadocia, Asia, Lycia, and Galatia. I even teach in Mesopotamia, where I am especially well-received. Their ancient legends are filled with the stories of the gods, and to hear of the liberation of Earth is good news. By 130 AD, my Christian Church is the largest Christian Church in the world, and I know that the time to enter Rome has come. This I dread, because Rome is the temple of all the gods. Jesus, Paul, and I are Jews by birth, and I have said a little about Yahweh being one of many gods, essentially different than the supreme Creator, the father of Christos.

I can no longer remain silent on the identity of Yahweh and the many gods of the Romans if I come to the Imperial City. The words of Jesus are being falsified, especially in Rome where the Roman Emperors have declared themselves as the gods, "the Imperium." Jesus said, "I am not come to fulfill the laws of the gods, I come to break the laws," but the Romans have interpreted his words as "I have come not to abolish the law, but to complete it." And so Jesus is being made into a puppet of the Romans.

I enter Rome shaking with the power I will take on. I am as disturbed as I was on the day of my vision of the ancient dragon. The city stinks with human perversion, as if the Demi-Urge is violating the Goddess in response to the opening of hell. The Romans hate the Christian belief in freedom from evil resulting from baptism. The good people are being stripped of their possessions, the city stinks of sexual perversion and disease, and people are dying in the streets. People step over babies on their way out the door to go to the temples of Mars, Venus, and Jupiter. Ministers of my church are healing the sick, but evil is a tidal wave.

I go to the Roman Christians to ask to be made bishop of Rome, so that my Church can grow there, teaching the words of Paul and Jesus. Paul taught the true Gospel, yet his wisdom has barely penetrated Rome. As I preach, I am heckled and called an arch-heretic. I do not understand this, for many doctrines are new. Jesus himself was a revolutionary. At this time, we are attempting to develop a ministry which will offer the teachings of Jesus to future generations. We know Christos will return when the world is ready to receive him. I see that I will have to enter into the dispute between Paul, who became Christian, and the Jews.

There has been a dispute about attaching the new Christian scriptures to the Hebrew scriptures because Paul and others were converted Jews. But if Yahweh is a Demi-Urge, then how can the teaching of Christos about the new order survive? Adamah made the Old Covenant with Yahweh, who asked him to serve Yahweh over the Goddess. But Christ loved women, the mirrors of the Goddess, and women baptize and teach in our Church. I preach and teach on the basis of the ancient testimonies from the Nazareans and Galileans. But the new works written in Greek and Aramaic of the life of Jesus tell a false story. The Roman Christians are burning as many copies of the original testimonies of the disciples as they can get their hands on. What if they attach the Hebrew scriptures to Greek and Aramaic sources on the life of Jesus? Later in time, the real truth will be completely distorted.

In my meeting with the leaders of the Roman Christian Churches, I go right into the crux of the conflict. I ask, "Who is Yahweh of the Hebrew scriptures? Who is Christos of the Christian scriptures? Yahweh says, 'An eye for an eye, a tooth for a tooth.' But Christos says, 'If anyone strikes you on the cheek, turn the other cheek to him to see if he will strike twice.' How can you say the God of the Hebrew scriptures is good when Jesus says, 'A good tree cannot bring forth evil fruit.' How can you justify attaching the new scriptures to the ancient ones when you know Jesus said, 'Put not new wine in old wine skins,' and 'Do not sew old cloth on a new garment'? How can you mix the ancient ways with a new creation when Jesus said, 'Those who are now last will be first, and those first, will be last'? The Jews hold many of their teachings in secret, yet Jesus said, 'No one lights a lamp to cover it with a bowl and put it under the bed.'

"Verily, as I meet with you today in the center of the Empire, you deny me my right to teach the truth, you deny me my right to communion, and you judge me as separate from the truth, thus acting out the law of the Demi-Urge. The Goddess will not be proscribed against. She has welcomed Christos into herself and, at the end of time, she will erupt out of your control. Like the opening of hell, those you call heretics will be freed. Their teachings will again free the people of the Earth."

They read me their verdict: "In the ancient wisdom of the Emperor Augustus, we declare that Augustus adored Jesus Christ as being born of the virgin, and Augustus refused to be called 'Yahweh' himself, out of respect for Jesus Christ, who is Lord."

This statement adorns the base of the obelisk which is in front of the gate to the pope's summer residence in Rome. These sentiments were the basis for the condemnation of me, the arch-heretic, Marcion. A large vulture eats the body of a black dog outside the doors of the Vatican.

I walk out of the meeting place of the early episcopate held in Hadrian's tomb, and I walk out into the sunny streets of Rome. I am dizzy. I am struck by a missile of magnetic blue light in the center of my forehead. Sirius Teaching Four, 1795 AD, encodes my cellular essence:

The powers of the Goddess are fully released from the underworld in order to create balance with the powers of the gods, the patriarchy. Slowly, woman within will awaken just in time to prevent ecocide, the suicide of planet Earth.

Chapter Ten

LAKOTA
MEDICINE WOMAN

"The crucifixion must involve the dying of the old self so that the resurrection is possible." What part of my soul was not yet crucified? I could feel the power within me preparing for resurrection. The male side of me appeared to be resolved. In the midst of all the stories, all the legends, all the cultures which form an intellectual matrix for me, I could see the same pattern being repeated again and again. In my male form of expression—as priest—I had gotten involved in not trusting the cosmos, in not trusting people, and in continually investing in the belief that priests knew what actions were best for the the world. I had continually played guardian of the secret and sacred sanctuary into which women were never permitted.

Now I am on the verge of releasing the power of the Goddess, whether the power is her womb or her fury. I do not care, for the ecocide of my times is the greatest sin since the beginning of time. There are many blasphemous stories in this epic, but nothing is as evil as the murder of the Earth. I wash my hands of all of my own male control of the Earth as a priest—a channel of the powers of transformation—no matter what the consequences. My heart cannot bear the pain of the betrayal for one more minute. I will look right into the Smoking Mirror.

I have participated in the cover-up lifetime after lifetime because I have remembered just how powerful the Goddess really is. I will release the power of the Goddess teaching whether the information can be tolerated or not. I must return to a life when that power of the Goddess—the matrix of the cosmos—was first compromised. We must bring light into every resistance, every shadow, so that we may truly know the power of woman's medicine.

I am moving into my solar-plexus area, where I feel a blockage that I sense is from anger that I could not express when I was once abused. I am angry at Dion and my fear lies in my heart. The fear feels like a river running from my crown, through my body, down through my heels and into the

Earth. In my third eye, I feel I would have been killed by him then if I had expressed my anger. I bring light into my crown, the fear runs down my body and out, and I scream a loud, ghastly scream that fills the room. Now my fear is collecting in a pool in my solar plexus. I go down into the gravel and growl, "Arghhh!" Now I feel a blockage on my left side where my hip connects with my leg.

I breathe into the feeling and send healing light into the flow of energy, into my legs and out into Mother Earth. I breathe deeply and hold, as I see the explosion of mana sending light to the area. Pow! I expel the anger lodged there. Again I breathe and hold. I look into my solar plexus to see if the area is clear, and there is still anger being held. Red residue in my left side is holding anger. I scream the word I really wanted to say to him then—"No-o-o-o-o-o!!" The word fills the room with a deafening, ringing sound and I cough as I begin to open my throat chakra. I scream, "Stop! Don't go in!" And I scream, "Monsterrrrr! Monsterrrr!"

I look at the etheric lines to see where I gave him the power of being my monster. I see that the location is my crown and third eye. I cut the cord that leaves him connected to me. My soul does not need me to see what that monster is, or whether or not I can even call love in and channel love power through my creative being. I excoriate that connection now to create inner emptiness, which will attract my pure Goddess self to me. There is a vacuum in my crown chakra, and I fill the void with purple crystal. I breathe the healing purple in and then I look to find the place in my heart that wanted to see him be destroyed. I breathe into that vortex of murderous desire and fill the need with forgiveness, for he served me in that experience so that I could experience living backwards. I can actually feel how he served me. I am filled with wonder at the release of inner hatred. I see. . .

I'm standing by a stream and I am very beautiful. I wear a white dress. My hair is long and black, my eyes are brown, and my skin is olive with oil on the surface. He is a warrior made of black obsidian, shiny, and he has an insect quality to his appearance. He wears a costume, a kachina costume which covers him. His skin is black and he has very beautiful eyes filled with curiosity, desire, and a possessive wish.

I am Diana of the forest and I am frightened of his lust. I am afraid that he will take my soul! My soul is my sense of being, my sense of who I am, and that is all I have. Once, a long time ago, a spider told me that my soul could be taken. As soon as I began my Moon time, a spider lived with me in a small, enclosed room. There was not even one window to the outside, and this was after I had lived as a child of the Sun, wind, and water. The other priestesses had put me in that ancient oracle room so that I could communicate with the spider. The spider gave the priestesses messages that could only come through me. I was used by them my whole life for their own purposes, and I became blind and rapaciously thin, like a sick sparrow. Before that, when I was still beautiful, I was released from the room after the spider told me that my soul would be taken away by a god who came down to the Earth. I believed the spider, and the stories the spider told me. I believed, because I was being used as a channel for the priestesses and I was not allowed to contemplate how I felt about the information that came through me.

Ever since then, I have been afraid that an alien power could enter me and take over my soul, but that is a lie. No one can steal my soul now, for I do not offer myself as a channel for information that other people want me to bring in at their will. There is still fear, though, because I was once bewitched, taken over. Once I believed that someone who had power over me could use me as a channel. I no longer fear being overtaken. Being used as a vehicle for the energies of others is a past issue, as I was once afraid of spiders but now am not. Now I know that spiders are the sisters who help me remember the ancient teaching that I have been asked to bring in this time. The spider is the astrologer's totem spirit, the teacher about cosmic cycles, the spinner of webs of cosmic connection.

The spider is the Earth creature which receives the Nibiruan vibration. She knows of all the pain we have suffered with Nibiru since we have become conscious. In the center of her tensile web, she is like a miniature Sun, attuning her being with all the planets and stars. She knows that we no longer need to fear being controlled. Yes, I was once bewitched and possessed. Great harm came to me, and I remember it well. But we are living in a new world now, in which the planet is again being gifted with the wisdom and power of magical healing. This new wisdom is being manifested by the Earth, not as a teaching from some other place.

Power coming through us is the only way. We must clear our resistance to owning our power, which is simply dysfunctional judgment from old memory. As we tap into these sources, we remember each trauma from the past. But we are also enlightened with a new truth that frees the mind: We can no longer be possessed or manipulated by energies outside ourselves if we have cleared all the inner hooks which attract such energies. We need no protection, no shield. We need a clear spirit.

But the body may not be clear even if the mind appears to be. My body still believes I can be taken over because of an ancient trauma that was re-encoded when I was raped in this life. I will let all of the memory go! I breathe, and let the pain flow all the way through my fingers, my hands, and into

Mother Earth. But still, the residues of pain are not all gone. My source of enlightenment is third-eye consciousness—opal light in my third eye. I move quickly into the flashing opal light where I see that, in this lifetime, I need to be a channel for an Earth teaching about going beyond the fear of star beings having once mated with the women of Earth. Cellular evolution is no longer accomplished in this manner, and if we do not see this, we will repeat it all in laboratories for genetic manipulation. In 0 AD, when the Nibiruans last visited, these teachers gave us special wisdom in a new way: babies conceived during the return of the Star of Bethlehem had special abilities to exist on both Earth and Nibiru. But sexual union with Nibiruans did not occur. Sexual interference exists on the astral level. This invasion is being dealt with over time, and the apex of the fear surfaced in the witchcraft trials. Medieval maidens dreamed of being taken by a succubus in the night, but this extraordinarily real nighttime drama was an example of the power of the subconscious mind to project inner fear. The legends of Dracula were a similar manifestation.

I need an etheric opal implanted in my third eye, so that this teaching can be clearly seen and brought in. The news of our absolute liberation from possession by entities in other dimensions must be transmitted into the cellular frequency of this planet. We must become aware that fear of possession and control lurks in the deep memory bank. The collective subconscious mind creates much of the community reality we live in. The primordial memory of the use of woman for the satisfaction of male lust causes the same abuse now. The rapist becomes infected with a godlike sense of his own power, and this superiority complex is a primary block against the power of the Goddess. There are countless traumatic memories in men and women of both using others and being used themselves. Part of moving beyond this block involves remembering how rape began. By clearing such deeply buried memories, we can agree to cease an activity that all participants loathe. The men need to be freed from their own lust and from the inflated energy triggered by women who fear the abuse. The women need to be freed from their fear! We cannot grow wherever there is fear.

I see my opal now. The stone is deep within my pineal gland, lighting my inner mind with a blue-green ray. It can be activated only by better understanding the original people who acted out this genetic experiment with us on Earth. The gem can only be activated by understanding the process of Nibiruan evolution on Earth or elsewhere. As long as we believe that the archetypal form of the outermost planet of our solar system is frozen in time, and that the hologram of the intervening gods is unchanging, then past experience cannot be understood and cleared.

There were at least twelve different civilizations that did this seeding, and I only have access to the civilizations in which I had direct involvement. To clear planetary blocks about this issue, I must first clear my own blocks. I see the beauty in the fire of the opal. The jewel flashes a pure, peridot green, and I follow the ray of light to a door that says, "Starseeding—Pastlife."

I open the door and see a humanoid being about three to four feet tall. He is called Non-Non, and is from Io, one of the Moons of Jupiter. I knew him 300,000 years ago! We worked with glass vials filled with mercury in a laboratory on Io. On the mercurial surface we reflected light from Andromeda Galaxy, our home. We brought to Io an essence to be seeded into this solar system. These photons were a matrix of soul/spirit material that was coded 2010 AD.

In the beginning, the Tree was revered as the gift from the gods that symbolized the ability of Earth to nurture life. These magnificent life-forms are the circulatory system of Earth. Their veins circulate the water and air of solar energy, and they are the sacred symbol of immortality which was placed on Earth as a gift, in hopes that the people of Earth would never forget to protect life. In the vegetable kingdom, a tree is the same as a human in the animal kingdom. But, over time, the people of Earth forgot the meaning of the sacred Tree. They lost the magical teachings about how to nurture the sacred sites which balance the deep watercourses with the solar winds to keep the Tree of Life alive. They began to believe that the Tree was the source of individual immortality, but actually the roots and branches are the source of resolution of the duality of the goddesses and the gods, the Earth and sky.

I see a giant oak tree with huge, perfectly balanced limbs, branches, and leaves on the top of a round hill. I stride quickly to the top of the hill and stand in front of the tree as I become aware that the root system of this great tree is puny. My legs and groin become the root system as I stand in front of this magnificent oak tree. My gut and heart are the same as the trunk, my throat and head are the branches and leaves. The root system begins to grow into the soil with great throbbing power, and I speak from a source that goes back to the beginning of our symbiotic formation with Nibiru. These are the Green Records of the Tree of Life.

I am Dion, the stellar male self of Barbara, usually only encountered when visiting the stellar home. However, she has asked for an opening of the Emerald Records of the Tree of Life—the bringing to Earth of woman's medicine from Andromeda Galaxy. So let me tell you the story of my relationship to this woman who now lives the life of Barbara on Earth. This is the story of the original splitting of the animus and anima on Earth. Within this ancient legend lies the healing of the stress between male and female.

We first brought you the Tree as a primary teaching about war for your whole solar system. From the great spiraling galaxy, Andromeda, we observed wars in your solar system caused by beings from the Orion galaxy. The men from Orion tried to eliminate life from your solar system, called Maya by us, out of pure jealousy! The Orion scientists assumed that Orion was the only location of life and civilization in the universe, just as Earth now believes. This is cosmic ego. When Orion saw life on Mars and Earth, the scientists were enraged! Great was their force—the force of I AM—and Orion decided to eliminate life elsewhere. Orion was to be the only conscious civilization in the mind of God, the chosen star.

Orion destroyed life on Mars, and many people hold the ancient memory bank of those wars. Earth astronomers have now sighted and photographed a mile-high human face on Mars that is staring at Earth. This face is in the midst of an ancient temple complex with pyramids and a great henge which very much resembles the henge of Avebury. Soon, Earthlings will travel to Mars and discover that a civilization existed there which was destroyed. Two countries who are enemies on Earth will send a joint exploration ship to Mars and see that war destroyed it. Mars was the Roman God of War. In 1992, the scientists of the Soviet Union and United States will cease destroying Earth once the history of Mars is recalled.

The Tree of Life was given to Earth in the hope that this symbol would remind Earth to never do what Orion did to Mars and attempted to do to Earth. Mars' atmosphere—all that was required to sustain life—was destroyed in a nuclear winter caused by atomic bomb detonation. Many on Earth remember the event very clearly. It is impossible for us—visitors from another galaxy—to ever know Mars again! That is loneliness. On Earth, life can connect with galactic forms. Humans can experience the perceptions and feelings of the stellar body, worshipped as the KA by the ancient Egyptians and explored in the kachina ceremonies of the Hopi. Do not ever create such cosmic loneliness for yourselves, because your stellar body is your unique knowing of creation. If humans destroy Earth, we cannot come to Earth from the stars, for we visit you on Earth by manifesting our selves in your own minds. What if you are not there anymore?

I created the Tree in the laboratory along with other new lifeforms, and the stellar body who is also Barbara agreed to manifest such forms on planet Earth. All humans have known such participation—the Goddess who willingly births the lifeforms desired by creation. But these galactic functions by humans who inhabit Earth involve the splitting of the soul into the anima and animus, for that is how existence takes form. Therein lies the pain of life. This separation is healed in orgasm. The desire for this union of the anima and animus fuels all sexual union. The soul of Barbara became a fragment of a portion that was a combination of both of us, for all life is both stellar and earthly. We once resided in the same body and then we were in ecstasy. But when she came to Earth, the anima was split from the animus to fuel the fires of evolution, to create movement. She then had, as all humans have, the freedom to manifest male and female bodies so that she could know her own soul. The records of this story are on Io, the home of the Galactic Federation, for this solar system and this story still exist in the legends of Isis, who wanders Egypt in search of her male part.

Now, Barbara's pain comes from both my need to know Earth and from her confusion about that first time when she awakened to her separation from herself—the primal duality. I visited her as her animus so that she could know me. This is why all knowing of stellar self is essentially sexual on Earth. You can only find your other side when lost in orgasm, the energy which causes the Tree to reach for the sky and to drive its roots deep into the Earth. This spiral energy exists in the very center of all galaxies. The spiral form of Andromeda, which is seen easily from Earth, is a mirror of the Milky Way Galaxy. The Milky Way teaches Andromeda Galaxy about the orgasmic spiral, and Andromeda teaches the Milky Way about how matter comes into form. A child was born of sexual union which occurred on Io, and then the soul of Barbara came, with the child in her womb, to begin her first experience on Earth. She will complete this story, her truth only from her own experience. I merely seeded her.

In this lifetime as Barbara, I have a residue from this primal sexual experience that makes me prone to have my power taken away by men, to seek to unite with men, for otherwise I feel incomplete. My heart tells me I still have a need to clear. The need has to do with changing from human to animal form. This is primal shapeshifting, which is one facet of matter going into form. I once had an experience in which I changed from human to jaguar form and I did not possess the cellular energy, the body power, to undergo this transmutation. Part of me got caught in the jaguar. But now I feel I must find peace with that animal's energy until the oneness occurs. My whole heart is filled with fear. I breathe into the emotion. I am willing to feel the shapeshifting, and I blow it out. I have felt for so long that I gave part of myself to the jaguar, lost part of myself to the spider, lost part of myself to a man; but these are all the fragments of self I am looking for! I need to reclaim these aspects; I want them all back.

I want to see the face of every animal form, every elemental form, every demon, every devil, every priest, every priestess, every human being, every extraterrestrial, that I have given my power to. I want to see anyone that I believed made me think I was not beautiful, equal, whole, or complete. I want to review all the past, and I want to reclaim the light I left with each one. I want to start recollecting the fragments of my light. I see all the facets of my being, and I roll the images of the facets of my soul into an enormous golden ball. I breathe all the parts of my soul back into my solar plexus and start breathing and pulling in every single fragment of self still hanging in time and space. For that was past and this is now. That light belongs to me, and I breathe the radiance in and feel my own love for the cosmos. I release my belief that any union I have ever known would betray me, and my trust flows back into me.

I feel the replenishment of my energy, the life-force coming back, being fed from the solar plexus to the heart, the throat, the third eye, the crown, the liver, spleen, and root. I breathe in, hold the breath as long as I can, and I move the wind out, so that every cell absorbs my radiance. I feel my physical body with the power it needs to transcend any dimension. I allow the force to ignite my root chakra, solar plexus, liver, spleen, heart, throat, third eye, and then I go three inches behind my forehead to the cave of Brahma, the pineal gland.

I walk inside the dark cave carrying my radiance, my torch, with me. In the back of the cave, in hiding, I find my Goddess self that had not collected the fragments of her own beautiful being. I see the love that she has for me. I open my arms and allow her to step forth. She is blonde, light, all light. There is a halo of light, a crown of leaves around her head that is made of opals. Her name is Alinni. I feel her come into my arms and I hold her. I feel her energy go into every single cell of my body. I feel the grief of not having collected my own light wash away, and I feel the grieving being replaced by joy. I flow with Alinni gently out of the top of the cave, and into the universe. I go to the sea of light as I feel the connectedness moving through my being from the sea of light in the the universe. I swim in the stream of the Milky Way as if I am the Earth nursing the galaxy down through myself. I loop the shimmering stars through Mother Earth, and then back up through myself, like the figure eight, like Avebury glowing in starlight at the New Moon. I feel, for the first time in eons, the love that every lifeform is sending through me. I feel the honor of what I am doing, the road I have traveled, the burdens I have borne, the love that flows to me from all creation.

I feel the centeredness, the serenity. I feel the waveform from my crown to my feet. I am air, earth, water and fire. The whole of the universe is my desire. I want to reach the stars, to kiss the sky, to love the Earth. The time is nigh that the Goddess within me does breathe and grow. The love and beauty of my selfsame soul touches the sky, brings that within, becomes my own exalted friend, as I honor the light and the beauty that is mine. And then I begin to take form into a lifetime of unity, into a lifetime when the culture I was born into was so worshipful of Mother Earth that I was able to live a whole life with no division between the anima and animus.

I see a small, bread-loaf-shaped habitation which is constructed with skins stretched over a frame of willow or larch poles. I live in this home and I sit inside holding my infant. My baby is wrapped very tightly and I am encased in tight blankets. It is a cold winter, and the baby is suckling as the wind snaps the frozen skins against the poles. He is about six or seven months old.

The elements are very primal and we feel them very intensely. We are wrapped up tightly together because of the bitter wind. I feel abandoned. We are waiting for our men to return. There is not much else I can do but feed my baby. My people are not hungry, there is still food, but keeping the fire going is difficult. My main interest is to keep us warm. I am young, only seventeen, and this is my first child. My body is very strong, vital, and healthy.

I am worried about where all the men went. My husband is a warrior and he is gone with the other men. Normally, the party would have gone hunting, but this time the men have gone to war. That is why I do not know when my husband will return. I do not know what is going to happen. Our warriors are fighting the Shawano, and we are the Lakota. I live on the plains in the center of the land. We travel great distances and I have a sense of my geographical location. I am just west of the Big River. We are the people of the Sun. In other places, nearby, people of the Sun live. There are other villages nearby and we are all usually in communication. But right now we are all in our homes, and the weather is cold. We must fend for ourselves without men.

This child is the son of a warrior. He is very healthy and I am very proud of him. I am proud that my first child is a son, and he has a great future for our tribe. But this is a strange time. These Shawano people never used to come here. Their people used to live further toward the rising Sun, but now members of the tribe come here to hunt and travel through our land. The intrusion is disturbing our village confederation.

We have many villages on this plain and we have been people of peace. These people are pressing on us from the East as their tribes have been driven out of their own homelands.

This is very confusing because, once upon a time, in the olden days, we all agreed on which territory was for which people. As for these Shawano, we know this is not their fault. But their warriors are invading our territory because they have been pushed out of their own land. We cannot allow this, but we do not wish for violence. Neither do they. Yet they need hunting grounds and places to settle.

Our land is very balanced. We have wisdom about how people can live in harmony with the animals, the trees, the land, and the plants. We let the old people die when they are ready. We lead the weak children into the wilderness to die or develop survival skills. We are equal with the animal. We do not take over animal territory and we limit the number of people in our villages. We do not take more trees than we require for simple shelter and fire. We only plant enough food for our village people, with some extra for wanderers and the hungry insects. This invasion has created imbalance, which is not right for the land, the people, the animals, and the trees. Just as the old people and the sick children must die, the Shawano must die unless they can find their place in balance. I am heavy in the heart about this problem as I hold my son of a warrior.

The men are gone away. I hear twigs snapping and soft footsteps on the ground. My astral body is very trained. I can jump out of my physical body and go to other places and other times. I sit quietly and fly out of my body to view the home I sit in. There are warriors—not my people! I take my child, cover his head, hold him tightly to my body, and I immediately leave my home. I go to the next home and pull aside the skins and say, "I-sha-na-ya-na-wa-na," which means " Shawano danger!" I go to the next tent and say, "I-sha-na-ya-na-wa-na." All of us do this. We move together to the edge of the village, but the actions are too late. We see many warriors, who have terrifying faces with red, white, and black war paint.

Suddenly these men all run after us! The warriors have long sticks which make thunder! I am clutching my baby and looking back, and I see the people falling with a look of shock on their faces, as if they are being exploded from inside just when the sticks thunder. A warrior grabs me by the shoulder, turns me around, and puts his arm heavy and tight around my shoulder. He grabs my baby with his other arm and throws my baby away from me! My baby screams as he lies on the ground. A warrior stomps on the baby. I am begging this man with my eyes not to leave my baby on the ground. This man's grip is so strong, I cannot escape. His arm is like iron. He starts to drag me away, holding me tight, and the last thing I see is one of the other warriors hitting the baby with a stone club. I see blood gushing out, and I know my baby is crushed. I pass out. That is the last thing I see. My heart is broken as my son dies.

When I wake up later, I find that I have been abducted. The warriors have taken the young women and a few of the young boys. The rest of our village must have been slain. The men are moving us west. Horses are pulling bundles along behind them, lashed to their sides with tree poles. The murderers are marching along, forcing the last of my village to keep up. The warriors watch us, making us move along with them. They are going toward the direction of the setting Sun. Stopping to set up a camp, they make a fire. We prepare food from the meat, vegetables, and grains taken from our village. The warriors are very hungry, but I am not. I will not eat, but then a man forces food down my throat. My breasts hurt from making milk for my dead son. I know what is coming next, as the warriors choose women.

The one who grabbed me is not the one who takes me. A young warrior who does not look at me takes me and rapes me. I leave my body while this is happening. I am in a state of utter and numbing grief. All I feel is the pain from losing my baby. I cannot talk—these people speak another language. I do not tell my sisters how I feel. We are all in numbing pain. We have lost our grandmothers, parents, children, and babies. We are so heavy in the heart, we just look at each other. The warriors even rape the boys. I am just sickened. This has not happened to these boys before. I have never seen such a thing. We are used in the way sick men use animals.

We are taken a great distance. Each day we walk and move. The war party is trying to get far away from our homeland because the leaders know that our men would kill every one of them if they caught up. I am used constantly by different men and I have to cook for my abusers. These people have been completely dehumanized. I can feel that these men once had their humanity, but that their identity has been totally stolen. The warriors are doing to us what has been done to them. I wonder . . .

After three moons, I begin to live with the loss of my child. The way I do this is to meditate on the plants and trees. Children are like plants. We are all like plants. We are born, we live and die, and we are reborn again. I know that my child's spirit will return again, just as I have once known his spirit. This teaching is very deep for me. I also live through the pain of the long journey, knowing that I might die, or I might not die. I am like a tree — maybe I will attain my growth and maybe I will not. But I know I will come back again and again, just like the deep soil sprouts a new field of grain every spring. My heart and soul have room to absorb much pain because of our teaching about life and death. Some are seasons of pain. Some are seasons of joy. This is such a deep teaching among my people that the message holds true for me as I endure intense suffering.

After three moons, we start to learn how to communicate. The winter ends, spring comes, and we have arrived at a territory where we can stop. Possibly there are few people here. Possibly the Shawano know the tribes of this area. For whatever reason, we set up a village near the river. This is a flat, muddy plain with much flowing water and few trees. This is the Platte River. The people who live on this river are fishermen. We can stay here for the summer without harm. We begin to learn to talk with each other, first with our eyes, then by sharing our words for the tools we work with.

I am chosen by one of the men. He pushes the other men away one day and he takes me into his teepee. This house has sticks which come to a point with an opening to the sky. The lodge poles are wrapped with buffalo skins. He lets the other men know I belong to him. Then we begin time and space together. My consciousness is that I am like the leaves in the trees which blow with the wind. I have blown a long, long distance, and now I have blown into a shelter. Now I am with another tree and we will grow together.

I am sitting in meditation wearing a deerskin dress with a secret pocket sewn into it. I remove an ancient turquoise from this pocket. This turquoise is a sacred stone that has been with my people for many years, and now I can finally sit alone and listen to the voice of the stone for awhile. I go into the Dreamtime by making spirals in my mind. I enter into a dream about all time before this moment. I make the four directions within the circular tent, using pieces of painted deerskin: white for North, yellow for South, red for East, and black for the West. I enter my heart and thank the universe for my place with this man in this sacred space. I move very deeply into the Dreamtime and I ask Wakan Tanka for my woman power again.

When these men took my body, I held my seed. We can control the time when we have children by watching the Moon and holding the seeds of the ancestors deep within. All of us have done this since we were taken from our homeland. I now release my seed and I call back my child. I do not do this out of my own need, for I do not need this child. Children come through us as gifts from the universe. We must survive. These are my people now and I will bring a child from the universe. I ask for the return of my child because, in my meditation, my child called to me from the other side. This is a very, very great miracle which ends all my pain.

We cannot release our seed if we are in a state of anger or fear. I go deeper and deeper into meditation. I enter a state in which, even if this man who chose me is the man who killed my child, I will still love him as father of the new child. I cannot know if this man who chose me is the one who carried me off or the one who crushed my child, because the war paint masked all the warriors on that fateful day. I assure Wakan Tanka that even if he is that man, I will still carry love for him in my heart and soul. We are the Lakota people, and we see our relationship to another as "I am yourself." We cannot bring forth a child if we are angry in our hearts. If we did that, the child would be unable to feel Wakan Tanka as its spirit enters Earth. The child would be like a tree with no roots that is unable to reach for the Sun. We only seed a child from love and wonder. These warriors do not understand that teaching. Perhaps their own women knew? Our children are very great, very evolved, for we are the spiritual teachers of this land. We are Lakota.

I enter a state of preparation so that I can conceive this child. Soon, six moons away, my belly swells and this man is pleased. This man is becoming more kind to me every day, for I use my woman power to please him. I give myself totally to pleasing him. As he learns that I am his center, his humanity returns. The pain of these people begins to leave their skins, their hands, their minds, their energetics. I see swirling circles of colors at their primary body energy points such as their hearts and stomachs. His red and brown is gone now, and I can see when his body is clear of the pain. I watch the rays of light, the waves of energy, passing off his body, and when his light is completely clear, I fuse my light with his during lovemaking, once, before our child comes. We become a star together and a new silence enters his soul. I spend much of my time in meditation, passing pain, passing anger. I am a being of great peace, filled with the wonderment of the black night sky. I am one of great endurance and patience, like a rock. If I just wait, then all will be beautiful again. I have complete trust in Wakan Tanka. I only ask when I am in need, and when I ask, my request is given to me. I am a priestess. But, in my tribe, all women are priestesses. We are the sisters of the Moon.

We modulate our energy with the Moon. We draw deep within, go into silence. Then there are times when we are shining. We do moon sign, moon talk, by looking into each other's eyes. Words are never spoken. When I was a young girl, I was trained how to reflect the Moon by the grandmothers. The waxing and waning of the Moon is the breath of the Goddess who draws in and exhales the winds of the Sun, the breath of God. The men exist to shine like the Sun, and I give my energy to this man so he will be the Sun as he readies to be a father. I wonder if he was a father before his heart was broken? Were his own child and woman destroyed by warriors? When he shines like the Sun, there is life. We hunt our game and fish, and gather the berries, with no worries. These men are receiving wisdom from us because they are willing to feel again. Their need to hurt others is spent.

I bring forth a child with the spirit of my son, but she is a girl child! In the survival teaching of this man's tribe, when a man's first child is a daughter, the child is put out on the rocks to be eaten by the vultures. The vulture and the maggot are the transmuters of life. There is space for many beings, and we all are transmuted by the vultures and maggots eventually. My center in the divine order of the universe is so absolute that I can even accept letting go of this daughter, this returned spirit of my heart, if her death is to come. For if there are too many female children, there will be too many babies born in the seasons and not enough hunters and warriors for survival. My heart is suspended because my first child was the warrior gift, and now my child has returned as daughter of the Moon.

I have entered into oneness with this man. My heart beats when his heart beats, and part of my respect for him is not to speak out of turn. So I am silent. My sharing of my heart is so pure that I see he is going to allow me to keep this child, and I lower my eyes as my daughter moves her mouth for milk. Now I see with my astral body that he is the one who killed my son. I could not have received that wisdom until he took my female child and accepted her. I am overwhelmed by this teaching: If I had not given from my heart to this man since the very beginning, he would not have chosen my female child, because he would have been incapable of feeling love for her. I followed the wisdom of Wakan Tanka and my daughter is saved. I have saved my own child by loving and not being angry in my heart. This is a great teaching for one so young to receive. In another life, this child will be my mother, and I will patiently wait for her to choose life over death. We will also have divine sight together in that life.

In my life as Ti-a-no, Water Woman, I became a great medicine woman. This child was a great teaching for the universe, the gift of the life-force. I held faith in that powerful life-force for the people, and for myself, during a period of great agony for the native people of the land. I made my heart large so that pain could blossom into total love. This was about 200 years ago. I was born in 1720 and I died in 1795, the period when Tecpatl, the Solar God, returned to the Blue Star, Sirius, and gathered the new teaching of the reemergence of the Goddess. There was much more suffering, more thundersticks, and great pain. The period was a time of darkness before the light. The worst pain that I experienced was my people being attacked by other native people. There was tribe against tribe, our people against the white people, and warriors against children. But the time has come to open the secret teachings of the Blue Star.

When Tecpatl reached the Blue Star, the Sisterhood of the Moon released the pain into water—Quiahuitl. White Buffalo Woman came to the men of my tribe carrying the Sacred Pipe of peace, the pipe of sacred red stone which hardens into granite in the Sun after removal from the Earth. This stone is the blood of the Goddess.

The time of trial goes on and on, but the Sacred Pipe is smoked, always signifying the patience of the people waiting for the time when the red pipe will transmute into white stone. There is much movement of peoples from their homelands, many thundersticks, much death, much disease. I simply use my power to love and heal. I have great wisdom. The power is given to me by my new people because I know the medicine of herbs and animal spirits. I watch the people coming and going. The seasons hold great pain and loss as our blood washes Mother Earth, and we thank the Earth for transmuting our blood into stone for our smokes for Wakan Tanka.

I am very close to my daughter, but she is also independent. I raise her until she is fourteen. She learns my ways, she works hard, and when she is fourteen, she is taken away to another tribe. I cannot control that part of my reality. I am under the rule of the Shawano. She is given by my mate to another tribe as a Maisu, a wife. Her people move a great distance away. She returns three times, once with two children, later with a third. I cannot leave to go to her, but my staying does not matter. She and I have moon wisdom. We are both stars in the galaxy, eternally, and we are never out of touch with each other throughout all time. All I have to do is look into her eyes to see that she has no anger. Our greatest teaching is to not hold anger, and the greatest joy a mother can have is for her own child to share the wisdom teaching with her. This teaching is later hidden by my tribe for a long time, but my daughter shares the knowledge with me. Because of the moon wisdom in her eyes, I am able to let her go with no pain, and we both keep Moon lodge at the New Moon, thirteen times a year. You will know when peace has returned to Earth when the New Moon lodges are again kept by women, and when the men manifest the white pipe after the Earth has been saturated with the blood of native people.

That lifetime was a time of great change, of great difficulty, and we gained a wisdom teaching about survival. Life and death, and coming into our own power through time, is the wisdom teaching I bring forth in my current lifetime. That teaching is the wisdom that kept me alive then and now. I knew in this life as Barbara, from the very beginning, that there are many lifetimes. I had this knowledge in early childhood, and the larger perspective helped me remain strong during times of abuse. I always knew that happy times would come again. Whole species were annihilated before my very eyes. My brother and I didn't even know that when rabbits died in the fields and did not decompose during the hot midwest summer, that this was a sign of a grave disorder. We lived downriver from Dow Chemical, and the chemicals in the bodies of these animals preserved them. All the while we lived in the midst of a new media culture in which the pain experienced in past lives was replayed daily at the movies and on the television sets. But, I have been sure that a time of Earth harmony and spiritual perfection would come again. Think about it . . . Every day now, you watch atrocities that once might have happened to you! All the war, rape, pillage, and plunder are being quickly rerun in front of your eyes, as if your own inner brain has become a video-cassette microcosm of history. That is because history is almost finished.

But, in my present life, I had forgotten the teaching about not holding anger in the heart, because there was so much anger around me when I was very small. This is a teaching that is only accessible to those who are protected against the corrosive effect of anger when they are very young, usually by a mother who is at peace. There has been no peace on this planet for mothers during this century of war. Then, as the child grows and begins to be subjected to experience, the child must have the means to assimilate its experience. The assimilation of experience is possible for children in a culture which values and transmits myth—the story of growth through time. History is not the story of the people, it is his-story—the judgment of males. History is a convenient invention of facts designed to keep the people in place. Myth, our story, empowers the people to birth their creativity—their participation in the divine unfoldment. The culture of the fifties in which I grew up offered no wisdom. There were no initiations, no ceremonial attunement to the cosmos.

The teaching of the Lakota medicine woman is very similar to the wisdom that was being given at the Light Institute in Galisteo, New Mexico by Chris Griscom while I was writing this book. Now this teaching about releasing anger from the emotional body is spreading through the world. We are beginning a time of death, pain, and destruction similar to the genocide of the indigenous people, only this time the experience is planetary. Our inner anger is destroying this planet. We all know this, as signaled by the mass cultural movements to let go of addictions—material abuses which enable us to hold anger. But if we do not release the anger, we are doomed. We must now see that we return many times, fully choosing each return, driven by the hope for freedom which is the destiny of our souls. We are not alive until we honor the need for survival, for survival is the key to a species-level redefinition.

For two thousand years under Christianity, we have come and gone as if asleep— a Piscean Age humanity stumbling through life as if we were still stuck in the primordial slime, as unconscious as amphibians not knowing whether we were on land or in water. When you come back again and again as if you have never come here before, you have no access to your own lifetimes of power or oppression. You do not know your own shadow, so you cannot recognize your oppressor from any other person. In my last lifetime in the Victorian era, I was like that. I woke up my own Victorian lifetime! We must wake up from our long sleep or we will not love the planet enough to save her, or to save ourselves. We must remember the Indian ways which lie deep within us all: If we take the soul of another human or animal, or if we harm another being, in the long run we will have to return that stolen energy. If we see that we return again and again, then we will not disturb other lifeforms. My wisdom teaching as an Indian was to be able to give away everything that had been taken from me until my soul was given back by the person who was my oppressor. My power of love offered my oppressor the chance to feel love again.

As Water Woman, Tiano, I observe that my daughter adores my mate. He is to her all the elements, the cosmos, the animals. He gives her his male spirit because she loves him so freely. I love him for that. There are deep teachings in this: The person who murders us is often the one who loves us most deeply. By allowing myself to release anger towards him, my time with him opens me for such great love. By not responding with anger, I do not steal my own capacity to love from myself. As for my daughter's relationship with her husband, she is well taken care of, and she freely loves her own husband because her father has loved her.

I move to my death. . .

I am lying on a bier dressed in white deerskin, beads, and feathers. I am in full high-priestess dress because I know when I will die. I have chosen this time of my death, and I am not even organically ill. I've decided that my teaching is complete.

I have asked for the ritual of I-ah-sha-ni-na-wah-ni, "the Eagle flies to the Sun," the ritual of Shawano passage after being teacher for the tribe. I am lying on the raised platform with rocks supporting the wood. Dressed in the beautiful white deerskin, I am feeling dizzy with wonderment about the energy in my body. My hair is braided, I am cleaned and prepared, and I am very beautiful. Standing closest to me are three medicine men covered with feathers who wear bird masks. One of them is the hawk, one is the eagle, amd the last is the raven. The birdmen are standing above and behind me. The eagle is above my crown chakra, the raven is on my left, and the hawk on my right behind my shoulders. All around us are the people, the grandmothers. The priestess who was taught by me sits below my feet. She is the priestess of White Buffalo Woman! And I am dressed as White Buffalo Woman!

This is incredible. Because of my healing and wisdom ways, I have been given the opportunity to bring to the Shawano the teachings of White Buffalo Woman at my death. I am Lakota—from the Ancient Ones—and I will give to the Shawano our deepest wisdom. The energy of the priestess at my feet is to hold the force of the red pipe. Each bird priest has a basket with a small opening at the top which he holds at his solar plexus. Each birdman will receive, in this basket woven of reeds from the river, the true teaching of woman's wisdom. Energetically, White Buffalo Woman is sending the energy from below me, through my feet, through my body, out through my head, and into the baskets held in waiting by the birdmen. As I give them my life, the Shawano, an ancient tribe which almost lost faith in the future, receives the Lakota high wisdom teaching about not holding anger. This comes from body/woman/Earth.

This is an amazing ceremony. The year is 1795. We see that the white people are going to take our spirit and our land, and will try to kill the animals. The white people had great council fires of thirteen states in the East and even used our Native American wisdom to create their own confederation. I am rushing all these visions from our seers through my body, as our wisdom about not holding anger is placed in the three baskets at my death.

I am going to go to the other side to Wakan Tanka, and I am shooting through my body a force, an energy which rushes through all my chakras, my heart. I am shooting all of my life-force from White Buffalo Woman, through me, into the baskets.

I become numb from white light, as if I am an electrical conduit, and I feel lightning go through my body. I hold the energy, encoding every cell with the liquid light, and I pass. I walk forward above my body, across the land where I became medicine woman, back to my ancient land by the Big River that I left when I was young, and then I go to the stars. My teachers welcome me with open hands. I am dressed for my return. The Sirians take me back when they see me, and they are joyful. Sirius shines my Lakota heart until I return to Earth.

The three baskets are buried deep in a cave, and petroglyphs are carved in the rocks at the cave entrance by the medicine men. A long phase of violence is about to intensify against the tribes. Our hunters and warriors will become strangely passive, waiting out the long siege. Our men will act very much like the Aztecs did at Tenochtitlan when Cortez arrived with ships adorned with great crosses, ships that were filled with disease and accompanied by a Catholic priest on Good Friday, 1519 AD. Each summer, the medicine men will return to this sacred cave until it is time for the resurrection. For two hundred years, the birdmen and Moon priestesses will return to the caves to pray for their people during the trials and tribulations with Waisachu—the white people. The Lakota will abuse themselves with fire water to hold down their justifiable anger. Alcoholism will be chosen over hatred. Ironically, as the time of healing draws nigh, the Waisachu will drown their own spirits in alcohol. The keepers of the Mother will contain the pain of abuse in their livers and not in their hearts. The Native American self-esteem will sink to a point where only death is desired, but still the keepers of the dream will not become angry. Their story will be seen in their eyes. Warriors will defend their women and children, but they will not hold anger in their hearts. At times the Waisachu will even abuse the Native Americans only because they are meek.

Beginning in the 1970s, the Native Americans began to communicate with white men and women who were remembering the medicine ways. The Native Americans began to teach white people of pure heart. The prophecies had said that these teachers in white bodies would come, and that these people would be capable of learning medicine ways once the new planet of healing, Chiron, was seen in the skies. At this point the spirit in the land quickened as the cycle began moving to a convergence. The white sons and daughters of the divine found their own parents turning on them for their medicine ways, and these children also had to learn not to hold anger in the heart against their oppressors—their own mothers and fathers. The medicine ways they had been given attuned them to the way Mother Earth expresses herself, and they found patience.

The greatest teachers in Peru, Mayaland, Australia, and Africa, who had been in seclusion for hundreds of years, hiding the most powerful medicine teachings within their lineages, were called out to quicken the Earth at sacred sites starting in early 1987. Teachers of new lineages discovered their power in sacred circle with them. The Nine Hells of the Aztecs, which was a phase of teaching about no more retribution—learning that the ultimate choice is to not become angry at beings the Creator loves—at last was complete. The time had come to open the baskets.

In May of 1987, the medicine men and the priestesses returned to the sacred cave of the baskets to read the ancient signs again. The baskets were brought out and carried in the long walk to Pine Ridge. At Harmonic Convergence, the Sun Dance was performed to remember courage. The pierced dancers went beyond fear, opened their hearts which contained no anger, and felt hope in the future again, as all indigenous people awaited the New Dawn. The gift was given, and the Red Pipe which contained all the pain of their oppression was given away to a Catholic priest—carrier of the cross. The baskets were taken into secret ceremony so that the priest could not steal the power for himself. On Harmonic Convergence, the baskets were opened, the peace force was dispersed to all four corners of the planet, and the Rainbow Warriors of Peace began a new age of knowing the spirit with no anger in the heart.

White Buffalo Woman, at the exact moment of the setting Sun on the last evening before the New Dawn, August 17th, was flying in a great bird, leaving the planet from the land of the Great Lakes. She, a little girl of a few years of age, was in the center of the purification fires of the passing age of technology. Like the elixir in the alchemical fire, she was found alive, magically sheltered by the lifeless body of her mother. She survived the time of fire to serve as messenger of the Goddess. The legend of Icarus, the male spirit who flies into the fires of the Sun, was reborn as a symbol of survival in these times. She was amidst the rubble of the end of the Nine Hells, her moon eyes peering out of the ashes.

THE NEW DAWN

WERNEKE © 1989

Chapter Eleven

MESSAGES FROM THE PLEIADES

We all exist as a symbiosis of our stellar and third-dimensional selves. Symbiosis is the living together of two dissimilar organisms. Such associations are advantageous or necessary to one or both organisms, and are so close that one body may be unconscious of the other. The organism may think it exists alone. You may think you exist alone.

Like the deep and resonant tone of a great organ in the sanctuary of an ancient cathedral, the sound of the stars is being heard by us now. And, as if they have been existing in a great mansion and are just beginning to realize that a tiny heart is beating in one of the empty rooms, the stars are now listening to Earth. This remembering of the story of Creation is a holometamorphic awakening that brings ecstasy to Earth reality. Suddenly we know that we do not exist alone. Our threat of self-annihilation is not so paralytic when we remember that we are not the only planet in the cosmos journeying to the divine.

We have reached that point when we must open to mystery. There is no other way. Remember, the male principle evolves, the female principle is everlasting. At this point, we are ready for ascension, for reunion with our stellar selves.

I first felt lonely when I realized there was a part of me that was located in a place far away. I could not imagine where this place was, but I began to miss that place more and more. As my loneliness intensified, my emptiness within got bigger and bigger. My maturation process was enlarging me for the capacity to contemplate infinity. More and more, I stared into the deep night sky, the place of truth which the Age of Enlightenment has tried to obscure by drowning the Earth's surface in artificial light.

In their modern ways of obsessive control, scientists sense that we will finally remember the truth by recommuning with the stars. They waste the resources of Earth to put men in spaceships. Scientists attempt to disprove astrology as they compulsively try to claim all space as a new laboratory for instruments of war and the technology of space exploration. But still the microcosm resonates with the macrocosm.

Beware, patriarchy! For in my crazy labyrinthian journey to the farthest reaches of consciousness, I reconnected with my stellar self. While you spent all your time and all of the resources of Earth's people on your shuttles, satellites, and rockets, I and the people remembered an ancient home. In your desperate attempts to control the next frontier, to find another land you could annihilate with your inner hatred, you also awakened the goddess of the sky. Now the eye of the Creator is fixed on you again. The ancient dragon has awakened. Let us return to Alcyone, central star of the Pleiades, said by the Mayan, Hunbatz Men, to be the very center of the Milky Way Galaxy . . .

This universe is astral blue and lime green. I see radiant light extending from a white building complex 200 yards away. I am standing on a pure white, polished marble step which is at the top of white marble steps coming out of a Greek classical building. The rays of light are sensual, and the shapes of the buildings are similar to Art Deco.

I am a woman and my name is Allini. I wear a silver robe which falls to the step from a jewelled catch on my right shoulder. The robe has slits for my arms. Underneath it I wear a sheer, long, draped pink dress which is very feminine. My sandals are silver and I wear diamonds. The jewels hang from my ears and sparkle in my tiara. One stone is set in a band on my forehead over my third eye. Another large, diamond pendant of 35 to 40 carats is on my throat, its diamonds set in platinum. My hair is straight, long, and black, and pulled tightly under the band. I have perfect, delicate, light skin, and blue eyes. My lips are thin and well formed, my nose is straight. You know me on Earth as a statue of Athena. I am a paradigm of feminine beauty. My hands are white, my fingers long and thin, and the diamonds sparkle, sending sensuous rays of color in every direction. We rarely have clouds here. There is always sunlight captured in the diamonds reflecting on the white marble.

I am standing in a courtyard. The building behind me has nine, forty-foot-tall, fluted columns. The people walking around are all wearing long capes of deep purple, astral blue, and green, which flow to the marble. Only those of the most clear consciousness wear diamonds. The other colors show different levels of spiritual growth. I stand alone looking at the courtyard and the people, and I am in balance, health, and peace. The climate and colors are perfect.

I see this universe in my pineal gland. The building in front of me is the Hall of Records. I watch the people go in and out. I can change my perceptions to see absolutely no people here, or I can tune into frequencies of people, or I can tune myself out. I am in contact with a very fast level of vibration and can move time backward and forward.

I move to the center of the Hall of Records. In the middle of the building is a pool with a water fountain surrounded by green grass, plants, and flowers. The scene is as beautiful as the most exquisite painting ever created on Earth. I am sitting infused with my own beauty and the beauty of this place. I have come here to meet a young man. I do not wait, for time does not exist. I am at peace in the midst of a total communion with my environment. There is no time or place. I can be either on Earth or on Alcyone as I sit here. I am simply a part of an energy field, just existing. When he appears, that is when he exists.

When I return, the people of Alcyone find me here, since I actually live on Earth at this moment. There are five steps down to the pool. First a unicorn appears, standing on a stairway; then the young man appears. He sees me and is happy as he walks toward me and sits down next to me. The vibrations are not physical like they are on Earth. This is a non-physical dimension and he is a visible energy field. He is young, handsome, and dressed in white. He is my peer. We communicate with our third eyes. I am welcomed back for a rest. My third eye is throbbing as he questions how I am.

I have come back because I am out of touch. I have been trying hard to figure out how things work on Earth. I have returned for more guidance about my search on Earth, and for the peace and harmony I feel here. I have returned to find a way to be more on Earth as I am here—the Goddess. I must manifest the Great Goddess on Earth, for I love Earth and the planet is close to self-destructing.

I come to this courtyard only when I have come for a gift. I am asking for the opportunity to take energy from this place to Earth because the Earth is changing now. I want to take this energy to Earth as others are doing. We have met here in the courtyard of the Hall of Records so that I, as teacher, may be given more instructions about how to resonate this energy field more powerfully on Earth.

He takes my hand, stands up with me, and we walk behind the pool to a cascading waterfall. There are stairs on each side of the waterfall which rise up to a temple. Overhanging trees and flowers canopy the stairs. He walks on the left staircase and I walk on the right, as we hold hands with the water falling between us. We walk up to the temple, which is made of a huge, open shell backed with white marble and blue glass. Then we walk up a staircase in front of the seashell to a raised pulpit. We stand together and turn around in the pulpit to look back down on the temple floor. Arches behind the seashell rise and curve like the inner bowl of the sky, and below, a throng of people dressed in green, purple, and astral blue robes is waiting for us. My teacher stands slightly behind me with his left hand in-between my shoulder blades, pressed firmly on my back. I feel like I am in the center of a star with energy waves moving out. I move forward, raise my hands, and speak to the people of Alcyone, central star of the Pleiades:

"I have returned from Earth to bring news to you. I have come here to make an announcment about the Earth. The Earth has become conscious of its time cycles at last! I have returned here to tell you that Earth succeeded in awakening sacred sites on Harmonic Convergence. Various humans felt the waveform of our beam on Earth! We resonated the Earth's core crystal into a correct resonance with the center of the Sun. The connection happened as the song of the Rainbow Warriors went to the Earth's core crystal. This set up solar resonance and then reawakened the Earth vortexes to the spiraling of the Galactic Center! There is molten iron in the center of the Earth like the center of an egg, and the liquid in the shell is in balance with the Sun. Now, Earthlings will reawaken ancient memories of themselves as Mayans. The humans will begin to feel our seven stars as their center, and our star—Alcyone—as their exact center point. For the first time in the history of Earth, Earth is in correct balance to its own Sun, and the stellar self of Earthlings awakens as they attune to their Sun as a star.

"I have accomplished my mission on Earth, which was to exist on Earth with many other star teachers as willing receivers of Earth energy so that this harmonic could activate. All will shift because this has happened. I am now able to return to you more frequently, to exist here longer, and to give complete reports about the status of the Earth. We will now have galactic consciousness on Earth. It has been hard to be lost on Earth for so long, to not know our origins as we entered material form. I will exist on Earth from now on in perfect contact with the Galactic Center, along with the other Rainbow Warriors. We remembered our origins once we were quickened. Like a new species coming into form, we woke up. Because the Earth-core/Sun balancing has occurred, the possibility exists for a being of our density to exist simultaneously on Earth and on a star, and to be conscious of both places.

"As all of you know, I have been monitoring the rocket technology on Earth. We have decided in the Alcyone Council that Earth will not be able to do certain activities in space. When space technology is for scientific purposes which will further the evolution of Earth, then scientists will be permitted to advance. Examples of such advances are the brilliant successes of Pioneer 10 and Voyager. However, as soon as space technology is utilized for military purposes, a different situation prevails, and Alcyone will block the militaristic use of space. That is the desire of the goddess of Alcyone. I am known on Earth as Nut and as her daughter Isis, as Artemis, Inanna, and Erishkigal. My power to save creation is enhanced by freewill support from Earth people who do not support the use of space by the military.

"If the men and women of Earth do not want to extend war into the skies, such conflict will not continue. People have long forgotten the dormant synchronistic law: that what Earth desires either assists or inhibits the stellar dimensions of the cosmos. Individuals on Earth have gotten lazy because the methods of stellar fusion have been lost to them for a long time. But fusion was remembered during the spring equinox of 1989. Now the Mayan temple complexes are being opened by the Rainbow Warriors, the bridges to us are being rebuilt, and people are remembering how to attune to the stars again. At the spring equinox of 1989, when Mars and Jupiter were conjunct the Pleiades, the Mayan initiatic centers were opened. Earth people are remembering stellar language, remembering the cosmic symbols, and if the ancient bridge can be reconnected—from the pineal gland in Earth people to the Galactic Center—then war will end.

"The difficulty with Earth is that the secret covens of the military are much more evil there than most people can imagine. At this point, we have succeeded in the following way. We have reached the most influential military scientists and political leaders, and these humans know we are real. We have told them that we will not allow military use of space technology, and the scientists are really dumbfounded. First of all, scientists know that UFOs exist, and we have programmed some of our messages into Earth computers. Humans can't stop us. The scientists are so disturbed by our interference that they are considering polluting the atmosphere with radiation, specifically plutonium. The scientists know that the one element which Pleiadians cannot tolerate is plutonium, and they are actually considering releasing plutonium even if it destroys all life—including their own sons and daughters! We cannot incarnate into Earth form if the atmosphere of the Earth contains much more plutonium, for our vibration is intensely disturbed by this element. We are very sensitive. This element causes cancer and destruction of the immune system—protection against viruses from space—which took billions of years to develop. The purpose of the Space Shuttle Program is to send liquid plutonium out into space from Earth, so that we cannot return to Earth and Earth people will not remember their stellar selves.

Scientists who are trying to do this are the Men in Black from Orion."

At the mention of the Men in Black from Orion, I had to let myself know! Great Goddess of the stars, if you have any place in your being that even believes the Men in Black can steal your exquisite integrity, it will weaken you! Within your soul is the Lakota medicine woman, since all time is spherical. If these Men in Black are outside herself/myself, this will darken the heart.

Into my body . . .

The left-shoulder, galactic point to the right brain is severely blocked and full of pain. All the gall bladder and liver points are open, for I have cleared being violated in this life. The galactic point is severely stressed because this spot is a connection point to the energy hologram making it possible for scientists to participate in deliberate murder. I want to know the source of the evil, to know how abuse works, allowing humans to destroy life and the future of their own species. I ask for the release of the Emerald Records of Orion, and a rasping voice comes in rather reluctantly. The voice of Khnum, the oldest god of wisdom in Egypt before Thoth, speaks:

The Men in Black from Orion have infiltrated Earth at this time because of the level of technology attained. In the last Orion battle against Earth 26,000 years ago, when Pisces last precessed into Aquarius, the chance for the cosmic leap—total attunement to our center, the Pleiades—was available. But Earth people were still too primitive to accomplish an evolutionary leap because they were enslaved to the will of the gods, their teachers. The Men from Orion caused a great cataclysm—the Fall of Atlantis—but the Men in Black did not succeed in their ultimate goal, which was to wrest the minds of men from the gods. The "official sources of information"—historians, anthropologists, archaeologists, and psychologists—deny the history of Atlantis because, if they admitted to it, people would remember that destruction has occurred before. Then humans would have a greater hope of identifying the way evil works to trick them out of their freedom. 26,000 years ago, Earth could have evolved into autonomy—an evolution of conscious lifeforms freely choosing the highest good—love. Once love is freely chosen, control and blind obedience are overcome.

The Men from Orion once had the opportunity to become autonomous beings. Refusing to do so with full awareness about their choice, the Men in Black opted for the brave path of negative polarity. For, balance can only come from positive and negative polarity. But let us recognize their part in the present crisis on Earth. Their ancient battle was with the Nibiruans and Sirians, and their struggle is recorded in the many legends about fratricide: Horus and Set in Egypt, Cain and Abel in the Hebrew Bible, and Quetzalcoatl and Tezcatzlipoca in Mesoamerica. As long as one is in a karmic cycle, one must choose a role until one's own part in the drama is recognized. We are not free of the struggle if we believe that opposing forces are different from our own selves. In that recognition lies the truth.

The Men from Orion are the ones who set up the paradigm of good against evil, of original sin against grace, of all hierarchies involving judgment on Earth. Due to this paradigm of one part against another—the essential flaw in human DNA, which will be repaired in 1989—Earth people are always "against" instead of "for". That is the test of the times. That is why the symbol for the Age of Pisces is two fish swimming in opposition in the water, which represents the duality of the emotions. The Pleiadeans have been radiating the Earth with love energy since the incarnation of Christos, for the Piscean Age is the time to prepare for the critical leap into Aquarius. The Mayans are the ones most conscious of the stellar source of integrated energy systems available for Earth to find peace. And, the Mayans made great progress at the beginning of the Age of Pisces when these medicine teachers taught the Nibiruans about the Dreamtime. This caused the ancient Sirian teachers to release Earth like a bird leaping into flight.

The twentieth century is the greatest critical leap time in the cycle, because the Men in Black are heavily incarnated on Earth during this period. This is the same transition time when these men caused a war on Earth before. Their particular skill is in setting up situations which encourage evil choices during phases of high technology. These covert cosmic visitors often wear dark blue suits with white shirts and red ties. Most people on Earth remember their influence during the Fall of Atlantis, and this fear of ancient cataclysm causes an almost total mental paralysis upon encountering the Men in Black. The Men in Black are involved in dilemmas of moral choice at this time which are similar to earlier periods of choosing control over love. Even the Men in Black may be capable of choosing life over war at this critical leap time, and thus forever cease choosing to be conscious agents of evil. If they do so, then evil will turn to light.

The Men in Black are being given this chance by being offered conscious experiences of their own love, their own positive energy. This is the Goddess at work. She is succeeding when you see priests getting married and soldiers ceasing to fight because men can no longer stand to kill innocent civilians. Since August 16th, 1987, people have been finding themselves in the middle of some very confusing emotional relationships. Many individuals are realizing that souls on the dark side are drawn to them in order to set up situations in which the dark forces might be given their last chance to choose to cease evil action. Positive energy predominates over negative, but the Men from Orion have charged the karmic memory pattern with much negative experience, which people tend to revert to. It is important to be in the present time after August of 1987, for, by 1992, every individual with whom you have ever experienced evil in past lives will manifest in your life. Welcome them as your teachers.

The exact moment when the Men in Black rejected creation is the only moment in which they can feel! So when you see sexual addiction, love of violence, hatred of self, know that these human poisons are a desperate cry for release by the imprisoned soul which is seeking surrender. Orion first learned to feel while using power and control, not by letting go to a larger force. So, when you find yourself hating another, being enslaved to an addiction, or enjoying the bizarre outward expressions of the inner evil of the End Times, then go to the love, to the light exploding within the chakras of your body.

We have received the Records of the Orion Wars from Khnum, and we return to Allini speaking to the people of Alcyone:

"I am a member of the Galactic Federation whose main work is starseeding—birthing creative forms for the knowing of dimensions higher than the third. I have gone to Earth from Alcyone often during this time to participate in the third crisis with Orion, with the Men in Black. In the first crisis, the Earth was in danger of collision with a comet from the early days of galactic formation. During deep meditation in the galactic core, we discovered a method to correct such catastrophes by creating a harmonic—a perfect waveform—an integrated, solar-system hologram which would then exist in harmony with the larger hologram of the universe. We discovered, quite to our own amazement, that when any form initiates harmony, form cannot be disrupted, for a form in harmony breathes with God. We were shown a series of visions by the Creator about how this works. Next, we were imprinted with the awareness that harmony is eternal only if we consciously attune to the resonant form by breathing with the Creator. This is why the Mayans are opening the temples and teaching seekers how to breathe with the Creator again. Then the harmony needed to resolve the third and last crisis with Orion can be attained. Earth must be energized to reflect upon itself so that the opportunity to free Earth and Orion is not missed.

"The Creator showed us how this works by allowing us to look into the mirror which reflects creation back upon itself. This is the supreme teaching that harmony comes from seeing oneself in the essence of all that is. The Creator showed us that this teaching is survival itself, for if the Creator forgot to look into the cosmic mirror to know that he/she was there, existence would cease at that moment! That is why initiated native peoples celebrate the rising of the Sun each morning. The Sun would not rise if it were not prayed with by those it shines its light upon! That is why the Sun—Hunab Ku—needed to be prayed with at sacred sites on the morning of the New Dawn. Existence happens only by the knowing of existence! When you are in the soul, within the temple, contemplating, you see the mirror—the living energy of the Pleiades—center of the Milky Way which spirals out symbols and ages of time, which form dimensions.

"The Men from Orion are the agents of the big lie. In the beginning, we were instructed by the Creator about how to attain harmony, and we each selected different teachings which are reflected in our work today. We have only become conscious of the full extent of the agenda since 1982, when the signals from Arcturus broke through the control of Orion. At that point, Arcturus activated the Mayan centers in the brains of certain individuals, and we began receiving clues from the main galactic brain circuit. This was a breakthrough, because Orion had been monitoring technological developments on Earth with great sophistication. The Men in Black have held the dominant paradigm on Earth: The belief that Earth is the only place in the universe with conscious lifeforms, and that any human who thinks there is life anywhere else in the universe is a cuckoo brain. Meanwhile, as the presence of high intelligence in space has become increasingly apparent to many intelligent humans, Orion has engaged in a program of seeding walk-ins—Orion robots—on Earth. The walk-ins, or stellar personalities in human bodies, are attempting to end their Earth debt by releasing themselves from previous evil acts. They do this by means of particular learning experiences which will cause them to either again choose evil or to surrender to the exquisite breathing with God. There is little time left, for soon, evil is to cease being an agent of evolution. The path of negative polarity has already contributed its full teaching about choosing love, and its agents will be sucked into negative space/time in 1992. All must listen to the screaming of the souls within—the uncleared evil experiences—and learn to love all manifestations of the self again.

"Many Men from Orion live on Earth now because these are the End Times. If you ever doubt the outcome of this magnificent time of choice, know that God suffers with you. The Creator can barely tolerate holding this time of freedom open as he/she waits for the last sheep to return to the keep. You know many in your own life in the midst of this struggle.

You can observe people at this time wrestling with the test of taking power as if free will is a boa constrictor at their throats. Offer them love during their terrible tests. The teachings are coming from pain and ecstasy, and you cannot wisely choose one side or the other until you have experienced both. That is why so many of the teachers at this time had childhoods of great pain and suffering. They needed to totally free themselves from emotional conflicts at an early age, so that they could open up to remember the ecstasy of being alive on Earth.

"We, the Pleiadians, are teachers about love, but we have things to learn at this exquisite leap time. We are timeless about how we love; we simply radiate love; but now we are to personalize our love. Love is an experiential resource which only exists if we are loving. We are now being put to the test by our physical incarnations on Earth, and many of us have chosen experiences that have made us scream in the night—desperate sounds heard all the way to the stars. Our Pleiadian heart has opened as we now hear Earth crying in the night. The beam from us has become a Rainbow Bridge from the stars to Earth.

"Now my Pleiadian galactic point—the pineal gland in my third-dimensional self—is activated, and I will tell you exactly the events transpiring on Earth. The Men from Orion have decided to commence their third battle, which is going on right now. The Men in Black are tempted to trigger humans into a nuclear conflict in order to gain ultimate control. The pollution of the Earth and the paralysis of well-meaning people is a behavior pattern from the first two wars in this solar system. For these Men in Black, who are true fallen angels, this is their third and last knock, and could open the door to reunion. If they make the conditions on Earth bad enough, no one but themselves will be left on Earth, for beings from Orion can tolerate high levels of radiation because the stars there are extremely dense. Orion immune systems are very strong, since their low level of vibration enables them to tolerate the typical modern diet and exposure to pollution and toxic chemicals. And, since their agenda is negative, the Men in Black are not agonized about the genocide of the species.

"In the last battle, 26,000 years ago, crystals were implanted in the etheric bodies of people by the Orion Atlanteans. The Arcturian Atlanteans made a deal with the Orion Atlanteans: The Arcturians agreed to set up a planetary stabilization program in this solar system that would culminate in a great balancing between 0 AD and 2012 AD. The Arcturians did this with the full agreement that Orion would not interfere with the cosmological stabilization until 2012 AD. The Men from Orion were

allowed, in return, to implant crystals in the etheric bodies of certain people which were set to be released between August 16, 1987 and August,
1992. These crystals contain programs which trigger beings from all parts
of the galaxy into karmic experiences required by the Men from Orion
to offer them one more chance to discover free choice. To put the matter
simply, players in the game were put into process in the midst of the End
Time cycle, because this is actually a game that most people would rather
sit out. The way out of this labyrinth is the Dreamtime.

"The apotheosis of the End Times has created a unique opportunity
for souls who have failed tests before to move into galactic synchroniza-
tion for all beings. All beings involved with Earth will be present to play
out this drama. Every lost sheep will be heralded by the shepherds,
which is why the Hebrew Bible emphasizes that the Creator will wait for
the last one. This is the Orion Factor—the chance to consciously reflect
on all that has been, as the Creator reflects on creation eternally in the
mirror of time. This is the Mayan teaching of the Smoking Mirror—look
in the mirror without your mask, and contemplate the very thing you do
not want to see—your own participation in evil.

"Now the crystals are being removed. This solar system is stable, but
that does not mean a cosmic catastrophe cannot occur. This solar system
is stabilized—in harmony with the Galactic Center. The crystals are
implanted with a variety of interesting programs which are now being
cleared from consciousness and the PSI bank—the accumulated knowledge of all time. The Men from Orion knew that Earth would undergo
another struggle at this point between the positive and negative forces.
Therefore, many of the key crystals were programmed to help their
cause. The end phase of the plan is to bring in walk-ins from Orion in
order to use the crystals to maximum advantage. This paradigm was first
contemplated by Earthlings at the Nuremberg Trials, when inferior warriors were found guilty of obeying the Nazis who ordered them to commit atrocities. These warriors obeyed their commanders because these
commanders controlled them like robots, due to the crystals. Earth began
to look at the evil resulting from the following of outside orders.

"The people containing these crystals have been under tremendous
stress since Harmonic Convergence. The only way to rebalance is to
allow yourself to look at your own dark side and to observe, very
intently, the individuals who have come into your life and triggered you
into actions which you would rather avoid. If the Nazi warriors had
already faced their past participation in evil, Hitler could not have triggered them. Orion has even programmed a scenario in which the people

who can stop the radiation on Earth and space will cop out at the last minute. If this seems like an outlandish scenario, consider that computers have now manifested which can teach us about how programming works. Now is the time for us to get to know all the 'write protected' programs in our lives.

"The Orion crystals are programmed to convince you that the radiation will not really hurt your children, your Earth. A military man on Earth, when asked about putting liquid plutonium into space, said, 'It can't pollute anything up there!' Clearly, like all of us, he has been in other star systems and galaxies, he knows the statement is a lie, but his crystal is programming him to says something utterly stupid. You can see how deepseated the problem is by considering the American election after Harmonic Convergence, when all participants acted like robots and wore dark suits with red ties."

I am getting a headache as the thoughts about crystals make me think of Tikal, the hardest issue I have been looking at. There is still a part of me that feels separate from me! I return to Tikal to ask about the bargain I made in that ceremony which caused me to take a drug that blocked my freedom of choice.

I am inside the pyramid with six priests. I am the seventh. "I am the kachina, Itzanna. I chose to come down here as the stellar body of this priest. I have agreed to be in this place for this ceremony."

Priest: "You are kachina—star-being—but we have a special little treat for you. We need you for another task today. . . I am from Orion. I am also kachina, and I want you to know that you are acting according to the desires of the Orion Factor today. I am here to make sure that you *feel* every action you commit on this last day of the Nine Hells."

I am shocked. I was trained to be the agent for carrying out a certain evolutionary program, but now he tells me that this ceremony activates Orion. He is a major Man in Black from Orion. I realize that the only way he can be here is because my auric field is damaged. I am filled with guilt that my auric field has allowed an Orion intervention here. Now the ritual of seven can set up a planetary program. Just like the etheric body crystals, the temple sites are programmed on the etheric plane to time-radiate forms into Earth historic processes. I also know that this will create time repercussions for me, that my participation will result in the creation of karmic experiences which will later activate this part of my brain circuitry. I see it all. . . the future.

Priest: "You are my agent for feeling all that happens here today so that this feeling hologram will be activated in 1942. For example, in you will be energy cells that will block Einstein from feeling his actions. Einstein is a Pleiadian leader who will be incarnated for the opportunity to feel the crying in the cells, the pain in the water, the agony of the forced fire. Your program at Tikal will assist him in not feeling the truth he intuits. In your program, in your own body, will be the Fall, Edward Teller, NASA, and Dow Chemical. This will exist in you until you let go of the big lie—that Tikal, or any crystal, or any matter, can hold negative programs from any source. As long as you believe that, you will come again and again into situations just like this one, and you will agree to play the game rather than let go. You, yourself, cause the evil you hate."

Itzanna: "But, I really don't want to play a role in this ceremony."

Priest: "Fine. Do you see that sexual aggression/possession is not separate from you? Do you see your nascent female being crying from within for balance with your form—your male self—in this life? If so, leave right now!"

He stares at my auric field as I feel dulling in my head. I go within, searching desperately for any female within. I know I only have a second. My heart is pounding! I see an infinitesimal little girl in my gut who tries to scream, but she has no voice! The Man in Black from Orion gestures impatiently to the priest next to me who carries the pulque, the drug. It will blow open all my chakras, all my feeling centers, and force me to take it in. He says, "Taking control is always so easy here."

He disappears and I am staring into the face of the kachina who was there before the Man in Black walked in. In my life as Barbara, I have a memory of this mask encapsulating a male essence frozen into a warrior. It soaks the feminine heart with pain, to sprout its inner seed of the Tree, and obsessively drives me to monitor the military/industrial space program. As Barbara, I can recognize the Men in Black, but they cannot recognize me. They think I am a cartoon character because I have been served up to the culture as Boopsie—a stereotypical, female airhead. I went down to Tikal to defuse my part in the program of male control by claiming my own male part of the warrior teaching. My ability to clear my own guilt and emotions, all my own shadows within, opens energy to help break down the control which is strangling Mother Earth. Again, I must feel the obsessive hatred of the feminine which creates ecocide, so that I might change the feelings of just one human.

Back in my right shoulder, the galactic point is cleared and there is no pain left in the muscle. My auric field will clear because I know that I am controlled by no being or galactic point. I do this work because I love this planet and believe that every hideous violence against nature first originated in a dark place within a human. When I see a dying tree, I feel the poison of my own blood system. When the lake I lived on as a child died, every fish gasping for breath was an inner voice of my own. I have lived a long time so that I would be ready to help remove all the barriers we have created against the power of the Goddess. I am prepared to know my teachers from the other side. I am beyond responding to them with judgment. I am ready to be a child in the cosmos instead of a parent who fully knows the universe and controls reality. If holding myself quietly until my inner child is free seems odd, remember that any communion with the other side is numinous—fully conscious of the holy.

I return to Alcyone, to the central record temple with my teacher. I have asked him to instruct me about the Luciferian Rebellion, for now that I have cleared my own experience of turning from divinity, I want to know about the primordial rejection of the Creator. I am having great difficulty understanding how this has functioned because I have been trying to look at the rebellion from an Earth perspective. My teacher has come from Andromeda Galaxy, the spiral form which represents the physics of the universe—the central laws of creation. The rebellion can only be understood from Andromeda. My teacher instructs me about the rebellion of the angels.

In the beginning, the light was created like the diamonds all over my body. The creation exploded and exploded and exploded. Matter had no limits and the cells spread out to infinity—the zero point which accesses holiness. There were some energies present that wanted to be able to contain the light, but these forms could not define themselves unless the light could be contained. So, the first forms uncomfortable with infinity thought the very first thought of all time: If existence could limit a primordial form, define that form, explain how it works, then matter would be comprehensible—both physical and definable. This thoughtform came into being by needing definition—by moving out of zero. These first forms seeking identity created self-definition which made existence in zero, in numinosity, impossible for them. As soon as this thoughtform materialized, identity formed a hierarchy—a structure of existence called Jacob's Ladder.

I can feel this process happening as thought and thought and thought. This idea created itself into a series of processes and beings who defined, limited, and controlled matter. This universe of processes and experiences was not made by the universal cosmic Creator: This world with a beginning and end was created by a lesser urge, the Demi-Urge, which expressed itself as "the gods." On Earth, we have experienced this creation as the Luciferian Rebellion, the Orion Agenda, the communion with the cycle of the gods who came down which is now coming to a close. Before the creation of the third dimension—a universe brought into existence so that we could consciously learn how to be in a holy state, zero, the numinous—before matter, time, and form, there was only the infinity of God and the Void/feminine. Once consciousness or thought occurred, the Void was threatened by the possibility that nothingness had no existence. The Void felt the desire to define nothingness! Once this process of separation began—a duality into self/other—a whole series of experiences was initiated in order to manifest existence. At this point—the Alpha—the Creator withdrew its name, for the opposite of definition is naming—unifying. Listen to me very carefully now, for the scientists on Earth are trying to steal the Creator's name by calling the first laser for Star Wars, Alpha.

If you know yourself, you can name yourself. If you name yourself, you are not defined, you simply exist in the numinous. You are centered in the nothingness. The animals named themselves and God was blessed.

Isis tricked the Creator God into giving her his name. He had defined himself as lesser God and called himself *he*. Isis saw this and tricked him into naming himself for her, and he fell to the Earth in flames.

Propitiation and sacrifice began, the first burden of Earth. For no one sacrifices to the divine. Sacrifice is the definition of self of the lesser gods.

I have lost this need for definition in creation, but once ego—who am I?—obsessed me. Definition is the original confusion which has been reverberating down through time on this planet. The only thing that counteracts this process is naming the self by exploring one's own creativity. Our link to the galaxy is through art, beauty, and love, which frees us from materialism—addiction to things we are conditioned to believe we need. Creativity, or moving into experience with the Creator, is more powerful than any force, even materialism. We can only create if we trust the process and let go of control. There must be no judgment about results or about reasons for creating in the first place. Any judgment instantly catalyzes the numinous into form. If healers stop to ask why they heal, artists why they art, lovers why they love, then experience falls back into definition, which blocks God's delight! Just by asking a question about existence, one is open to the negative path.

The pathway is simple trust. If we trust in the cosmic plan, we do not have to question anything. It is fine to be curious. Curiosity is a high function of being. But the trick is to never lose total trust in the eventual outcome of existence. The fallen angels lost total trust in existence and defined themselves in separation. Definition was their sole reference point.

My teacher on Alcyone speaks:

"This has been the ultimate struggle in the universe and on each planet. Alcyone passed through the struggle and established communion in zero relationship to the Galactic Center, a long time before Earth came into existence. The stars, including the Sun, are fourth dimensional and beyond. The goal of the Pleiadians, beginning 26,000 years ago, was to quicken *Homo sapiens* so that the divine could penetrate the third dimension. God seeks to penetrate all essence, and, while looking into the cosmic mirror, the divine saw Adamah. The divine felt a desire to have Adamah name the third-dimensional form. The last 26,000 years have been the time of the Creator desiring to know the name of Adamah. But Adamah could not name the self until the learning was complete. In 2012 AD, Adamah will vibrate this name throughout the cosmos, as God desires.

"Alcyone is in communion with the solar system, which precesses or walks backward in the sky around this central star of the Pleiades. One equinox precession cycle equals five Mayan Great Cycles of 5,125 years each, according to the Mayan Calendar. The interface of these two cycles is the Rainbow Bridge from the solar system to the Pleiades. By crossing this bridge in your mind, you attain creativity, or contact with your own name in your pineal gland, the home of God in your mind. God has not forgotten you: you have forgotten creativity. Earth will attain creativity and synchronicity with the Pleiades because the Mayan daykeepers are again attuning the Sun to the Galactic Center. But individuals will participate in this magical awakening only if they are aware of it, dance with it, or delight in the swimming photons they see as little stars when they shut their eyes. Earthlings must work now to remember the symbols and language of the divine—the most sacred gifts given to Earth during the last 26,000 years.

"Are we afraid to remember that we are merely a desire in the mind of God? Then what if God may need to let go of desire? Christianity has been especially critical of the fallen angels because, if Earth names itself, then the forces of definition will have no place to attach in physical form. Such energy will dematerialize. If the fallen angels dematerialize and feel for the first time the gap to ecstatic creation, the angels will feel separation from creativity. The angelic manifestors who are, for us, the closest beings to God, would be devastated. The fallen angels have sidetracked themselves by playing around with various experiments which have been creative but without wisdom. As the third dimension has become increasingly complex, especially during the last five thousand years, the angels have amused themselves by being voyeurs of the results of materializations. Technology with no divine inspiration or wisdom has been the latest project of the angels.

"If, by means of healing and love and a fusion of the light, we can create a balance, then negativity will discover its own ability to feel good. There will be no more desire to create the definition in form—the fall into matter. A child, for example, feeling the difference between good and evil, will choose good. There are many cultures and individuals who have no idea what feeling good, balanced, and harmonious is like. A person who does not know harmony is like a person who has never heard Beethoven.

"On the Pleiades, we teach harmonics and balance by means of light, art, gems, healing, and sound. We sounded to Beethoven even when he was deaf! We trust the divine potential of each soul. From the beginning, we have used light and rays in the planetary harmonics like eternal perfect resonating notes. If we can succeed, the forces of separation will end because the Luciferian angels will move into greater harmony and dissipate. The angels will not let go as long as they have a place of attachment—the memory bank of humans. Even St. Michael will have to drop his spear! The prophecy about the last sheep means that even Lucifer will be called by God in the night to return to the fold."

I return to the elevated podium and speak to the people of Alcyone:

"On Harmonic Convergence, we sent the message of the need to return to sacred sites on Earth. This was an attempt to create a resonant field of balance which would help more people remember good feelings. Many people on Earth responded to the call who had already realized how their own lack of feeling causes evil.

"The Rainbow Warriors succeeded in awakening the Earth, but the negative forces continue to hold on with even greater desperation as the possibility of going to the light gets closer and closer. Going to the light demands letting go of ego or identity in the third dimension, and most people will hold ego until the shift into numinous form. The shift is happening, and the only real question left is whether the last sheep will come into the fold.

"The greatest crisis of the end of the Mayan Great Cycle—2012 AD—is the threat of liquid plutonium polluting space. This desire to pollute is the last gasp of the dark forces. The shuttle that was supposed to send the plutonium into space in May of 1986 was called 'Atlas Centaur,' a confession by the scientists that they believe they hold up the world with their evil desires. Because the divine did not allow the flight of Atlas Centaur, the military scientists will next attempt to put plutonium in space by means of a shuttle called 'Atlantis.' The scientific community, which universally denies the existence of the ancient kingdom of Atlantis, will demonstrate publicly, by calling their fire-powered phallus Atlantis, that they are an ancient technocratic cabal of scientists who were previously the cause of the fall of civilization on Earth. Beware!

"If the plutonium is released, this element will limit the Earth to the third dimension. All higher dimensions will be blocked, and Alcyone accesses Earth in the fourth or higher dimensions. The effects of plutonium are like a higher vibrational hologram of emotional body pollution in Earth's atmosphere. The soul cannot exist in the body of a person who is in an extremely negative state of mind or emotions. The atmosphere of Earth will not be capable of admitting higher vibrations such as the Pleiadian energy if the air element gets much more polluted. Beware! Your barometer of emotional body pollution is cats. Nearly fifty percent of the cats in industrial nations have cancer. We are able to exist on Earth unaffected by the crippling emotional body pollution which afflicts so many unevolved humans. But the plutonium will carry emotional body pollution into the fourth dimension because this element has feelings! The planet Pluto is a higher vibration of Earth, and represents humans' most intense feelings. Since the splitting of the atom, even the elements on Earth can feel. Earth radiation is cutting us off because Earth must take responsibility for the pollution. The time to take responsibility has arrived, and an emotional body polluted by negative experiences cannot be penetrated by the light. We wish to keep on radiating light as long as possible, but people must clear their own emotions.

"We are becoming concerned now. We have been able to work on balancing individuals, hoping that enough people would clear emotionally so that the critical leap could occur. We have radiated light to individuals who have become servers and healers, and then these individuals have gone on to reach as many others as possible to help them clear their emotional bodies of pollution. But, what if we cannot penetrate the Earth PSI bank anymore? That is why we have been contacting so many people to let them know how dangerous the situation is. Those of us who live on Earth as servers can return to our places of origin, such as Alcyone, but we will not be able to return to Earth again.

"Every person who experiences the light energy will gravitate immediately to its source, so the trick is to get them to feel. People respond to what has happened to them, to their own experiences. So the goal is to increase the vibratory nature of experience. We have helped to increase the number of healers. The light infusion has been increasing since the planet of crystals—Chiron—was sighted in 1977. This brought light technology into third-dimensional form. Since Harmonic Convergence, we have been increasing the voltage, and a lot of people cannot take the dosage. Those of great density are burning out, but an individual lifetime is not what matters. What matters is the alignment with the greater balance for all creatures of Earth. Humans are not meant to be parasites. Individual agendas are not the most important now. Humans have had thousands of years to learn about cause and effect.

"The time for the individual agendas to be played out is coming to a close. We are coming to the end of experience, and the time of choice is almost here. Lifetimes of the same soul test over and over again have been repeated opportunities for people to experience the dark and the light, so that they could choose between them. Now is the apotheosis. The planet is going to move out of third-dimensional linear space and time.

"I am calling on my people on Alcyone to go into light-body transmission phase at this time. If our light bodies can exist while we are in human incarnation, as Christos demonstrated, we can break the control of the dark forces. The fourth-dimensional light-body transmission phase from Alcyone cannot occur unless the dark forces are transmuted out of the third dimension. Three major light-body transmissions assisting Earth during 1989 are accompanied by major solar flares. Earth is going into the fourth dimension no matter what. The only remaining question is whether Earth will have light-body connection to the Galactic Center or whether our planet will be a cold, dark rock in space with no consciousness, like the asteroids.

"The sighting of the face on Mars offers Earth people the chance to see what could happen to Earth if the contact with Alcyone ceases. Earthlings work by seeing the range of possibilities caused by their actions. When a factor goes wrong, Earthlings choose whether or not they will take action to remedy the situation. When a man is evil, he may see evil, but he does not know what the experience is like to feel not-evil. Earth is entertaining a choice of good feelings.

"Have you ever looked into a beautiful diamond? That is what I feel like! I have compressed the carbon of my body with fire power until every cell has become diaphanous. Individuals who clear their emotional bodies by deep experiences at the Plutonic level no longer have any fear. All that remains inside is a reflection of that which penetrates me. So, when something enters me, I can see it clearly because I reflect it with clarity. People naturally prefer being reflective once the inner mirror is discovered, because this inner refraction is the end of confusion. Intrusive and hostile beings are repelled by the light, and beings who feel love and shared joy are naturally attracted to it. This is why people can completely change their lives after they have had one ecstatic experience. The diamond clarity is like emerging from a swamp, washing the mud off, and laughing at your whole life, and at all your lives, because you see that the only person in your reality who genuinely loves you is a frog! The diamond faceting is so much more exquisite than any other feeling people have ever had. We have been very successful with many individuals, but we would like Earth to feel diamond clarity now. Here on the Pleiades, light is so strong that the darkness cannot penetrate form. Instead, the darkness defines the form of light. Like a diamond or crystal, we are fully grounded and sensual in our stellar field, the darkness. Negative influences are repelled, and the darkness is as visible as the light. Darkness takes form like a ray in a rainbow."

Down in the audience, the people I see as I speak on Alcyone are also now on Earth. As I speak about events on Earth, the ability of the people to radiate light intensifies. My brothers and sisters wear purple, green, and lapis lazuli, clothes that absorb and reflect back spiritual energy. Because of the power of the people on Earth who desire peace, the power of Alcyone to awaken stellar bodies of people on Earth is intensifying. People on Earth are sensing that they are actors in the dream of a distant paradise—their existence is the dream of a star! My people feel empowered by hearing about the progress on Earth. As I feel my people on Earth, my awareness on Alcyone also intensifies. Suddenly I feel incredible energy, as if light is shooting into every cell of my body. I am in the Dreamtime! Christos began this intensification of energy from the Pleiades two thousand years ago. He explains:

I shifted the way I transmit this energy, shifted the power into quartz crystals. Quartz crystals are the medium for bringing in the light. I am soon going to shift more of this energy directly into the diamonds of Earth. I have already been energizing diamonds, but the force will become more intense. These diamonds have caused cancer in many humans. The light force is so strong that light goes into the cellular matrix, speeding up the cell mutation and causing cancer. Cancer is the speeding up of the life-force. The body speeds up too much in individuals who have not sufficiently awakened and cleared negativity from their body imprints. Hot vortexes of emotional body imprints form tumor masses in the body organs which hold uncleared anger and pain over separation from God. The diamond alters the blood chemistry by speeding up the blood cells. I energized diamonds on the planet so that people could begin to see in their normal experience how the Luciferian Rebellion works. By manipulating reality and speeding up the processes on Earth, the truth about the negativity captured in the body is being shown. Lucifer is caught in the universe, just like your pain is caught in your body. AIDS has manifested to teach humans not to seek the divine in the third dimension through pursuit of sexual ecstasy without love. Only love can go into timelessness. Love can let go of control and move faster. Beware: never seek ecstasy without love.

From the podium, again I speak. "Christ is the energy that has the most power on Earth for energizing crystals and diamonds. There have been imbalances from these energies, which have all been teachings. We have been experiencing a speeding-up process resulting in death. Death, of course, is not real and only results from things speeding up and people going out of form. The energy that was directed into diamonds and then into crystals is now being directed right into the crystalline cells of the human body, and the healing light is more balanced by its presence in all cells. The diamond sets up a light ray that is too intense in one place in the body. Christ is speeding up the crystalline light cells right in the body, and those who are balanced in the light are clearing very fast as the crystalline matrix floods with light. All bodies must go into balance with the light at the time of apotheosis.

"Our problem with working on Earth is that we are not sure exactly how Earth functions. Here, diamonds are very healthy. These dense stones balance me, and I bring people around me into balance by wearing them. On Earth, light often reflects back in the wrong way, and so we have gone deep into the body of humans to detect the sources of perverted force on Earth. Healers are working with deep, cellular, body techniques. Flower essences are very potent. The enzymes of master plants go into dark places in the body such as the pineal gland and bring the light right into the cellular matrix, inviting less danger of reflection. Those who have been damaged in this diamond-body process are those who have needed to learn the most about speeding up the body. Therefore, those who have speeded up their sexual forces without opening their hearts have burned out. Some wealthy women who have worn huge diamonds, exhibiting their desire for power, have not been able to handle the reflection of their inner anger and have gotten cancer."

Christos speaks again about the diamond teaching:

The image to use at this time is the diamond, with a ray of light going into the cave. We are now going into the diamond light body as a result of the work we are doing to clear the emotional body. Shining the light into the cave, looking for where the light must go and how the shining must be transmitted, we are to identify ourselves at this time as diamonds. Diamonds are the provenance of the divine, and these stones of star light will now be returning as power objects to those who carry stellar frequency. Diamonds were originally cut by the Atlanteans. These jewels have gone all around the planet to return to their original possessors. The point is coming again when the light within an individual must be equivalent to the solar light within the diamond. Otherwise, the emotions in the body cells will activate into physical cancers as virulent as the emotional poisons of inner anger and longing for connection with the divine. I came here two thousand years ago and quickened myself on Earth. The time of learning from my teachings is coming to a close. There are many who will be of greater light and healing powers than I am.

There are many on the planet who have been experiencing contacts with stars and galaxies since early childhood. Some report being pulled to another level either through energy or in a direct physical way. Some report being observed and trained by extraterrestrial agents. My teacher will tell you the story of how this happened to me on Earth as Barbara when I was four years old . . .

She is walking in the woods of Earth. She is four years old. She is in communion with the nature around herself, which she loves. As she walks down a pathway in the woods, she walks right out of her body. This is very easy for her to do, and she only comes when I call her. I call her when I need to give her teachings. She comes. I sit with her in the temple, very much like I await her return to the temple of Alcyone now. I give her teachings about the cycles of the galaxies and planets. Later, she will search through human records—archaeological, historical, mythological—for traces of my teachings. She will not consciously know the source of her inner knowing until she is 45 years old. Her parents will tell her about the many times she disappeared for hours when she could barely walk, and she will always wonder about those stories. We began teaching her when she was a tiny child, for only an innocent child could absorb the full and simple truth without question. Her mind had to be free of Earth impressions. Then, as an adult, she could trust her own inner knowing so completely that she would be hungry for any human report which validated this resonating core of galactic teachings within her being. Gradually she would reassemble from Earthly records the teachings from Alcyone, the center of the precession of the equinoxes. All humans will be awakening to these ancient stellar knowings, but she will be one of the teachers who will tell the story to help awaken the inner memories of many.

Many times, we removed her from the physical and returned her a few hours later in excellent condition. It was necessary to remove her from the physical in order to encode her consciousness with the teachings in a way that would remain in her third-dimensional Earth mental body. This could only be accomplished by removing her from the Earth field for that encodement. That is why, to the great dismay of her family, we took her and delivered her back. She does not fear being taken away because her experiences began before she knew how to talk. Once a person can speak on Earth, the process of definition has started and the person will automatically judge us to be separate. She has special wisdom teaching about not fearing other dimensions, which she will now describe:

I am on a path in the woods in communion with nature. I start to feel happy because of the beauty. I begin to speed up my physical body form by making each step a step into another dimension that becomes a distance. I go into a rhythm within myself that shifts me to another dimension and then I am in the other dimension. The best way I can describe the rhythm is to say that time becomes equivalent with the distance of my step. I go because I am called. I am sitting with my teacher in this beautiful place and learning how the universe functions. The beings do not teach me technical skills, such as how to heal on Earth, because I am already encoded with such skills from past lives. The teachers merely awaken my own memory about past-life skills. What is new for me in this life is that they teach me about how the universe works in cycles of time. Later on I am to bring these teachings to Earth.

At any moment in time, I often feel what needs to happen next and I act upon that foreknowledge. In this way, I differ from many people. But anyone would act upon valid future knowledge beyond third-dimensional consciousness! This gift of sight makes my life very confusing at first, because my understanding about Earth cycles is so clear yet I have no source on Earth for that knowledge. When I go to school, I find that most of what they are teaching is incorrect. The Galactic teaching I have within me turns out to be more correct and useful. I am very pragmatic. That is the way of the Pleiades. As for Earth records, I sift through thousands of pages in a book just to find one sentence that is correct or even relevant. There is a lot of totally useless information on this planet.

My Earth job from Alcyone is to sift through all this information, to find the vestiges of truth, and to use these accepted facts as vehicles for reawakening the memory of the real teachings in the intellectual field of Earth—the search from the ancient rem-

nants. We on Earth are not able to open ourselves to the ancient truths contained within all of us unless these truths are first offered to us in a format which the left brain can process. This format involves agreement with scholarly sources and the results of "official" scientific experiments. This method is tedious, and meanwhile another Earth process goes on which is very destructive. The Men from Orion were the Earth people's first experience with polarity. This experience awakened curiosity, and taught Earthlings to believe any idea that was presented to them through official left-brain channels. The left brain, analytic, scientific, teaching process has become a major tool to lead people astray from our birthright—knowing the truth of the divine.

Humans have been almost completely blinded for the last four hundred years, since the beginning of the Age of Reason, when the dark forces injected the left-brain channel into the consciousness field. This is why the legend of the forbidden fruit, the apple in the Garden of Eden, fascinates humans so much. We know we are being led astray by knowledge, but we do not yet see how the execution works. We are about to graduate from the Garden, because the fruits of ruling Earth with the intellect have culminated in the Bomb and a technology which threatens all life on Earth.

We are now looking for truth in the intuitive mind, the right brain. We are hearing the new story of the universe because we are hungry for a life-oriented cosmology. I have returned at this time to help integrate the sources found in scholarly research with the right-brain skill of searching the memory bank. I end with a question for my teacher: "I want to know—what is the meaning of the encapsulation of consciousness in stone statues that has come up for me throughout this journey? What is the meaning of my existence in the fourth dimension on a star in the Pleiades simultaneously with my encapsulation within a stone statue, a Nagua, at the archaeological park in Villahermosa, Mexico?" My teacher explains:

"The sacred objects were re-energized on Harmonic Convergence, and the secrets which the objects contain about galactic history will be released to seekers as repositories of ancient wisdom teachings in relation to Earth's unfoldment. The stone statues contain the primary experiential holograms that need to be cleared from 1987 to 1992. Each one of the stones is encoded with a particular karmic pattern which needs to be explored by individuals so they can move into free choice at the End Times. End Times? Do these words sound apocalyptical? No, the time has come to see the reality of the desires of the divine—the divine can only be known in the material, the Goddess. The Goddess cannot release herself when her creations are called 'idols,' when her own forms of self-expression are banned. These encapsulations of conscious experience on Earth are extremely potent and exquisite. One of the strongest power forms on Earth, they were often buried in the Earth after being polished by the rain and wind. Power encapsulated in stone that is now ready to be released is the correct archetype for the release of the soul.

"Power objects tell the stories of the last Mayan Great Cycle, 3113 BC-2012 AD. Some of the stones are from the earliest stages of the cycle, when the primary holograms of divine communion with Earth first became conscious in the minds of Earth creatures. Like the joy in the heart of a mother who sees her baby smile, this was a time when the full being of God became known here. Some power objects are energy forms of the gods and some are Earth heroes. The stones represent desires and wishes which have become known over the last 26,000 years! They are half of the stars and half of Earth, as are all the desires and wishes of humankind. The Great Goddess calls to you from near and far to return to your original complexity, to again release all your exquisite creativity, to let go of your judgments about gods and idolatry, and to call your own name into the cosmos, which has always waited for you to remember who you are. She wishes consciousness to take form in her being, her body, the Earth."

Chapter Twelve

THE EMERALD RECORDS OF
THE HOLY GRAIL

I am vibrating with chills of mystery. Like a little child who watches the wind rustling the leaves outside the window near the crib where she can be alone, suddenly the other side is present. For just an instant, all is vertical. I am my own metabolism, my own coursing blood, as if I am in the exact center of a figure eight, skating with all the weight and balance of my own body, and I become a point of matter with a swirling galaxy of stars manifesting as my other half of being. I am in the home of the blessed and that home is Earth. I go to the first time I saw Christos in this lifetime.

I am with a group of eight people at Teotihuacan—eight being the number of manifestation of other dimensional issues here on Earth. Breakfasttime is at hand after sneaking under the fence to get into Teotihuacan at five in the morning. Our group was not going to be dealing with rules when the real issue was sacred sites. We crawled into Teotihuacan under a cyclone fence, got totally filthy in the dry Mexican dirt, and then got sent packing back under the fence by a pair of guards and their dogs.

Back to the hotel for some coffee! We all sit around a table as the Sun begins to rise over the adobe walls, and we talk about the Harmonic Convergence to come in a few months. As we talk, Supernova 1987 is being sighted in telescopes around the world. I suddenly become acutely embarrassed when I am pulled out of my body! Usually that happens only when I am alone, because I keep the frequencies toned down when I am in the company of others. I am seeing The Christ flying in on a beam of sunlight which is coming through the window and hitting the floor next to our table. I look at my friends around the table as if through a veil, wondering if any of them can see me as I am disappearing before their very eyes. I take off with the exquisite ray of white seed light and fly into the sky! I become my own orgasm, as if I am shooting through the body of a serpent and exiting the serpent's mouth. I can feel myself in the jaws of a great cosmic serpent, as if I am the Sun emerging from the mouth of the serpent.

I am flying over the main north/south avenue of the temple complex, bathed in white light which I see is composed of billions of stars! I am flying in the Milky Way and coming to the central axis of the site, which is an east/west line crossing in the front of the Pyramid of the Sun. There is a great round altar stone there where the stars swirl into a spiral. The central axis point is the center of our galaxy, and I am in the center of the galaxy. As I exist in the center of the spiral, I become a tree, with my roots planted deep in the sacred Earth and my branches and leaves dancing in the stars. A great eagle flies in a huge circle around the circumference of the Milky Way Galaxy. She flies north to an energy vortex in the plaza in front of the Temple of the Moon. I see a whirling form of light—it is Christos!

Christos creates a circle of diamond lights. The circle forms a tight spiral, which spins out billions of droplets of crystalline lights. The lights are the whipping spiral of Andromeda Galaxy, so close to the edge of the Milky Way, our roadway of stars. Christos smiles the mysterious smile of a child lost in reverie, in delight over a great prank, and I am back at the table again! My friends are still trying to get the waiter to understand that we want coffee. I go deep inside, finally ready to understand a past-life transmission I received exactly one year before. When I emerged from hypnosis after the transmission, I remembered none of the experiences. I listened to the tape and I could not understand the meaning. The words went into my brain but meant nothing. Now I see—I return to myself as stone...

I see bare feet in sandals and my body is very tall, muscular, and wiry. My hair is cut short and the locks are very curly. Because my hair is cut so short, my head feels bald. My skin is rough and not clean-shaven on my strong jaw. My mouth is powerful—the mouth of authority. My lips are full, and my nose feels like the bridge was broken, like I got shoved. I have prominent cheek bones and my cheeks feel chiseled and sunken. I am very elongated—about fifteen feet tall. Oh! I am a being...

I perceive myself as a stone statue; that is the form I inhabit. There are leather straps crossed in an X over my chest which support a heavy object on my back. This thing is so heavy that I also have a loop over each of my shoulders to assist in holding it on my back. It is an apparatus which enables me to fly. The larger straps crossing my chest are supported on my hips, where there is a wide leather belt which rests firmly on my waist. This can carry a lot of weight, and the material is flexible so that I can move. I wear a short fabric skirt and I have heavy, leather, protective boots up to my knees. My arms and hands are filled with incredible power as if electrified. I am here to protect the divine child on Earth, the child of the jaguar who becomes snake god when born on this exquisite planet.

I keep my palms on the ground, or my hands hanging down by my sides with the palms facing my legs, or I cross my hands across my chest with my palms facing in. When I aim my hands at a person or animal, my power is sent to the receiver, so I hold my healing powers close. My healing hands are controlled by my helmet, which covers my whole head and has flaps over my ears. I am a guardian warrior being and I am completely mentally clairvoyant, so I need no oracular information in my ears. I do not have to listen here, as I am fixed on the divine mission. Because of all the power coming into my brain and the power in my hands, I hold my palms to my own body or to the perfectly balanced mother, Earth. On the backs of my hands, I wear knuckle dusters with straps around my wrists. My hands underneath are white and very delicate, the hands of a surgeon. My knuckle protectors balance the electrical power in my hands. I can rebalance any living thing by scanning that being with my open hands. I keep my hands encased because I am on Earth to hold the divine child. My knuckle dusters are connected to the apparatus on my back. The connectors feel like a pulley device, like a wing apparatus? I wear a flying machine! If I move my fingers or clench my fist, I activate the flying machine on my back, the metal tanks which can propel me through the air.

I am standing on a stone pedestal which is about four feet long. I just came out of a tunnel of time. The landscape is very beautiful, very green. There are papaya trees here, rolling hills, beautiful blue sky. The weather is warm and temperate, breezy, sunny, and very nice. The pedestal I stand on is a landing device. I came here and landed just as I was called into time! I came here because I am ready to have a meeting about the deepest secrets of the universe in relation to planet Earth. Earth is ready at last to know the most important truth. I am a god who landed here just for this meeting. I have arrived!

The colors here are so beautiful: the green is so lime, the blue so turquoise, the pink so exquisite. There is such great vibrance, as if the vibrance extends down into every blade of grass. The temple is pulsing with the long wavelengths and vibrations of the astral-etheric plane. I must come into even more physical form in order to tell the secret I have kept for three thousand years. Listen carefully now! A fourth-dimensional form is shifting down into the third-dimensional vectoring of the form which is identified as me. This process is the revelation about individuals on Earth interfacing with extraterrestrials. I clutch my fists, which activates the device on my back, and I come more deeply into form. Now I have a head like a chicken and I shoot energy up. This strange shape is my Earth headdress. The gear is tall and elongated and my face is like a chicken from the side and a jaguar from the front.

I can turn into a stone statue at any moment I desire. I can get dense if an interloper appears. I can turn into a tree and park myself next to the road so a person cannot see me. Actually, my appearance would shock a person who happened to see me. In the past, I could be seen more easily, because people in the ancient days did not judge their perceptions. I can be seen easily now by those who are not closed to mystery. I am a shapeshifter, and people can see me when I am in a form which they need to integrate, such as a jaguar. But they must loosen up their own molecules if they really want to understand the great secret. Before we unravel the mystery . . . if they want to know . . . what people see is what they are able to see. Do not worry. I am about to quit playing games, but perception is what is fun about the third dimension! Listen! People trust what they think is real, so loosen up!

The fear of all living things is of changing form, of transmuting, of getting caught between dimensions—in purgatory—and not knowing who they are when they return. To them, having identity means being unwilling to release anger, to surrender themselves, and that identity cuts them off from any other talent or energy that they could otherwise emulate. So, let us play our way out of this limitation.

As chicken-foot, snake-brain, silver-god extension of my spine, I can change into a stone, a tree, or an animal. All I have to do is vibrate with the cellular matrix of my next form and become that new manifestation. I feel perfectly safe in this nine-dimensional Mayan temple because I can change form if necessary. I go down a pathway which is an elevated roadway—a sacbe—and I move through a magical forest, a very childlike veil of dancing ceiba trees. I go into the Temple of Jupiter, which has a rounded top resting on twelve fluted columns. I have entered magicland and I am delighted. I go into the temple and stand in front of a person sitting on a throne. The pathway into the temple emerges into the temple, like it is going through the lower end of a keyhole, a place within all of us. Each event going on here is created by my mind. There is a throne in this room, and on it I can create any great power with which I would like to become acquainted. I can create Tezcatzlipoca or Quetzalcoatl, Horus or Seth, Isis or the god she named, just by standing here holding the force in my presence. Or, I can sit on that throne myself and summon one being who is curious about me.

On the throne, a humanoid male with an elongated face and high forehead manifests. Within his body is a small, red baby. I focus on the child and see an Olmec baby serpent god. I am seeing the alchemical homunculus, the first time a demi-god existed in the Western cultural matrix as the Olmec divine snake child found at La Venta. I can actually see the child matrix, the form created on Earth from other realms as we prepared for our birthing. The baby is a spaceman, jaguar-human, composite human, Goddess/snake. These are the inner archetypes we find when we attempt to contact other dimensional parts of ourselves. That is why the remains of great temple sites were covered with vines and earth until we were ready to know the truth. That is why Coba, the temple of descent, was only discovered recently, and why the secrets have been carefully protected by the teachers. No religion alien to this land, such as Christianity, will ever be able to eradicate this knowledge from the hearts of the people. All sacred forms that have survived the ravages of weather, of catastrophe, or of the destructive habits of humans, are the codes of our origins. We of the Western Hemisphere are spacebeings, jaguars, snakes, stars, and divine children. The blocks to knowing our origins are merely the limitations we ourselves place on our imagination—our ability to form images of our source and our future.

My own ability to form images is limited by my own experiences with the Luciferian Rebellion—the fall into identity, the turning from the light of the divine—for I still believe the angels fell away from God. The Incarnation was a dimensional fusion experience that transmuted our understanding of our relationship to the divine. Christos showed the world that no person falls from God. One by one, we have said no to delivering the divine child, because our low self-esteem has believed that our inner male cannot give birth. I return to my life as a Druid when I first thought that I fell from God. This was a time when fundamental dimensional vectoring sucked the ninth dimension into the sacred sites of Earth, and the divine child—fruit of the vine—was carried to his temple in Mesoamerica.

I wear leather boots which fit my feet like slippers. I am of medium height, muscular, and I wear a cape, with leather pants tied at my waist. The cape is hooded and the heavy fabric falls over my leather shirt and pants. I wear a tunic of rough, woven sheep's wool. Sheep are sacred to us because our sheep graze on the grounds where they were born. The sheep will not cross the lines of their keepfield even if the stone walls were moved. The animals know the land better than their herders. I hold a wooden, carved staff in my right hand which has a human skull on the top. The skull contains the sacred teachings of the seven directions: horizontal—North, South, East, West; and vertical—sky, Earth, and center, or inner self.

I am standing here in touch with a lifetime in Atlantis which I can feel but not remember. Something happening in this time—the sixth century AD—is related to an Atlantean seed teaching from eons ago. My only access to the powerful memory within me is the present time, and I am very energized and upset because I can feel the Atlantean hologram but my mind cannot access it. I am like Moses with his rod. I am Druid—one who worships the Tree —and my present reality is affected by the events in Atlantis. My memories are not literal, and so I simply stand here, aware of the ancient days in relation to the present. I am feeling my power connection with Atlantis. I am getting in touch with it now because I have to recover the memory in order to be able to tell a story of the ancient times, a forbidden story, a story which all will remember when they hear it again.

I just returned from the Rhine, where I am head Druid, and I have come back to Briton, bringing with me an important esoteric secret. As I stand here, I am swept by waves of power, because for the first time my connection to Atlantis is coming back into my essence. I am a storyteller, and it is extremely exciting to feel the winds of time rushing in. I stand with my feet rooted into the ground, my head held erect in the magnificent swirling clouds. My heart burns, then opens like a magnificent fire filled with glowing red coals. Everyone, all people, are suddenly held in my skull as I tell the forbidden story of the bloodline of Jesse of the Tree of Life. I will sing even if I am threatened by all the priests and kings who spilled blood to bury the truth. I feel higher-head-center vibration activation. My upper head is all lit up.

The skull on my staff is the Druid teaching tool for activating the higher head centers. A skull is made of the bone which encases the brain, and the brain is a complete holographic resonation center. Humans can willfully attune to any frequency in the cosmos by visualizing the photons in ray form bouncing off the inner skull bones and vibrating the brain matter at the appropriate frequency range. We did not write the skull teaching down in words because the vibrational-frequency-attunement techniques passed to us from the Atlanteans can only be transmitted by means of a quartz crystal skull that is equal in size to the skull of a human. If people just stop thinking what they think is thinking—left-brain, computerlike access of informational fields—they could feel and see photons traveling on their paths. Photons, or cells of light, contain all the information we need. I have activated the staff with my skull. I have the Atlantean power source and I am ready to activate storytelling.

I start walking to the meeting place of a secret male order of priests—no women allowed! We are near Avebury, which is over three thousand years old in my time, and I see the tent of sheepskins supported by circles of posts. In the front are the staffs of each clan, topped with skulls like mine. The Druid skull teaching has nothing to do with cannibalism. The skulls of humans contain the science of brain frequencies.

We are not barbaric—this same form exists in the twentieth century as the secret society, Skull and Bones. I have a lot of energy in my right hand that is shorting out the muscles. I enter the tent.

Inside, there is a group of thirty Druids of lower rank, and there is great power in this lodge. I go to the center with my rod, jam the base into the soil, and the vertical axis is immediately activated like lightning. The staff sends a ray of white light to the sky which the other Druids can see. As we watch the light, the force of the radiance establishes that this is a time of highly charged Earth energy. This is a very rare time, caused by the arrival of photons to Earth from a distant exploding star, a time when the course of civilization can shift. The Druids have come from Eire, North Gaul, Briton, Scotland, and our ancient homeland, Iberia. This is a major convocation of the Druids, totally secret. None of the political figures know about this, and the story will never be found in historical annals. The political people never know when we convene on this level, because if they did know, kings would attempt to influence the sacred timing.

This is the Liber Frater—the Brotherhood of Freedom—and we return to Earth again and again. We know the whole story exactly from the beginning of time. Our only questions are what we are going to do about certain things at certain times to make the traveling on the road of life easier for the people, the ones we serve.

We have gathered here today because this is a time when the outposts of the Roman Empire are collapsing. Starvation, disease, and murder are universal. I called this meeting because a brother in this circle knows a secret that he has not shared in the Brotherhood. Whatever that crucible of knowledge is, the time has come to reveal it to us, for we hold up the planet. I put my rod down and say, "Let's cut the secrecy at this level. I want to know who in this group knows the real story behind what is going on with Aethelberht! There is a brother in this room who knows the real truth."

Merlin is not in this room because he has removed his vibration. He is not accessible to us, but he was once our main conduit to the political center. What has happened to cause him to abandon the field of action and go into seclusion in the forest? He would be where I stand if he had not withdrawn his participation. The loss of Merlin's participation is one of many stories of failed teachings. The failure of these teachings will end in 1989 AD.

A man in this room knows where the Grail is hidden and he is not telling us. The Grail is Earth's repository for the photons of new creation.

The Grail holds the DNA, the Emerald Records of the full birth process of Earth when Christos came. The cup contains the planetary codes of the unfolding story of the penetration of divine blood into the Earth. The blueprint of Earth DNA has always been the creation of many dimensions and star systems, but when Christos came, he grounded that star energy into the Earth. He shifted the Earth hologram so that any individual living on Earth could become divine, could become conscious of being a Divine Son or Daughter. He created a new energy form—a fusion of the seven directions—which then became accessible to all human beings from that point forward. That energy form is human free will—full activation of consciousness.

In the esoteric orders, we protected the repository of this power by protecting the Grail, because we saw that organized religion would continue to try to curtail our freedom. Like the Ark holding the positive and negative pair of each species, the Grail is the holder of the liberation form. It is now 583 AD, and the Grail is gone. I returned from the Rhine when I heard that the cup was removed and that Aethelberht was involved in the disappearance. A man in this room knows what happened to the Grail, and we must be told the truth.

If we do not know the truth at any given point in time, we lose hundreds of lifetimes of service as storytellers, for we are the holders of the legends of the ages—the Dreamtime. Our thoughts create the cycles which manifest reality, as do everyone's thoughts. We have come back here over and over again, from Lemuria to Atlantis, and finally the resonant field of the planet has been set for the divine to incarnate into the Earth, the Goddess. This new energy form was to be introduced gradually, so that it could be recognized and chosen by individuals who were ready to open their hearts. Now all the work is on the verge of being lost, which would be like going back to the stone age. We have to know the story now, and so does everyone.

Who in this room knows what happened? I feel him in the second row. I see him sitting there with grey curly hair and white skin, sitting there thinking about whether he is going to tell the truth or not. What could be funnier than the way we masters act? All of us can read auras and can see the one who knows about the Grail, but the guilty one's pride causes him to hope he can hide. He sits on the ground, balancing himself by gripping his staff around the middle, and he looks up at me. He knows that I know that he knows the secret. We are all masters here. Immediately, all the Druids in the room know he knows. He says:

"Aethelberht had the cup released to a priestess!"

We are furious, and I thunder, "How did he ever get it?"

"Aethelberht was holding the court together," he replies. "In the middle of trying to maintain military order over four castles in remote locations, the Grail was given to a woman who is a priestess. The sacred cup was given to her by Merlin who then disappeared. She is the main priestess of the Tor, and now that she has gotten the Grail, she has become the Grail. That is the way the power works. Female energy has taken over the Grail and this priestess is in every woman who is in her power. Merlin gave her the Grail. She hid the power object in one of the sacred Goddess caves, and then she was able to learn who her child, Wotan, is. The Grail released the ancient legend to her. This is a disaster."

I say gravely, "We have lost the power which we have held for thousands of years. We have to know the facts about how this happened." I am watching the Druid who just spoke and I can see that his aura has been invaded by the energy of this priestess. We are unprotected now!

He goes on, "I watched her and I could see that she had incredible power. It was the result of having gotten hold of the Grail during a time when Aethelbert was very weak. I discovered that I was powerless in the face of this priestess, Mordreth. That is my truth."

To be in this group, one cannot be vulnerable to women. We once were invulnerable because Merlin was our leader and we held the Grail—the secret of the new order. The Grail was our central connection to the Pleiades, and we have been warrior priests who have held the great treasure for almost 600 years. I have believed that this group had the right to hold and protect that energy, that men must control the secret of the liberation by Christos. Male secret societies do not open this energy to women, for we control the evolution of the species.

I stand in the center, feeling my whole belief system begin to crumble. We all know the story now; we sense the beginning of a great shift, but we are not yet ready to let go of control. My future life at Tikal kaleidoscopes through my mind at this moment, and even so, I will still not let go! But time is spherical and my soul has chosen liberation in the twentieth century by agreeing to bring the story to the public. I begin to spin in the midst of the circle, slowly at first, causing fantastic shock to all the Druids in the sacred tent. I become a whirling dervish before their very eyes as I begin a journey into my own body!

I am trudging along the left side of my spine, which is like climbing along an old stone wall encasing a sheepkeep. I keep trying to get off the wall and walk along the ground, but I am pushed back by the wind onto the canyons and peaks of the stones.

There is deep and intense red pain all around me. I come to the cause—a small black crystal implanted during Lemurian times in this ancient wall. As I approach the crystal, it emits a hideously annoying, high-pitched sound. I hear an encoded program that has been dormant until its activation time—843 AD, at Tikal. Now, the black crystal screams out its program!

This black stone was dormant so that I could attain certain levels of mastery, initiation, and power before the program was to be activated. The program of the crystalline matrix contained the proper device to activate stickum or cellular pollution on Earth, so that I would experience sufficient negative and positive polarity. This was needed to prepare my physical body for surrender to magnetic force. This magnetic force is the infusion of the divine, the power of Neptune. The force cannot flow freely without overwhelming the evolutionary matrix pattern of any form in creation. Divine infusion, samadhi, ecstasy, only occur at the point of complete surrender when the resistance to letting go finally ends. The polarity creates action for experience and will become unnecessary at the precession into Aquarius, the Water Bearer. The black crystal was programmed so that this soul would lead the sacrificial ritual at Tikal in 843 AD and find out what separation feels like. This separation from the divine causes the soul to make a commitment to the arduous path back to the Creator—back to timeless existence in the center of the galaxy.

I reach down and grab hold of the crystal, feeling like it must be hot. I pluck the program that once served me out of the ancient wall and throw the dead crystal over a cliff near the side of the wall. I am laughing as I hear a nighthawk catching insects in the early evening light. I am suddenly in the twentieth century, laughing at myself walking along my own spine. I get the point! No teaching can be known unless that teaching is lived first, and I am chosen for many experiences because my nature is to be an evolutionary trigger. I come into form during times of great turning. I am an alchemist, and I must be present to know all the solutions which create form in order to know individual function.

I was present when the lesser gods came to Earth to participate in the evolution of DNA. As I walk along the wall of myself, I begin to dissolve in tears as I feel how much I love this place. I want to be mindless like the sheep I contain, to know exactly where I am within my field, while my own body cells know the positions of the stars and feel the winds on the face of the Earth and the surface of the Sun. Moving into my spine, I remember the Lemurian time when I was an alchemist, working with metals and mastering frequency attunement, the key to elemental resonation. I required mastery of alchemy to know Saturn. I created crystalline forms when I learned to read photons in Atlantis. This ability was required in order to know Uranus, since I am a teacher of electrical evolutionary timing. But with Saturn, I encountered resistance, because Saturn is denser and I could not master this confusion until now.

I study the rocks in my wall more carefully. They are granite, with many embedded, *white-quartz, crystal clusters. I contain many programs within my intracellular matrix, but I could not activate my original Uranian crystalline frequency until Earth quickened itself in August of 1987. I see! The stone wall of my own spine transforms into a rainbow bridge, and I realize that I am walking on Chiron, the small planet between Uranus and Saturn. I have a massive vision of the spectral colors of matter, and I receive Saturn's wisdom.*

Saturn teaches that we must experience all levels of life on Earth. Saturn is the planet that reveals that we are not separate from matter, that density is an illusion, that vibration is what forms reality. By letting go of holding onto my identity, I can activate the crystalline-form matrix of my consciousness, I can experience many forms by accessing vibration. Forms will proliferate endlessly in creation, but the frequency of matter is the pathway to oneness. The divine is the frequency. The creation is the proliferation. We are mere thoughts in the mind of God. I see reality as a thoughtform while I stride on the rock wall of myself, but the field I divide is one.

Knowledge on this planet is only accessible by experience. I have lived the high and the low, the dark and the light, in order to access the universal frequency, which is love. In my experience, I forgot. In the course of a long journey through the pathways of time, I have been able to remember the creative frequency. Suddenly, all is dark and I am held by thick bloody masses of tissue. I am in my own liver!

I am in the middle of my own anger. I have agreed to experience this pain like a mother agreeing to have a child. Humankind will not know love until the ancient anger is released. I strive to see through the thick blood and I see Yahweh—the avenging, male, fire-god of Earth. But I am the avenging fire-god! The agenda at Tikal was to release astral negativity so that we could look at violence and abuse. We cannot ever allow other people to control us; we cannot turn other people into our gods. I committed the worst atrocities in full consciousness. That was during a time when I explored extreme taboo. In the late Mayan phase, I was drawn back in to be the killer, the henchman, the sacrificer, so that I could know how it feels to abuse. Like a polluted liver, I drown in the midst of my own blood, unable to cry for a vision. I move into my heart, that cave of non-being that I once pulled, beating, out of the body. In its many rooms, I can consider being honest.

The souls who participated at Tikal are now back on the planet, leading the restructuring of frequency resonation. We are literally traveling through all the organs of the body, searching for denial of the exquisite union between the Goddess and the divine children. As soon as our part in the hologram of Tikal is released, then the next dimension of negativity will be released. I move into my mind, where I see crystals which interface directly with the organs of my body. I move into the crystals and realize that these stones are programmed so that it is possible for people on Earth to destroy our planet with radiation and chemicals, and not feel their actions.

I move right into the center of my heart, willing to see any residue of anger. In the very center lies the Goddess, who says:

"All who have invaded me are rejected as I hold my mirror up to you. The poison you pour into my body is the poisoning of your body, and soon you will hear the screams of the protozoa in the seas. Your skin will turn to fire when you wear my sacred animals, and the radiation you steal from my body will burn the cells of your brain. The people you neglect cause your heart to spasm into death. I am the house of the divine, and only the divine may enter me now."

I stop spinning and return to the center of my sacred circle of twenty-nine. I am in the center, the Sun. As the oldest mockery of female ways, we steal women's Moon wisdom to oppress the Goddess, just like the Christians oppress the Jews by stealing their ancestral scriptures. My men play the days of the Moon even though we do not know how to wax and wane. There is to be no sharing of this story outside of this group—and never with women! Why has Merlin abandoned the Druid Council at this time?

The Druid who is a traitor of men replies, "Mordreth told me that she possessed the Grail because she was the mother of the Divine Son. I believed her because she said she celebrated the hierogamous with Aethelberht. The king is a carrier of the sacred blood, and his first son, Arthur, carries the divine line of kings. But if Mordreth was telling the truth, then Wotan, her son with Aethelberht, would also be the Divine Son of Earth, because Mordreth carries the ancient bloodline of females who came to this planet from the stars. Eons ago, the priestesses of the Goddess carried a higher genetic code than the humanoids on the planet. When the goddesses came and mated with male humanoids, this created the gene of Isis. Our secret records of male gods who came down and mated with human females are filled with races of monsters and composite creatures which resulted from the gods who came down. Even the Hebrew scriptures chronicle this story. The Isis records—the vine and the branches—are the story of love, female wisdom, and the healing of the lesser gods. Only the birthing goddess, who shared her womb and sacred seeds, could heal the ancient pain and anger. As you all know, our sanctuary at Avebury and Silbury Hill was built to honor the gene of Isis. Avebury is our eternal hope for peace on this planet at the end of time.

"She got the Grail, the sacred receptacle of the vine and the branches, from Merlin by convincing him that the higher DNA factor—in a child conceived with no memory of ancient pain and separation—could only be released within a freely conceived child, the child Wotan of Aethelberht and Mordreth. All other births would be defective and filled with pain. A time would come when all children would be born without pain, when the ancient pain would be released from the memories of humanity. She said that Mary was Isis, who agreed to bring in Christos, and that Mary Magdalene was the Earth priestess who was to be the teacher about Christos. She claimed that she was Mary Magdalene. She said it is true that the gods came down—the Nephilim—but that if the gene of Isis is honored as the female side of the DNA factor, instantaneous healing will occur. She said that women are not just vessels for the male seed, but that females are the vessel, the Grail, the carriers of the vine and the branches."

I listen to this, thinking about the whole foundation of our group, the Liber Frater, which is to help protect the genetic bloodline of Jesus as it has continued through the children he fathered with Mary Magdalene on Earth. Is the whole foundation of our esoteric order faulty? We exist to protect/conceal the teaching about Christos. He brought divinity into form on Earth by being born here, by delivering a new freedom to humans, and by putting himself indelibly into the phylogenetic code by reproducing himself. Was there something even bigger going on six hundred years ago? Is it possible that we have been double-duped by the Roman Church? I have become exceedingly heavy in the heart since Sigebert was assassinated, for he was one of the direct carriers of the bloodline from Christ and Magdalena. Are the symbols of the bloodline, the vine and the branches, not the whole story? Is there another way that the sacred bloodline is being transmitted, such as through a dark and potent priestess cult? It was rumored that Sigebert was murdered because his wife, Brunhilde, was a pagan priestess. Are we—the male secret societies—simply a front for the Roman Church, which is sytematically eradicating the true story of Christos from the planet?

"Mordreth told me evolution would not proceed without the addition of correct vibrational resonance with the female attunement to the star matrix—that DNA codes involve balanced power in male, female, child, all species and elements. She said that as long as we retard the power of the woman, we will degenerate. Christos came here in order to set Earth into galactic balance. The secret that Christos revealed was that the actual balance of the solar system is the vibration created when a man and woman make love. The Incarnation was an Earth-shaking change of frequency, because the birth waves of Mary, his mother, created an erotic form in the cosmos. This erotic form became Earthly when the mother received her child and God laughed. Now God desires the ecstasy of birth and will wait patiently for the new waveform. Isis attempted to incarnate Horus 3600 years before Christos, but it was not the right point in the Mayan Great Cycles. Her divine child, Horus, lost his left eye to his brother, Seth. There was no fratricide when Christos came, so the animus is intact. Mordreth said that there would be no fratricide with Arthur and Wotan. Arthur will inherit Excalibur—Imperium—the Secret Society of the Round Table which will hold the secret and designate knights to protect the Vatican—Church and Empire. Wotan would leave to found a new temple of the divine kingship of Earth, not sky. I believed Mordreth. I still believe her, and I chose to give her the Grail so that she could protect her son of the Earth and sky."

I stand in the middle of the temple, having killed seven men with the sword of the Imperium—Excalibur. I know all about my previous lives that had involved total male dominance as a priest. As Druids, we are given the privilege of knowing all of our incarnations—as men, that is. This initiation into male dominance is the basis of all secret societies which have kept the world from falling into darkness. Now I wonder if I have ever been a woman before. Did my initiators not take me into such a memory? I have recognized one thing from the speech my colleague has made today. My need now is to be receptive, to notice how I feel. I cannot continue to take orders from the king, to kill people when the political situation calls for such acts. I can see why my brother responded to Mordreth as he did. I wonder if any of the others in our circle feel the same way? Do they feel tired of the Druid roles with the kings? How many hundreds of years will pass before all men tire of dominance? We sit in silence as candles burn and dogs scratch the soil outside.

We begin to realize that we are dysfunctional, which is the worst end point for a male. Can we bear to look at that? My God, I utter silently to myself, our whole teaching is dysfunctional. We have all been serving an elaborate structure designed to deny that birthing is always female. Priests and kings have formed an elaborate cultic structure that was created to deny the ecstatic cosmic release of a child's arrival. We take all the male skulls, even the one on my staff, and we dig two ditches out in front of the temple, one on each side. We bury all the skulls in the ditches. I release myself to my shrunken anima.

We come back into the temple as the stars shine brightly above the newly turned earth. I stand in my center, no longer the Sun, and I feel myself becoming a great tree! For just an instant I am very afraid of shapeshifting into the first gift of the gods, but the energy coursing into my feet from the Earth who has received her son is so intense that my body becomes an earthquake. The electricity forces me to reach rigidly for the sky. I become the sky. I become Earth and sky! I am the storyteller!

On the night of the frothing seas and boiling night clouds over the face of the Full Moon, I, Mordreth, take my sacred son to the new holyland as ordered by the Grail. The violence in the heart of my times is like the wild, wild wind, and I am called to the eternal return. Merlin has come out of hiding from the northern forest, his love for me compelling him to gather the men for the ship of the ancient crossing. At last we are ready to leave. My priestesses are with me as we board the great ship. Wotan is but four years of age and is sleeping next to my breast.

Aboard ship, with the great sail set, we stand on the prow and move into the passageway. We watch the land of birth fading from sight as the wind pummels the sails. Standing in the damp night air, I see the passage of time in the old home. The power of priests and kings will grow and widen, and days will come when the blood of the priestesses will soak the Earth to guard the lie. This ancient land will be soaked in blood by the great evil one, who will hold Excalibur and spill the blood of the line of David. But then a time will come when the exhaustion of the struggle will weaken the male will. My son will return someday, and the people will know it when the Druid skulls resurrect as crystal skulls across the sea.

Days pass, weeks pass. Our voyage is without danger. As if the very gods push our sails, we pass through the waters of old pain. Our storage is excellent, and no man or woman wants for food or water. Ours is a voyage into the new life, a voyage blessed by the gods of the ancient days. But nothing could have prepared me for the greeting we receive in the new land.

We sail into a great sea of calmer waters, a sea my men call Atlan. No one knows the names which the people of this land call their cities, waters, or rivers. We anchor our ship, come to shore in our smaller boats, and are all stunned by the exquisite beach and the thick jungle of tall trees, flowers, and vines encroaching on the sand. We marvel at the colorful birds, with long feathers and plumes on their heads, which we have never seen before. Later we learn that this is called the Quetzal bird. We marvel also at the clarity of the water and the brightly colored fish swimming in the reefs. I go to the moment when we come ashore in the new land.

A great eagle circles overhead, and we see a man in white robes with bronze skin waiting for us. We approach with no fear, for I know he is waiting for my son. This is the brown man who has been in my dreams since I was a little girl. I move into a state of ecstasy, for I finally understand! He has been dreaming about Wotan and me, and now my dream is becoming real.

I push my feet through the salty water, step on the sand, and walk up to him, holding my child. He smiles with great joy and expectation. His eyes are brown and he wears huge gold earrings which sparkle in the Sun, making Wotan laugh. I see great tears in the eyes of this man in white, as if my laughing son is the beginning of time. Soon many people arrive who help us. We go many miles down a road through the jungle, to a temple which is built up high above the sea. As we arrive, I see high stone walls and an observatory overlooking the sea from whence we came. There are many buildings and temples. I am amazed by the libraries filled with colorful, hand-painted books and exquisite murals of ferocious snakes with long tongues. The people are beautiful, with brown skin, and long robes of many colors. Most wear gold jewelry set with blue-green stones in very elaborate settings.

My priestesses are given clean robes and jewelry, and Merlin and I are led to a beautiful small palace. We are feasted, but we are very tired. As I fall asleep, the jungle throbs with bird calls and the sounds of animals I have never heard. The background of high-pitched insects sounds like waves of singing as I drop off to sleep. Wotan is delighted by the sounds, and seems to be coming awake. I am tired the next day, but the people in this temple are anxious to worship the stars and Moon with me even though we cannot talk to each other. This temple is called Tulum, and I am filled with wonder because the people have been waiting for us. These are a people of peace and childlike grace that I have been looking for since before my birth. This arrival is happening in my soul.

We arrive at the New Moon, and, at the Full Moon, the people make preparations for a long journey to our destination. We never question their plans because we can see that we are their dream. We can see that our arrival is part of their own cycles of emergence. As if I am coming out of a deep sleep, and as we learn to talk to them, we discover that many of our words and ideas are the same, as if we both came from the same source many years ago. We are a great joy for them, and our deliverance to our new home is their pleasure. I tell them of my oppression in my homeland but my story already seems to be another life.

Hundreds of carriers are to attend us, for our journey is to be very long. We are all to walk except for Merlin, Wotan, and myself. The three of us are carried the whole way in elongated boxes covered with colorful handwoven cloth. Eight men carry each of our three carriages. As we move along, I study the marvelous jungle for hours. I am amazed at the great raised roads called sacbes which they have built through the jungles. I see monkeys and many wonderful birds. We hear great cats screaming in the night.

Every few days, we come to one of their temple sites. The first one is the sanctuary of the descending jaguar, the animal totem teacher of Itzanna. We walk on the sacbe out of Tulum and proceed through the jungle near the shore of the sea. We walk into the rays of the rising Sun. We turn into the jungle, walking in a deep state of meditation. After many hours, we come to a deep pool of fresh water in the jungle. Along the sacbe is the Temple of the Descending Jaguar, which has just been built. The paintings on the walls are fresh and exquisite, but the whole temple is miniature, as if it has been built just for the child—for Wotan! He is delighted, and they are happy to see the joy in his eyes. The temple has a very small inner chamber with a small altar. Its walls are painted with lovely reliefs of jaguars, turtles, hummingbirds, and many other animals of this new land. Wotan goes into the sanctuary, sits in lotus position in the room of animal reliefs, and the priests sing him into the Dreamtime for hours.

The second temple site on our journey takes many days of walking on the same sacbe from Tulum that passed by the Temple of the Descending Jaguar. This second temple is on a huge site with many, large, freshwater lakes. There is a pyramid which is so tall that it seems to reach the clouds. I wonder how they ever built such a huge mountain. It is very steep and four priests carry Wotan all the way up to the sanctuary at the top. As they climb, there are huge iguanas everywhere, staring at us as if they are participating in the ceremony. This temple feels like a library of the ages to me. When they reach the top, they see two large reliefs of Itzanna, diving down as if he is entering the Earth, as if he is coming into this dimension. Again, the priests pray with Wotan as he experiences his rebirth into this new land. When he walks down the pyramid, the iguanas watch him with wise old eyes. I know he has become a new being on this planet.

The great mounds of stone which they call pyramids are models of star patterns, or are cyclical markers for Venus, the Moon, the solstices, or the equinoxes. There are great ball courts where contestants play games which put them in relationship to cosmic forces. These people, the Maya, are very spiritual, and seem to be in touch with the stars and the other planets. Yet they are very happy and live simple lives of devotion. We do not linger long, but at each temple site we are feasted. Our arrival is the cause of great mad joy, as if a legend has come true. We are part of the unfoldment of their story, but the only one among us who seems to understand the meaning is Wotan. As if he has been brought home after being in exile, Wotan is the teacher of these Mayas.

Wotan gazes at the beautiful people and they laugh when they see him. When the warm and soft jungle rains come, Wotan runs madly out into the downpour with no clothes on, and the people cry with joy. The people say he is in the stars when he runs in the rain. Eventually there are no more temple sites, and the journey through the remaining jungle is long and arduous. Finally we come to a temple site that is mostly new. I am amazed! I wonder if the structure has been built for us! We must be an arrival of great teachers who are a dimension of the cycles of time. Time, that is what the Mayas are obsessed with, and our arrival is the opening of a new cycle of time in action—history—which will be a new stage of unfoldment for the people.

The temple is different from all the other ones I have seen. I see a great palace with a courtyard that is backed by stone carvings of their gods. There is a north palace which is to be the home of Merlin. Wotan and I are to reside in the central palace, the Palace of the Divine Tree. I get chills from the murals and symbols of the Tree, for I have been severely traumatized by the Christians' destruction of our sacred oak groves. There is great festivity as we ascend the stairs for the first time. We are ensconced in the courtyard. Wotan is placed in a throne on the east side of the courtyard and I sit next to him. Men and women dance and play flutes and drums. I begin to hear other-dimensional sounds for the first time since I left Briton. I can hear the angels in the sky above the courtyard, for this is a holy place. Soon I am aware of the arrival of a group of people dressed in bright colors. These people have come from the Temple of the Sun. Three of these people climb a mysterious tower which resembles the castle towers in Briton. The structure has four stories, and there is an altar at the top. One priestess climbs to the altar on the top and lies on it as if she were preparing for hierogamous. I begin to wonder if there will be a mystery play to recreate Wotan! But she lies on the stone slab as a contingency of priests from the Temple of the Sun brings forth a statue that was made before we arrived. The object is a very old, stone statue of Wotan! The contingency passes by the lowest level of the tower containing the priestess, comes through a portal, and enters the courtyard where Wotan, Merlin and I sit. We instinctively rise from our seats.

We form a line of two. Wotan and I follow the priest, who carries the statue and walks next to Merlin. We leave the palace complex, descend wide stairs, and walk along toward the south in the glorious day. We turn east by a great foundation for a later tomb, and approach a complex of tall temples with remarkable decorative structures on top that look like lace. The wind blows through them as we pass into their center. There are four temples, one placed at each of the four directions. We are climbing to the East temple. As we climb, the sound of the wind in the roof combs causes me to go into an altered state. I hear the teachings of the Grail in the wind.

Merlin, Wotan, and I go into the central room of the East temple, where there is a bare wall. A man stands on each side of it, holding red paint and brushes. I realize I am to direct them in a new inscription. I go forward as Wotan stands with Merlin. I move my hands slowly on the smooth stone surface, and the painter adept marks the energy forms I indicate. We are there for a long time, drawing a great tree with vines and branches. This is the cross on which the Son of God was crucified. Later they paint one of their gods on each side of the tree. As the wind whistles in the roof combs, at last the mural is done. The image is of a cross, with the vines and branches of the new land, a sacred seal of trust in the evolution of humanity. I turn around to leave. Merlin has vanished again, and I return to the palace with Wotan.

Thus begins the life of Pacal Votan, the sacred Earth King of Nah Chan, Palenque, Mexico. This is the entrance into Mesoamerican history of the New Kingdom of Atlantis. It will be revealed in the sequel to Heart of the Christos—Signet of Atlantis.

SELECTED BIBLIOGRAPHY

Alcock, Leslie. *Arthur's Britain*. Middlesex, England: Penguin, 1971.

Allegro, John. *The Dead Sea Scrolls*. Middlesex, England: Penguin, 1964.

Angus, S. *The Mystery Religions*. New York: Dover, 1975.

Arguelles, Jose. *The Mayan Factor: Path Beyond Technology*. Santa Fe, NM: Bear & Company, 1987.

Ashe, Geofrey, ed. *The Quest for Arthur's Britain*. Chicago: Academy Chicago Publishers, 1987.

Augustine, Saint. *Confessions*. Translated by R.S. Pine-Coffin. New York: Dorset Press, 1961.

Bachofen, J. J. *Myth, Religion and Mother Right*. Princeton: Bollingen, 1967.

Baigent, Michael, Richard Leigh, and Henry Lincoln. *Holy Blood, Holy Grail*. New York: Dell, 1983.

_____. *The Messianic Legacy*. New York: Henry Holt, 1986.

Baran, Michael. *Twilight of the Gods*. New York: Exposition Press, 1984.

Bernal, Ignacio. *A History of Mexican Archeology*. London: Thames and Hudson, 1980.

_____. *The Olmec World*. Berkeley: University of California Press, 1969.

Blackman, E. C. *Marcion and His Influence*. New York: AMS, 1978.

Bradley, Marion Zimmer. *The Mists of Avalon*. New York: Ballentine, 1982.

Brennan, Martin. *The Stars and the Stones*. London: Thames and Hudson, 1983.

Brindel, June Rachuy. *Ariadne*. New York: St. Martin's Press, 1980.

Brown, Norman, O. *Life Against Death: The Psychoanalytical Meaning of History*. New York: Vintage, 1959.

Budge, E.A. Wallis. *Babylonian Life and History*. New York: Copper Square, 1975.

_____. *The Egyptian Heaven and Hell*. La Salle, IL: Open Court, 1905.

_____. *The Book of the Dead*. New York: University Books, 1960.

Burl, Aubrey. *Prehistoric Avebury*. New Haven: Yale University Press, 1979.

Campbell, Joseph. *The Mysteries*. Vols. 1 & 2. Princeton: Bollingen, 1955.

Capt, Raymond. *Missing Links Discovered in Assyrian Tablets*. Thousand Oaks, CA: Artisan Sales, 1985.

Ceram, C.W. *The Secret of the Hittites*. New York: Alfred A. Knopf, 1956.

Chan, Roman Pina. *Chitzen Itza: La Cuidad de los Brujos del Agua*. Mexico: Fondo de Cultura Economica, 1980.

_____. *Guide to Mexican Archeology*. Mexico: Minutiae Mexicana, 1970.

_____. *Quetzalcoatl: Serpiente Emplumada*. Mexico: Fondo de Cultura, 1977.

Chenu, M.D. *Nature, Man, and Society in the Twelfth Century*. Chicago: University of Chicago Press, 1957.

Churchward, James. *The Cosmic Forces of Mu*. New York: Paperback Library, 1968.

_____. *Understanding Mu*. New York: Warner, 1970.

Clow, Barbara Hand. *Chiron: Rainbow Bridge Between the Inner and Outer Planets*. Minneapolis: Llewellyn, 1987.

_____. *Eye of the Centaur: A Visionary Guide into Past Lives*. Minneapolis: Llewellyn, 1987; Santa Fe, NM: Bear & Company, 1989.

Coe, Michael D., and Richard A. Diehl. *In the Land of the Olmec*. Austin: University of Texas Press, 1980.

Coe, Michael D. *The Maya*. London: Thames and Hudson, 1966.

Coe, William R. *Tikal: A Handbook of the Ancient Maya Ruins*. Guatemala: Asociacion Tikal, 1986.

Cohen, A. *Everyman's Talmud*. New York: Schocken, 1975.

Cory, L.P. *Ancient Fragments*. Minneapolis: Wizards, 1975.

Cottrell, Leonard. *The Bull of Minos*. New York: Grosset and Dunlap, 1953.

Coxe, A. Cleveland, ed. *Ante-Nicene Fathers*. Vols. 1, 2, & 3. Grand Rapids: Eerdmans, 1986.

Craine, Eugene R., and Reginald C. Reindorp. *The Codex Perez and The Book of Chilam Balam of Mani*. Norman: University of Oklahoma Press, 1979.

Cumming, Barbara. *Egyptian Historical Records of the Later Eighteenth Dynasty*. Fascicles 1, 2, & 3. Warminster, England: Aris and Phillips, 1982.

Cumont, Franz. *The Mysteries of Mithra*. New York: Dover, 1956.

Dames, Michael. *The Silbury Treasure*. London: Thames and Hudson, 1976.

Davidovits, Dr. Joseph, and Margie Morris. *The Pyramids: An Enigma Solved*. New York: Hippocrene Books, 1988.

Davies, Nigel. *The Ancient Kingdom of Mexico*. Middlesex, England: Penguin, 1987.

_____. *Voyagers to the New World*. Albuquerque: University of New Mexico Press, 1979.

Doresse, Jean. *The Secret Books of the Egyptian Gnostics*. New York: Viking, 1960.

Doumas, Christos G. *Thera: Pompeii of the Ancient Aegean*. London: Thames and Hudson, 1983.

Drake, Raymond. *Mystery of the Gods—Are They Coming Back to Earth?* Self-published, 1972.

Eisler, Riane. *The Chalice and the Blade*. San Francisco: Harper & Row, 1987.

Eliade, Mircea. *Death, Afterlife, and Eschatology*. New York: Harper & Row, 1974.

_____. *Myth of the Eternal Return*. Princeton: Bollingen, 1954.

_____. *Rites and Symbols of Initiation*. New York: Harper Torchbooks, 1958.

_____. *Sacred and the Profane*. New York: Harcourt, Brace, Jovanovich, 1959.

Eusebius. *The History of the Church from Christ to Constantine*. Translated by G. A. Williamson. Middlesex, England: Penguin, 1983.

Faulkner, R.O. *The Ancient Egyptian Book of the Dead*. New York: MacMillan, 1985.

Fell, Barry. *America B.C.* New York: Simon and Schuster, 1976.

_____. *Bronze Age America*. Boston: Little Brown, 1982.

Finegan, Jack. *Archeological History of the Ancient Middle East*. New York: Dorset Press, 1979.

Fontenrose, Joseph. *Python: A Study of Delphic Myth and its Origins*. Berkeley: University of California Press, 1980.

Fox, Hugh. *Gods of the Cataclysm*. New York: Dorset Press, 1981.

Fox, Matthew. *The Coming of the Cosmic Christ*. San Francisco: Harper & Row, 1988.

Fox, Robin Lane. *Pagans and Christians*. San Francisco: Harper & Row, 1987.

Franck, Adolphe. *The Kabbalah*. New York: Dell, 1940.

von Franz, Marie-Louise. *Alchemy: An Introduction to the Symbolism and the Psychology*. Toronto: Inner City, 1980.

_____. *Puer Aeternus*. Santa Monica, CA: Sigo Press, 1970.

Friedrich, Otto. *The End of the World: A History*. New York: Coward, McCann, & Geoghegan, 1982.

Galanopoulos, A.G., and Edward Bacon. *Atlantis: The Truth Behind the Legend*. Indianapolis: Bobbs-Merrill, 1969.

Gallenkamp, Charles. *Maya*. New York: Viking, 1976.

Grant, Michael. *History of Rome*. New York: Scribners, 1978.

Grant, Robert M. *Gods and the One God*. Philadelphia: Westminster, 1986.

Graves, Robert. *The Golden Ass by Apuleius*. New York: Farrar Strauss and Giroux, 1951.

_____. *The Greek Myths*. Vols. 1 & 2. Middlesex, England: Penguin, 1955.

Graves, Robert, and Raphael Patai. *Hebrew Myths*. New York: Greenwich, 1983.

Greer, Rowan A., trans. *Origen*. New York: Paulist, 1979.

Gregg, Robert C., and Dennis E. Groh. *Early Arianism: A View Of Salvation*. Philadelphia: Fortress, 1973.

Griaule, M., and G. Dieterlen. *The Pale Fox*. Chino Valley, CA.: Continuum Foundation.

Griffen, Miriam T. *Nero: The End of a Dynasty*. New Haven: Yale University Press, 1984.

Griffiths, J. Gwin. *The Conflict of Horus and Seth*. Liverpool: Liverpool University Press, 1960.

Guignebert, Charles. *Christ*. New York: University Books, 1970.

_____. *Jesus*. New York: University Books, 1956.

_____. *The Jewish World at the Time of Jesus*. New York: University Books, 1959.

Gwatkin, H. M. *The Arian Controversy*. London: Longmans, 1914.

Habachi, Labib. *The Obelisks of Egypt: Skyscrapers of the Past*. Cairo: The American University in Cairo, 1984.

Haich, Elizabeth. *Initiation*. Palo Alto, CA: Seed Press, 1974.

Hall, Nor. *The Moon and the Virgin*. New York: Harper & Row, 1980.

Hammond, Norman. *Ancient Maya Civilization*. New Jersey: Rutgers University Press, 1988.

Hanson, L. Taylor. *He Walked the Americas*. Amherst, WI: Amherst Press, 1963.

Hapgood, Charles H. *Maps of the Ancient Sea Kings: Evidence of Advanced Civilization in the Ice Age*. New York: E.P. Dutton, 1979.

Har-El, Manashe. *The Sinai Journeys*. San Diego, CA: Ridgefield, 1983.

Harleston, Hugh. *The Keystone: A Search for Understanding*. Self-published, 1984.

Heidel, Alexander. *The Babylonian Genesis*. Chicago: University of Chicago Press, 1951.

Heschel, Abraham J. *The Prophets*. New York: Harper & Row, 1955.

Hitching, Francis. *Earth Magic*. New York: William Morrow, 1977.

Hoffmann, R. Joseph, trans. *Celsus on the True Doctrine*. Oxford: Oxford University Press, 1987.

Howard, George. *The Gospel of Matthew According to a Primitive Hebrew Text*. Macon, GA: Mercer University Press, 1987.

Jaynes, Julian. *The Origins of Consciousness in the Bicameral Mind*. Boston: Houghton Mifflin, 1976.

Jonas, Hans. *The Gnostic Religions*. Boston: Beacon Press, 1963.

Josephus. *Antiquities of the Jews and a History of the Jewish Wars*. Translated by William Whiston. Philadelphia: David McKay, n.d.

Jung, C. G. *Aion: Researches into the Phenomenology of Self*. Princeton: Bollingen, 1959.

_____. *Memories, Dreams, and Reflections*. New York: Vintage, 1963.

_____. *Psyche & Symbol*. New York: Doubleday, 1958.

_____. *Psychological Types*. Great Britain: Pantheon, 1962.

_____. *Psychology and the Occult*. Princeton: Bollingen, 1977.

_____. *Synchronicity*. Princeton: Bollingen, 1960.

_____. *The Visions Seminars*. Books 1 & 2. Zurich, Switzerland: Spring Publications, 1976.

Kerenyi, C. *Goddess of Sun and Moon*. Irving, TX: Spring Publications, 1979.

King, C. W. *The Gnostics and Their Remains*. San Diego: Wizards, 1982.

Kushner, Lawrence. *Honey from the Rock: Ten Gates of Jewish Mysticism*. San Francisco: Harper & Row, 1977.

Lamy, Lucy. *Egyptian Mysteries*. New York: Crossroads, 1981.

Lemesurier, Peter. *The Armageddon Script*. England: Element, 1981.

Lichtheim, Miriam. *Ancient Egyptian Literature*. Vols. 1 & 2. Berkeley: University of California Press, 1973.

Lost Books of the Bible and the Forgotten Books of Eden. Newfoundland: Alpha House, 1927.

Luckert, Karl W. *Olmec Religion: A Key to Middle America and Beyond*. Norman: University of Oklahoma Press, 1976.

MacGregor, Geddes. *Gnosis: A Renaissance in Christian Thought*. Wheaton, IL: Quest, 1979.

MacMullen, Ramsey. *Christianizing the Roman Empire AD 100-400*. New Haven: Yale University Press, 1984.

_____. *Paganism in the Roman Empire*. New Haven: Yale University Press, 1981.

Mahan, Joseph B. *The Secret: America in World History before Columbus*. Columbus, GA: 1983.

Maier, Paul. *The First Christian s*. London: Mowbry's, 1976.

Maltwood, K. E. *Enchantments of Britain: King Arthur's Round Table of the Stars.* Cambridge: James Clark and Co., 1982.

Maspero, G. *The Dawn of Civilization: Egypt and Chaldea.* London: Society for Promoting Christian Knowledge, 1896.

Masters, Robert. *The Goddess Sekhmet: The Way of Five Bodies.* New York: Amity House, 1988.

Matthews, Caitlin, and John Matthews. *The Western Way: A Practical Guide to the Western Mystery Tradition.* Vols. 1 & 2. London: Arkana, 1985.

Matthews, John. *At The Table of the Grail.* London: Routledge & Kegan Paul, 1984.

_____. *The Grail: Quest for the Eternal.* New York: Crossroads, 1981.

Mavor, James. *Voyage to Atlantis.* New York: Putnam, 1969.

Mazar, Benjamin. *Recent Archeology in the Land of Israel.* English edition by Hershel Shanks. Washington, DC: Bibilical Archeology, 1985.

McGlone, William R., and Phillip M. Leonard. *Ancient Celtic America.* Fresno, CA: Panorama West Books, 1986.

McMann, Jean. *Riddles of the Stone Age: Rock Carvings of Ancient Europe.* London: Thames and Hudson, 1980.

Men, Hunbatz. *Los Calendarios Astronómico Mayas y Hunab K'u.* Juarez, Mexico: Ediciones Horizonte, 1983.

_____. *Religión Ciencia Maya.* Merida, Mexico: Comunidad Indigena Maya, 1986. (Available in English in 1989 by Bear & Company, Santa Fe.)

Mertz, Henriette. *Atlantis.* Chicago: 1976.

_____. *The Mystic Symbol: Mark of the Michigan Mound Builders.* Gaithersburg, MD: Global Books, 1986.

Meyers, Carol. *Discovering Eve: Ancient Israelite Women in Context.* Oxford: Oxford University Press, 1988.

Mitchell, John. *Secrets of the Stones.* London: Penguin, 1977.

_____. *The Earth Spirit.* New York: Crossroads, 1975.

_____. *The New View Over Atlantis.* New York: Harper & Row, 1983.

Moscati, Sabatino. *Ancient Semitic Civilizations.* New York: Putnam, 1960.

Moss, Richard. *The I That Is We.* Millbrae, CA: Celestial Arts, 1981.

Mullett, G.M. *Spider Woman Stories: Legends of the Hopi Indians.* Tucson: University of Arizona Press, 1982.

Murray, Margaret A. *The God of the Witches.* London: Oxford University Press, 1970.

Musaios. *The Lion Path: A Manual of the Short Path to Regeneration for Our Times.* Berkeley: Golden Sceptre Publishing, 1987.

Negev, Avraham. *Archeological Encyclopedia of the Holy Land.* Princeton, NJ: S.B.S. Publishing, 1980.

_____. *Archeology in the Land of the Bible.* New York: Schocken, 1977.

Neugrosschel, Joachim. *The Great Works of Jewish Fantasy and Occult.* New York: Overlook, 1986.

Nyssa, Gregory of. *The Life of Moses.* New York: Paulist, 1978.

O'Brien, Christian. *The Genius of the Few: The Story of Those Who Founded the Garden in Eden.* Wellingborough, England: Turnstone, 1985.

_____. *The Megalithic Odyssey.* Wellingborough, England: Turnstone Press, 1983.

Ochoa, Lorenzo. *Olmecas y Mayas en Tabasco.* Villahermosa, Mexico: Gobierno del Estado de Tabasco, 1985.

Ogilvie, R. M. *Early Rome and the Etruscans.* Glasgow: Fontana, 1975.

Oppenheim, A. Leo. *Ancient Mesopotamia.* Chicago: University of Chicago, 1977.

Pagels, Elaine. *Adam, Eve, and the Serpent.* New York: Random House, 1988.

_____. *The Gnostic Gospels.* New York: Vintage, 1979.

Pelikan, Jaroslav. *Jesus Through the Centuries.* New Haven: Yale University Press, 1985.

_____. *The Emergence of the Catholic Tradition, (100-600).* Chicago: University of Chicago Press, 1971.

Perera, Victor, and Robert D. Bruce. *The Last Lords of Palenque: The Lacandon Mayas of the Mexican Rain Forest.* Berkeley: University of California, 1982.

Petrie, W. M. Flinders. *Religious Life in Ancient Egypt.* Boston: Houghton and Mifflin, 1924.

Petronius. *The Satyricon.* Translated by J.P. Sullivan. Middlesex, England: Penguin, 1965.

Pettinato, Giovanni. *The Archives of Ebla: An Empire Inscribed in Clay.* New York: Doubleday, 1981.

Phillip, Brother. *Secret of the Andes.* Bolinas, CA: Leaves of Grass, 1976.

Piggot, Stuart. *The Druids.* London: Thames and Hudson, 1975.

Pritchard, James B. *The Ancient Near East.* Vols. 1 & 2. Princeton: Princeton University Press, 1958.

Radice, Betty. *Early Christian Writings.* Middlesex, England: Penguin, 1968.

Ragette, Friedrich. *Baalbek.* Park Ridge, NJ: Noyes Press, 1980.

Randers-Pehrson, Justine Davis. *Barbarians and Romans: The Birth Struggle of Europe, A.D. 400-700.* London: Croom Helm, 1983.

Recinos, Adrian, and Delia Goetz. *The Annals of the Cakchiquels. Title of the Lords of Totonicapan.* Translated from Quiche by Dionisio Jose Chonoy. Norman: University of Oklahoma Press, 1979.

Redford, Donald B. *Akhenaton: The Heretic King.* Princeton: Princeton University Press, 1984.

Reed, Bika. *Rebel in the Soul: A Sacred Text of Ancient Egypt.* New York: Inner Traditions, 1978.

_____. *The Field of Transformations: A Quest for Immortal Essence of Human Awareness.* New York: Inner Traditions, 1987.

Reich, Wilhelm. *Character Analysis.* New York: Farrar, Straus & Giroux, 1933.

_____. *The Function of the Orgasm.* New York: Simon and Schuster, 1974.

_____. *The Sexual Revolution.* New York: Farrar Strauss & Giroux, 1974.

Robinson, James M. *The Nag Hammadi Library.* San Francisco: Harper & Row, 1977.

Rostovtzeff, M. *Rome.* New York: Oxford University Press, 1960.

Rudolph, Kurt. *Gnosis.* New York: Harper & Row, 1987.

Russell, Jeffrey Burton. *Lucifer: The Devil in the Middle Ages.* Ithaca: Cornell University Press, 1984.

_____. *Satan: The Early Christian Tradition*. Ithaca: Cornell University Press, 1981.

_____. *The Devil: Perceptions of Evil from Antiquity to Primitive Christianity*. Ithaca: Cornell University Press, 1977.

_____. *The Prince of Darkness: Radical Evil and the Power of Good in History*. Ithaca: Cornell University Press, 1988.

Sanders, E.P. *Jesus and Judaism*. Philadelphia: Fortress, 1985.

Schillebeeckx, Edward. *Jesus: An Experiment in Christology*. New York: Crossroads, 1981.

Schneweis, Emil. *Angels and Demons According to Lactantius*. Washington, DC: Catholic University Press, 1944.

Schodde, George H. *The Book of Jubilees*. Thousand Oaks, CA: Artisan Sales, 1980.

Scholem, Gershom G. *Major Trends in Jewish Mysticism*. Jerusalem: Schocken, 1941.

_____. *Kaballah*. New York: New American Library, 1974.

Schonfield, Hugh. *The Essene Odyssey*. Shaftesbury, England: Element, 1984.

_____. *The Passover Plot*. Shaftesbury, England: Element, 1965.

_____. *The Pentecost Revolution*. Shaftesbury, England: Element, 1974.

Sejourne, Laurette. *El Pensamiento Nahuatl Cifrado por los Calendarios*. Mexico City: Siglo Vientiuno, 1981.

_____. *Pensamiento y Religión en el México Antiguo*. Mexico City: Lecturas Mexicanas, 1984.

_____. *Supervivencias de un Mundo Mágico*. Mexico City: Lecturas Mexicanas, 1985.

Sharkey, John. *Celtic Mysteries: The Ancient Religion*. New York: Crossroads, 1981.

Shearer, Tony. *Beneath the Moon and Under the Sun*. Santa Fe, NM: Sun Books, 1975.

_____. *Lord of the Dawn: Quetzalcoatl*. Happy Camp, CA: Naturegraph, 1971.

Sheehan, Thomas. *The First Coming: How the Kingdom of God Became Christianity*. New York: Random House, 1986.

Sheldrake, Rupert. *A New Science of Life*. Los Angeles: Tarcher, 1981.

_____. *The Presence of the Past: Morphic Resonance and the Habits of Nature*. New York: Times Books, 1988.

Shorter, Alan W. *The Egyptian Gods*. London: Routledge & Kegan Paul, 1983.

Sitchin, Zecharia. *The Twelfth Planet*. New York: Avon, 1978.

_____. *The Stairway to Heaven*. New York: St. Martin's, 1980.

_____. *The War of Gods and Men*. New York: Avon, 1985.

Smith, Morton. *Jesus the Magician*. San Francisco: Harper & Row, 1978.

Spanuth, Jurgen. *Atlantis of the North*. London: Sidgwick and Jackson, 1979.

Spence, Lewis. *Atlantis Discovered*. New York: Causeway Books, 1974.

_____. *Myths and Legends of Ancient Egypt*. New York: Farrar & Rinehart, 1911.

_____. *Myths of Babylonia and Assyria*. London: George Harrap, 1916.

_____. *The History and Origins of Druidism*. New York: Rider, 1942.

_____. *The History of Atlantis*. New York: Bell, 1968.

_____. *The Occult Sciences in Atlantis*. New York: Rider, 1978.

Stevenson, J. *The Catacombs: Rediscovered Monuments of Early Christianity.* London: Thames and Hudson, 1978.

Stone, Merlin. *Ancient Mirrors of Womanhood.* Boston: Beacon Press, 1979.

_____. *When God Was a Woman.* New York: Harvest, 1976.

Szekeley, Edmond Bordeaux. *The Discovery of the Essene Gospel of Peace.* Cartago, Costa Rica: International Biogenic Society, 1977.

_____. *The Gospel of the Essenes.* Great Britain: C.W. Daniels, 1984.

Temple, Robert. *The Sirius Mystery.* New York: St. Martin's, 1976.

Tolstoy, Nicolai. *The Quest for Merlin.* Boston: Little Brown, 1985.

Tompkins, Peter. *Secrets of the Great Pyramid.* New York: Harper & Row, 1971.

_____. *The Magic of Obelisks.* New York: Harper & Row, 1981.

Trench, Brinsley Le Poer. *Forgotten Heritage.* London: Neville Spearman, 1964.

_____. *The Sky People.* London: Neville Spearman, 1963.

Trento, Salvatore Michael. *The Search for Lost America: Mysteries of the Stone Ruins in the United States.* London: Penguin, 1978.

Turner, Frederick. *Beyond Geography: The Western Spirit Against the Wilderness.* Princeton, NJ: Rutgers, 1983.

Vallee, Jacques and Alan Hynek. *The Edge of Reality: A Progress Report on UFOs.* Chicago: Henry Regnery, 1975.

Velikovsky, Immanuel. *Ages in Chaos.* New York: Doubleday, 1952.

_____. *Earth in Upheaval.* New York: Dell, 1955.

_____. *Mankind in Amnesia.* New York: Doubleday, 1982.

_____. *Oedipus and Akhnaton.* New York: Pocket Books, 1960.

_____. *Peoples of the Sea.* New York: Doubleday, 1977.

_____. *Ramses II and His Time.* New York: Doubleday, 1978.

_____. *Stargazers and Gravediggers: Memoirs to Worlds in Collision.* New York: William and Morrow, 1983.

_____. *Worlds in Collision.* New York: Dell, 1973.

Waite, A.E. *The Hidden Church of the Holy Grail.* London: Rebman Limited, 1909.

_____. *Lamps of Western Mysticism.* New York: Alfred A. Knopf, 1923.

Wand, J.W.C. *The Four Great Heresies.* London: Mowbray, 1955.

Wasson, R. Gordon, Carl A. P. Ruck, Albert Hoffmann. *The Road to Eleusis.* New York: Harcourt Brace Jovanovich, 1978.

Weigle, Marta. *Spiders and Spinsters: Women and Mythology.* Albuquerque: University of New Mexico Press, 1982.

Wentz-Evans, W.Y. *Cuchama and Sacred Mountains.* Chicago: Swallow Press, 1981.

West, John Anthony. *Serpent in the Sky.* New York: Harper & Row, 1979.

Wicke, Charles R. *Olmec: An Early Art Style of Precolumbian Mexico.* Tucson: University of Arizona Press, 1971.

Wilhelm, Richard. *The Secret of the Golden Flower.* New York: Harcourt Brace Jovanovich, 1962.

Wilson, Ian. *Jesus: The Evidence*. San Francisco: Harper & Row, 1984.

Wilson, R. *The Gnostic Problem*. London: A.W. Mowbry, 1958.

Wood, David. *Genesis: The First Book of Revelations*. Tunbridge Wells, England: Baton Press, 1985.

ABOUT THE AUTHOR

Barbara Hand Clow is a noted astrological counselor, spiritual teacher, writer, and editor of books on New Age consciousness. Her first book, *Stained Glass: A Basic Manual* was published in 1976. She received her master's degree in theology and healing from Mundelein College in 1983 after writing a thesis on "A Comparison of Jungian Psychoanalytic Technique and Past-Life Regression Therapy."

Clow believes that everyone on Earth possesses memories of all times and places within their cellular matrices, and that anyone can remember everything that they have ever known if they have the courage to go deep within and experience themselves. She feels, as do many Native American and Mesoamerican spiritual teachers, that the purpose of the late twentieth century is to go beyond time, and beyond history. Her *Mind Chronicles* series is a journey into the archetypal memories of the human race. It is a redefinition of his-story to include and empower the experiences of women, animals, plants, and rocks.

As a result of her extensive personal work with ceremony at sacred sites and its role in the evolution of consciousness, Clow wrote the first volume of *The Mind Chronicles* trilogy, *Eye of the Centaur: A Visionary Guide into Past Lives*, in 1986. In this book, she embodies the shifts in dimensionality experienced by many people during the Harmonic Convergence in 1987. Her continued work on clearing the emotional body, and emptying the contents of the subconscious mind through shamanic journeying, compelled her to author *Heart of the Christos*, the second volume of the trilogy.

Clow is also the author of *Chiron: Rainbow Bridge Between the Inner and Outer Planets*, 1987, a definitive astrological work on the new planet Chiron, which rules the current redefinition of the species. She is married and the mother of four children: Tom, Matthew, Christopher, and Elizabeth.

Due to her continued commitment to her writing and her exploration of the subconscious, Barbara Hand Clow is not currently available for doing personal astrological readings.

ABOUT THE ARTIST

The artist, Angela C. Werneke, received her B.F.A. in graphic design from Kent State University and has been an illustrator and graphic designer for twenty years. She has received numerous awards for her work, which includes Bear & Company's *Keepers of the Fire*, *A Painter's Quest*, and *Medicine Cards*. She sees her work as a means of healing and nurturing the Earth and its inhabitants. Angela makes her home near Black Mesa in northern New Mexico.

COMMENTS BY READERS

"Like the tree-ring and the carbon-14 methods needed to date anthropological material, Barbara offers her cellular memory to be used as a yardstick, reaching far beyond the memories of present-day humanity.
"Through the often tragic experiences of a forgotten past, she is helping all of us to re-experience the agonies, the horrors, and the ecstasies of a world slowly emerging from the chaos of its birth."
Robert Boissiere, author of *Meditations with the Hopi* and *The Hopi Way*

"Barbara Clow's excellent rendition of her own shamanistic journey into the past is a strong catalyst for each of us in journeying into our own depths. This book also provides invaluable information on esoteric rituals from the past which explore in depth the themes of female and male energy, sexual initiation rites, and the role of the Goddess."
Marcia Stark, author of *Earth Mother Astrology* and *Astrology: Key to Holistic Health*

"In *The 12th Planet* I have retraced the story of mankind on Earth as recorded by ancient peoples from the tales they had heard from the *Nefilim*, the "gods" who had come to Earth from the planet Nibiru. Now, Barbara Clow enhances in *Heart of the Christos* the overall tale by bringing it to the level of individual experiences; and the mythology of nations becomes the mystical tale of the self."
Zecharia Sitchin, author of *The Earth Chronicles* trilogy

"*Heart of the Christos* is a fascinating book that is a true addition to the New Age movement."
Edith Fiore, Ph.D., clinical psychologist, lecturer, and author of *The Unquiet Dead* and *You Have Been Here Before*

"A shamanic journey of shattering intensity that gripped me from the first page. Herein lies a fascinating account of how humanity has suffered at the hands of patriarchy. Barbara Hand Clow delivers an urgent message: that we cannot enter the age of enlightenment without reclaiming the power of woman, the Goddess."
Rosemary Ellen Guiley, author of *Tales of Reincarnation*

"In *Heart of the Christos*, Barbara Hand Clow journeys through the hidden archetypal memories which lie buried in the heart of Western culture. Through her inner struggle to understand her own psyche, she discovers and reveals the mysteries behind the myths of our evolutionary past."
Dr. Richard Gerber, author of *Vibrational Medicine*

"Barbara Hand Clow has the gift of interweaving history with explorations of the human soul. She is a brilliant scholar and writer who utilizes the pain and the anger from personal nightmare not only to find her own peace but to help objectify the human journey and its meaning. Although *Heart of the Christos* is quite controversial and bound to elicit all manner of comments, both negative and positive, the book *is* a worthy read."
P.M.H. Atwater, author of *Coming Back to Life*

"Our souls tell us stories which draw us ever deeper into our own mystery. These dream stories (daydreams and nightdreams) are given to us in a picture language which dissolves the boundaries of our present time and space. We marvel at their startling immediacy, the intense intimacy, the wealth of memories manifest in our dreams. Where do they come from? Why do they come?

"In her quest for self-knowledge, the author answers these questions. Listening to her memory stories and looking into her mind images, she trusts them to lead her into the unknown. Her journey often leads to frightening places and adventures where she re-collects herself in her past lives. The treasure with which she returns belongs to all of us. It is a priceless gift because her journey is an invitation to walk more quickly and more graciously toward our own mystery, encouraged by a true teacher."
Meinrad Craighead, artist, and author of *The Mother's Songs*

"To watch Barbara courageously dive into our collective unconscious and expose the unspeakable, is not only timely, but inspirational. It is a sign of our planet's emergence from denial into conscious responsibility."
Rick Phillips, president of The Deva Foundation

"Amazing! Barbara has sent her spirit soaring among the ethers of history and come back with a story that binds the great mysteries of the world. Her adventures ignite the imagination and illuminate the present and the future. A *tour de force* of the spirit."
Steven S.H. McFadden, journalist, astrologer, and author of *The Legend of the Rainbow Warriors* and *The Farms of Tomorrow*.

"Mining the archetypes of the mind in that wilderness zone where personal and collective unconscious intermingle is a nearly lost art in modern times, which is sad, for as Barbara Hand Clow shows in *Heart of the Christos*, many of the pure springs of health, creativity, and wisdom arises from these fertile waters of consciousness.
"This book helps lend value to consciousness exploration of the depths of the human soul, for through Barbara's writings we not only gain fascinating glimpses into human nature, but we witness the work of claiming the shadow which lives within us all. And what clearly emerges is that we must own this dark side of our reality of being human to become truly powerful and manifest what Carl Jung called the 'Mana Personality', which is when we are bisexual, human-animal, light, and dark all at once. Gifted athletes know these spaces, transforming the 'killer' within into the tackle that saves the game. From coming to befriend this gray region of being she explores, we see how great minds of the past were able to make sense out of reality without the scientific tools of today, and have the wisdom of the owl priestess or the jaguar shaman come alive. Our nervous system hasn't changed for over 10,000 years. These voices and their brothers and sisters live within the reach of all of us. *Heart of the Christos* will inspire more people to undertake the journey Barbara has taken. And from making this trek, we will return with new energies, symbols and insights, as well as integrations which will then enable us to

express these themes in daily life in wise ways, with greater and greater potential to express new creativity in many realms of life."
James A. Swan, Ph.D., California Institute of Integral Studies; organizer of the "Spirit of Place" symposium

"A spell-binding *tour de force* of ancient mysteries and archaic consciousness drawn into present time and space. The book is hypnotic and *initiatory*, speaking to the reader at different levels of her/his consciousness and being. As the Mysteries and the God and Goddess forms re-emerge in our time, so there is beginning to appear a new literature which does not just speak of the Sacred and the Numinous, but brings them living into the body/mind and soul dimensions of the human. Then the experience is not just one of reading, but of energetic participation in the revelation of Forces reaching through vastnesses of history and pre-history, human and non-human, the domains of the Powers and Principalities. Barbara Clow has worked such real magic with this book."
Robert Masters, director of research for the Foundation for Mind Research

"Some people talk about karmic law, and yet very few truly understand its principles enough to write about it. Barbara Clow's newest book, *Heart of the Christos*, is a mystical journey into the experiences of past, present, and future lives—beyond the veil of illusion—making it readily accessible to the public in a unique polyphonic style."
Iron Thunderhorse, Thunderbird Shaman; author of *Return of the Thunderbeings*

BOOKS OF RELATED INTEREST
BY BEAR & COMPANY

BRINGERS OF THE DAWN
Teachings from the Pleiadians
by *Barbara Marciniak*

ECSTASY IS A NEW FREQUENCY
Teachings of The Light Institute
by *Chris Griscom*

EYE OF THE CENTAUR
A Visionary Guide into Past Lives
by *Barbara Hand Clow*

SECRETS OF MAYAN SCIENCE/RELIGION
by *Hunbatz Men*

SEXUAL PEACE
Beyond the Dominator Virus
by *Michael Sky*

SIGNET OF ATLANTIS
War in Heaven Bypass
by *Barbara Hand Clow*

THE 12th PLANET
Book I of The Earth Chronicles
by *Zecharia Sitchin*

Contact your local bookseller or write to:
BEAR & COMPANY
P.O. Drawer 2860
Santa Fe, NM 87504